HIGHWAY TO
HELL

HIGHWAY TO HELL

CAN **YOU** SURVIVE THE ZOMBIE APOCALYPSE?

MAX BRALLIER

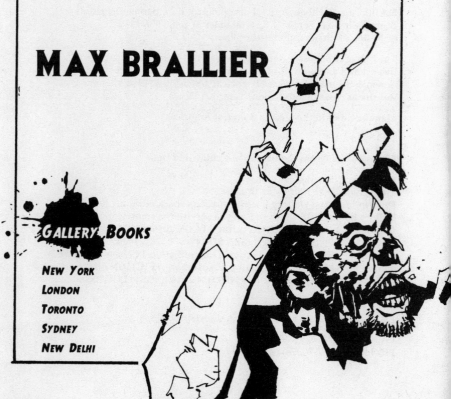

GALLERY BOOKS

NEW YORK
LONDON
TORONTO
SYDNEY
NEW DELHI

G

Gallery Books
An Imprint of Simon & Schuster, Inc.
1230 Avenue of the Americas
New York, NY 10020

First Gallery Books trade paperback edition August 2016

GALLERY BOOKS and colophon are registered trademarks of Simon & Schuster, Inc.

For information about special discounts for bulk purchases, please contact Simon & Schuster Special Sales at 1-866-506-1949 or business@simonandschuster.com.

The Simon & Schuster Speakers Bureau can bring authors to your live event. For more information or to book an event contact the Simon & Schuster Speakers Bureau at 1-866-248-3049 or visit our website at www.simonspeakers.com.

Manufactured in the United States of America

10 9 8 7 6 5 4 3 2 1

Library of Congress Cataloging-in-Publication Data

Names: Brallier, Max, author.
Title: Highway to hell / Max Brallier.
Description: First Gallery Books trade paperback edition. | New York : Gallery Books, 2016. | Series: Can you survive the zombie apocalypse? ; 2
Identifiers: LCCN 2016006456 (print) | LCCN 2016008054 (ebook) | ISBN 9781476765679 (paperback) | ISBN 9781476770376 (ebook)
Subjects: LCSH: Zombies—Fiction. | Horror fiction. | Choose-your-own stories. | BISAC: FICTION / Action & Adventure. | FICTION / Horror.
Classification: LCC PS3602.R344455 H54 2016 (print) | LCC PS3602.R344455
(ebook) | DDC 813/.6—dc23
LC record available at http://lccn.loc.gov/2016006456

ISBN 978-1-4767-6567-9
ISBN 978-1-4767-7037-6 (ebook)

*George Miller, John Carpenter, Roger Zelazny,
and George Romero—your characters and stories
continue to inspire. Thank you.*

*Also, much gratitude to the fine folks at Think Coffee
on Fourth Avenue—thanks for keeping me caffeinated
and letting me write, write, write.*

You want . . . some kind of explanation . . . ? Here's one as good as any you're likely to find. We're being punished by the Creator. He visited a curse on us. So that man could look at what hell was like.

—*DAY OF THE DEAD*

It's amazing how quickly things can go from "bad" to "total shit storm."

—*ZOMBIELAND*

They say the mind bends and twists in order to deal with the horrors of life. I think my mind bent so much it snapped in two.

—*TWISTED METAL: BLACK*

Good. Bad. I'm the guy with the gun.

—*ARMY OF DARKNESS*

HIGHWAY TO
HELL

You're in a five-by-five cell that smells like piss and disease.

Been in this cage for fifty-eight months. Only light is the dim bulb in the hallway beyond the bars. The cell is sparse: stained mattress, rusted sink, and a toilet you unclog with your hands.

You were a soldier.

No—to call you a soldier, that would be an insult to decent men who fight for concepts like honor and "the right thing"—men who fight because they *believe*. To call you a butcher, a killer, a dealer of pain, a breaker of faces, a general *bad man*—that would just be skimming the surface.

You were the youngest on the ground in Desert Storm. Lied about your age to join. Killed nine men in a war where almost no Americans died. Sliced off a man's ear. That's when you got the feel for it—the metallic taste of sprayed blood on your tongue and a thirst that wouldn't leave.

Came back to the US in '92. Tried to fit back in. "Normal." Married your high school sweetheart.

She was far from sweet.

Can't blame her. She didn't love the drinking. The fists through the walls. The steel-toed boots shattering the TV, ruining Thanksgiving because the Lions lost again. So she left, and that was just fine.

'Ninety-five you reenlisted, recruited to black-bag missions.

Twenty-eighth birthday, you were in a brothel in Turkey, taking a ball-peen hammer to a man's eye socket, when you turned to the TV and saw the towers fall.

It all got bigger then. More jobs. More killing. Your life was a splatter-work painting—blood here, agony and execution there. Death on a grand scale.

Seven years of that, in deserts and caves and towns so hot the sweat poured off you until it felt like some second, liquid skin. Seven years, until your stomach was so hollow the only time you felt anything was when you were fighting or drinking.

The military cut you loose in '08 when they found you drunk, racing a Humvee through an Iraqi minefield on a bet.

You made it to the other side of the minefield, safe and sound, but they shipped you back to the other side of the world, battered and broken.

Two years bumming around the States: New York to Detroit to Alabama to who-knows-it's-all-a-blur-at-the-bottom-of-a-bottle.

Then 2010, back in Afghanistan behind a big rig, doing the Kabul–Jalalabad run. Most dangerous drive in the world.

You forgot about the feel of your hands on a man's neck—replaced it with the feel of your hands on the wheel of an armored transport.

That's when you found your true love: driving.

You felt like Mad Max, the Road Warrior—that big ending. Always loved that movie. You watched it with your old man and he gave you your own six-pack of Iron City. You finished your beers just before the grand finale, when Max steers the rig through the wasteland. You were nine years old.

But they cut you loose. Someone frowned upon a 1.2 BAC while driving through the Korengal.

Back to the States again. Had some money saved up. Bought yourself a gift—your dream car.

A '67 El Camino.

You were thirty-eight years old.

That's what normal guys do, right? Workaday fellas? They have midlife crises and they buy dream cars.

But racing through Baltimore one neon dreary night, you

said fuck it, and you drove that mother head-on into a brick wall, just to see what would happen.

Whiplash happened.

Six broken teeth happened.

Shattered cheekbone, nose broken in three places, arm dislocated, five broken ribs, one punctured lung—that happened, too.

But the impact. The pain.

Goddamn. It got your heart kicking like a bronco with a shock rod up its ass.

You checked yourself out of the hospital, went straight to the impound, got the El Camino back, and started repairing it and fitting it up for the New Mexico Demolition Derby.

You took the racing name "Jimmy El Camino." You drove all the circuits. Most days the demolition derby, other days off-road races. You rarely lost, and you'd rarely felt better.

But your past caught up with you.

That's what pasts do.

You came home drunker than usual—blacked out on your feet. You were celebrating your fortieth birthday, first with a hired girl, who you scared away, then alone, with your ol' buddy Johnnie Walker.

The spooks came in the night, needle in the neck, your legs turning to rubber, knees giving out, collapsing, and then you waking up in this cell.

This cell, where you've been for one thousand seven hundred and forty-three days.

CL—CLINK.

A door opens at the end of the hall. A triangle of light. Keys rattle. Footsteps. Two voices.

"John Casey?"

You squint. Two men at the bars.

"John Casey, stand up."

"The name's Jimmy El Camino," you say. Your voice is a croak. Haven't spoken a word aloud in who knows how long.

"Hands behind the back, against the bars."

Usually they come twice a day, slide you food and water through the bean slot—always while you're asleep. This is new. You go with it—rise and turn around, stepping back, placing your hands against the horizontal opening. Cold handcuffs hug your wrists and clink shut.

"You get much news down here?" they ask.

"What do you think?"

"So you don't know, then?"

"Know about what?"

"Hell."

"Oh, I know hell. I know hell real well."

"Not like this. *Real* hell. Bad shit. Came to earth a while back. Man wants to talk to you about it."

You turn that one over in your head for a moment before saying, "Cool."

They let you shower and shave. You see yourself, fully, for the first time in almost five years. Muscles still there. Muscle tone, lean and cut, could pass for thirty-five. Your face, the blood-shot eyes, the heavy lids, the bags beneath them, the scars—a stranger might ballpark you at sixty.

You don't like looking so vintage, so you leave most of the beard, still thick, to cover up some of that sad countenance.

The same two soldiers—one tall and thin, one boxy and angular—come to retrieve you. Thin One leads you through a mostly dark, mostly cement complex. Place smells like decay. Down two halls, a flight of stairs, and into a dim room. Boxy refers to it as a briefing room, but it looks more like the back hall of a VFW. One TV, empty cups of coffee, a flag on the wall, plastic folding chairs.

A man in uniform stands behind a desk.

Thin One and Boxy push you down into a chair, so you're facing the uniform.

"Uncuff him," the man in uniform says. You squint, still having trouble with the light. Name on his uniform reads *Eigle*.

Thin One and Boxy hesitate.

"Uncuff him," Eigle repeats.

Boxy does as he's ordered. You place your hands on your thighs and wait for them to get out the butter knife and start spreading on the bullshit.

Eigle looks you over. He's medium height, bony, pale as powder. Needly eyes gaze down a sloping, angular nose. His hair is white and thin, his gray mustache is stained with coffee. He steps forward, sticks out a rough hand. "Major Eigle."

You reach out. Shake it.

Eigle starts, "John Casey, I've been—"

"Jimmy El Camino," you say.

"Sorry?"

"Call me Jimmy El Camino."

He shrugs, tired. "Sure. *Jimmy.* You've been underground a long time. Any idea what's been going on up here? Out there?"

You don't respond.

Eigle takes a leaning half seat on a flimsy wooden folding table—the type you sat at as a kid at the weekly Methodist fish fry. The table sinks in the middle and creaks as Eigle reaches for the remote from the table and points it at the TV. He hits a button. Hits it again. Looks at the remote, frustrated, bangs it twice against his palm, takes out the batteries, eyes them like they might provide some clue, slips them back in, then points it at the TV and clicks again.

The TV flashes on. Flashes on to terror, disaster, mass hysteria. It's a prerecorded video, telling the story of what's happened since you were gone.

You've seen what chemical weapons do to people, but you've never seen anything like this.

Zombies, like the horror comics you read in grade school. Humans, consuming the flesh of other, still-breathing humans.

You see New York City, smoking. You see rotting cannibals, stumbling through the streets.

CNN headlines:
- *Los Angeles burns*
- *London falls*
- *President to speak*
- *President's speech delayed*
- *President unaccounted for*

Fox News headlines:
- *Is this the Rapture?*
- *An angry God takes revenge*

Images, clips: soldiers dying, tanks overrun, police turning their service pistols on themselves while monsters tear flesh from bone and chase it down with a blood cocktail.

In fast-forward, you watch the country crumble and the world fall.

Eigle clicks the remote again and the TV flashes off.

"It happened soon after you went into the cell. You didn't see the world devolving, changing. Didn't see society break. I realize this will take you some time to process, but—"

"I got it."

"You got it?"

"Zombies. Zombie apocalypse. Society in ruins. Probably a few cities still fighting. Roving bands of cannibals, marauders, highwaymen. That about it?"

Eigle nods.

"So what—you want me to save the world or something?"

Major Eigle's lip curls into what, strictly speaking, could be considered a smile. "Something like that. I have a mission for you."

"Why me?"

"Because you're a killer and you're a driver."

"No tap dancing. The whole deal. Lay it out."

"Not yet, Jimmy."

You glare.

"I need you to prove yourself," Eigle continues. "Prove you didn't lose your mind down there in that hole. Prove your reflexes haven't withered away to nothing."

"How?"

"You drive."

"Drive where?"

"In the Death Derby."

"Sounds fun," you say. "What is it?"

"What it sounds like. You interested?"

"It get me out of the cage?"

"Only way."

"Then I suppose I'm interested."

Eigle nods. "Okay, then. Follow me."

Zombies? Death races? You should be shocked, scared, surprised—but you've seen so much hell, you're more curious than anything.

But there's one thing you don't like: taking orders from assholes. Especially the assholes who kept you locked in a cage. Even the small orders, like "Follow me."

You can sense the two guards behind you—Thin One and Boxy. Nine feet and some inches separating you from Eigle. The TV remote. You could grab it, crack it—a quick shiv. Have it to Eigle's neck, use him as a shield before Thin One and Boxy have time to realize just how useless they are . . .

Do you want to follow Eigle and discover what exactly the Death Derby is? If so, turn to page 75.

If you hate taking orders and you'd rather take prisoners, turn to page 24.

GETTYSBURG

The El Camino's oversized, steel-lined gas tank is almost empty. In the rear, twelve tanks of gas in fire-safe canisters—but that's emergency only.

You check the map. A red circle around a place in Gettysburg: a Texaco station that belongs to friendlies. You don't like the idea of stopping, but you can't skip the chance to refuel.

It's nearing noon when you find the station, just across from the Gettysburg memorial. Old junkers form a makeshift fence around the station, with a metal gate, wrapped in barbed wire, in front.

You leave the car idling and step out, carrying the Remington sawed-off. A bell hangs from the gate. You ring it, and the sound is loud and hollow, like a church bell—made louder by the silence of the Pennsylvania countryside.

You ring again.

No response.

You nudge the gate. It gives. You give it a hard push, and it swings open.

The gas station looks typical but run-down. Four pumps. Beyond that, a small shop. Sun-washed soda cans in the window. Beside that, a garage with a REPAIRS sign over it. An old Chevy pickup and a newer BMW, along the side, waiting for repairs that never came, put on permanent hold by the apocalypse.

"Well?" Iris calls from the car.

You slide back in, drive the El Camino to the pumps. The credit card machines on the pumps have been smashed. A small piece of cardboard says *See Ed for barter.*

"What's the name on the map?" you say. "Who's it say to speak with?"

Iris looks down at the map, squinting, then says, "Ed or Nancy."

You nod.

Surprisingly, the pump works with no problems. You fill the car up, then tell Iris you'll be back.

"Where are you going?"

"See if there's something we can fill up, take some more gas with us."

"Be quick, huh?"

You lead with the sawed-off, doing a full circle around the outside of the station. Coming back around, you see Iris watching you.

Into the small store. Nearly empty. No food or water on the shelves. A few old bottles of Pennzoil. Two packs of cigarettes behind the counter. You take them both.

Cash in the drawer. Worthless.

You come to the garage. It stinks like oil. You inch open the door with the Remington and the stench of oil is replaced with the stench of death.

You peek your head back out the door. Iris is leaning out the window, tapping her hands on the car door while she keeps watch.

You step down into the garage, sawed-off raised. There's a Subaru in the center. You walk around it, and that's where you find the bodies. Two of them in a pool of dried, caked blood, beginning to bloat. Dead five, maybe six days. Flies buzz.

A man and a woman.

The man has been stabbed multiple times.

The woman's head has been removed, impaled through the hood of the Subaru with a blade. You step closer. The blade is an Arkansas toothpick—the Bowie knife–like weapon much loved by Confederate soldiers during the Civil War.

You remove the Arkansas toothpick and the woman's head

rolls down the hood, falls to the floor, and lands beside the man with a smack. On the man's blue jumpsuit you see a name tag. *Ed.*

Ed and Nancy.

On the wall, scrawled in blood, are the words *Yankee Scum*.

A scream causes you to spin.

Iris.

Carrying the blade and the sawed-off, you charge out of the garage, through the store, into the parking lot. You expect Tanner's men at first—you think they've found you, but no. Instead, a thin man—all skin and bones—dragging Iris across the lot, out toward the street. He has a blade to Iris's throat.

"Fuck'n Yank," Bones says, hissing in your direction. "See y'n hell, boy."

Iris lifts her leg, drives her heel into Bones's foot. He howls and pulls the blade closer, drawing a trickle of blood. Iris stops fighting then. The ferocious look on her face, though, says she's eager to break the man.

There are two zombies in Confederate soldier garb on either side of Bones. "Hee-ya!" Bones shouts. He kicks one in the rear, sending it sprawling toward you.

You charge after them. The larger of the two Confederate zombies—a fat man, with guts spilling out and seeping through his uniform—tries to grab hold of you. You take out its leg, dropping it to the ground.

You don't understand. Confederate soldiers? And in Pennsylvania? Zombies pulled from their graves? This isn't a horror movie, with old men crawling out of the earth. Doesn't make sense . . .

The other Confederate zombie, this one with a thick beard and a tilted hat on its head, lunges. You drive the Arkansas toothpick into its skull, black blood bubbling, the body crumpling.

You look down at the thing, spot a large tribal tattoo on the zombie's rotting arm, and you realize—

Reenactors. They're goddamn Civil War reenactors.

Bones is across the street now, dragging Iris into the Gettysburg memorial graveyard. You unhook the gas hose, sliding into the El Camino. Foot down, tires howling, crashing through the gate, darting down the street, then spinning it back—the El Camino bounces through the cemetery entrance, slewing onto the yellowed grass and gravestone-dotted lawn.

You spot Bones, pulling Iris, knife blade glinting in the sun.

Hope this car is as tough as Hank said . . .

You spin the wheel, driving *through* the cemetery. The heavy metal thresher plows into headstones, cracking them in half, ripping them from the ground.

The skinny Confederate reenactor weaves through the cemetery, using the larger monuments to keep you from getting too close. Iris is quiet—no screaming for her life, no begging for help.

Bones lets out a howl—a banshee shriek. *Ah, hell.* A rebel yell, you realize.

And then they're coming over the short hills and from the thick woods, swarming like roaches. Undead reenactors by the thousands. They hear Bones's yell, and they come for him—but it's you they see first.

They rush, staggering with that telltale hobbled gait—slow, usually, but quicker than shit when they smell human flesh.

And, Christ almighty, the man leading the charge is atop an undead horse, strapped across the broken animal. The animal's flesh is rotted away and its rib cage visible, but it still gallops.

It's a zombified Major General George Pickett reenactor, you realize, and this is Pickett's Charge. The entire army of Northern Virginia is coming for you. This is your own personal battle of Gettysburg.

Pickett's Charge failed spectacularly, near ended the war for the South—and this isn't gonna end well for these undead bastards, either, you think.

Bones, currently ducking behind a headstone, waits for the army to pass, then yanks Iris to her feet. He drags her toward the memorial museum and gift shop—a long building, beyond the headstones.

You flip open the trigger block on the gearshift, pressing your thumb onto the firing button.

Northern hell is unleashed.

The M134D minigun is deafening, pumping round after round of thundering fire.

Bullets punch fist-sized holes in the monsters—wet globs of flesh and chipped bone splashing headstones. Pickett's horse goes down first—the animal's head opening, then the legs chopped apart by scorching rounds. Gray uniforms jerking, convulsing as the minigun deals death at four thousand rounds per minute.

You lay off the gun then and grip the wheel tight, the El Camino screaming into the charging army. Replica rifles drop from the monsters' hands as they're mowed down, chewed up, chopped apart by the thresher.

KRAKA—BOOM!

The ground ahead of you erupts, an explosion tearing open the earth, chunks of dirt splashing.

What the . . .

You wrench the wheel, the El Camino slicing across the field. Through the thick horde of reenactors you glimpse four men—*living men*, like Bones the skinny Confederate. They're manning two rusted howitzer guns, cramming them with homemade ammo.

Another earsplitting bang and a dozen Confederate zombies are liquefied. Bodies burst, muscle and tissues and brain matter spraying the cracked windshield.

You try to steer left, away from the guns, but—

SLAM!

A headstone plays roadblock, greeting the El Camino, throwing you into the wheel, punching the wind from your lungs. The headstone is cracked, but not pulled from the ground. Another headstone snags your rear right tire.

Pickett's undead men coming from all sides. Reaching through the window. Clawing at your face. Climbing onto the car.

You jerk the stick, throwing the El Camino into reverse, but the tires just spin, kicking dirt, and the headstones grind against the car's undercarriage. And all around you, the moaning of the hungry dead . . .

Abandon the El Camino? Turn to page 366.

If you'll continue trying to get the El Camino free, turn to page 184.

DEATH FROM ABOVE

The float, advancing slowly down the packed street, will pass your location in six, maybe seven minutes. That gives you just enough time.

Up the block is the Bourbon Orleans Hotel. Balconies jut out over the street. You take the ax from the El Camino, hop a guardrail, and creep toward the hotel.

Zombies crowd the sidewalk. You hug the wall, moving past them. One of them smells you, turning, and you see its skin rotted away to nothing, its face almost entirely skull—only yellow eyes and a few strands of hair making clear it's something alive. Quick as Doc Holliday with his Colt revolver, you lash out with the ax, splitting open the monster's head.

Three more turn, rushing for you, but you're already stepping into the hotel.

The lobby is crowded. Full of undead sorority girls and rotting frat boys.

You hack apart three of the things, then push through to the stairwell. At the second floor, you peek your head out the door. The hallway is choked with the undead.

You have better luck on the third floor. Only a dead housekeeper bumping into a wall. You kill it, then try the handle on a Bourbon Street–facing room. The door is locked. You kick it in.

The room smells of death. Stale and exhausted.

Somebody was having a helluva good time when the apocalypse began. Drugs on a glass table, along with half-empty bottles of expensive vodka.

The door to the balcony is open. A breeze blows the curtains and pigeons flap about.

It takes a moment for the two undead monsters in the room to notice you. When they do, they come hard and fast.

The first is a man in a suit, his face sunken and skeletal. A pigeon flutters, then squawks as the monster steps on it. The monster's ankle rolls, and it falls through the glass table. You bury the ax in its head before it has time to get up.

Stumbling behind it is a disgusting undead thing that once—years ago—was probably a very attractive woman. Topless and thin.

You need to keep it alive.

It trips over the undead man but regains its balance. You hit it with the blunt side of the ax, knocking it to the floor.

You step over its body and out onto the balcony. The float is rolling down the street and will pass underneath you any minute. The man in the tracksuit's hate-filled voice floats up.

Time to interrupt his speech, you think as you step back into the room, grabbing the topless zombie by the shoulders, holding the thing's mouth away from you—its teeth snapping. With one strong toss, you hurl the moaning monster over the side.

The topless zombie lands on the wife, hitting her like a ton of bricks. She's screaming, falling backward, trying to kick the zombie off, but the thing is already gnawing her leg.

Rattail yanks the topless zombie away, kicking it back so the zombie tumbles over the side of the float. The wife continues screaming.

The appropriate amount of chaos has begun, so you jump—one hand on the railing, leaping over.

The float gives a little when you land, breaking your fall. You're up in a flash, burying your ax in the belly of Sunglasses as he raises a rifle.

The wife, blood pouring from her leg, spins, raising an old pistol, but you're already swinging, slicing off her hand. She shrieks and watches, bewildered, as her hand drops onto Bourbon Street.

The old man drops his bullhorn, curses, stomps toward you. At the same time, Rattail comes from the other side.

You stick the sawed-off in the old man's face and hold the ax against Rattail's throat. The wife is on her side, wailing while blood pumps from her wrist like it's a garden hose.

To the old man, you say, "Shut that woman up. Or I shoot her."

She stops sobbing then, and starts whimpering.

Above you, the young girl looks on, holding her comic book and not seeming much impressed, shocked, or scared by the sudden violence.

"Now," you say loudly. "To the man beneath us, driving this float. It is now mine. Honk if you understand."

Silence, for a moment, and then *honk*.

"Good. Drive it to the hospital up here on the right, and stop."

"What do you want?" the old man says.

"Your help," you say, a moment before you slam the ax into the wife's head, ending her before she transforms into one of the undead.

When the driver of the float steps out, you're surprised to see he's a young boy, seven years old at the most.

You're in the hospital's storage garage. You sit the boy down beside Rattail, the old man, and the girl, and hold the gun on the four of them.

"You two," you say to the old man and Rattail. "You're going to load these four generators up onto that float."

Rattail and the old man move slowly. It takes them near an hour just to use a big hunk of wood to build a ramp up to the float. Then another hour to get the first generator up.

You drink and watch. The boy and the girl sit beside you.

"That your brother?" you say, raising your flask in Rattail's direction.

The boy shakes his head. "Cousin. I think."

"And the old man's your grandfather?"

"Our dad," the girl says.

"Awful old to be your dad," you say.

"But not too old to be awful," the girl says.

You look down at the boy and girl. They seem generally unaffected by the whole situation. No shock at the death of their family. No anger. Either they've seen so much hell for so much of their lives that they're completely numb, or they just don't much like their family.

Three hours later, you're good and drunk and Rattail and the old man are finally loading the fourth generator onto the float. They stumble down the ramp, soaked in sweat. "Now what?"

"What are the kids' names?" you ask. You're not sure why you care, but the words just tumble out. You're slurring now and the "s" comes out with a lisp.

The man shakes his head. "You filthy drunk. You should know what the Lord said about alcohol. 'And do not get drunk with wine, for that is a great debauchery, and you should be only filled with the Spirit of our Lord and—'"

"Tell me the names of the children!" you shout, your voice booming in the tight, low garage.

Neither the old man nor Rattail says anything.

"Suzie-Jean," the little girl says at last. "I'm Suzie-Jean."

The boy looks at Suzie-Jean like she just gave away the location of his Halloween candy stash. But she glares back and he finally looks up and says, "My name's Walter."

"Thank you," you say, then take a deep gulp from the bottle. "Suzie-Jean, Walter—please go sit in my car and cover your ears."

"You don't tell them what to do!" the old man shrieks. "No one tells my li'l darlings what to do!"

You glare at the children until they go and squeeze into

the passenger side of the El Camino, Walter piling on Suzie-Jean's lap.

"You covering your ears?" you ask.

"Yes!" they both call back.

"If you were covering your ears you wouldn't be able to hear me asking you. Cover them for real. Like you're trying to cave your head in. You know what that means, cave your head in?"

"Yes!" they both call back.

"Good, now do it."

They place their hands on their heads.

"You covering your ears?" you ask again.

No answer.

"Good."

You shoot the old man first, in the chest. Then Rattail is running at you. He's quick, athletic. Probably played high school ball. You shoot him next.

The father doesn't die immediately. He crawls toward you, dragging his bloody body across the garage floor. "Please," he says. "Please don't kill the children."

"I'll try not to," you say.

Then you finish him off.

When you slide into the El Camino, Suzie-Jean says, "Did you think we wouldn't hear gunshots with our ears covered?"

"No. But I didn't want you hearing them yell or cry."

"You killed our family?" Walter asks.

You nod. "I did. And I'm sorry for that."

"Why did you do it, then?"

"Because I'm doing something very important. And they were in the way."

"We weren't in the way?"

"No, you weren't."

"If we were in the way, would you have killed us?"

You light a cigarette. "I'm not certain."

Walter looks you up and down. He looks at the ax on the

seat beside you. He sits up and looks out the windshield, down the hood at the thresher in the front, and then he examines the strange buttons on the dashboard.

"Are you like Batman?" he asks finally.

"No."

"Are you like another sort of superhero?"

"No."

"What's so important, then?"

"I'm trying to save the world."

"That's what superheroes do," he says.

Lighting a cigarette, you say, "Well, I guess I am a superhero, then."

Walter smiles at that. Suzie-Jean does, too, just slightly.

"I like Batman," Walter says. "Suzie-Jean likes Captain America. She thinks he's cute."

Suzie-Jean elbows her brother.

"There are superhero movies," Walter says. "But we never saw them. We never saw any movies."

"You never saw a movie?" you ask.

"No. Movies weren't allowed."

"They made a Captain America movie?" you ask.

"Yep! Lots of them, I think. I've seen the posters and stuff. *All* the posters. You're old. Didn't you see the movies?"

"I was in jail for a little while. I remember something about a Batman movie. But I never liked movies much. Just Westerns."

"What's a Western?"

"You wouldn't like them."

The three of you sit in silence for a while. You take a drink. "I'm sorry I killed your parents," you say. "But like you said, I'm a superhero. Kind of. And I need your help to save the world. Will you help me?"

"You don't need our help," Suzie-Jean says. "You're just saying that because you feel bad."

Smart kid. "That's not true. I need it badly. Will you help?"

They look at each other, thinking it over, Walter getting excited. At last they say, "Okay."

You stick out your hand. "Superheroes."

They take hold of your hand, all three of you shaking together. "Superheroes."

You exit the garage, using the El Camino to tow the float. You take back roads, avoiding the undead wherever possible.

"What's this?" Walter says, pointing to a red button.

"Don't touch it."

Walter touches it anyway. There's a loud KRAKA-BOOM! and a rocket launches from the side of the El Camino. It spirals through the air, into a roadside bar, exploding the front of the building in a fury of brick and fire.

Walter and Suzie-Jean both say, "Holy shit."

It's a long, slow drive. Outside Woodmere, you spot an army of undead Klansmen in bloody white sheets. Bunch of good old boys probably took the zombie apocalypse as their cue to rise again, get the whole Klan back together. It's like the apocalypse gives people an excuse to be just as damn awful as they always wanted to be. You run one over. The rest come after the El Camino, following you around a corner, stumbling fast, before you lose them.

You're approaching the turnoff when you recall something you passed earlier. You turn hard to the right, nearly flipping the float.

The kids scream.

"Sorry," you say. "Thought of something."

You round a corner and see the small video store. Run-down. Windows shattered. A sign on the front, hanging off, reads *One Video Place.*

Pulling into the small parking lot, you say, "Stay here."

"Where are you going?" Walter asks.

You don't answer. You climb out and step closer to the store. The door is half off the hinges. You kick it open and raise the gun. A rat skitters out, over your boot.

Inside, it's like something left over from the late nineties. DVDs on shelves. Piles of VHS tapes. Candy racks, overturned, all the food gone.

You do a circle through the store. Coming around the comedy aisle into the drama aisle, a zombie jumps out at you. Once a pimply-faced kid, no more than fifteen. Its jaw is rotten away and its skin is mostly gone, but pockmarks still dot its forehead. You throw it to the ground, then reach up, grab one of the big hanging TVs, and rip it down, squashing its head.

You find the movies in the action aisle. Something called *Batman* and something called *Captain America: The First Avenger*.

You shove the DVDs into your back pocket.

On the way out, you rip another TV from the wall, along with a DVD player.

"What did you do?" the kids ask as you walk back toward the El Camino, carrying it all.

"We found a generator—you can watch movies now."

They grin.

When you return, Dewey's waiting out front. "Hell took you so long?" he calls. "Thought you went and got yourself killed! And what in hell are you towing there, a float?"

"Never mind it," you say.

And then he sees the two kids. "Wait. Jesus hell. What the . . ."

"C'mon, Dewey, help me with these generators. Need to hurry."

"No shit you need to hurry. Girl's body's starting to turn to cheese."

Dewey rolls a dolly out from his junk collection. It takes

some work, but you're able to get the generators down off the float and together, you wheel them around the house.

Dewey hooks them up and you go down to see Iris.

Standing over her legless body, you pour a tall drink. "I'm sorry about this, Iris. I'm sorry you're dead. I'm sorry you've got no legs. I'm sorry we have to do this strange thing."

"Hurry, hurry, need to hurry," Dewey says, racing down the steps and yanking open one of the tubes. "Put her in."

You lift her body. She weighs no more than seventy pounds now. You slide her into the tube. Feels like putting yesterday's steak sandwich into the microwave.

Dewey slams the tube shut, punches in a few numbers, then turns it on. It hums, loud as hell.

"That's it?" you say, practically screaming over the rumbling.

"That's it!" he calls back.

"Always this loud?"

"Extra generators!"

You nod. Then you head upstairs. Been a long day. Going to finish your drink and pour a few more.

TURN TO PAGE 85.

You launch off the balls of your feet, grabbing the remote, slamming it down on the table, splintering it—then spinning, holding it to Eigle's neck as you pull him close. Boxy and Thin One, eyes bulging, pulses visibly speeding, raise their M4 rifles.

"You're going to take me out of here," you say.

Eigle shakes his head. "I'm not."

Eigle snaps his boot heel up—quick for an old man—and into your groin. Heel connects with your left testicle and pain shoots through you, drops you to your knees.

"You've been in a cell for fifty-eight months, John Casey," Eigle says, spitting out your name like it's rotten. "You're slow and old and dumb."

Smiling through the pain, you say, "The name's Jimmy El Camino . . ."

"Interrogation room," Eigle says.

Clutching your balls, you watch Boxy draw his sidearm, train it on your chest, and fire. There's no bang. Just a sharp, sucking sound of compressed gas and then a punch in your chest. A fifty-caliber tranq dart, just above your heart . . .

You wake up on a cool, metal floor in a small room not much bigger than your cell. One door. A long glass panel on the wall—double-sided. You've been on the other side of that glass plenty of times. It's the preferable side, you think.

A metal table. Two metal chairs.

You get to your feet.

The tranq dart is still in your chest. Your vision is a little foggy and it feels like you're moving through water—you guess etorphine in the dart.

The door opens.

A man stands there. Barely a man. No . . .

Not a man.

The thing wears fatigues, but they're torn and caked with old blood. Much of its chest cavity is visible. Its muscles are atrophied to the point of nonexistence.

Its face is cracked—a horrible, shattered thing. Much of the skin is gone, and its jaw juts out. Its hair is thin in a sad way, like someone deep into chemo. Eyes are cloudy and the pupils, irises, and scleras a murky yellow.

It's one of the monsters Eigle showed you on TV.

A zombie.

A piece of paper has been attached to its chest by way of a nail, driven through the flesh. It reads: "KILL ME. —LOVE, EIGLE."

The door shuts and the monster suddenly lurches toward you. Its arms spring up and it crosses the short distance near instantly. You sidestep, and it only gets one clammy hand on you—bony fingers raking your shoulder, and then you're bringing a fist down, hard, onto the thing's forearm. The bone cracks like balsa wood.

You twist away—it follows you across the small room. Its mouth biting at air, teeth snapping against each other with such force that you expect them to shatter.

You let it lunge, then sidestep, sticking your foot out like it's a schoolyard tussle, and the monster trips. Before it hits the ground, you catch it by the back of its thinning hair—then you use that hair to slam the monster's face into the table edge five, six, seven times.

You drop the thing. It moans and continues biting at invisible flesh. But its head is split wide open, and its skull is visible.

You rip the dart from your chest and bring it crashing down into the monster's braincase. It breaks through, piercing the cerebrum.

It stops moaning then.

You kick it over onto its back, yank the paper from its chest, and slap the note against the double-sided glass. "That work?" you say.

A moment later, the door opens again. Eigle stands there, saying, "It's the Death Derby or the cell, your choice."

That's no choice.

"Death Derby," you say.

"Follow me."

And this time, you do.

TURN TO PAGE 75.

BULLET IN THE GUT, TROUBLE IN THE BRAIN

Hours turn to days. Endless driving. Everything you pass broken, gray, rotted. Horses gallop, free. Lone men hitchhike. The undead stumble across America.

Iris is buckled in beside you. Her freeze-dried body jostles back and forth as the El Camino rumbles over dirt roads, races down short sections of highway, navigates crumbling urban sprawl.

It's early morning and the sun is beating you down when you pass the *Welcome to Texas* sign.

The pain in your side is becoming unbearable. You have it roughly bandaged with fabric and duct tape, but you can't continue long like this: vision closing in, blackness intruding on the sharp light of the high Texas sun.

You come to a small gas station along a thin, tree-crowded country road.

"I'll be back," you say to Iris's dead body.

Her eyes stare out the window, vacant.

"You want anything? Bottle of water? Snickers?"

It appears she does not.

"All right, I'll just be a minute."

The cocktail of poison and booze and the blood loss and your festering gut flesh have you half-deranged. Three-quarters deranged, even, closing in on full-on brainsick demented. Your hands no longer feel like they're *yours*—your sense of touch is distant, numb, weak. Stepping out of the El Camino feels like watching a stranger step out of the vehicle.

The gas station is small: three pumps and a locked, bullet-proof booth. Rough neighborhood, you guess. Inside the booth is a zombie, once a man, now a broken figure—all maggoty flesh and visible bone. A John Deere hat rests on its head.

"First aid?" you say to the zombie.

It moans and slaps a hand at the dirty glass.

"First aid?" you repeat.

It moans again and its teeth snap.

"You're not very helpful."

It gurgles, then smacks the window with two hands and tries to bite you through the glass, its teeth scraping against it. A tooth falls from its decayed mouth.

"Are you laughing at me?" you say, tapping the ax blade against the window. "You shouldn't laugh at me."

More gurgles. More moans.

You sigh and walk to the side of the booth. You kick the door twice. Searing pain shoots through your gut. Another kick, more pain, and the door finally pops, thumping the zombie in the face.

"When a customer asks you a question"—you bring the ax crashing into its face—"you should answer."

Savage, vicious swings of the blade. Large thrashes across the monster's chest. Slashing limbs. Darkness crowds your vision, until you see nothing but pinpoints of light, and you keep swinging, a flurry of hacks, and then you're stumbling back, collapsing into the corner.

You awake to see the result of your blind fury: a pile of bloody flesh with a John Deere hat perched on top. No more body, no more human figure.

You use the ax to help yourself to your feet. "Sorry about that. But customer service is important. Especially these days."

You find a first aid kit under the cash register. You tuck it beneath your arm, grab two cartons of cigarettes, and stagger back to the car, thinking, *My God, I'll soon be insane . . .*

In the passenger seat, with a pair of pliers. A long swig of whiskey and a look to the cold body beside you. "Iris, you might want to look away. This could get messy."

She doesn't look away.

"Okay. But don't say I didn't warn you."

You dig the pliers into your side. It takes three attempts to get hold of the bullet, and when you finally yank it out, the blood comes in streams. You stuff fabric inside the wound and press it tight. Another swig from the flask and then, mercifully, you black out.

When you wake, the sun is dipping behind the horizon. The pain in your side is sharp. You could sleep longer. You'd like to sleep for hours. But Iris's body won't allow that.

You drive through the night in silence. No music. No Iris chitchat. Every few hours, you re-dress your wound. Blood loss is severe, but not yet critical.

Undead coyotes howl occasionally. The poison mixes with the booze and mixes with the wound in your belly until you think you're going blind.

Texas is endless. All oranges and browns and collapsed bars with faded paint and shit-kicker boots on the front, the neon lights long since broken.

Back roads lead you past a long string of car dealerships and restaurants plastered with the names of old Houston Oilers stars.

You stop for gas outside the Alamo. Gunshots ring out. You sit on the hood of the El Camino and drink and watch men fire off shots from the roof of the country's most famous mission-cum-fortress. Zombies stumble toward it and get cut down.

You flick your cigarette butt and continue driving.

As you cross into New Mexico, a good-sized pool of blood

has formed at your feet. The El Camino's seat is caked with it, and it cracks when you move.

"Things aren't looking good, Iris," you say. "Not good at all . . ."

The highway is clogged, forcing you onto Route 54.

You already thought you were going clinical, and you're near certain when you spot the towering, three-story pistachio nut on the horizon.

"Hey, Iris, do you see that big pistachio nut?"

You wait a moment.

"No, huh? So I'm hallucinating now?"

But as you drive on, you realize, no, this isn't some cartoonish Tom and Jerry mirage. A sign marks it as the World's Largest Pistachio Nut. It looks like a massive alien pod ship. Like some interstellar vessel became trapped here, out of space gasoline or whatever, unable to move on.

It's thirty feet high—the tallest structure for miles. Surrounded by almost pure nothing. You spot a small gift shop and country store.

You pull over and step out. You need to re-dress your wound and refill the gas tank—might as well do it here, beneath the shadow of the world's largest nut.

"WELCOME TO PISTACHIOLAND, USA," a voice calls out.

You stumble back, pulling the sawed-off. You swing it around, searching for the source of the voice.

"WELCOME TO PISTACHIOLAND, USA," the voice repeats.

It's an animatronic cowboy, sitting on a wooden barrel on the porch of the gift shop. The half-grizzled, half-whining tin voice goes on—telling you all about pistachios and the history of McGinn's Pistachio Tree Ranch.

You step inside. In a back room, you find a first aid kit. There's a small sewing kit for sale, which you grab as well.

Back outside, you sit down on the porch beside the animatronic cowboy. It's nice in the shade, and you disinfect the wound and fix yourself up. Then you drink and smoke. The cowboy tells you more about the place. And you think, *Well, isn't that perfect? Me here, at the world's largest pistachio nut, when I may in fact be the biggest nut in the world right now.*

When you first see the smoke, you again think you're hallucinating. Two thin columns, rising up from a yellow field, a few miles out.

But you're not hallucinating. They're real. And they look like smoke signals . . .

If you choose to examine the smoke signals, turn to page 379.

Pedal to the metal, continue driving, hoping to outrun the poison? Turn to page 280.

Iris has a point. The train will follow a safe route—and you can trail it, at least until its usefulness comes to an end.

"All right," you say.

You roll through the intersection and turn, hugging I-66, following the tracks. You lose the train for a time amidst the hilly countryside, but coming into Virginia, Iris sits up and points. "Look there. The train—it's stopped."

The train is just outside a town named Fork Station. Town looks to be a few dozen storefronts lining a single, long main street, encircled by a heavy chain-link fence. Zombies claw at it.

The train horn blasts three times, then two men swing open the gate. Other men fire rifles from guard towers, holding off the monsters while the half-mile-long train enters the town at a crawl, finally gets entirely inside, and then the gates are shut again.

Iris looks at you. You see a small hint of excitement splashed across her face. "We should check it out."

At the gate, you honk twice. Zombies begin to shuffle over. A guard shouts down from his wooden tower, "Reason in town?"

Before you can respond, Iris sticks her head out the window and shouts, "What do you think? The circus!"

"What you got to trade?" a second guard calls back. "Need to trade to enter."

"Well, I got this girl, here . . . ," you call out.

Iris ignores you.

"We can spare a few guns," you call up. "And some food."

The two guards look at each other, exchange a series of shrugs, then, at last, open the gate. You roll inside before the monsters can follow.

A fat man with a bad sunburn directs you to a barter station. You trade two rifles and a bag of popcorn kernels for a single night's stay in the local inn, two tickets to the circus show, a hot meal, and a half tank of gas.

You park the car in the local garage—an old auto-repair shop—and give the keys to a pimply kid. The kid looks at the car in awe.

"Don't touch her," you say. "She's got a temper."

In no hurry, you and Iris stroll through Fork Station. It used to be a typical small town. Most of the houses, the Walmart, all that shit, were left outside when the fence went up.

An old paint store is now a saloon, complete with bat-wing doors. The town hall has been turned into a large gambling hall and brothel.

It's mostly men in town. Some woman sell wares—blankets and scarves—from carts. You pass what was a Rite Aid—a wooden sign out front now says, *Dr. Jack Brayer's Dentistry, Oral Surgery, Bone Setting, and Adequate Haircuts.*

By the time you've walked the length of the main thoroughfare, the circus train is nearly unloaded. A few activities, carnival games and the like, are already up and running in a field at the edge of town. Kids scream from a run-down Tilt-A-Whirl while a generator rumbles.

"What time's the big show?" Iris asks a carny.

"'Bout an hour 'fore the sun goes down," he says as he unloads torches. "Don't miss the fights. The fights are primo. Prime cut. Worth everything you bartered."

You spot a booth near the train, serving the carnies. A sign reads *Old Grandma Till's Homemade Whiskey*.

Grandma Till doesn't look much more than fifty, but apparently that makes her an old grandma these days.

"How much?" you ask, eyeing the bottles of moonshine.

"What have you got to trade? Bullets? Tobacco? Books? Magazines?"

You reach around behind your back, pull out a curved blade.

Grandma Till is unimpressed. "Plenty of those around. Don't need a blade." She spots the sawed-off hanging from your hip. "That spread gun, though. Like that. Give you one full case for it—that's twelve bottles, that's a bargain."

You shake your head. "Can't part with her, but this piece is good." You reach down into your boot and pull out a small pistol. You hand it over, and Grandma Till feels the weight. "Six bottles," she says.

"Deal."

A slow-looking boy begins filling a cardboard Coca-Cola box with six bottles of Grandma Till's moonshine. You pluck one from his hand before he can place it in and take a swig. It burns down to your balls.

Together you and Iris walk alongside the train, past the roar of screaming children and churning rides and howling drunks.

You hear the moaning then. It comes from a train car near the front of the convoy.

It's the wounded, breathless growl of a zombie. Other strange sounds, too—different from the monsters you heard back at the derby. These are ghoulish, almost exotic sounds.

You sense danger: your stomach getting tight and the back of your neck feeling electric . . .

If you want to see what, exactly, is inside the car, turn to page 166.

If you'd rather march back to the El Camino and blow this joint, turn to page 50.

HOLLYWOOD
FOR UGLY PEOPLE

The train passes and you continue forward, following. Iris curses you and falls back asleep, soon snoring.

It's early morning when you enter DC, driving down Rhode Island Avenue, rolling past abandoned military vehicles and stumbling monsters.

You see nothing living. No raiders, no gangs.

Zombies stagger around the White House lawn. The iron fence has been torn down in parts—in other parts, it's bent, mangled. Two of the building's front columns have collapsed and much of the building is now black with fire damage.

Farther ahead, the capitol building. Windows and entrances are barred up, covered in wooden planks. You wonder if there are still people inside—senators and congressmen, holed up for half a decade. Or maybe they're all monsters now—feasting on themselves. The thought makes you smile.

An explosion snaps you back to attention. A missile, flying just over the roof of the El Camino, even skimming the surface, then detonating against a cherry blossom tree, filling the air with smoke and fire.

It's the little white Porsche driven by Lucy Lowblow—who you battled on the streets of Manhattan days ago. Smoke pours from the launch tube fixed to the Porsche's front right fender.

Iris curses. "Fuckin' A, she found us."

"Someone radioed," you say. "Tanner has men everywhere, Eigle told us."

There's a puff of smoke and another rocket is whistling

toward you. You stamp the accelerator, cutting the wheel, neck stiffening as the rocket slams into the armored rear of the El Camino, cracking metal, splitting it open. Your small armory spills out across the street, instantly lost among the zombies, leaving you with only the sawed-off, the Smith & Wesson 500 revolver, the grenade launcher, and your beloved fire ax.

Another rocket, whooshing past the El Camino, slamming into the US Treasury building, raining concrete and fire down on the zombies beneath.

You shift into third, fishtailing onto Pennsylvania Avenue, jumping the pedestrian walkway in front of the White House. Machine-gun fire pounds the ass end of the El Camino, the Porsche keeping pace as you charge ahead, spinning the wheel, the rusted, battered White House fence crumpling as you ram through, up onto the lawn, slamming into a zombified tourist—his body catching in the thresher.

You cut across the famous White House Rose Garden. The roses are thick and wild—a small jungle, shredded beneath your tires as you swoop around.

The supercharged Porsche barks behind, fast as hell. Playing possum like this could get you dead. With the rear of the El Camino damaged, you may need to take a risk to finish off Lucy . . .

Take a risk and leave the car? Turn to page 207.

Never leave the El Camino! Turn to page 262.

STEPPING INTO
THE RING

You stand in the torch-lit arena, Ring beside you, shouting to the crowd.

"Hope you enjoyed your appetizer," he yells. "Now the real show begins! A new gladiator! A man, paid by Boss Tanner"—at that, the crowd hisses and boos; apparently word of his particular brand of awfulness has gotten around—"to drive cross-country. But I've intercepted him, and he will now fight for your amusement!"

You turn, eyeing the bloodthirsty spectators. They whoop. Bottles clink together.

Louis walks over and drops two weapons to the ground: a meat cleaver and a long, wooden spear.

You want to take the spear and run it through Ring. He sees it in your eyes. The anger. They all do. His men step closer to the edge of the cattle ring, guns up, aimed at your chest.

You look down at the weapons.

The meat cleaver you can wield with deadly skill.

But the spear can attack from a distance, allow you to keep the monsters away.

"Louis," Ring says. "Send in the clowns!"

Louis crosses to the train. The big cattle-car door rumbles open, he steps up, and a moment later he's leading out five undead circus clowns. One long chain, wrapped around their throats, connects them all.

They're smothered in paint and blood. Faces half-gone. Flaps of skin hanging over big red bow ties. One missing an arm. Louis leads them into the cattle ring, then unlocks the chain. It clatters to the ground.

"Good luck, Jimmy El Camino," Ring says as he slams the gate shut.

Again, the crowd roars. The monsters shuffle forward, moaning. You eye the weapons at your feet.

If you choose the spear, flip to page 271.

Are you a meat cleaver fan? Then turn to page 91.

GOOD-BYE, IGOR

"You know what," you say, pulling the gun and firing, "I'll handle this without you."

Both barrels are emptied into Igor's chest. He's lifted off his feet and propelled backward. His body lands in a heap, at the feet of zombie [REDACTED, LEGAL].

You watch it eat as you reload the gun.

"C'mon, Iris," you say, carrying her through an *Employees Only* door and down stairs. There's a large industrial freezer there, for storing the wax.

Carefully, you lay Iris down. You pull the sawed-off, twist the handle on the freezer, and then—

They're on you! As the door opens, two dozen zombies rush forward. You squeeze off a shot, hitting some obnoxious B-list celebrity in the face. Another shot hits a very old James Bond.

More of Igor's celebrities. You can make out the faces of some. Faces you recognize, through the decayed skin. And then it's [REDACTED, LEGAL], delivering the final bite—teeth at your throat, tearing the flesh.

AN END

Suddenly, a plan. A terrible plan. But when death is this close, a terrible plan is better than no plan.

You rip your shirt off, jam the Smith & Wesson into your waist around your back. You grab a handful of shriveled, rotten grapes from the ground, squash them on your face and chest, creating the illusion of gory, blood-soaked skin.

You begin shuffling through the field—moving like one of the monsters. Zombies surround you, but none approach, yet.

The Lincoln rolls into the clearing, first snapping the stalks, then creeping through the tall grass. Mr. King is searching for you.

You—battered, broken, lean from years in that damn cell, with one arm hanging from its socket, and covered in your own blood and chunks of grape—look nearly as horrific as the monsters.

Mr. King rolls toward you. You slowly shuffle to the side.

You look up, carefully.

The long Lincoln begins to roll past you.

This is your moment.

The cracked driver's-side window passing you.

You pull the Smith & Wesson from behind your back.

You tap the butt of the gun against the glass. You smile as he turns. His mouth opens, just slightly, and you thrust the barrel through the cracked window and fire two rounds. The glass shatters first, and Mr. King's head shatters next. At point-blank range, from the Smith & Wesson, there's nearly nothing left. Smoke and gore fill the car.

"Gotcha . . ." you say softly.

And then they're on you. Zombies, stumbling toward you, smelling the rich scent of blood. You race through the fields, darting down the long rows, scooping up Iris's body with your good arm, passing the smoldering El Camino, never slowing.

You scramble up the hill, back out onto the highway. San Francisco's skyline towers off in the distance.

You begin walking.

Coming to the San Francisco airport, you're close to the point of exhaustion. Sore, dehydrated, sharp pain all through you.

You're greeted by a great barricade, forty feet high, stretching the length of the entire city. It's built of rusted vehicles, steel beams, and anything else they could dredge up. Men with rifles stand atop the barricade, like medieval soldiers at parapets.

"Hold it!" a soldier calls down.

"I'm Jimmy El Camino," you say, tired.

"That supposed to mean something?" the soldier barks.

Pride, suddenly—a foreign feeling—as it hits you that you're really here. You look up and say, "You're damn right it means something. Call your boss. He knows I'm coming."

"Guy, this is an open city. But we get a little nervous when a man shows up carrying a woman with no legs."

"Just get your boss on the line."

Before the soldier can argue further, there's a rumbling, and a section of the barricade ahead of you opens. A car rolls forward and out steps a man in full military regalia. He's bald, with a thin, precise mustache.

"Jimmy El Camino," he says.

You nod.

"Come with me."

You shake your head. "The antidote. Not going anywhere

until I see it. And you better hurry—the girl gets any warmer, this'll all have been for nothing."

He seems to have forgotten. "Yes," he says, raising an arm and snapping his fingers. Out rushes a man in a white lab coat. He hands you three small pills. You swallow them.

You look up at the guard, give him a fuck-you smile, and follow the military man through the door and into the city to a waiting Humvee.

"So that's Iris?" he asks.

"What's left of her." Sliding into the rear of the Humvee, you say, "Need to move quick. Eigle said if I kept her cool, there was still a chance."

The Humvee races through the streets. You sit in the back with Iris's head in your lap. Her face is shriveled and lifeless. Her hair feels like straw.

You look away from Iris's dead eyes, out the window. It's a real city. Not like New York. San Francisco is bustling. Full of people, full of energy. It's certainly not what it was before, but it's civilization.

The base of operations is Fisherman's Wharf—buildings there turned into laboratories.

When you step out of the Humvee, a soldier tries to take Iris. "No," you say. "I'll deliver her."

You follow them, moving quickly, carrying her warming body into the bowels of a building that was once part of City College.

You come to a room full of scientists. Zombies in cages line the wall. Others lie on tables, cut open. Monitors glow dimly.

The lead scientist, a long-haired man in a lab coat, steps forward. He looks at her body and frowns. "What happened?"

"A lot."

"I'll see what we can do . . ."

TURN TO PAGE 154.

Not long after you see the WELCOME TO LOUISIANA sign, you pull into a gas station and cut the engine. You wait for a moment—listening, watching for monsters or highwaymen—then step from the car.

There's an old phone booth at the edge of the station. Inside, you find what you're looking for: the yellow pages.

You flip to the Ts. Taxidermy. There are a number of entries, all with awful names: *Big Billy's Beaver Work*; *Reedville Taxidermy, Liquor, Cheese, and Flowers*; *Aunt Jude's Famous Turkey Stuffing*.

Not what you're looking for.

Any real business will be long since abandoned. But a small place, out of the way, work done out of the home—some backwoods survivor just might still be living there.

It's a long shot, but when it's your only shot, it's the shot you take . . .

One looks promising: *Dewey's Taxidermy and Freeze-Dry Preservation—Call for Appointment. 87 Broken Pelican Drive.*

Freeze-drying preservation—a process that eliminates decaying and leaves the tissue unaltered.

Back inside the El Camino, you scan a map of local Louisiana. Dewey's Taxidermy is forty miles from your current location. You throw on your sunglasses and hit the gas.

An hour later, just past an old video rental store, you find Broken Pelican Drive. Two huge trees bridge the entrance, and as you take the turn, it feels like you're driving into some different, dark world.

Broken Pelican Drive is a long, twisting road that runs south, into swampland. Narrow and thick with shadow. Cypresses and massive oaks loom overhead and overgrown bushes crowd the dirt road. *No Trespassing* signs are nailed to trees.

You drive slowly, checking addresses on mailboxes. The few houses you spot are two- and three-room shacks set back in the woods.

Roughly a half mile down the road, you spot the tin sign nailed to the side of a thick oak: *Dewey's Taxidermy. No entrance without appointment. Trespassers will be shot on site.* You assume he means "shot on sight"—but both apply, you suppose.

You turn down the muddy path. At the end of a quarter-mile trail, backing up to the swamp, you find Dewey's Taxidermy.

It is a tumbledown backwoods place. A chain-link fence in front vaguely delineates something of a yard. Inside the fence, between the drive and the porch, is an impressive collection of junk. Toilets and refrigerators. Old car parts. Moonshine bottles and street signs and mattresses. Stuffed animals are posed out front: muskrats, coyotes, red foxes, and armadillos. Perched on the roof is a plastic Santa Claus and a few overturned reindeer. A wind chime jingles away, adding an eerie sort of sound track to the scene.

You turn to Iris's dead body in the passenger seat. Her mouth hangs open and her eyes stare forward. "Well," you say, giving her a friendly slap on the knee, "we're here."

You step out of the car, carrying the sawed-off. A sign on the fence gate says, in scrawled letters, *Holler for Dewey.*

If you want to "holler for Dewey," turn to page 371.

If you'd rather go around back and try to get the jump on the man, turn to page 190.

"If you've got something else for me, give it to me now—why this charade?"

"You need to prove you've still got it in you," Eigle says. "Live through the Death Derby. Don't make a fool out of yourself. Get some kills."

"And then?"

"And then one job. One mission, and you get your freedom. Unconditionally."

You grit your teeth. "All right."

A sly, thin smile from Eigle. "Boss Tanner!" he calls. "My man will drive."

Boss Tanner strolls over. He grabs your cuffs, rattles them. "I suspect you'll die very shortly. I will enjoy that."

Major Eigle pulls you away. Descending the stairs, you hear the announcer say, *"Hold on just one minute, folks! It appears we have a late addition to today's derby card. That means you've got a few extra moments to get your bets in! Place 'em, place 'em, place 'em!"*

Thin One and Boxy move quickly now with Eigle, hurrying you downstairs.

You tell Eigle, "It's taking everything I have not to slam your head into this wall right now. And snuff out your two boys here."

"I know that, Jimmy. I know that."

At the ground floor, you're led out a back entrance. The street is empty. Papers whip across the ground. Rats dart. Eigle marches quickly down Forty-Fifth Street, to the east, toward Broadway.

The soldiers are behind you, hurrying you along. Graffiti on building walls—REPENT NOW! and, scrawled in blood, I FOR ONE WELCOME OUR NEW ZOMBIE OVERLORDS!

The whole city smells of rotting meat.

You're now three blocks north and two avenues east of Times Square. You're halfway between streets, past abandoned drugstores and a Starbucks and a McDonald's.

You see it on the corner.

A black Jeep Wrangler—heavily armored, heavily armed.

Speakers screech, kicking feedback, and the announcer barks: *"Five minutes! Drivers, take your positions! Gamblers, final bets! Everyone else, get ready for electric entertainment!"*

Eigle uncuffs you, gives you the spiel. "Jeep's heavily modified. In the back, everything you need if shit gets hairy on the ground. But I'll say it now—shit should *not* get hairy on the ground because you should never *be* on the ground because you should *never* leave the car. Now, inside . . ."

Eigle opens the door. The interior looks like something from a low-budget seventies sci-fi flick.

"On the shifter, you've got the machine guns. Those are located on the front of the car there, as you can see. Fifty-cal. Triggers for sidewinder missiles on the dash. In the back, frag grenades here, a fire ax, and a sawed-off Remington—"

"My favorites."

"I know."

The announcer's voice echoes off the buildings: *"Two minutes!"*

You slide into the car and settle in behind the wheel. Pull the rearview mirror down. Check yourself out.

You look good.

You look alive.

Good enough and alive enough to kill a whole mess of undead monsters and maybe twist some metal, too.

Eigle looks down at you—stern, like the whole world depends on you. "Want to reiterate: the rules are simple. Ten points for every zombie you kill solo, twenty-five points for combo deaths—that's killing more than one at once. Fifty points for knocking a driver out of the race, and one hundred for killing another driver outright. The whole thing lasts ten minutes. You don't have to win—just don't get dead. I can't explain the mission yet. But just—please *don't get dead*."

You nod.

Eigle hands you a fifth of whiskey. You take a swig, tuck it between your thighs. You don't say anything. You only glare at the man who held you in a cage as he marches away, back to the tower to watch you fight for your life.

You put it in gear, steer the Jeep toward the Times Square starting line.

The announcer: *"And here we have him! Our stunning surprise, our newest racer, our late addition! Mr. Jimmy El Camino, driving a 1999 Jeep Wrangler!"*

The crowd erupts. Some cheers, some boos, some bottles thrown.

"This is Jimmy El Camino's first official race, and we have absolutely no idea what he's capable of behind the wheel. But we'll find out soon enough . . ."

You tune out the chatterbox as you bring the Jeep to a stop at Forty-Eighth and Seventh, the tip of the Wrangler just poking over the crosswalk.

Across from you is Mr. King: Boss Tanner's handpicked man. The reigning champion, in the 1965 Lincoln Continental.

"And here we go, folks. Hang on to your seats and your hats and your drinks and your betting stubs, because we're about to begin!"

You watch the numbers count down on the big Times Square screen:

Five . . .

You take a gulp from the bottle.

Four . . .

You twist your left hand around the wheel.

Three . . .

You take one last glance down at the strange controls. Missile launchers and machine guns at your fingertips . . .

Two . . .

You rock the gearshift side to side, eyes focused ahead.

One . . .

TURN TO PAGE 205.

You step out of the house, tommy gun leveled at your side, bucking as it fires, you feeling like an old bootlegger. You unload from your waist, laying down hard, heavy fire that blows sections of the approaching army to pieces.

You've killed a dozen of the rotting bigots when a moan comes from your right. One is at the fence, coming over, half-falling, half-leaping. The monster tackles you.

As it lowers its head to bite, you get the gun up, jabbing it beneath the white hood, into its mouth, teeth cracking as you force it inside. And then you fire. Everything shakes as you pump the monster's head full of two dozen rounds. The close fire sets the hood aflame, and the thing's head burns as you continue firing slug after slug and blood and brain and charred, flaming flesh splash over you.

And then you're up, firing again at the approaching horde, but the gun just clicks.

Empty.

TURN TO PAGE 290.

You feel it in your gut. There's more to this circus than just animals and games. There's something cruel here. Something macabre and grim.

"We're leaving," you say, pulling Iris along.

She yanks her hand away. More strength than you expected. "The hell? We just bartered to get in here—now we leave?"

"This isn't right. None of it."

Iris eyes you. She takes a step back and looks around: at the games, the carnies, the eager townsfolk. And then she nods in agreement.

Quickly, you and Iris move away from the train, through town, with your head up. It feels like every man is watching her and watching you: the man in the El Camino, the one who brought her.

Inside the garage, the pimply kid is sitting on a stool, flipping through a tattered issue of *Hustler*. "Keys," you say.

"Not staying for the show? Circus only comes through once, maybe twice a year."

"Places to be," you say, walking past him, so you're deep into the garage and he's closest to the street. You don't want the street at your back. "Keys."

"Sure thing," he says, shrugging and turning his back to you, reaching to the key box.

As he reaches for the keys, you reach for the sawed-off. You bring it up, holding it steady. When the kid comes around, he's gripping a pistol.

He swallows as he sees the sawed-off pointed at his chest.

"Drop the peashooter," you say, "and give me the keys."

He grinds his teeth. He's probably read stories of these new-style wasteland warriors. Maybe fancied himself one. Thought this was his moment to prove himself a gunman.

He was wrong.

He places the pistol on the cracked garage floor. Then, slowly, he retrieves your keys and tosses them to you.

Iris nods to you, then gets inside the car.

Two men step in from the street, then into the garage, blocking the exit. One, a heavy, carries a baseball bat. The second, a skinny man, carries an AK-47 that's about as big as he is.

Skinny says, "We heard tell on the radio about a bearded man in an armored El Camino, driving around a long-haired blond whore."

"Coincidence," you say. "Dime a dozen, bearded men in armored El Caminos with long-haired blond whores."

Skinny smiles. "They said, dead or alive, worth a lot."

"Well, shit, I'm honored."

"Not you. Her. You're not worth nothin'."

"Just like my ma used to say."

There's a silence then. No one speaking. The heavy with the bat steps closer.

You break the silence by breaking his jaw, slamming the butt of the sawed-off into his face, dropping him, then stamping your boot down on his throat. The sawed-off stays level, pointed at Skinny. "I suggest you move. The 'blond whore' and I are leaving town."

The kid steps forward, looking to impress these local thugs. He wants to be some sort of pulp fiction legend. Instead, you make him a footnote—turning, squeezing, the explosion of the gun loud as all hell inside the garage. The kid is lifted off his feet, chest opening as he slams into a row of tools that runs along the wall.

Skinny opens fire with the AK.

Then it's Iris lunging, swinging open the driver's-side door, you following, diving inside the El Camino. Skinny lights up the windshield. It cracks, splinters, but the bulletproof glass holds.

You jam the keys into the ignition and, mashing the pedal, the front of the El Camino slamming into Skinny, pushes him into the thresher. He shrieks, convulses, firing into the air, into the crowd, as you speed out onto the street.

Chaos now.

The townsfolk running—most away from the scene, some toward it. More men with guns. One shouts, "It's them two Boss Tanner radioed about!"

Grandma Till dives behind her booth, shouting, "One year's free booze to the one who stops them!"

Goddamn it, Grandma Till . . . Can't even trust a kindly old-lady moonshiner . . .

You glance toward the main gate. A dozen men with guns blocking it. You need those gates opened. You stomp on the accelerator and spin the wheel, racing toward the far end of town.

"Gun!" Iris barks over the roar of the engine and the screams of the townsfolk and the heavy fire of the enemy.

"M16. In the back."

As she goes for the weapon, you steer the El Camino through town, doing your best to avoid those scrambling for cover, doing your best to run down the men firing on you. You plow through Grandma's stand, bottles shattering and whiskey splashing over the windshield.

Near the end of the town, you pop the e-brake and the car whirls, sliding up next to the circus train.

"Blast open the doors!" you bark.

Iris rolls down the window and rests the gun on the door. She squeezes and the gun shakes and kicks but she holds it damn steady and the M16 fire blows open the train door locks.

You drive and she continues, opening three, four, five, six train cars, and then there's a tremendous moaning and an undead, ungodly howling.

In your rearview, you see zombies pouring out of the cars. But not just humans.

A fucking menagerie. A circus. Zombie tigers, zombie horses.

A zombie giraffe runs alongside the El Camino. Its muscles are too deteriorated to keep its head up, so it just lopes around, its neck flaccid and its head dragging along the pavement.

A gunman, ready to fire on you, is knocked off his feet by a zombie horse, then crushed beneath its hooves.

Old carnival workers, long since turned undead, stumble about. Two, done up in fresh clown makeup, tackle Grandma Till. Their teeth penetrate her skin and soon the blood mixes with their red makeup, creating a gory, indistinguishable mess.

At last, you hear someone scream, "The gates! Open the gates! Get those fucking animals out of here!"

Good. Now you just need to get to the front of the town without dying.

You cut the wheel, swinging, racing down an alleyway. And there, blocking your path, is a zombified rhinoceros—plucked from a zoo, you figure. It is a massive, hulking beast. Its skull is exposed and bits of rotten gray brain are visible. Its eyes are red. Its flesh has broken down so that in certain parts nothing but bone is visible.

Yet the zombie virus keeps it "alive." It keeps the strange animal on its feet. It keeps the strange animal thirsting for human flesh. *Your* flesh.

If you want to unload, giving the zombie rhinoceros everything you have, turn to page 129.

This fight looks unwinnable. To throw it in reverse and try to escape, turn to page 292.

It takes nearly an hour to get the El Camino free—it's a final whirring of the thresher and a kick of the nitrous that does it. The whole time, zombies are gathering, harassing you. You kill almost two dozen before you get the car loose of the headstone, and you're happy as hell to ride out over the beasts' broken bodies.

The sky is the color of rust when you cross into Ohio. You drive down long, winding roads, past weather-beaten houses with caved-in roofs and sunken porches.

"You need to sleep?" Iris asks.

"Not yet."

"You've been driving sixteen hours."

"I can drive sixteen more."

"There's a place near here. In the guidebook. I'd like to stop there. And sleep for the night. I'd prefer it."

"This isn't a sightseeing tour."

"You need to sleep."

"When we sleep, we sleep in the car. We don't get out of the car. We stick to the map."

She holds up the guidebook. "I need to see this place."

"What place?"

"The Museum of Divine Statues. In Lakewood, Ohio."

"Why?"

"Personal."

You don't say anything. After a moment, she says, frustrated, "Well?"

"What personal reasons?"

"I can't explain."

"Then we don't stop."

"I'll explain when we get there. That good enough?"

You look over at her. Her face looks heavy, tired—more than before. Some backbreaking weight on her shoulders, nearly crushing her. "Find it on the map," you say. "Get me there, I'll see if it's safe. If it is, we can sleep there tonight. But if I get a feeling, we leave."

A barely perceptible smile on Iris's face. "Good."

"What are you smiling for?"

"I'm not. Asshole."

You grin at that, and you continue driving down the endless, depressed Ohio back roads.

For the first time, you feel the poison in your system. A fogginess in your head. Brief moments of blurred vision. Nausea. You ignore it and press your foot down harder on the gas—the sooner you get to San Francisco, the sooner you can get right.

The Museum of Divine Statues is in fact a church, located a few blocks from Lake Erie. It's a beige brick building, vines up the sides, surrounded by houses gone to rack and ruin. Some burned down.

In the parking lot, you stop between two long-abandoned cars. If Tanner's men are onto you, you need to keep the El Camino out of view.

You shut off the radio, grab the sawed-off and a flashlight, and step from the El Camino. "You stay, I'll check it out." Iris ignores and follows you. You don't fight her. You circle the building once. No cars parked anywhere.

The wooden church doors are half-open. You shine the flashlight and lead with the sawed-off.

Faces stare at you.

Pink faces.

You take a step back, muscles tightening—it's a long two seconds before you realize they're not real.

Iris reads from the book. "'This gutted, renovated church now houses dozens of restored statues.'"

You walk the museum, slowly, gun up. You hear nothing. Not even rats skittering or roaches scattering. The kitchen is empty. There's a workspace in the back, where the people who ran the place did their restorations. Paint supplies, easels. You check the bathrooms, the closets. Empty.

"Okay. We can sleep here," you say, stepping back into the main hall, statues surrounding you. "I'll secure the doors."

You move from room to room, building makeshift barriers in front of the few doors that can't be locked. When you return, Iris is kneeling in front of a cross, praying. You begin to say something, then stop. Let her be.

You find a pew. You kick away a small wooden divider, the wood splinters, and you fully lay your body out.

Iris lies in the pew one over. You can't see each other. You stare up at the roof of the church—it's full of subpar paintings. Adam and Eve and angels and other nonsense.

You say, "Let me sleep for four hours. You stay awake. You hear anything, see anything, wake me up. Then we leave. You sleep in the car. Understood?"

"Okay."

You take a swig of whiskey, slide the flask between your legs, and shut your eyes.

Five minutes later, sleep not coming, you say, "Why were you eager to stay here?"

"It's a holy place," Iris says. "I need that now."

"Why?"

She doesn't respond, so you don't press. You're half-asleep when she next speaks. "Do you believe in this?"

"What?"

"All this. The statues. God. Whatever you want to call it."

"No."

"Really?"

"Really."

"How can you not believe?"

"Just don't. Don't think none of it matters. Think it's bullshit."

"Do you think what we're doing, it's the right thing?"

"Yes."

"I hope people pay attention to this," she says. "I'd like it to matter."

You sit up, grab the flask, and rest your arm on the back of the pew. You light a cigarette and you drink with the gun across your lap.

"It doesn't have to matter, Iris. What matters is that we're doing what we set out to do. If we get there, and it doesn't work, well—at least we tried. Nothing lost."

"No."

"No what?"

"I'm going to die, Jimmy. When we get there."

"Huh?"

"I'm going to die. Eigle told me. In San Francisco they'll have to kill me. To learn how my body works. Why it's—y'know."

You pull at your cigarette.

"Real nice, huh?" Iris says after a minute.

You just drink.

"That's why I wanted to come here. I need to be saved, before I die."

You drink more.

"Damn it, you going to say anything?" she asks.

"I think you'll be giving your life for something. Which is more than most people get."

"But you just said it's all bullshit!" she says, voice raising, angry.

"No. I said *this* is bullshit. Statues to God. But helping people to live—that's not bullshit."

"No, I think you meant it's all bullshit. People. Humans. Us. We should just give up. Maybe I agree."

"No. I didn't. I've seen horrible things, Iris. And—"

"And what?"

"Nothing. I'm going to sleep. Wake me up like I said."

Two hours later, a heavy thud yanks you from a nightmare. In the corner of the room, a statue blocking a confessional booth has tumbled over.

Iris stands next to it. She looks at you, embarrassed. "Shit, shit," she says. "Go back to sleep. I just—I saw the booth. I wanted, ah—I wanted to confess."

"Iris . . . ," you sigh.

And then the confessional door flies open.

A priest in a torn black robe bursts out. Its face is maggot-infested and its eyeballs have been plucked from their sockets. It dives at Iris, biting into her throat, teeth sinking into flesh.

Iris howls, grabbing at it, punching.

In a second, you're hopping over the pew, gripping the ax.

The zombie priest is on top of her, clawing.

You bring the ax down with such force that for a moment you're worried it will go all the way through the monster's back, split it, and hit Iris. But it doesn't. You yank the ax back, pulling the body with it. With a tremendous heave, you throw the undead priest over three pews. It slides into a statue, knocking it over, pinning it.

You rush to Iris. Blood oozes from her neck. She's immune to the zombie infection, but not immune to having her throat near ripped out. You slip off your shirt and wrap it around her neck. "Hold it tight."

You find a first aid kit in the kitchen.

Coming back out, you see her lying next to the pinned zombie. She's holding the monster's hand. Her lips move, praying.

You kneel beside her and examine the wound. Her artery is fine, but the flesh is torn.

"Stitches would help. But for now, you'll be all right."

She nods. Her eyes are wet.

"It's time to go," you say.

"Yes. But kill the priest. Okay? Free him. It wasn't his fault."

A metal cross sits on a table nearby. You pick it up, raise it, and swing it down, crushing the undead priest. You pound away at the unholy face with the edge of the cross until the thing is no longer recognizable as anything human—it looks like a creature made of bubble gum and bone.

The thing's hand squeezes Iris's tight, then lets go, limp. The bloody cross drops from your hand and falls to the tiled floor. "Now we go."

Go to page 61.

Holding the ax, you step into the El Camino. You turn on the radio, and immediately Eigle's voice hollers: *"Jimmy! Jimmy, goddamn it, you there? Iris?"*

You sigh, slide into your seat, light a cigarette, and pick up the microphone.

"Go ahead."

"Jimmy?"

"Yes."

"Christ. Thought you were dead. Been radioing for an hour. Where have you been?"

"Went to church."

"Excuse me?"

Iris, shirt to her throat, laughs softly.

"Listen," Eigle continues. *"Things went bad here. Hank's dead. Came back to the garage to find him shot up, maps gone. I'm holed up back at the compound. Don't think they'll reach me here. Can't be sure. But Tanner and his men know your route now. They know the northern route."*

You lay the map out on your lap and look it over. "We could cut back, go south," you say. "Probably lose 'em."

"Take a lot longer," Eigle says.

He's right. If you cut back to the south now, you'll add weeks to your trip. But you'll most likely lose any drivers who might be following you. But God knows what other hell you'll encounter . . .

"What's it going to be, Jimmy?"

This is a big decision. No turning back, and you know it. Depending on which way you go, your and Iris's journey will be very different . . .

If you want to continue along the northern route, possibly dogged by Tanner's men every step of the way, turn to page 242.

Change direction and head south? Turn to page 65.

The tiny Porsche races down the avenue. Zombies lunge for it. One is hit, rolling up and over the top, then bouncing along the concrete like a rag doll.

You let loose with the fifty-cal. Bullets spray concrete as Lucy rockets ahead.

You glance down. Doing 65 miles per hour. And the Porsche is putting distance between you. You can't keep up . . .

But six blocks ahead of you, the Porsche pulls a 180 e-brake turn, whipping around so it's facing you, and you can see the beautiful driver, and her thick blond hair, her big blue eyes, and the two M2 cannons on the front of the Porsche, unloading—

BLAM! BLAM! BLAM!

Your windshield cracks. You duck as the Porsche races toward you, full steam, hammering your Jeep with gunfire and then roaring past you.

You want this girl. Want her dead.

You cut the wheel, pedal hitting the floor, giving chase. The Porsche weaves across the road, up on the sidewalk.

What's she doing . . . ?

You follow. And then—

Something drops from the rear of the Porsche. There's a deafening explosion. And suddenly, in front of you, a gigantic hole. She blew the ground apart. Directly over the 1 subway line.

You hit the brakes and wrench the wheel, but there's nothing you can do—

The Jeep, at 40 miles per hour, goes over the side, plunging into the gaping hole. The car falls, dropping forty feet onto the 1 2 3 subway line . . .

Your head slams into the wheel, and everything goes . . .

Black, all around you, when you come to. Takes a moment for your eyes to adjust. Ringing in your ears. Over it, you can just make out the announcer: *". . . appears Jimmy El Camino has dropped onto the subway! And we all know who lives down there, don't we, folks?"*

The headlights are shattered. You reach up. Tap the overhead light, and—

Pale faces, all around you. Yellow eyes watch you and dirty teeth chomp. Thin hair hangs over bloody skin. The ringing in your ears fades and you hear a new noise. The famished moaning of a thousand undead.

You reach for the seat belt buckle, but one of them grabs your hand. Cold fingers paw at your face. Another tumbles over the passenger-side door, reaching for you.

You get the belt buckle undone just as the teeth sink into the base of your neck. Fangs pierce your scalp. You're swinging a fist, trying to knock it free, as another undead beast bites into your shoulder. Your flesh splits. Another falls into you, teeth in your neck.

"And it looks like Jimmy El Camino's first Death Derby will be his last . . ."

☙ AN END ❧

It'll be the south, you decide—a longer trip, yes, and the more time on the road, the better chance some monster or highwayman gets you. But if it allows you to avoid Boss Tanner's drivers, so be it.

You cruise alongside 81.

Iris soon falls asleep. The madness she's witnessed would tire anyone.

Late afternoon: a band of roving marauders, like something out of *Mad Max*, forces you back east. You drive straight through the evening and into the night. Iris snores softly while you listen to Waylon Jennings and smoke cigarette after cigarette, lighting each with the last.

You notice, curiously, that you have a slight smile on your face.

It's early morning when you come into southern Philadelphia. You drive up a winding suburban road, to a point overlooking the city's skyline. Through binoculars, you see that the city is overrun—thousands upon thousands of undead filling the streets.

Goddamn it.

That forces you even further east, as every possible southern route is blocked by hordes of zombies, marauders, or general destruction.

You're passing by something called the National Museum of Dentistry, getting close to Washington, DC, when you hear it. The sound starts in the distance, low at first, then turning to a thundering roar.

A train.

You stop in front of the tracks. No safety gates lower.

The train barrels down the track, rumbles past the intersection. At first you think it's some strange freight train, but it emits a different sort of noise: a calliope. Across the side, in tall stenciled letters, are the words *Ring's Most Wonderful Circus Show*. The growl of the diesel engine wakes Iris. She clears her throat, and spits out the window. "What's happening?"

"Circus train, believe it or not."

That brings her to like a bucket of cold water. "Circus? No shit, huh. Let's go."

"No."

"Never seen a circus. Be a break from the horror. Something decent, 'fore I die."

"Maybe there'll be one in San Francisco," you say, then immediately regret the words.

"We could follow the train. They probably know a good route."

The rickety caboose hurtles past you—must be the fiftieth car, at least—then the train winds around a bend, disappearing.

"I'm serious, Jimmy. Why not follow the tracks?" Iris says.

She has a point. The train is headed south and the crew, most likely, will follow a route that steers clear of cannibal dens, undead hordes, bandits, highwaymen, and the rest.

But there's a feeling in your gut, saying this decision is big. Saying that whatever choice you make, it'll result in two very different journeys . . .

If you'll continue into DC, turn to page 35.

If you think Ring's Most Wonderful Circus Show sounds like a grand ol' time, turn to page 32.

"You okay?" Billy asks.

"Yeah. Just can't sleep anymore right now."

"You like war?" Billy asks.

You blink. "What?"

"Do you like war?" Billy says again.

You shake your head, not understanding.

Billy shoves his hands into his oversized jean pockets and pulls out a beat-up, rain-damaged deck of cards. "We can play. I like it. Mr. Ring taught me."

"Oh," you say softly. "Yes. Yes, that'd be good. I like War. Keep me from sleeping. Let's play War."

Billy counts out the cards and gives you half. You pick up the whiskey bottle and you drink and you smoke and you and Billy play for hours.

When you get tired of War, you play Slapjack. Billy has never played it, so you show him how.

Your hands are strong. They come down hard, smacking Billy's. He laughs. You laugh, too. You laugh for the first time in a long time.

When the sun comes up, Billy sneaks back through the crack in the roof.

"Good-bye, Jimmy," Billy says as he leaves.

You nod good-bye. You don't thank him for the company. You fall back asleep, and this time you go under just fine.

The next day, just as dusk is beginning to settle over the horizon, you see Mr. King's black Lincoln. You're peering through one of the cracks, watching Wisconsin race by, when you spot the vehicle speeding across rough fields. It's off in the distance, following the train, kicking up dust.

You're surprised it took him this long to find you.

You smile, thinking about how disappointed Mr. King will be when he discovers you're no longer with Iris. How angry Boss Tanner will be that his man won't get to kill her.

The train rolls to a stop just outside the Amtrak station in Green Bay, Wisconsin. The air is refreshingly cool and you breathe deeply.

The door rattles open. As always, the gunmen are there. "Wrist," one says.

You stick your arm out, and they cuff one hand to the side of the cattle car.

Looking out, you're surprised to see there's no crowd waiting—no onlookers eager to ride the rides and watch the undead bloodshed. The area surrounding the train is completely desolate. Empty storefronts. Scorched houses. Forgotten vehicles. Garbage piled in the streets, scattered along sidewalks and avenues.

Not even zombies shuffle around.

"Some crowd," you say, and one gunman hits you in the gut with his gun barrel. You light a cigarette and keep your mouth shut.

Not far from the tracks, six large army transport trucks are idling. A man in a suit leans against the closest truck, and Ring greets him, shaking hands, chatting. Ring waves his hand at the train, showing it off. He points to the elephant cars, the lion cars, the giraffe cars, the undead-clown cars, and finally to you.

Ring and the man walk over. "Really packing 'em in," you say as they stop in front of you.

"Special show today," Ring says. "Off-site. Jimmy, this is Big Stump. He runs this area."

Big Stump smiles. He's got a toothy grin. "I keep my folks safe in a little town not far from here."

You puff your cigarette.

Big Stump continues, "We're all real excited to have you in town. Folks here, itching for entertainment like you wouldn't believe. Real excited to have you—just real excited."

You nod, then flick your cigarette butt into his eyes.

The man stumbles back, shrieking and wiping the sparks from his face. "Jesus Christ, Ring!"

Ring chuckles. "I told you, Stump. He's a wild animal. Why you think we got him caged up?"

Stump looks you up and down. "Yeah. Well, guess that's what you want in a gladiator."

Ring puts his arm around Stump and they walk off, Ring bragging more about his enterprise.

The carnies unload the wildlife only, no rides. They usher the undead animals into the large transport vehicles. It's not easy work—like trying to wrangle a bunch of oversized, rabid dogs.

You lean your head against the car door and shut your eyes.

Ring comes to get you around noon. You're ushered to the last transport truck, then cuffed to the rear bumper. "You'll walk to the stadium," Ring says. "That's for misbehaving, not being kind to our host."

The six-vehicle caravan rolls out. You jog to keep up. The chain tugs at your wrist and after two miles, your breath comes sharp and pained.

Over the Fox River, down South Ashland Avenue, onto Lombardi Avenue. You know exactly where you're going: Lambeau Field.

A little over an hour after leaving the train, you come to the stadium. It towers over the town that surrounds it.

The statue of Green Bay's legendary coach, Vince Lombardi, has been torn from the ground. It lies on its side. You wonder how they pulled it free. Was it ropes, like Saddam? You saw that firsthand.

A local crew at the stadium. They raise the gates to one of the large vehicle entrances, and the caravan rolls inside, through a tunnel, and then out onto the field. You hear the noise then. The crowd. And then you come out of the darkness, into the sunlight, and you're walking out on the legendary Lombardi turf. A goalpost towers over you and you can still make out the faded yard markers on the field.

It's a big crowd, though nothing near capacity—nothing like a Packers game in December. Stadium holds eighty thousand, you guess—probably not that many people alive in the whole region. But there are at least five thousand here, spread all around the stadium, leaning over the first few rows.

Big Stump shouts into a bullhorn. "Citizens! Thanks for coming out today! I know it's not easy travel for you, but I promise to make it worth the trip!"

The crowd cheers and whistles. Ring takes the bullhorn from Stump, then grabs you by the wrist.

"This, friends, is Jimmy El Camino! THE GLADIATOR. Killed five hundred zombies in just three weeks!"

Well, that's just a giant fucking exaggeration, you think. *No way it's more than two hundred.*

He continues, "Jimmy El Camino is the greatest gladiator Ring's Most Wonderful Circus Show has ever had! And today, he'll do battle for your viewing pleasure. But not against a few simple zombies. No. Would I have you come all the way out for that? NO! Today, it'll be six elephants, one tiger, five giraffes, two rhinos, and *one hundred* zombies. AGAINST ONE MAN!"

The crowd screams and stomps their feet.

"Folks, there's no point in delaying the action," Ring says. "So let's get to it!"

Ring hands the bullhorn to Big Stump and slaps you on the

shoulder. "Well, Jimmy, this is where I say good-bye," Ring says. "I doubt we'll see each other again."

"I don't know about that," you say.

"Oh, one other thing!" Ring says as he climbs up into his truck. "My son, Billy. I told him not to talk to you. He didn't listen. So now you can die together."

You hear a pained cry, and then the boy Billy stumbles around from the far side of the truck you're cuffed to. His eye is black. Bruises on his neck. He's been beaten.

Ring waves good-bye and his truck rumbles away, across the field, back into the tunnel.

The other transport trucks open their rear doors, then do a circle around the stadium, dumping out the horrible creatures they contain. Undead tigers tumble out. Elephants, falling over themselves. Soon, the arena is nearly full of undead animals.

But still, no human zombies . . .

A gunman tosses you the keys to your handcuffs, then climbs up into the truck as it begins pulling away. You have to run to keep up with the truck, struggling to unlock the cuffs before your arm is yanked from its socket. You get the cuffs off and stumble, falling into the mud, just as the vehicle pulls into the tunnel and the heavy security gate slams shut.

You're officially trapped inside the stadium.

Billy tries to help you up from the mud, but you swipe his hand away. "Just stick close," you say.

The zombie animals have begun to notice you. Some come slowly toward you, others move fast, galloping with their strange, undead gait.

And then the tunnel at the far end of the field opens and hundreds of human zombies flood out. Some of them are Packers players, still in jerseys and helmets. Others are local fans, turned undead. In a moment, they're rushing across the length of the field, toward you.

The crowd erupts.

You look around. You have no weapon. No cover. Need to find both.

Not far from you, one of the undead elephants lies on its side. Both its legs shattered when it tumbled from the transport truck, and it struggles to move.

Across the field, closer to the visitor's tunnel, is the ambulance the team used to carry injured players from the stadium.

There's little time to think—an entire army of zombies and undead animals is racing toward you. Billy tugs at your shirt. "Jimmy? What are we going to do?"

Take cover behind the elephant? Turn to page 120.

If you want to sprint to the ambulance, turn to page 215.

CITY OF ANGELS

When you see the *Welcome to Los Angeles* sign, you're low on gas, you're short on sleep, and Iris's body is starting to smell. It was those damn Klansmen—interrupted the freeze-drying process. You can find the gas, the sleep you can do without, but Iris's body . . . if her insides rot, then this was all for nothing.

You're contemplating the issue as you cross over the 101. The freeway is clogged—you've never seen so many cars. The sky is a dark gray and a haze hangs over everything.

On Hollywood Boulevard, you pull over to piss and refill the tank. A large theater looms over the street. The Dolby. A sign announces something about the Oscars. Looks like it was Oscar night when the zombies came to Los Angeles.

A few monsters, dressed up like famous movie characters, stumble around; most of them you don't recognize. You were never much for pop culture—a pirate, something that's either *Star Wars* or *Star Trek*, some other nonsense.

"You there!" a voice calls out.

You whirl around, drawing the sawed-off.

A man—hunchbacked, with a sort of Igor look to him—is hobbling out of the Madame Tussauds wax museum. He waves his hand, beckoning you close. "What is that marvelous smell?"

You raise the gun. "Go back inside, old man."

Igor continues across the street. "I mean you no harm. I've only come to help. That wonderful stench caught my nostrils."

"I don't want to kill you," you say, "but I won't much care if I do."

He stops then and meekly holds up a hand. His hair is white

and wispy. He has high cheekbones and large, deep eyes. "Let me speak, at least. From the smell there, and from the somewhat distraught look on your face, I suspect you are in possession of a rotting body, yes?"

After a moment, "Yes."

"Now, why would you be hauling around a rotting body?"

You don't reply.

"Well?"

"Trying to get somewhere with it."

"Need to put it on ice, I'd say."

You lower the shotgun, just slightly. "Keep talking."

"Come inside," he says, throwing a nod toward the wax museum. "I can help you keep a body cool, for travel."

"Talk here."

"No, no. Inside, I can show you. Much easier," he says, turning and limping back toward the museum.

Curious? Want to follow Igor inside? Turn to page 98.

No! No more delays. To keep moving, turn to page 386.

You follow Eigle down two long halls, through a steel door, and then up four flights of stairs. Thin One and Boxy keep their guns on you—and they keep their distance.

Twin doors open onto the world. Outdoors. It's early morning and the sun is dull, but still, it's been years since you've seen any sunlight, and you squint. Not helping much. You place your forearm over your eyes and focus on the weeds poking through the cement and your shuffling feet as you follow Eigle.

Sniffing at the air, you ask, "New Jersey?"

"Yes," Eigle says.

Whole time you were in that cell, you had no idea where you were. Didn't even know if it was American soil. Figured a black site somewhere overseas—Lithuania or Poland. But no—a black site in the goddamn Garden State. A nondescript factory with a second, more secretive use.

It's quiet. The white-noise hum of the highway is absent. The other sounds—the honking horns, the distant machinery, the steady buzz of humanity—none of it is there.

You pull your arm from your eyes, let your irises adjust. The sky is gunmetal gray. A filthy afternoon in a filthy world.

Thin One and Boxy push you into the back of a Humvee. At gunpoint, you're handcuffed to a ceiling mount.

"Play nice," Eigle says. "It'll be worth it."

Boxy drives, Eigle rides shotgun, Thin One sits beside you. The Humvee drives up a ramp, away from the facility, past abandoned factories, and out onto 95, headed toward New

York City. The highway is choked with rusted, abandoned cars. Undead figures shuffle between them.

You've seen horrors, but these undead things roil your stomach. This tastes like bile. The living dead. You want to look away—but you force yourself to watch. You pick one of the monsters, focus on it: a child. An undead corpse that was once a young girl. You see its clothes: A blue T-shirt, torn. Black pants, shredded and caked in blood. Its hair, once long and curly and red, now all but gone, just spots of scalp.

You don't look away. You force your eyes to accept the unacceptable. To believe the unbelievable, to understand it—doing that removes the fear. And it's the fear that gets a man killed.

A path has been sliced through the highway, cars pushed aside, allowing the Humvee through.

You lean forward, peering through the bulletproof window.

It's a bumpy ride. Zombies stumble out in front of the car, and you watch. You never turn away. The vehicle hits one, knocking it down and rolling over it. You can feel the cracking bones.

When the undead horde dwindles to nothing, you stare out across the river. Feels good to stretch your eyeballs. Past five years, never looked farther than five feet in front of you. You see Manhattan's skyline. You don't notice anything missing— no zombies snuck away with the Chrysler Building in the middle of the night.

But it's empty and dark. Even in daytime, the lack of lights is clear and stark and unnerving.

The Humvee rolls on, never topping 20 miles per hour as it navigates the makeshift highway lane. The cars are now tombs, full of people who never got out, just starved to death, died along their morning commute.

You come to the Jersey side of the George Washington Bridge. Trucks, parked horizontally across the highway, block every toll lane, forming an improvised wall across the bridge entrance. Six armed guards stand in front, bullshitting.

The Humvee stops in the center toll lane. A guard—a young kid, half-invisible mustache—steps to the window. "Morning, Major Eigle. Destination?"

"One guess," Eigle says.

"Uh. The Death Derby, sir? Right?"

Eigle nods.

The kid looks to the back, at you, then down at a clipboard. Nothing digital, you notice. Nothing that takes batteries or electricity. "I have no prisoner transfer on my island entrance sheet," he nervously reports.

Eigle glares at the kid for a long, hard moment. The soldier coughs. Nods. Turns a little red. Gives. "Uh, you can head on through, sir."

Eigle rolls up the window and the Humvee continues on as the kid shouts, "Major Eigle, coming through!"

One of the trucks rumbles to life, jerks forward and back several times until it can pull out and free the lane.

The Humvee rolls through the tollbooth and onto the barren George Washington Bridge. You cross, then come out in Manhattan. Boxy drives south on the Henry Hudson Parkway.

At Fifty-Seventh Street, the Humvee gets off the highway, onto the city grid. No zombies here. A scattering of living folks plod back and forth between a few operating storefronts. A grocery. A stand offering roasted pigeons, jugs of water, and park-grown fruit. Most things are shut down. Storefronts with shattered windows.

Armed men on the street corners. Militia: flannel shirts and thick beards and Mets caps.

The Humvee takes you downtown, toward Times Square.

As you approach, the population increases. But still, few on the street. Most of them hanging out windows. Holding up signs that read RACE LIKE A CHAMPION TODAY and ELWOOD'S MY LOVER and THE DEAD DO IT BETTER. Someone pukes out a window, then laughs. It's like they're tailgating.

At the corner of Forty-Sixth and Eighth, you see a zombie.

It's thin, rawboned, and nearly skeletal. It's standing in the center of the intersection.

No, you realize, it's not standing. Not really.

Its feet are enclosed in a large cement block.

It's like an ornament, almost. Its arms thrash out. Its mouth opens and closes in a pained, hungry, silent howl. You roll the thick, bulletproof glass down and the silent howl becomes a loud moan. The zombie spots you and lunges. But it just falls forward, hands smacking the cement awkwardly, like it has no idea how to catch itself. Head bouncing off the street. The block of cement doesn't budge. After a moment, the undead thing manages to rise again.

"Looks like they put them out early today," Thin One says.

"Christmas decorations?" you ask.

"Boss Tanner's toys," Boxy says. "Part of the Derby."

"Who's Boss Tanner?"

Eigle turns around to look at you. "Remember the name. Boss Tanner is the man who runs Manhattan."

The Humvee rolls into Times Square. Men in faded NYC Sanitation uniforms rush about, sweeping, lifting overturned benches, clearing the streets.

You stop in front of the Paramount Building, on Broadway between Forty-Third and Forty-Fourth. The towering structure overlooks Times Square and the building where the ball dropped every New Year's Eve.

You're uncuffed from the mount, led out of the vehicle, then pushed against it and your wrists are shackled again. Militiamen, drinking beer from metal steins, look on with curious eyes and action boners.

Eigle begins walking. "Electricity is spare. You get used to the stairs."

"How many floors?" you ask as you enter the Paramount Building.

"Seventeen."

"Delightful."

In the cell, you kept yourself in relatively decent shape: jumping jacks, body-weight squats. Four hundred push-ups a day, never less.

Seventeen floors later, you come through an emergency exit into a crowded sort of ballroom. A wide, open-air terrace circles the building. People rush around, preparing. Someone setting up a cocktail bar. Another testing a sound system.

"Get some rest," Eigle says. "The derby starts at noon."

"Cuffs in the front?" you ask.

Eigle thinks, then nods. The men keep their guns on you as Eigle uncuffs and then recuffs you, in the front.

Then you plop down on a plush leather couch. Christ, it's comfortable. You shut your eyes. You're intrigued, curious about all this. But you let your mind go to that quiet place—the quiet place that lets you get through the blackness without drowning in it.

You're asleep in seconds.

NOON . . .

Whiskey. Like smelling salts. It snaps you to. That wonderful goddamn smell turns you into a cut-rate Shakespeare.

Oh, my lover, how I've yearned for you. Longed for you.

Eigle is holding a thick crystal tumbler beneath your nose. You grab it with cuffed hands, open your mouth, and pour the whiskey down.

My darling, I've dreamed of your taste on my lips.

The liquor makes its way down your throat, tentacles of warmth, circulating through your belly and entering your system. Joining you. A symbiotic bond. An old friend, back again—that rare buddy with whom you can pick up exactly where you left off, no awkward "How's the family? How's the job? Tough commute?" No, the booze cuts straight to the chase—it knows exactly how everything is and exactly what it's here to do.

Christ, darling, how I've ached for you.

You swallow and softly smack your chapped lips. You blink twice, wide awake now.

Eigle pours another, then sticks his hand out and helps you off the couch. "The derby will begin soon. Need you to know a few things before you start."

The ballroom and the terrace are crowded now. A jazz band plays soft, sleepy, kill-me-now music. Waiters carry appetizers. You spot one carrying pigs in a blanket—it takes every ounce of restraint not to tackle him. You grab four. Your cuffs clatter against his tray, but he just smiles and whispers, "I've been there."

You shove two into your mouth.

You follow the major out onto the terrace. Seventeen floors up, you've got a full view of Times Square.

At the far end of the long terrace is a fat man with short, bright red hair. He laughs—a hyena cackle—and squeezes the two bone-thin girls at his sides.

"That's Boss Tanner," Eigle says.

"The man who runs New York," you say.

"Right. C'mon. Keep your mouth shut, I'll explain soon."

The major leads you across the terrace, past rich-looking folks, all dressed in their Sunday best.

"Boss Tanner," Eigle says, "I'd like you to meet Jimmy El Camino. Think he'd make a nice addition to your stable."

The fat man known as Boss Tanner turns. His cheeks are red, and a gold watch glitters in the afternoon sun. He looks you up and down, then says, "You look like shit run over twice, old man. A drunken bum."

Quick as snapping fingers, your cuffed hands flash out, right palm open, monkey's paw. An instant before your hand slams into Boss Tanner's face, Eigle throws you, gripping your cuffs, swinging you into a pillar.

The terrace goes silent. Bated breath.

After a moment, Boss Tanner chuckles. He's untouchable, apparently, and he knows it. At last, he says to Eigle, "He's mean."

"I know," Eigle says.

"That's good," Boss Tanner says.

The rich folks breathe a collective sigh of relief.

"Play nice, Jimmy," Eigle whispers in your ear. "It'll be worth it."

Boss Tanner tugs on your cuffs. Eigle lets go, and Tanner leads you to the edge of the terrace. Eigle remains close behind you.

"This is it, old man. The Death Derby," Boss Tanner says to you with a proud, sweeping wave at the city. He's a big man, but he's got a voice that sounds a bit like Kermit the Frog on helium. He wants you to be impressed; you want to laugh.

"It was all my idea," he continues. "After all the badness, people wanted entertainment. We went a bit *Roman*."

He looks at you like he's waiting for a hearty slap on the back. When he doesn't get it, he simply says, "Just pay attention when the announcer starts."

You peer down the long, wraparound terrace. You see 125 people, maybe more. Girls barely dressed. A few photographers with high-powered lenses.

An announcer sits at a table, a few yards away. When he speaks, his voice booms off jury-rigged speakers positioned around Times Square. You watch the speakers, and you notice cameras, too—CCTV cameras on every building, looking down.

The announcer's words are a squeal, at first; there's feedback, and then someone, somewhere, adjusts the levels and the sound settles in. Lightbulbs burst, electricity sparks, then a giant electronic monitor flashes on the front of One Times Square—the building that sits at the crux of the world's most famous intersection. The monitor shows the announcer.

"Ladies and gentlemen," the announcer begins, *"welcome to the*

Big City Death Derby. The ultimate in vehicular zombie combat! Violent! Uncensored! Death has been promised, fans, and death will be delivered!"*

The crowd cheers. They hang out of windows, like they're in one of those photos of V-Day, welcoming home the troops.

"You know the rules. The derby lasts ten minutes. Ten points for every undead killed solo, twenty-five points for combo deaths, fifty points for knocking another driver out of the race, and one hundred for killing another driver. And they all know to watch out for Boss Tanner's booby traps!"

Boss Tanner wears a wicked grin. The man is in love with himself.

You look back at Eigle. He gives you a solemn nod.

"Now," the announcer says, *"let's welcome our drivers!"*

There are seven of them. As they're announced, they pull out from different intersections, rolling into Times Square like NFL players running out of opposite tunnels.

"First," the announcer says, his voice echoing off the buildings, *"let's welcome Elwood. As always, behind the wheel of his 1974 Dodge Monaco."* The red-and-blue gumball lights flash and the sirens blare as he enters. Guns and missiles protrude from seemingly every inch of the car. Elwood, a big-boned man, steps out of the car and tips a black fedora.

Next, a tremendous roar as a Harley rolls into Times Square. Atop it is a big, tall, butch redhead, hair cut close. *"And here comes Sonja, atop her trademark 1991 Harley Dyna. She's gripping the steel mace that's bashed in a grand total of ninety-four undead skulls over the past five derbies."*

Next, a rusted 1981 Chevy pickup rolls out from Forty-Fourth and Seventh. A massive Gatling gun is mounted in the bed of the truck, its barrel just above the top of the cabin. Out steps a younger man, on the tall side, with a bushy brown beard. He wears dirty brown corduroys and a torn denim shirt. The announcer says, *"There's Buzzy, a young driver with a lot of promise. He tells us he used to hunt the undead on his fa-*

ther's property in Maine before they came to glorious New York City."

The announcer's voice raises an octave and he says, "Now, hold on, folks, we've got a real treat for you—a brand-new racer. The Desert Fox!" From the corner of Forty-Third and Broadway out rolls—Jesus—a German World War II–era Panzer III tank. Desert unit. The driver, presumably the Desert Fox himself, pops out of the top and waves his helmet.

"Next is Lucy Lowblow, in her little white Porsche. Who doesn't love Lucy?!" A cute little blonde steps out of the sleek vehicle and waves and winks. Men cheer and catcall. One is so eager to touch her that he leaps from a twelfth-story window, screaming, "Lucy!" as he falls. He splatters across the cement and the crowd whoops and hurrahs.

The announcer chuckles and then continues as a Ford van pulls into the intersection, smoke pouring from the windows. An old hippie sits behind the wheel, puffing on something fat. "Making a triumphant return from a terrible accident three months ago is the lovable onetime-pacifist slayer of the ungrateful undead: Stu Bean."

You take another drink. Boss Tanner leans close to you. "This next one's my favorite. My man. Handpicked."

A 1965, all-black Lincoln Continental pulls out into the street. The announcer says, "And last but not least, the man known as Mr. King. You know all about the Lincoln, folks—fully equipped: flame throwers, rocket launchers, machine guns of all shapes and sizes. He's Boss Tanner's best loved!"

It's then that Major Eigle takes you by the arm. He pulls you away, to the far edge of the terrace.

"So this is the government now?" you say. "This is what it does?"

Eigle shakes his head. "There is very little government left."

"You're military—"

"Yes. But I report to no one. I have a few soldiers beneath

me, staying out of loyalty. But most everyone else? They work for Boss Tanner. Guns for hire."

"Real government? Washington?"

"Like I said, not much left. Us here. San Francisco. Local bosses like Tanner control the major cities. I provide Boss Tanner border support. Just easier that way—if he really wanted to, he's got enough men to wipe me out."

You grit your teeth. "So who the fuck had me in that hole the past five years?"

"CIA, at first—but that was just for the first six months or so. Then all this shit happened. People started dying. People started running. Soon, it was just me. I wanted to free you, but Boss Tanner wouldn't allow it. He knows about your history. Wasn't sure he could control you. I pulled strings to get you here today."

"You want me to drive."

"Yes. One round in the derby. And then the real mission."

"When do I drive?"

"Right now. The Death Derby is beginning. We have a vehicle waiting for you downstairs."

You're hot. You're ready to kill.

Boss Tanner might be the asshole in charge of all this, but it was this goddamn Major Eigle—this military man—who held the keys that kept you in that cage.

If you'll do his bidding and drive in the Death Derby, turn to page 45.

Want your revenge? Want to hurl Major Eigle over the side? Turn to page 116.

THE WAITING IS THE HARDEST PART

"Can't believe you got fucking kids sleeping in my guest room."

"Guest room?"

"Fuckin' spare room, whatever. Lounge. Office. *Foyer.*"

You and Dewey are sitting on the front porch, drinking homemade hooch. It's just past one a.m. and the moon is tucked away behind the clouds. Dewey's handiwork is on either side of you: stuffed zombies, posed like waiters. You place your drink down on the world's strangest end table—a zombie child, stuffed, standing, wearing a top hat. The hat makes a good surface. You don't bother to ask for a coaster.

"Dewey, you get lonely out here?" you ask.

"No."

"Never?"

"No. I was alone a long time before this. Figure the end times changed my life a lot less than most folks'."

You nod. "Probably lonely and you just don't know it. Used to it."

Dewey shrugs and drinks.

"You any sort of pervert, Dewey?"

He turns. "What kind of question is that to ask a man sharing his bottle with you?"

"Are you?"

"Why? What, the magazines? You been snooping in my drawers?"

"No, Dewey. I mean a real pervert. Not skin mags. Kids, anything like that? You into that?"

Dewey stands up, then. He's got a drunk on and he's wobbly. "I should knock your teeth out."

"Sit down, Dewey, I don't mean any harm by it."

He glares and half-falls back down onto his rickety rocking chair.

You say, "Even now, all alone, a girl like Suzie-Jean in there. Young. You wouldn't do anything?"

Dewey shakes his head. "Never."

"Swear?"

"Swear on my family."

"You got family?"

"No, but I'm swearin' on 'em just like I did have 'em."

You nod. Silence for a while, as you smoke a cigarette and drink more. "Dewey, when we're done with Iris, I'm going to need to leave those kids here with you."

Dewey chokes on his drink. "Say again?"

"I need to leave those kids here with you. Can't take them with me. Slow me down."

"No."

"They'll be of help to you. They'll grow up. Be like family, maybe."

"I ain't got food to feed a family!"

"Figured you for a skilled hunter," you say.

Now he really wants to knock you out. He puffs his chest. "I get the biggest goddamn bucks in the county. Gators, too."

"So, there you go—you can feed three."

He leans back, sipping the rotgut. "I suppose."

"Dewey, you need to. I shot the family they had. You can teach the boy things. He didn't grow up learning anything but goddamn nonsense."

You see Dewey smile, just a little. He takes a long swig and his eyes water. He wipes his mouth with the back of his arm, and after a moment, he says, "Fine."

The month passes quickly. Dewey says Iris's body is handling the freeze-drying process well.

You spend the afternoons watching movies with the two children—Dewey has a big collection of old Westerns, and those put you at ease. You can feel the poison eating away at you, but you hide it—at night, you sit outside and drink and sometimes the pain has you lying prostrate, clawing at the ground, but it always passes.

When Dewey says there's just one day left before Iris's finished, you rummage through Dewey's piles of hoarder garbage, looking for a game for the kids. You end up with Chutes and Ladders. It's nearly dawn, and you wake up the kids early. You fix them breakfast, pour a drink, and you all four sit down to play—sort of a good-bye.

That's when you hear the bell ring. The trip wire.

Dewey rushes to the window, and you follow. Men in white hoods, coming through the woods.

"Klan . . . ," Dewey says, confused. "Ain't been Klan in these parts for years."

They come closer. None carry guns. Their white robes are splashed in blood.

Undead Klan, you realize. Like you saw on the bridge.

"What are they doing here?" Dewey asks then, turning to you. "You lead them here?"

"I ran one over. That was a month back, though."

Dewey glares. "Well, they move fucking slow, y'know!"

They're stumbling toward the house. A hundred, maybe more. Some coming down the path, others shuffling out from behind trees, through the woods. Flashes of white in the misty early-morning fog, like ghosts, closing in all around you . . .

Iris is nearly done—so why stick around? If you want to take her and leave Dewey and the children to fend for themselves, turn to page 145.

Join the fight? Help Dewey and the children fend off the army? Turn to page 356.

DEATH IN A CAN

You're sprinting toward the building, racing past a bronze statue of pigs. The door is half-open. You have no weapon, save for the splintered flagpole, so you move hesitantly, nudging the door.

Inside, it's SPAM heaven.

SPAM hats and SPAM office supplies and SPAM stuffed animals and SPAM umbrellas. You pass by a short history of SPAM, then into the gift shop. SPAM everywhere. Cans and cans—a pyramid, taller than you. You pull a can from the center and the pyramid breaks and cans topple to the floor.

You rip open the can, jamming your filthy fingers inside. You shove the cold meat into your mouth, so much you nearly choke.

You take a seat on the floor and eat slowly and steadily. After finishing your fourth can, you hear footsteps. Slow, ragged footsteps. Four zombies, shuffling in.

Each one wears a SPAM tour guide costume. You fling a can at one, dinging it in the head.

You slide back, behind the counter, as they charge.

You grab a SPAM-branded rolling pin. You limp toward the first, swinging. Its glasses shatter as you crack it in the head. You whack it twice more, dropping it, then continue whacking away until the rolling pin is covered in gray brain matter.

The next to come at you is a monster in a full-body SPAM costume. Its arms are stuck in the costume, down by its sides—not so dangerous. You give the monster a good kick, and it tumbles over. It rolls around, legs thrashing, like a turtle on its back.

Two remain. You grab a SPAM-branded umbrella and dash forward. You open the umbrella wide and charge straight through the next one, knocking it aside. You continue running, not looking where you're going, just holding the open umbrella out, when—

A mangled, meaty hand bursts through it, clawing at your face. You slide to a stop and jump back, closing the umbrella, jabbing the tip into the creature's face. Each jab pushes the thing further back. It stumbles over its own feet, tumbling back onto its undead ass.

When it rises, it comes at you full force like a goddamn bull. You set your feet, let it come at you, and then—

SPLURT!

The thing runs its eyeball directly through the umbrella's tip, stopping it cold. You grip the umbrella, keeping the monster at arm's length as it waves wildly, trying to grab hold of you.

Your hands slide up, opening the umbrella. Pushing with all your might, you're able to open it, cracking the zombie's eyeball socket. Old flesh breaks.

You continue opening it, shattering the socket. You begin laughing, cackling, as you open the umbrella wider and wider and watch the monster's face come apart.

You've gone mad, fueled by SPAM and pain and anger and lack of booze. When the umbrella is finally wide open and the monster's face and brain are finally shattered, you simply giggle.

You let go of the umbrella and the thing drops.

You find a SPAM gift bag. Fill it with about forty cans, throw it over your shoulder, then stroll out into the parking lot toward the SPAMmobile.

TURN TO PAGE 131.

You rush forward, grabbing the meat cleaver, charging toward the undead clowns. You let out a furious, guttural howl and the crowd cheers and you raise the makeshift weapon and then—

One swing, and one zombie clown's head is whirling through the air, its headless body falling to the cement.

The next clown is slathered in blue makeup. It trips over the headless one, reaching for your legs as it falls. Another clown, a juggler, stumbles over the decapitated one but keeps its balance and grabs for you.

You swipe upward with the cleaver, cutting off the juggler's hand, and then the juggler is poking at you with a bony, meaty wrist stub, not understanding it can't grasp you. You bury the cleaver in the juggler's head, then kick it in the chest, full force, and it tumbles back.

The one at your feet digs its fingers into your calf. Your thick jeans keep it from doing damage, but you're pissed— these are your only pants, and now they've got goddamn zombie-hand dirt on them.

You lift your leg and stomp. There's a sickening crunch as your boot smashes the thing's skull and forces it down into the pavement. You stomp again and again until its head cracks like an egg and bits of brain leak out like yolk.

The crowd cheers and roars and chants your name.

You grip the cleaver and lower your stance and beckon the two remaining zombies forward, growling, "Come on, you mother-fuckers!"

They stumble forward, headlong, into quick deaths.

The first lunges. You sidestep, it misses, and you follow through with the cleaver, hacking into the back of its head.

Anger and murderous rage pump through you. Not because you're forced to fight these undead idiot things, but because of Iris—you see her, driving through the wasteland, confused, lost, unsure. All because of men who care only about their own tenuous fortunes. You've been that sort of man, too, you know—but seeing Iris, seeing people treat her as a pawn in their silly games, it turns your blood to lava.

You tackle the last one, grabbing it by its silly bow tie and slamming it to the ground. Kneeling over it, you bring the cleaver down, over and over, like some sort of machine on the fritz, until it no longer has any sort of face at all.

You stand then. Breathe in and exhale slowly, calming yourself.

You swing the messy meat cleaver through the air, showering the crowd with a red stream of zombie carnage.

And in response, the spectators roar.

TURN TO PAGE 294.

THE HEALING DREAM

The man's cryptic words referred to a healing ceremony. It begins at sundown. You enter a tent. Sage leaves are scattered across the ground.

The leader sits across from you, cross-legged. Another man, a healer, you think, sits beside him.

The healer hands you a clay cup. "Peyote mixture," he says. "Bottoms up." The healer is shirtless, well built.

You swallow the bitter liquid, then lie on your back. The healer holds a rattle, made of a gourd attached to a stick. He passes it over you while the other man beats a drum.

Your eyes shut. They begin the smudging process—holding a bundle of dry herbs that burn thick, letting the smoke envelop your body. The healer says, "The smoke will cling to the illness, and when the smoke vanishes, along with it will the illness."

Your body feels warm first. And then it feels like nothing at all. The ground is quicksand, surrounding you. Pulling you under. Hands, on your back, reaching up through the dirt and trying to drag you down.

The peyote trip has begun . . .

Your eyes blink open. The leader's face has changed. So has the healer's. Their faces are very pale. Horror encases you like a pair of frozen, spidery hands—an icy chill, hugging you tight.

The tent and the buildings and the desert mountains and the cacti fall away like an old film set made of plank wood. And then you are entirely alone. Standing on an empty plain, looking up at the star-dotted sky above you.

For what feels like an eternity, you are solitary with your thoughts. Your mind feasts upon itself, like one of the roaming monsters feasting on the living—your mind is hungry, and it devours itself whole, swallowing your sanity.

And then the ground cracks. Men come, carrying muskets, stomping across the vast plains like great invaders, consuming all in their path. And the desert turns to dirt and the dirt turns to cement and great buildings sprout up like stony trees, constructing a concrete jungle.

You're back in Times Square. It's empty of people. The buildings are shiny and untouched. Advertisements glow and commercial jingles play. And then a song: Chuck Berry playing "Maybellene."

You turn, looking for the source of the music, and you see the El Camino directly behind you. Headlights blinking—on, off, on, off—slowly, like the beating of a heart—like the car is some possessed thing.

Just you and the car.

You understand it's a dream. A trip. Not real. Something fueled by drugs. But it feels *real*.

And then they come. The monsters. The zombies. So many of them that they choke the streets and pile on and above themselves, crushing each other, like a great flood of flesh. A rushing river of bodies. A tidal wave of diseased meat, rolling toward you, stacked a thousand bodies high.

Dread fills you. You climb into the El Camino and lock the doors.

Suddenly, the monsters stop heading toward *you* and instead they rush toward *each other*. They're launched through the air, whipped about, and then they join together, sticking to each other as if drawn by some great, invisible meat magnet. Undead Velcro. The bodies mix and combine until they form a single, towering beast—an undead monstrosity. Eyeballs made of bodies intertwined, forming circles. A beating heart at the center, made of a thousand zombie beings.

The skyscraper of a beast steps toward you and the earth shakes.

The El Camino lets out a mechanical shriek. It begins to change and transform, morphing like something out of a comic book. The driver's seat becomes a sort of space-age mechanical cockpit—the car now a robotic man, fifty stories tall.

You control the robotic man, wielding it with your thoughts in this dreamscape.

You step forward and the million-ton machine steps with you. You swing your arm and the great mechanical thing swings with you. Your metal fist slams the towering zombie monster in the face, shattering it. Undead bodies whirl through the air, crashing into empty buildings and tumbling to the peyote-drawn streets far below.

The giant zombie monster lumbers forward. It tackles your machine and you fall together. The monster stands and the machine melts away until it's only you, alone in Times Square—a five-hundred-foot beast above you.

The monster raises a foot made from the bodies of a thousand zombies, ready to crush you.

And suddenly they stop, all of them—frozen—like someone simply pressed pause.

"I did that."

You whirl around. It's Iris. She has no legs. She rests on the hood of the El Camino, which is again a car, perched like an owl. Iris, dead and blood-spattered and her eyes beige and cloudy and her body smelling of formaldehyde.

"My body did that," she says. "And this . . ."

She throws them all back—the bodies of the undead propelled, launched, with some telekinetic dream power. And the zombies disappear. More bodies come back, replacing them, marching down the avenues. Women carrying shopping bags. Men in suits. And the buildings all around you continue to grow, reaching up to the sky until they block out the sun.

You feel something on your hip. The sawed-off.

It's yanked from its holster and flies into Iris's hand. Iris places the gun to her head. You reach out, grabbing the gun, and she wraps her hand around yours, so together, you hold it.

She looks at you with her big, round eyes and she says, "What will you do, Jimmy? You're a man who has seen the horror of the human condition. You're a man who probably thinks, deep down in his booze-filled gut, that people themselves are a plague. A glitch in God's system. So, Jimmy, tell me, what will you do? Do we go on?"

Do you pull the trigger and kill Iris in the strange dreamscape? If so, turn to page 358.

If you choose to holster the gun and let Iris live, turn to page 383 .

There appear to be bodies stacked out front of Madame Tussauds, but stepping closer, you see they're only piles of clothing and lumpy masses of wax. Removed from the museum, dumped outside.

"So you need to keep a body cool, yes?" Igor says, limping past cash registers and velvet ropes and opening a door. You follow him inside, into the darkness of the attraction.

"Yes."

"I can certainly help," he says. "Certainly, certainly."

"Why a wax museum?" you ask.

Igor wraps his hand around a door handle. Two big double doors, which lead to the main exhibit hall. With a disturbed twinkle in his eye, Igor says, "Oh, they're no longer wax figures."

The smell hits you like a concussion grenade. You stumble back. A gale-force wind of undead stench.

Igor holds the door open, breathes in deeply, and smiles. "Wonderful, isn't it?"

You hold your hand over your nose and follow Igor. The wax figures have all been replaced with zombies.

"They're real," he says very proudly. "The actual actors! Stars! All of them!"

You scan the hall, not believing. You see at least forty zombified actors, each carefully placed within a set from a classic film.

Zombies. Chained. Moaning. In costume.

"I've hunted them," Igor says. "All over Los Angeles. Undead stars and starlets."

"You're insane."

"Not in the least."

"Then why?"

"A wax museum," he says. "It's just so *old*. So *passé. Baroque* even. I thought, why not the real article? Skin is better than wax, don't you agree?"

You follow him down a lantern-lit hallway. Film sets on all sides. Zombies moaning. One reaches out for you, brushing your shoulder.

"I was able to track most of them down myself," he says. "Silly, self-absorbed celebrities—they thought they'd be safe in Los Angeles. They thought the president would see to them first, I suppose. But no . . . "

"Keeping the body cold," you say. "Get to it."

Igor turns and grins. "Oh, I need something from you first, of course. An exchange."

You glare.

"There is a startling gap in my collection. I'm missing one very important actress. America's sweetheart, when this all began. You know the one—[REDACTED, LEGAL]. Oh, she's quite wonderful. I want her, here, in my museum."

It'd be fun to kill this peculiar man, you think.

"Find her," Igor says. He pulls a slip of paper from his pocket—a photo of the girl, on the red carpet. "This is what she was wearing at the Oscars. The zombies came that night. She might have changed clothes, might have lost her clothes, but I doubt she took this off," he says, pointing to a triangular, jeweled necklace.

You feel like Philip Marlowe. Fitting, as you stand just off Sunset, being asked to find a missing person for a madman.

"Find the girl with the necklace. Bring her back. And then you can leave with your friend refrozen."

"In a city of four million? Impossible."

"Not entirely. She was attending an Oscar after-party at the home of [REDACTED, LEGAL]. His house, up in the hills, beneath the Hollywood sign. I've written the address here, on the back of the photograph."

You look at the picture for a long moment. This man is a lunatic. But lowering Iris's temperature, being able to keep her cool, it might be your only chance of finishing this . . .

If you'll accept Igor's proposition, turn to page 229.

If you'd rather get back in the El Camino and drive as fast as you can, hoping you can get to San Francisco before Iris's insides rot, turn to page 386.

Would you prefer to simply kill the man and freeze Iris's body yourself? If so, turn to page 39.

The monsters come quickly—limping, shuffling death from all sides and some even over the top of the El Camino, reaching, tearing at you.

You shoot and you swing and you punch until you and Iris have no choice but to run.

The monsters get Iris first, barely twenty feet from the car. A zombie that was once a child hangs off Iris's leg and drags her to the pavement, fingers digging into her calf, muscle tearing, blood red and pulpy and fresh-squeezed. You're raising the ax, ready to cut into the small monster, when the sniper's shot rings out.

The ax falls from your hand and sticks into the highway cement. You clutch your gushing throat. A monster pounces on you then, teeth taking two fingers, clawing, blanketing you, dragging you down until you collapse on top of Iris.

"I will make it," Iris says, fighting off the zombie, struggling to squeeze out from under you. "I will make it."

Another shot rings out.

The bullet enters Iris's head just above her temple. Her eyes flash and her head mushrooms and the bullet exits, skimming along the pavement like a stone skipping across a lake.

You wait for the next bullet. But it never comes. At least not for you.

More shots ring out. The surrounding zombies fall.

You lie atop Iris, unable to move, covered in dozens of bites. You feel yourself begin to become feverish.

Sometime later—maybe an hour, maybe five—you hear footsteps. You're delirious, barely lucid. You look up to see a man carrying a sniper rifle. He wears rough jeans and heavy boots, and a hood covers his head. A large pack is on his back and numerous items dangle from a belt around his waist, clattering. A scavenger.

He kicks a monster off you, shoots it, then looks down. His face is lean and covered in stubble. "Boss Tanner says hello."

You expect him to shoot you. Instead, he simply walks to the overturned El Camino, stepping over the bodies of monsters, and begins rooting through the car.

He stuffs his pack with items, then walks away, leaving you to become one of the things.

You lie there, changing, your body going hot, *so fucking hot*, like your insides are boiling and—for one last, quick, coherent moment—you feel sorry for the next poor sonofabitch to drive down this highway. Especially if that next poor sonofabitch happens to have made an enemy of Boss Tanner . . .

AN END

At each cannon, one man fires and the other reloads—stuffing black powder, rocks, silverware, and anything else they can find down the barrel. Each dressed in Confederate grays manufactured in Taiwan or China. Jefferson Davis would roll over in his grave, and that's a thought that makes you smile as you move in a crouch, along the small path between the Gettysburg visitor's center and gift shop and the lines.

"You seen him?" one "soldier" says.

"Hard to see mucha anything with all them bodies. Few of them still walking. Not many, though, not many."

"Let's fire another, for shits."

The second "soldier" begins stuffing the cannon as the other turns the crank, aiming it.

You come up behind them with the ax raised. The soldier turns at the last minute, eyes going wide, mouth forming a final curse, as you slam the ax into his face, splitting it open.

The loader looks up, says, "Shit! No!" as you leap toward him, tackling him. He tries to scream but you're already up, slicing his belly, ropes of guts tumbling out.

Two dead. Quick and quiet.

You peer out from around the howitzer, and you spot the next two "soldiers," fifty yards down the line, ducked behind the wall, looking out on the battlefield and trying to distinguish undead stumbling body from living man—from *you*.

You eye the thirty-two-pound howitzer—the big wooden wheels and the short, powerful bronze barrel.

Hmm . . .

Still crouched behind it, you turn its large, rusty crank. Slowly, the cannon turns away from the battlefield, down the line, and toward the men. You yank the trigger cord and—

KA—BOOM!

The two soldiers turn just in time to see the shell coming at them. They explode in a mess of red and gray.

Now to retrieve Iris.

You move toward the visitor's center and gift shop. No time to look for anything useful.

You pull the sawed-off and kick open a wooden door at the end of the visitor's center and gift shop. It's a small room, maps laid out on tables. It's been done up to look like a Civil War tent.

Bones is standing to the side of a room, holding his pistol at his hip, pointed toward you.

In a chair at the back is a man done up like General Lee. He looks the part, you'll give him that. A thick, gray-and-white beard. His uniform is cleaner, sharper than those of the "soldiers" you killed earlier. He grips an empty scabbard.

Iris is on the floor, beside General Lee. She eyes you—like she's waiting for a sign to make a move, eager to kill the pair of 'em.

It's a warm welcome all around.

You say, "Give me the girl, and we'll be on our way. Don't like that, I'll kill you both and take her anyway."

Bones steps forward. His face is turning and you can see his jaw working overtime, teeth grinding. He blurts out, "Yankee coward! You ain't dare fire any dern shot in the war room of the great General Lee!"

You sigh, raising the Remington, squeezing as you pull it up, shooting Bones in the chest, lifting him off his feet and throwing him back into the wall. He lands in an awkward heap, one leg sprawled out flat, the other tucked underneath him, ass in the air.

You turn to General Lee, gun aimed at his chest. "Come on, Iris."

General Lee trembles, lip quivering, close to tears. "No!" he barks as he twists Iris's hair, causing her to wince. "She will be my lady! Together, we will birth an army of fine young boys, to lead a new army! An army that will rebuild this great nation!"

"Jesus Christ," you mutter, jamming the sawed-off into its leather holster.

You cross the room and slap the fake General Lee across the face, knocking him out of his chair. His scabbard clangs to the floor and he moans.

You yank him to his feet, turn him around. His face is down in the dirt. You reach into his back pocket and pull out his wallet.

"You are not General Lee," you say. "You are"—you're reading through the wallet now—"Bernie Muskovitz. You sell insurance for Pittsburgh Mercury Auto and Home Insurance—Go Local, Go Mercury. *That's* who you are. You have an outstanding speeding ticket and you have some flimsy paper card that declares you an honorary member of the First Corps of the Army of Northern Virginia Civil War Reenactment and Historical Authenticity Group. *That's* who you are."

The man is sobbing now. "No, I'm a general. I'm a great man. I am leading us against the Union zombie uprising. A general. A great man."

Iris gets to her feet. She gives the bullshit general a hard kick to his throat—he wheezes and slumps over, gasping for air.

"Do you want to kill him?" you ask Iris.

Iris's face is stone as she thinks. "No. Leave the sad bastard."

"You sure?"

"No."

"If you're not sure, don't kill him."

She gives him another kick to the throat and he spits blood. "Then let's leave," she says, "before I get sure."

Walking back through the building, you see a plastic jar on the ground. Deer jerky. You pick it up. Pop the top and offer some to Iris.

"What is it?"

"Deer."

"Never had it."

"You'll like it. Can't imagine someone wouldn't."

You take a piece and jam it into your mouth, and together you walk back to the El Camino—each of you chomping deer flesh.

 TURN TO PAGE 55.

You take a heavy slug from the whiskey. "San Francisco is safe?"

Eigle nods.

"The whole thing?"

"Much of it."

"I want a house there, in San Francisco. On the beach. Where no one will bother me."

Eigle shrugs. "You do what's asked of you, that will be arranged. Our friends there can get you what you want."

You look to Iris. Pain is etched across her face, yet she watches you; staring at you like you're the last man in the world she wants taking her anywhere. Hank has removed the rag and is now splashing her bloody arm with antiseptic. Iris grits her teeth, swallowing agony, as Hank begins stitching her up.

Christ, you think, *this girl's one tough cookie.*

You look back to Eigle. "Well, why the hell not, huh?"

"Good," Eigle says. "Good."

"When do we go?"

"Very soon. I need to prepare a few things. Hank, take him to the garage—I'll finish tending to Iris."

Iris eyes you. "This is my life on the line—"

"Mine, too," you interrupt.

"Listen when I speak," she says, and you watch her blood dripping on the floor and her torn flesh and you figure, fair enough, so you shut up. "This is my life on the line. Can you do this?"

You take the whiskey bottle and stand up. Crossing the room, you stand over her. "Listen, I've been in a jail cell, alone, five years. This prick's giving me a chance to drive for my freedom. So I'm going to do it. And I'm going to do a fan-fucking-tastic job of it, too."

"All right," she says.

"I'm not done," you continue. "That means us driving together—in a car, long days. I don't like to talk. I like to listen even less. When we're out there, you do a lot of yapping, I drop you off on the side and you can walk the rest of the way."

She swallows slowly, then leans forward. Her voice is a growl. "I don't yap. I say what I need to say, and that's it—no wasted words, if I can help it. As much as you don't want to talk to me, I want to talk to you even less. Just get me there alive."

"Deal."

With her good arm, Iris reaches into her pocket and fishes out two pills. She puts them in her mouth, takes the bottle from your hand, and washes them down. You watch her. "Vicodin," she says, finally. "For the arm."

You nod and knock back whiskey. "Booze," you say. "For everything."

Iris lies down on the couch and shuts her eyes. Eigle continues attending to her wound. You figure it wouldn't be kosher if humanity's last hope succumbed to gangrene. "Do what you all need. I'll be sleeping off this pain," she announces.

You half want to kick Eigle out of the room, stitch her wound, lie beside her. But Hank's calling, directing you down a long hall to the auto-body shop's garage. You follow him. Halfway down the hall, you hear it. The rumbling of the engine. That purr.

It can't be . . .

You step around the corner behind Hank and—

Well, I'll be goddamned.

Your baby.

Your El Camino. 'Sixty-seven. Right there, on the garage

floor, rumbling away. You clap your hands together. "Sonofa-bitch."

She's still a goddamn peach. Modified Big-Block V-8 transmission—baby kicks like a mule. M21 close-ratio four-speed transmission. Disc brakes. Dual exhaust. Added four-wheel drive. Forklift wheels. AM/FM stereo and eight-track. Bolero Red exterior, pretty as pie.

Hank rests against the door and grins. "Whaddya think?"

"I think you should stop leaning on my car."

Hank steps forward. "Right. Sorry, good fella," he says.

"How is this here? . . . I don't understand."

"Eigle pulled it, set it aside when they brought you in all those years back. Loved it so much, planned to keep it for himself. But then the world went to hell. And now—well, here she is."

You plop down on a stool. You light a smoke and you just stare at her. Your better half. Your woman. Your El Camino.

A few drinks, a few smokes, and a few hours later, you're back in the front room. Iris is on the couch, stitched up, snoring lightly, while Eigle goes over the route. Maps of the United States are duct-taped to the shop's cinder-block wall. Each map is covered in highlighter, traced over different routes. Each route connects New York City to San Francisco—some across the northern part of the country, some running south, some through the Midwest.

"Routes are as safe as can be expected," Eigle says. "Of course, everything can go to shit in about five seconds. High-ways are bad, small towns are worse, and the cities all depend—some are like here, halfway civilized, some are just rats' nests teeming with the undead."

"Highways are out?"

"For the most part. Only Interstate 80 can be navigated, and she's got highwaymen up and down. But the back roads come with their own dangers. It's not just the undead. It's the marauders, it's the cannibals, it's the animals."

"The animals?"

Eigle nods. "Wasn't just humans infected. Mammals of all sorts. It's gonna be hell all the way there, Jimmy."

"Fun."

Major Eigle pulls a map off the wall, folds it up. He taps it against his open palm, like he's thinking, then finally hands it to you. "If you run into trouble, just stick to the map. Something's blocked, you find a different way. The map's got location markers for friendlies—people who will help you. The car is stocked with local maps, too."

"What about communication?"

"HF radio. Powerful transmitter in the El Camino. Hank and I will be in touch every step of the way."

Iris moans. Her lips smack together. She speaks softly in her sleep—but the words and the tone, even in whispers, sound like the stuff of nightmares.

Eigle crosses to a big, green metal desk—the type your fifth-grade teacher sat behind. He reaches into a drawer and pulls out a bottle of good scotch. He takes out two heavy crystal glasses, pours some in both, then hands one to you.

"To the future of humanity, Jimmy El Camino," he says.

You take it. "All right, then."

You knock it back. Eigle's eyes flash as he watches you drink.

"What?" you say.

He shakes his head. "Nothing. Cheers." He knocks back his.

"I'll take this," you say, grabbing the bottle. You leave the glass.

With nothing to do except wait, you walk down the hall, past Hank in the garage, through a heavy metal door, and up two flights of stairs. You step out onto a roof and stare out at the city.

The sun is setting.

You drink and you smoke.

You could have been a star here.

You could have driven and drank and whored your days away.

But you made your choice. Now life heads in a different direction.

As you stare out at the darkness, faces flash before your eyes. Men you've killed. Families you've destroyed. Lives you've taken in your hands—felt the breathing, felt the spark of life, the light, and then snuffed that light out.

But now you've got a chance.

A chance to get some of that back.

A chance for just the tiniest bit of redemption.

A chance for that house, your seat in the sand—a comfortable place to drink yourself to death, in peace.

You toast to that, finish the bottle, and stumble back down the stairs. You collapse in the corner of the garage. The cold floor feels like your old cell. You sleep like a newborn . . .

 TURN TO PAGE 137.

What's one life, factored against the future of humanity? The life of a small boy? It's nothing, a drop in the bucket.

You're up on your feet, crossing the car, pulling at Billy's feet as he struggles to wriggle through the crack in the ceiling.

He cries out, "Help! Help! Mr. Ring! Help!"

You yank him down, pulling so hard you feel his knee pop out of its socket. He continues crying and screaming until you slam him to the floor and his small head bangs and his eyes go dull.

You get on top of him and wrap your hard, scarred hands around his thin neck and squeeze. Don't even need to choke him to death—he's so small, his neck so frail, that you simply crush his windpipe and he stops breathing.

You roll off him and crawl back into the corner of the car. You drink. You drink and you observe his small body, lying there, unmoving. The boy's eyes seem to watch you.

You crawl to the other corner of the car.

Still, the boy's dead eyes watch you.

In Newark, Ohio, they bring you out to fight.

You're so drunk that Louis has to take your hand to lead you from the car.

In the ring, beneath the shadow of a building shaped like a giant wicker basket—one of the stranger things you've ever seen—a massive undead man comes at you. But you don't see it, not really. Instead, you see Billy's face, plastered onto that of the undead man. You blink, but it's like Billy's face has been seared onto your eyeballs.

And you hesitate—just long enough for the monster to tackle you and sink its teeth into you. You don't fight back. You just let it straddle you and hurt you and take your life, like you took Billy's.

AN END

At the last moment, speedometer clocking 120, you swerve, spinning past the Lincoln, drifting, and then the El Camino is up on two wheels.

The car flips a dozen times, rolling through the remaining zombies, crushing them, bodies practically exploding. Your seat belt snaps and you're thrown around the interior. Something sharp, the ax, maybe, cuts you open.

When the El Camino finally skids to a stop, your body is going into shock. Your gut is split open, your legs are shattered. You won't live. The El Camino's doors have broken off, smoke pours from the hood, and the reinforced metal is crumpled. The car is upside down.

But Iris is alive. She's held tight by the seat belt. Blood streaming down her face, but alive.

You manage, "Iris, go . . . Please, hurry. Go . . ."

Iris releases her seat belt and slips to the ground. She grabs your hand. "I'm getting you to the end."

"Fuck you," you choke out, laughing as blood comes from your mouth. "*Go.*"

She gives you a long last look. Then she's out, crawling away, staying low, pushing her way through the legs of the few remaining undead.

You hear the engine. The Lincoln, turning, coming back. Gripping your stomach, holding your insides *inside*, you drag yourself out of the car, onto the bridge.

You hear footsteps.

You roll over, and you see Mr. King. His face is a twisted, scarred, burned thing, looking down, uncaring.

"I win," you say.

He steps past you. Peers into the overturned car. "Where's the girl?" he barks.

Your head rolls to the side. And you point.

You both see her. Iris is through the zombie horde. A man in a white coat hugs her. Others tend to her wounds. Soldiers, at the edge of the Golden Gate, guard the entrance to the city.

Mr. King growls, and you begin laughing hysterically. "We won!" you say. "We won!"

"Yes," he says. "Yes, you did."

And then Mr. King turns, walks back to his car, and drives away—but you're still there, cackling, howling like a fucking madman . . .

AN END

Your fingers grip Eigle's jacket.

"Don't do it," he hisses. "I told you. Do this, this one thing, and then I give you a job. A mission. And your freedom."

"You kept me in a cell for nearly five years, for no reason."

Eigle mutters something but goes silent as you smash his face into the guardrail. There's a crack as his nose explodes. Blood like paint.

You lift him up by his collar, blood pouring from his mouth, over the guardrail, and then you raise him, his feet up, into the air, but—

You're slow.

Reactions dulled.

And it was stupid, banging around his face like that. If you're gonna kill a man, just do it—don't play with him first.

Scorching pain shoots through your body. You convulse. Your hands clench tight, your head rocks back, your legs give.

You're still gripping Eigle, and he shakes with you as the voltage pumps through your body.

It stops. You collapse.

Major Eigle stumbles away, still shaking, then falls to the floor. Catches his breath, stands, roars at Thin One. "You zap him while he's holding me, *you halfwit*? You shoot him, it goes into me—get it? Basic electricity? You go to fuckin' elementary school?"

"I'm sorry, sir, I didn't—"

Eigle slaps the stun gun from the man's hands.

Suddenly, Boss Tanner appears. He snatches the big rifle that's slung over Boxy's shoulder.

"No, no. It's okay, Boss Tanner," Eigle says, holding up his hand. "Jimmy here's just a little hot."

Boss Tanner shakes his head. "Can't let a driver act up like that. Once, maybe. But twice? No."

You try to stand, but Boss Tanner is over you, barrel aimed at your face, finger on the trigger.

Eigle looks on.

Then Boss Tanner stops. A smile slowly appears on his face. "Actually, I have a better idea," he says. Then he flips the rifle around, winks at you, and smashes the butt of the gun into your face.

When you wake, you're on the street—Forty-Fifth and Madison, from the signs. You squint. The sun is a little higher in the sky. Maybe thirty minutes have passed.

You're on your ass. You try to stand.

Something's pulling at your wrist. You hear a moan.

You look up.

Shit.

You're handcuffed to a zombie, wrist to wrist. It looks like the same rotten, broken thing you saw on your way into the city, but who knows. You look down the avenue behind you. It's lined—a zombie with its feet in cement in the middle of every intersection.

This one lunges at you and snaps its teeth. You slide back on your ass. And then a sound—

Speaker feedback. Echoing off forty-story buildings. You look up, spot a camera as well. The voice booms: *"LET THE DEATH DERBY BEGIN!"*

All right, so you're a part of this thing. Officially . . .

People lean out of windows. A woman whistles. Flashes you. "Hey, tough guy, who'd you piss off?"

"The wrong person, apparently," you call back.

"You get out of this, you come see me. And bring the cuffs!" she hollers.

You give her a nod and a wink.

The roar of a Harley engine echoes down the almost-empty avenue. Each of the undeads-in-concrete-shoes turns.

It's Sonja. She's racing down the avenue, toward you, swinging the steel mace.

WHACK!

She bashes in the head of one of the concrete-shoed monsters.

SMASH!

Another. The zombie's head cracks open like an egg. She's coming up fast. Pushing 50 miles per hour on the Harley.

KRAK!

This next one's head gets spun around completely. It falls down, staring at you, dead eyed.

You're next in line.

You stretch the cuff chain as far as possible, pulling the zombie so it's nearly falling over.

The engine barks as Sonja twists the throttle, closing in, one arm out, gripping the mace. Eyes blazing, afire—this woman is a fucking banshee.

And then she's upon you . . .

You *leap*, back toward the undead thing, looping around its back. You're like a bullfighter, using yourself as the red cape.

The Harley blasts past you and you hear her scream something that sounds like "Motherfuck!"

You step away from the zombie. It looks *puzzled*, if that's possible.

"That was close," you say to the thing. "You owe me, buddy."

The zombie doesn't look particularly grateful.

The Harley roars and Sonja is turning back. She's not satisfied cruising down the avenue, smashing in undead brains. She wants living brain. *Your* living brain. She wants it splattered all over her mace and splashed across Forty-Fifth Street . . .

If you want to let Sonja get close and then go for the clothesline, turn to page 171.

Prefer to use brute force to escape? Then turn to page 174.

TUSK

Your feet pound grass as you race toward the fallen elephant. Billy chases, trying to keep up.

The elephant trunk waves about slowly and its thin tail slaps at the ground. You slide up next to the creature's belly and peek over the side of its thick, rotting hide.

The zombies are at the twenty-yard line, then they're crossing the fifty, and they'll be on you soon. The lions have run through the horde, devouring some of the undead humans, buying you a little time.

You need a weapon. Now.

The elephant snaps at you and struggles to push your body away with its big feet. But with its shattered legs, it's the most harmless thing here.

Its tusk, jabbing at the ground, gives you an idea.

"Sorry, fella," you say, getting to your feet, placing one boot square on the elephant's head, grabbing hold of the tusk, and pulling. The elephant has been undead for a long time, and its skin is soft and poor.

You twist and pull, finally wrenching the ivory spear from the animal's face. You have a weapon now: the tusk, roughly the size of a baseball bat, curved and sharp.

Suddenly, an undead lion appears—roaring as it leaps over the body of the elephant. Billy screams.

You swing the tusk, jamming it into the throat of the leaping beast. It doesn't slow the monster. Undead creatures don't need to breathe. The animal has you pinned, snapping with long, thick fangs, when—

Something crashes into it. A bright red cooler, thrown from the stands. Two dozen beer bottles spill out onto the grass and someone in the crowd cheers.

The lion is knocked aside momentarily, which is all you need. You jam the elephant tusk up through the lion's throat and into its brain, then kick the lifeless animal off you.

You grab one of the nearby beers, pop it open, and guzzle it down. You throw a thankful wave to the cheering crowd.

Six undead humans charging toward you now, up and over the still-moaning elephant. You swing the tusk, knocking them aside. One—a man in a bloodstained Brett Favre jersey—continues forward. Its hands latch on to Billy and the boy cries out, "Help, Jimmy! Help!" and then you're there, slamming the sharp ivory into the monster's brain.

Ahead, two lions are devouring a pack of humans, giving you a second to think. You eye the gate behind you. You see Ring, watching, enjoying the show. Big Stump, too, grinning. Gunmen at their side.

No escaping that way.

But the far gate, all the way down the field—the visiting team's tunnel, where the rush of monsters originated from. It's shut, but if you could break through somehow . . .

You pull Billy along, racing through the thick crowd of monsters. A zombie in a football helmet lunges for you. You swing the tusk, dropping the beast.

Another comes. This one a shirtless man wearing a foam cheesehead. Chunks of dried gore cover the headpiece. You ram the tusk through the thing's gut and leave it lying on the field behind you.

The crowd roars and lions rip bodies to shreds and elephants roam awkwardly and zombies reach for you—but you keep your head up, running hard, pulling Billy along, swinging the tusk when you need to.

And then, as you approach the gate, a massive explosion

blows it apart, sending hot metal flying. The ground shakes and the stands rock and fire burns and thick clouds of black smoke roll forward across the turf.

 TURN TO PAGE 234.

INTO THE PIT!

You charge forward and leap into a fifteen-foot drop. Your ankle rolls as you land on the hard-packed dirt floor.

The rounded pit is filled with nearly forty zombies. In the darkness and the flickering candlelight, you catch glimpses of faces. Women who look like burn victims, their faces disfigured. Men with flesh that hangs in shreds, so you can see the bone beneath. The stench is thick and foul.

A legless monster hangs on to Iris, digging into her side. You swing the sickle, slashing the beast right down the middle, then pushing forward, cutting through their numbers. The blade chops bone, cutting some clean in half, so their torsos simply topple off their legs.

One grabs you from behind and you whirl, pulling your shoulder back and unleashing a vicious punch to its skull.

But they tug at Iris from all sides, draped over her, hanging off her, dragging her down. She fights. Kicking. Ripping flesh. Doing what she can to stay alive.

A fat one gets in your way. You roar and swing, cleaving the thing horizontally across the face, revealing its gray matter.

But there are so many of the filthy, rotting, hungry bodies.

You drop the sickle and begin grabbing the undead, dragging them off Iris with your bare hands. As you do, her flesh tears—their teeth clamped tight on her skin even as you pull them away.

They're upon *you* now. Climbing up and over you. You feel teeth in your hand. And then in your back. One clawing at your thigh muscle, rupturing tissue, dropping you to one knee.

Iris lets out a bloodcurdling shriek and you look up, just in time to see one large monster—recently dead, still strong, muscles swollen, veins popping—tear out her throat and shove it into its mouth.

It's over.

A female grabs hold of your stomach flesh and pulls it open, so your entrails splash down onto the dirt.

Looking up, you see the cult members leaning over the pit. Smiling. Laughing. You killed a few of their friends, but not enough—the remaining ones are plenty happy to watch you and Iris die. One pulls out his penis and begins to urinate.

Iris reaches out. Blood bubbling from her throat with every attempt at breath. She feels for your hand. Grabs it.

And as the zombies reach further into both of you, pulling, tearing, eating, turning you into an undead monster and sending Iris into the endless darkness of death, the Man in Antlers watches and howls with laughter until he's hunched over, sobbing, tears rushing down his cheeks.

AN END

You stamp the accelerator, steering the car toward a tight gap between the towering zombie rat king and the tunnel wall.

But the monster raises a thick paw, a foot made entirely of brother rats, and the thing roars—a screeching hiss. Inside the narrow tunnel, the sound is deafening.

The paw slams down and blocks your path. The rat king's tail—a disgusting appendage built of a thousand interconnected undead rodents—whips around, hitting the El Camino with the force of a wrecking ball. The car tumbles, end over end, then skids to a stop—upside down. You hang, held in only by the seat belt.

Through the cracked glass, you watch as the giant rat-king beast dissipates—disassembling, collapsing, almost crumbling—transforming from one giant monster to a flooding movement of individual, undead rodent-monsters. They stampede toward you, skittering up and over the El Camino and through the shattered glass.

They claw at your face. Iris begins to scream, but she's cut off as one wriggles inside her open mouth. She claws at it, turning to you, her eyes wide in indescribable terror—her cheeks puffed out. The rodent-monster is halfway inside her mouth, and its pink tail protrudes and wags. She yanks it, but it's too late—her throat grows thick, like a snake swallowing its meal, as the rodent-monster crawls down her gullet.

And then you feel one clawing at your ear. You feel its cold, furry snout pressing against you. Then claws, ripping you open—pain as your ear is torn, and then the rodent-monster is chewing a path into your brain.

AN END

GIVE IT HELL!

The undead rhino lowers its head, its massive horn looming like some great saber. Primal, undead eyes skim over you, over the car.

And then it charges.

"Give it hell!" you shout, and you unload with the M134D minigun as Iris leans out the window, squeezing the M16's trigger, screaming like a banshee.

Bullets pound the stampeding beast, slugs piercing its rough hide, chunks of gray flesh blown away, one eyeball bursting.

Yet it continues its wild rush forward.

"The legs!" you call out. "Shoot the legs!"

Iris lowers her fire. Bullets pound bone until the left leg gives out and the giant, undead monster stumbles. You lean out the window and fire the sawed-off—two shots to the front right kneecap, and the monster collapses, crashing to the pavement.

It moans and kicks and blood pools around it.

You slip two fresh slugs into the smoking sawed-off, step out of the car, and fire twice into the rhino-monster's head. The first shot breaks through the skull—the second destroys the brain.

Stepping back into the car, you see Iris holding her throat—where she was bit by the priest. Blood trickles through her fingers.

"The kickback," she says.

"We'll get you fixed up. Once we're out of here."

You blast out of the alley, plunging yourself back into the chaos.

An elephant charges through the front gate, smashing it open, crushing gunmen beneath its feet. Surrounding the gate, undead humans feast on hired guns. A light red mist hangs over the whole town as throats are torn open and brains are devoured and flesh is ripped to pieces.

Giraffes stampede through the gates with their heads hanging, bouncing behind them. Undead horses and zebras follow.

You race forward, flicking the nitrous, burning rubber as you blast through the gate and leave the town and the screams and the horror in your rearview.

Ten miles down the road, you stop to dress Iris's neck wound. You wrap gauze around it and douse it with disinfectant. Iris grits her teeth.

"The gauze should hold."

"Hope so," Iris says. "I'm used to some hurt. But this isn't fun."

After you check your map, it's clear the best course now is north. You press on—driving for two days straight, no sleep, just booze and cigarettes and the need to be rid of Eigle's fucking poison pushing you forward.

 TURN TO PAGE 242.

The SPAMmobile is one big mother—a full-size RV. You step inside. It smells stale. You find the keys beneath the driver's seat.

You stamp the ignition and steer it out onto the highway, thinking *goddamn* it feels good to be driving instead of draped across an undead elephant.

It's just after dusk when the SPAMmobile rumbles into its destination: Cawker City, Kansas. First thing you think is, *Well . . . "city" is being pretty goddamn generous.*

You roll past a few zombies that stumble around the outskirts of the town. You don't see many. Maybe the Midwest is too empty—too picked over—to allow the cannibal monsters to survive.

It's clear that before the world ended, an entire economy popped up around the World's Largest Ball of Twine. Driving through town, you're inundated: from one window the Mona Lisa stares out at you—hugging a ball of twine.

The World's Largest Ball of Twine is housed in a gazebo at the top of something called Prairie Dog Hill. The SPAMmobile rumbles as you drive up the hill.

You pull to a stop, step out, and stretch. The gazebo is in front of you—inside it, the World's Largest Ball of Twine.

Will Iris be here?

You haven't allowed yourself to think about what you would do if she *wasn't*. Looking around, you don't see the El Camino anywhere.

Your stomach feels hollow.

"Iris?" you say.

No answer. You pull open the gazebo's screen door. The air is damp and sour. You circle around the large ball.

You think she's dead when you first see her. Iris is sitting on the ground, her back against the big ball, looking out at the prairie. She cranes her neck to look up at you. "What took you so long?"

Relief floods through you, but you don't show it. You simply smile and say, "That *is* one big damn ball of twine."

"It stinks like sweat and dog."

You light a cigarette and wave your hand at the damp air. "I noticed."

You lean against one of the gazebo's pillars and rest there for a long time.

"I thought you weren't going to come," Iris says after a while.

"I told you I would."

"I've learned that doesn't usually mean a lot."

Very lightly, your shoulders form a shrug.

After another long silence, you say, "Where's my car?"

"Down there," Iris says, getting to her feet and pointing. At the bottom of the hill, about a hundred yards from where you are, you can read the big, sun-faded orange sign: *Prairie Dog City—Home of the World's Largest Prairie Dog.*

Also, according to the sign, it's home to a six-legged steer, a miniature donkey, and a five-legged cow.

"Don't get your hopes up. It's not real," she says.

"Huh?"

"The world's largest prairie dog. It's just a big wooden thing. I saw it when I put the car down there. I thought I should park it away from where I was, in case someone came."

You nod.

"What happened to you?" she asks.

You shake your head. "If I told you, you wouldn't believe me."

The sun is setting behind you. The sun sets big in Kansas—orange and red and pink streaks, filling the whole sky, like the man upstairs dumped a few buckets of paint across the horizon and called it a day.

"I need to sleep," you say. "We'll start again first thing in the morning. We can sleep in the SPAM truck. Plenty of room."

"The what?"

"You'll see. Outside."

"Forget that," she says. "Upstairs, above the gazebo. I made a small room."

You shrug. "Lead the way."

You climb a ladder through a small door in the ceiling to the room above the gazebo. It's there for storage: all the World's Largest Ball of Twine–related–item storage anyone could ever need. The ceiling is low and you have to duck. A small pile of discarded food packaging sits in the corner—Iris survived on jars of peanut butter and ramen noodles. A mailbox on its side collects rainwater.

You can see the sky.

"There's a hole in the ceiling," you say.

"It's nice," she says.

"It's nice there's a hole in the ceiling?"

"You look up at the stars while you sleep."

Iris has built a sort of sleeping bag from things taken from the surrounding stores. She lies down on it. You take a seat on the wooden floor.

"We can share," she says. "It's not much of a bed, but . . ."

"Floor's fine for me."

She shrugs. "Whatever you want."

You lie on your back. Stars are beginning to peek through the purple sky. Your stomach is tight, like your insides are wrestling. Too much SPAM, you think—but then you realize it's the poison, beginning to rot your interior.

You and Iris lie in silence for a long while. "You run into much trouble?" you ask at last.

"Nothing I couldn't handle."

"How's the car?"

"It's in one piece."

"Good."

"Jimmy?"

"Yeah."

"Appreciate you coming."

"Uh-huh."

As you drift off to sleep, half-awake, your vision nothing but purple sky and silver specks, you say, "Iris?"

"Yeah."

"The hole in the ceiling is nice."

"I know."

You wake up to a screeching sound. You sit up, holding your gun.

Iris is snoring.

You step onto a crate, poking your head through the hole in the roof. It's morning now and the sun is huge and bright, coming over the horizon like it's rising for the first time. You put your arm above your eyes, blocking it. And then you see them—

Prairie dogs. The whole fucking Prairie Dog City—they've surrounded the gazebo. Thousands of the little bastards. All infected. They have beady red eyes and their hair has wilted away. Probably some infected wolf tried to eat one—now the whole damn city is an army of overgrown fucking rodents.

Something tugs at your pants. You wheel around, looking down, and see Iris.

"What is it?" she asks.

"Goddamn prairie dogs. You see 'em before?"

"No. Had no problems with them."

"Must have heard the RV coming in last night."

They're an army, disgusting, zombified. They gnaw at the screened-in walls.

You slip through the hole in the floor, back down the ladder, and into the gazebo. "Where are you going?" Iris calls.

You ignore her. You have an idea. A stupid idea.

The rodents are clawing at the fence around the gazebo. Little teeth picking away. They'll be through in moments.

You put your weight into the ball of twine and push, struggling, sweat pouring down you and your arms pulsing in pain.

"Iris, get down here and help!" you call.

Iris slips down. She immediately gets to it, digging her feet into the cement floor and pushing against the ball.

And then it goes. The ball of twine is upended and, very slowly, begins rolling. You keep pushing, and finally it bursts through the fenced-in gazebo, tumbling down the great hill.

"Holy shit," Iris says.

You don't say anything. You just grab Iris's hand and chase after it.

The World's Largest Ball of Twine barrels over the rodent monsters, crushing them. They make rotten squishing sounds as they're smashed. The things nip at your heels as you run the length of the long hill. Your foot hooks in one prairie dog hole, and you wrench your ankle. But you keep moving. Limping. Following the ball of destruction.

Suddenly, Iris shrieks. You turn. Her foot, too, has been hooked by a prairie dog hole and she's on the ground, a zombie prairie dog bursting up from a hole beside her, digging its teeth into her flesh.

You step forward and kick the thing off her, then pull her to her feet.

Her neck is bleeding. "I'm fine," she says. "Keep moving."

You continue running.

There's a thunderous crash as the ball slams into the side of Prairie Dog City, taking out the porch and knocking down the main wall.

You barrel inside the building. Animals run free—a menagerie of terror. Strange creatures. At first, you think they're mutated—but no, they're simply what was promised on the sign: six-legged steers and five-legged cows and snakes, overgrown, slithering at your feet.

You rush through the back and into the El Camino. Then turn the key, stamp the pedal, crushing monster rodents, leaving a scattered trail of undead prairie dogs behind you.

TURN TO PAGE 308.

AND YOUR JOURNEY BEGINS

Just before dawn, Major Eigle wakes you with a kick in the side. "It's time."

You piss, drink a glassful of dirty water, and step into the garage. Hank slides out from beneath the El Camino's chassis. "Just finishing up, Jimmy."

"Fine."

"She looks pretty, but she's tough as hell. Heavily reinforced, two-inch steel plating, sides and rear. Military-grade bulletproof glass." You watch Hank run his hand over the hood. "Dillon Aero M134D minigun mounted on the roof. Three thousand rounds a minute. Turn a zombie into mashed potatoes quicker than—well, hell, quicker than you can say 'mashed potatoes.' Here, on the front fenders, mounted rocket pods. Only get six rounds on each side, so use them sparingly."

You whistle. "No joke."

"In the bed, twin nitrous tanks. Browning M2 machine gun along the passenger side. Those stay hidden away in a compartment until you roll them out."

You nod, impressed.

"Now, up front, the best part—the thresher. A long line of blades, they'll spin when you stamp the accelerator—like a lawn mower. Anyone gets in your way, they'll chew 'em to hell."

You follow Hank, walking around the car.

"And in the bed, your favorites: fire ax, Remington Spartan sawed-off. Also, food, drinks, spare ammo. And a cooler full of beers and a case of whiskey."

"You're all right, Hank."

He grins, palms up. "I do what I can."

You open the door and climb inside. Been five years since you sat in the El Camino. The cracked leather seats feel like home. When you wrap your hands around the fake-walnut wheel, it's like the familiar touch of an old lover. The leathery, oily scent of the car brings back a flood of memories.

Iris steps into the garage, sipping coffee.

"Time to do this," you say.

"All right." She goes off to the bathroom. A few minutes later, she comes out, teeth brushed, face wet with water, clean. She slides in.

In the glove box, you find your scratched-up aviators. Same pair you wore for twenty years. You slip them on and light a smoke.

Eigle opens the rear garage door. "You'll take the George Washington Bridge," he says. "I have a man there who will let you through."

"Okay."

"Head low until you're out of the city. This car, hard not to draw attention, so be quick. Boss Tanner's men are everywhere."

You nod.

"And good luck."

"Not needed," you say. "Just stay on the radio."

Eigle stands over the car. "Iris," he says. "Thank you. You don't know—"

She cuts him off. "I do know."

Eigle swallows. For a second, you almost think he might start crying, but he's just tired, you see—exhausted. The type of exhaustion that comes from years of fighting a battle that seems unwinnable. "Be safe. Be smart. Don't die."

He gives the hood a slap, and with that, you roll out.

The sun is coming up. Blinding and bright. Same sun as always, and it doesn't give a damn about your mission. Doesn't give a damn about Death Derbies or zombie attacks or old stories like the broad with a heart of gold and veins full of special blood.

But you do.

Right now, you give a damn because you have to. If you're going to survive, if you're going to get that house on the beach, your attempt at some sort of peace, after all these years, then you *have* to care.

You have to drive the best you've ever driven. Kill the best you've ever killed.

You make it just six blocks before the trouble starts. Boss Tanner's men, standing on the corner, holding their AKs and eyeing you.

"They're watching us," Iris says.

"They are."

"They know about me."

A moment later, you find out she's right.

The big speakers—the ones used to announce the race—crack and hiss. A voice comes on. Boss Tanner. *"Jimmy El Camino. Stop now, hand over the girl, and I may allow you to live."*

No hesitation, you stamp the accelerator, slicing around the corner as Tanner's men open fire. You reach over, push Iris down on the seat, and floor it. The men dive as you race toward them.

Your radio crackles. It's Eigle. *"Jimmy, that got started quicker than I expected. Forget the bridge. Too far. Drive to the Lincoln Tunnel. My two men there can get you through."*

Locals scatter as you weave through the busy streets, pushing 50 miles per hour. Boss Tanner's voice continues to boom, like he's some sort of unseen god—the man behind the curtain. *"Jimmy, you will not get off this island alive!"*

You cross Eighth Avenue. The tunnel entrances—three of them, set into filthy gray and brown brick—visible now. Two of Boss Tanner's militia stand guard. They raise their assault rifles, aiming, and then they both fall to the ground.

Thin One and Boxy come out of the shadows, knives in hand, plunging them into the throats of Tanner's men.

You drive forward. Each of the three entrances is blocked by heavy concrete walls chained to trucks. Thin One and Boxy climb into the trucks and slowly drive forward, pulling the concrete walls aside, revealing the middle tube entrance.

The soldiers nod. You nod back. And then you enter the Lincoln Tunnel.

"Jimmy El Camino, stop now or else I—so fucking help me—I will . . ."

Boss Tanner's voice fades as you drive further into the tunnel. You flash on the headlights and the twin beams slice through the darkness.

The tunnel is nearly empty of cars. Water drips from cracks in the ceiling. The fusty odor of rust and decay and death is trapped within the tight walls.

But no zombies.

"Anyone live down here?" you ask Iris.

"When it happened, they locked the tunnel down. A lot of people trapped inside. All of them turned, though."

"They must be dead by now," you say. "Truly dead. What could they have been eating?"

Iris straps on her seat belt. "We'll find out."

Then comes the sound.

A clicking, almost—a wet snapping and hissing. When you hear it, you no longer wonder what the zombies have been eating—you wonder what's been eating the zombies . . .

"Stinks like death and shit," Iris says.

"Yeah . . . ," you say, pushing harder on the gas. "Not a good sign."

You push the El Camino faster through the tunnel. Rounding a bend, you see them coming down the tunnel like a tidal wave of black death, leaping over cars, scampering over the bodies of decomposed, starved zombies.

Rats.

Zombie rats.

New York City rodents, now changed, zombified—almost mutated—the size of goddamn pit bulls.

Iris begins to shriek but swallows the sound. Your boot punches the pedal, plowing into the undead things. Three of the rotting rodents roll up onto the windshield. Others are caught in the thresher and ground to bits.

"Gun, in the back," you say.

Iris doesn't hesitate. She grabs the sawed-off, rolls down the passenger window, and—

BLAM!

She blows four rodents off the hood. A clean shot.

You swerve, jerking the wheel, as Iris fires—and the blast blows a hole in the windshield. You both curse. Not off to a great start . . .

A zombie rat leaps off a rusted old Civic and slams into the window just as you're accelerating. The glass cracks further and its head bursts through. The snout snaps. It writhes, foul claws scratching, trying to wriggle inside.

You veer right, narrowly avoiding a horde of the creatures.

"C'mere!" Iris barks as she reaches across you, grabs the rodent by the face, and yanks it through the glass. The massive thing bulges in her hand, snapping and hissing. It leaps for you, but she throws her other hand around the long tail. A second later, she hurls it out the window. Its fetid odor hangs in the car.

Rounding the next turn, finally nearing the end of the tunnel, you see more: hundreds. Thousands. And—Christ . . .

"Hey," Iris says, swallowing hard. "What is that?"

You clench your teeth. "I was gonna ask you . . ."

Something's happened to these rodents—something changed after they were zombified. You know what it is. You don't want to admit the truth, but there's no denying it.

"It's a rat king," you say.

"Huh?"

"Never seen one. Urban legend; myth—when a mess of rats are in a tight space, their tails get intertwined, caught together. Blood, piss, dirt, shit—all mixed together. They form one giant sort of rat—but this? This is enormous. This shouldn't be real."

And this isn't just any rat king. It's a *zombie* rat king. As big as a tank.

And it's wriggling and clawing and snarling as it drags itself toward you.

Want to hit this vile beast with the heavy artillery? Go to page 325.

If you'll lay on the gas and try to squeeze past the beast, turn to page 127.

Sitting inside the El Camino, you key the radio. "Eigle."

A moment later, *"Go ahead."*

"She's dead," you say matter-of-factly.

Silence. Then his voice comes back, thin, sucker-punched. *"How?"*

"Does it matter?"

"Christ . . ."

"But, Eigle, is there any chance? Her organs—could they still do anything with them?"

A moment later, Eigle says, *"Get her to San Francisco."*

"Will it work?"

"I don't know."

"All right."

"You need to keep the body cold, Jimmy. Or keep it preserved. The men in San Francisco won't be transplanting the organs, so you have more than the half hour you'd have if it were a heart or a liver. But still, she needs to be kept cold. And beyond that—hell, I don't know, Jimmy . . . I don't know how you get her there without her rotting away to nothing . . ."

"Okay."

"Need I remind you, if you don't get her to San Francisco, then the poison . . ."

You clench your jaw so hard you half-expect your teeth to shatter. You want to scream at the bastard. Tell him what he can do with his fucking poison. But you don't. There's no point. Instead, you slam the microphone against the dash and pick up Iris's *Odd America* book.

You flip through it. Something catches your eye. An idea. You stamp the accelerator, light a smoke, and drive as fast as the old El Camino will let you . . .

TURN TO PAGE 43.

In moments, the zombies will be past the El Camino, and then it might be too late.

Without speaking, you rip open the door in the floor and hurry down into the basement. You yank open the freezer door, grabbing Iris's legless, lifeless body, then you're back upstairs.

Dewey is loading a rifle. "The hell you doing?" he says.

"Leaving."

"You brought them here!"

"There's too many. I can't risk failing now."

You throw a look back at the room. At Dewey, red-hot with anger. At Suzie-Jean and Walter, confused, scared, eyes saying, "Don't leave." Then you slam the door shut and step outside.

You pull the sawed-off as you cross the garden with Iris's legless body thrown stiff over your shoulder. Opening the fence door, you shoot the nearest undead Klansman in the face—its hood explodes in a mess of dirty old brain tissue and cheap white cotton.

To the El Camino.

Zombies approaching.

Setting Iris's torso down in the passenger seat.

Zombies near on top of you.

You're spinning, firing, killing a lunging Klansman, then sliding into the El Camino, starting her up, hearing the familiar rumble.

You throw a glance at the house. Walter and Suzie-Jean watch you from the window. You look away.

Shifting into reverse, rolling over two hooded ghouls. You're smashing into more, when—

BLAM!

It's Dewey, in the doorway. Firing. Not at the zombies. At you. Four bullets hit the door, ricocheting off the reinforced steel.

You throw it into first, and the car leaps, charging down the path. A glance at the side mirror. Dewey, ferocity on his face, drops the gun and steps back inside. He appears a moment later holding his Mauser 1918 T-Gewehr—an elephant gun. Strong enough to blow a hole through your door. Through your windshield. Through goddamn Superman, most likely.

You hear the elephant gun fire and you brace yourself for a hit, but it doesn't come.

The thresher tears through the undead Klansmen. You plow through the grand wizard in its ridiculous red-sheeted costume, and the thresher eats it, so all you see is its arms being flung about, its red robe being sucked into the blades, and then its hood being pulled in, the thresher snapping the undead thing's neck, wrenching its head and grinding it to nothing but cinnamon-colored cerebral matter.

Stomping the pedal, burning up the path, and then—

You feel it just a split second before you hear it. The car jerking to the side. And then you hear the blast—the tremendous echo of the elephant gun, still loud as all hell a hundred yards away.

Dewey.

A perfect shot, through the trees. Into the tire. The El Camino flips, crashing into the woods, rolling end over end before slamming hard into an oak tree. Iris's body is tossed from the vehicle.

Punch-drunk, seeing stars, you crawl out of the car.

And there, staring at you, is an undead alligator, with ferocious yellow fangs. You inch back, reaching for the sawed-off, but the giant reptilian zombie's mouth opens impossibly wide, snapping your arm off. Blood pours. And before you can run, another is upon you, jaws clamping around your skull like a vise, tugging, pulling, ripping, until finally you hear your neck snap . . .

AN END

RING

At the edge of town, not far from the train, Ring stands in the middle of a cattle ring. Lanterns surround it, lighting the scene. A crowd of a few hundred has gathered and they drink and eat and watch happily.

Ring stands on top of an old beer keg. He's wearing a gold sport coat now, looking less like a thug and more like a carnival barker.

Standing behind him, at the edge of the cattle ring, is a man in full-body chain-mail armor.

A zombie stumbles around the cattle ring. Its face is now dark and rotting, and it wears a muzzle.

You stand outside the cattle ring, smoking a cigarette. Two of Ring's thugs on either side of you, guns against your back.

Ring grins and begins his show. "You all know what this is, don't you?" he calls to the audience while pointing at the stumbling monster. His voice booms. "It's a zombie! Got a dozen other names for 'em. Walkers. Stumblers. Brainers. All the same. And I bet most of you fine folks out there have killed a few, ain't ya? That's why you're still alive today—still alive when the rest of the suckers, may they rest in peace, are either rotting beneath the earth or staggering mindless across its surface."

Ring points to a wide-eyed boy in the front row, not more than seven or eight. "How about you, boy? You ever kill one of these undead sons of bitches?"

The boy shakes his head. He has long, mussed hair, and it falls over his eyes. He wipes it away. "N-no, sir, never have."

Ring hops down from the keg and crosses the cattle ring. "Well, young man, would you like to?"

The boy is trembling. Nervous but excited.

Ring pats him on the shoulder. "Oh, it's not hard. Easy as—this!" Ring says, stepping back, pulling a pistol from his belt, placing it against the left side of the shuffling zombie's head, and pulling the trigger. There's a sharp *bang* and the bullet explodes the monster's brain and skull out the right side of its head, splashing gore on the audience. They clap and cheer.

Ring holsters the smoking pistol, then leans over the fence and takes the hand of a woman in the crowd. "Son, is this your mother?"

The boy nods.

"Ma'am, it's a pleasure to meet you. My name's Ring and this is my carnival train."

The woman blushes. This guy's Frank Sinatra as far as she's concerned.

"Maybe we should let your son step in the ring here? Get him his first kill, what do you say?"

"Is it safe?" she asks.

"Safe? Safe! Well, sure it is! I'll start him off easy," Ring says with a grin. "Safety's the name of the game!"

"Okay," she says.

"Louis!" Ring calls, turning to the man in chain mail. "Find the boy someone his age."

Louis exits the ring and walks the short distance to the train. The armor clatters loudly with every step. He slides open the door to the nearest car and climbs up. Moaning comes from the car. You catch glimpses of zombies, chained up.

A moment later, Louis steps back out of the cattle car, carrying a zombie in his arms. This zombie was once a young girl, maybe six years old. Now its blond hair has fallen out, and only a few strands remain. Its nose is gone—just a hole in its face. It's missing a large chunk of its left foot.

Louis places the girl in the center of the cattle ring. It tries to charge him, bite him, but he holds it at arm's length and easily places a muzzle over its mouth.

Ring smiles at the boy and his mom like a goddamn mall Santa and says, "Well, son, you ready?"

The boy seems unsure. He looks up to his mother, who nods. Ring then leans over the fence and helps the boy up and over.

Inside the arena now, Ring hands the boy a butcher knife. The boy takes it tentatively. Ring says, softly, fatherly, "Go on, son, you can do it."

Ring opens the gate to the cattle ring and steps out. Louis follows, so it's just the boy and the zombie girl.

The crowd watches, quiet. A few hushed whispers.

Then, with a throaty, wet growl, the zombie girl charges.

You can see the boy wants to run. But he doesn't.

It comes at him. Gets its hands on his checkered shirt and tears it. It has its face to his neck, forcing his head back—he'd have been bitten by now if it weren't for the muzzle.

At last, the boy swings the blade. The tip of the undead girl's ear comes off.

"Harder!" his mom shouts. *"Goddamn it, harder!"*

The boy listens. He swings the blade against the zombie's skull.

It bangs off.

Someone boos.

Finally, you see the boy clench his teeth, turn the blade, and jam it into the girl's eye. He does it four times, quick, fast, and angry. With the fourth stab, the blade goes hilt-deep into its eye socket.

The zombie stumbles back, almost confused, then collapses on the ground. The blade sticks out of its eye and blood pools around its head.

Ring steps back into the cattle ring and grabs the boy's hand, raising it. *"Let's hear it! Not bad for a first-timer, eh?!"*

The crowd roars. The boy is beaming as his mother helps him over the fence.

"Some show," you say as Ring walks toward you.

He leans close. "You like?"

You light another cigarette and say nothing.

"You better like it," he says. "Because now it's your turn. But it won't be no fucking girl in pigtails, and there won't be no muzzle."

TURN TO PAGE 37.

Your feet slap pavement as you race past the zombies. One lunges for you, tearing your shirt, but you keep moving. The Panzer's MG 13 machine gun opens up and bullets pound the cement.

You weave back and forth across the street, dodging the fire, nearing the tank, when—

BLAM! BLAM! BLAM!

White-hot pain in your leg. You crumple. Four, maybe five bullets in you.

The machine gun stops firing. You glance up. The tank rolls toward you.

"The Desert Fox has ceased fire! It seems he has other plans for Jimmy El Camino!"

Your fingers scrape at the concrete as you try to crawl.

Shadows fall over you. Shuffling monsters. One grabs at your hair, yanking, pulling it out in clumps.

You roll over onto your back, squeezing the Remington as you turn, and—

BOOM! The blast punches the zombie in the chest, lifting him off his feet, carrying him back through the air.

The ground shakes. Tank treads rumble. The Desert Fox shifts slightly, aligning the treads with your body.

Monsters claw at your face, paw at your flesh, begin to feast. But they won't be what kills you.

No.

It's the Panzer. It's rolling up over your legs now. And you feel it. The fucking zombie bites—they keep your body from going into shock. You feel it all, every organ bursting, every muscle liquefying, every bone exploding.

It's a relief when the twenty-five tons of tank finally crush your skull.

AN END

ALL FOR NOTHING

It turns out, what they can do isn't much.

You're sitting in a pub on the water, drinking beer, watching a closed-circuit "broadcast" of a baseball game—two local teams— when the military man comes in. He sits down next to you, orders a coffee, and says, "Jimmy, her body was too far gone."

You knock back your whiskey, order another, and light a cigarette.

After a time, you say, "I was promised a small place on the beach."

"All right."

"You're not gonna fuck me over?"

"No."

You nod. "Good."

You both drink in silence. You smoke two more cigarettes, watching the game. Something about baseball—that sound— feels right.

"What are they going to do with her body?"

The military man sighs. "Burn it, or put it out to sea. Cemeteries are full."

"Give her to me. I'll bury her, near the beach."

He thinks about that for a moment, orders another coffee, and says, "All right."

It's a one-room shack they give you, thirty yards from the Pacific.

You bury Iris far behind the house, away from the sand and the ocean.

When you're finished, you say, "I'm sorry." You say it again. And again. You sit on the dirt, her grave, and you drink and you drink and you say "I'm sorry" over and over, until the words lose all meaning.

Then you begin digging again. Another grave. You leave that one empty.

Finally, exhausted, you stumble back to your little shack on the beach. You sit on the porch and you drink some more.

You plan to keep on drinking until you're in that grave beside her.

AN END

You're close to the exit. The thick cloud of smoke looms ahead, completely filling the air, and pieces of the exploded gate are scattered across the field. Your leg is hurt, but you continue forward.

And then you hear a scream.

Billy.

You turn.

He's on the ground, ten feet behind you, shot through the leg. He's looking up at you and his mouth is open and he's emitting a shrill, boyish shriek. He attempts to stand but falls back on his face. He lifts his head again, covered in mud now, and his wide eyes beg for your help.

Seven zombies in Packers jerseys charge toward him— moaning, howling, eager to feast on the young boy's flesh . . .

Turn around and try to save Billy? Turn to page 224.

If you believe nothing is more important than getting to Iris, go to page 176.

Fuck it all, you say, and you simply drive off, headed west, freedom overwhelming you. The poison is there, too—but the longer you drive, the more convinced you become that Eigle was bluffing.

You smile.

You listen to music and drum the steering wheel to the beat. You smoke cigarette after cigarette with the windows down as you push 80 miles per hour along back roads, whipping around turns, not caring where you go—just feeling right, knowing that you can travel wherever you want.

The little girl darts out into the street outside Hattiesburg. She's just there, suddenly, in the road—a young girl, no more than seven or eight. Thin, straight blond hair, and dirt smudging her face.

She hasn't been bitten.

At least, it doesn't look like it.

You slam on the brakes, wrench the wheel, skidding and swooping around her. You wait a moment, seeing if she's with anyone—if it's an ambush—then you roll down the window.

"Hi," you say.

The girl has stepped back, off the road, onto the dirt. She's shaking. "You almost killed me!" she yells in a thick, almost Cajun accent.

"You darted out like a goddamn jackrabbit!" you bark back, then, after a second, you say, "Sorry about my language."

She glares at you and says nothing.

"What are you doing out here, all alone?" you ask.

"Looking for food for my family."

"Why don't they look for their own food?"

"They got hurt by some men. Takers. Thieves. They came and they shot my dad and my brother and cut up my mom. They're recovering at home. My dad lost both his legs and it's real sad, how he gets around. Real sad. They're starving now."

Again, you look around, expecting an ambush. Nothing catches your eye. You step out, walk around to the rear, and pull some supplies for the girl: jerky and trail mix and stale bread and a third of whiskey.

"Take this back to them," you say.

She looks at it tentatively. Unsure. Then she scampers forward and grabs it all and steps back. "You don't wanna kill me?"

"No."

"Could you drive me back to my house? I can't carry all this."

You think for a moment, then open the passenger-side door.

"Smells like shit in here," the girl says, climbing inside.

"You're too young to talk like that."

The girl just shrugs. She directs you back a few miles—she never gets lost, never gives you a wrong turn, and you figure this girl must be out here day after day, trying to find food for her family.

Finally, you come to a stop in front of a small brick house on a quiet street. "Will you help me carry this in?"

You eye the house. It's dark and run-down. The grass is overgrown and boards cover the windows. No light comes from it.

If you want to help the girl carry the food into the house, turn to page 339.

No helping. You'd rather return to your mission, searching for generators in hopes of preserving Iris. Go to page 396.

FORCE CHOKE

"Iris," you say, "it's simple. You can save the world, or you can be this man's goddamn property. He'll throw you aside, soon as he finds something he likes better."

"Now, that ain't so," Ring says.

You turn to him. "Speak again, and I kill you."

"I don't want to die," she says. "That so hard to comprehend?"

"Not hard. But this isn't about that. This is about you—you being the one person who can change things. The one person who can make people like Boss Tanner disappear. Who can make people like this piece of garbage here go away."

"They'll never go away entirely," Iris says.

You sigh. "Goddamn it."

With that, you holster the gun, drop the ax, and wrap your fingers around Ring's throat. His eyes go wide as he struggles.

Iris watches, face blank.

You continue squeezing. Ring's eyes are about to pop out of his head. He kicks. His hands lash out, slapping at you. You squeeze tighter. It's been a long time since you strangled a man, and you forgot how damn long it takes. You keep your hands tight around his throat for four minutes. Then piss drips down as he wets himself, and then you smell shit, and you know he's dead.

You pull your hands from his sweaty neck, wipe them on your shirt, and Ring slumps over. His face is purple.

"Iris, you're the only one who matters. Every other person on this journey—collateral damage. Me included."

Iris swallows. "I just don't want to die."

"Nothing that can be done about that."

Iris stares at Ring's purple face. Finally, she stands. "Okay. Let's get to San Francisco."

"Have to wait. Wait a long time, for the tracks to be cleared and for the train to begin moving. When it gets a good head of steam, we jump."

And you do just that. When the train finally gets rumbling again, you get ready—and on your word, you both jump.

Iris hits a rock when she lands, and her throat is cut open, bleeding. She holds her hand to it, shakes you off, and you walk. It's a long walk back to the El Camino. An even longer drive waits for you—and that drive takes you north . . .

TURN TO PAGE 242.

Steering the Panzer back toward Times Square, turning the corner, you see a scoreboard on the large monitor.

Mr. King—440 . . . Jimmy El Camino—380 . . . Elwood—310 . . . The Desert Fox [PRESUMED DEAD]—190 . . . Lucy Lowblow—100 . . . Buzzy—80 . . . Sonja [PRESUMED DEAD]—70 . . . Stu Bean—60

Rolling into Times Square proper, a sort of ceremony is under way.

Mr. King stands atop a platform. You see his face for the first time: his skin is burned and scarred, pocked and tight.

On either side of him are girls in just-barely-there bikinis, shivering in the afternoon breeze. Boss Tanner holds a microphone and announces, *"The winner of the Death Derby, for the eighteenth time, is Mr. King, driving the 1965 Lincoln Continental!*

Mr. King shakes Boss Tanner's hand. King holds up a trophy—a severed zombie head, brains scooped out, on top of a mount. Flies buzz.

When you finally climb out of the Panzer and the crowd sees you clearly, there's a roar. Thunderous applause.

Jim-my! Jim-my! Jim-my!

You don't smile.

But you can't fight back that feeling in your chest. A warmth. And that's just fine; you don't want to fight it.

It feels like the old days, after the wars, during the derbies and races. When you'd win. And they'd call your name. Never this big a crowd, you weren't NASCAR, just backwoods tracks. But still, goddamn, it was sweet as Southern Comfort.

From the stage, Mr. King watches you, his tight face blank.

Soon, the crowds flood out onto the streets. Drivers are greeted and hugged. Guys mug for photos taken with Lucy Lowblow.

Eigle makes his way through the crowd, accompanied by Thin One and Boxy.

Another man follows, wearing a mechanic's outfit with a name tag reading HANK. Hank has a gut, looks like he's smuggling watermelons beneath his jumpsuit. Type of guy, you'd bet, who has more hair on his ass than on his head. Eigle says, "Jimmy, this is—"

"Let me guess: Hank, the mechanic."

"Correct. He'll be working with us."

Hank's grabbing your hand before you offer it and shaking it like it gets him off. "Real happy to be working with you, fella. Real happy. Some driving today. Whoo-boy. Some show. See why the major here was so eager to bring you on board."

You pull your hand free and look back to Eigle. "The mission. Let's talk."

"Yes," Eigle says. "Come on, I'll explain everything."

But as you begin walking, a voice calls out, "Jimmy El Camino!"

Boss Tanner, making his way through the crowd. Still a girl at each arm—maybe they're sewn on. "Jimmy El Camino," he says. "Nice driving, son. Impressed even me, and I'm man enough to admit it."

You don't reply.

Boss Tanner turns to Major Eigle. "Where are you taking our new star?"

After a hard moment, Eigle says, "Buying the man a drink, to celebrate not dying."

Tanner shakes his head. "No offense meant, Major, but after the years this man has spent locked up, I suspect he'd like to celebrate his victory in the company of his many fans. Some girls, maybe? Or boys? No judgment in my city."

Thin One and Boxy move their hands down, slowly, toward their guns. Eigle shifts his weight, steeling himself. A subtle movement, but you notice it.

You're a chess piece here. A pawn in a standoff between Major Eigle and Boss Tanner. But you don't yet know the game or the stakes.

Boss Tanner throws his arm around you. One of the girls grabs hold of you, running a rough hand up your shirt, along your hard stomach. She smiles, and you notice a dead tooth. The girls smell good. Trashy and sweet.

Tanner flashes his big grin. "Well, Jimmy, what's it going to be?"

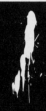

To go with Major Eigle and learn more about the mission, go to page 216.

Getting drunk and celebrating sounds like a good time! Turn to page 195.

You slice through the cult members like some avenging angel of death. You slash the closest one across the face, blood appearing in a sudden, thin line, like he was lacerated by a laser.

More gunshots ring out, but none hit you. For a moment, it's as if you're invincible—swinging, chopping, hacking, killing anything purple.

Soon, the floor is slick with gore and purple-red fabric. Only the Man in Antlers remains. He takes a nervous step back, hands up—suddenly appearing very human, very timid, very small. He is no god, and there is no divine being who will intervene.

But then Iris howls. The Man in Antlers grins sickly. "It's too late."

You look into the pit. Iris's stomach has been torn open. One zombie has her intestines wrapped around its hand. No one is immune to that . . .

You charge at the Man in Antlers, swinging the sickle up into his gut, lifting him off his feet; his body wriggles like a worm on a hook as blood pours from his belly, down the shaft of the sickle, and over your hands. And then you drop the sickle, dropping him as well.

You pull a semiautomatic rifle from a dead cultist's tight, lifeless hand and walk to the edge of the pit. You fire off head shots—methodical, mechanical, reloading, firing, until every undead monster has fallen.

You lower yourself down into the pit and grab hold of Iris. Her eyes are open but lifeless.

The pulley is still attached to her belt—now torn and blood-splattered. You pile the bodies, using them to climb out, gently pulling her up. Her body is mangled—skin flayed, flesh torn, bones broken.

You wrap her in a bloody robe and carry her down to the El Camino.

TURN TO PAGE 143.

You step closer, peeking through the wooden slats. You see zombies packed inside the cattle car, at least fifty, jammed so tight they can't move.

The next car is more macabre: it's filled with undead animals. An elephant with half its face rotted away. Horses with their ribs showing. Zebras, flesh torn away and hanging so that their stripes look like chessboards.

"Jimmy," Iris says, "think we should forget the circus."

"Agreed," you say.

Footsteps behind you. You turn and—

KRAK!

A gun butt slams into your nose and your vision flashes bright white. Your ears ring. You hear Iris scream.

And then the butt of the gun, again, hard into the back of your head, and your legs go weak and everything goes black.

You wake up on a cracked leather couch in a room that smells of smoke and spilled booze and mold. Iris sits beside you. Your head is pounding away like a sailor on shore leave.

Across the room are two windows, looking out on the town. It's darker now. Two men lean against the wall, guns pointed at you.

Another man, rounder, thicker, with long hair stands over you. He smells like feces. He leans in close to you and says, "We heard about a guy driving an El Camino. And a girl worth a helluva lot to Boss Tanner, back in the Rotten Apple. Seems like maybe that's you."

You rub at your forehead and you yawn.

"Hey!" he barks. "My name's Ring, and I run that train. I'm the goddamn ringleader of this circus."

"Clever."

"I know. I pilot that train all over this shit land. So be kind, huh, and listen when I'm talking to you—it'll make your life easier."

"Sure."

He nods to one of the gunmen, who crosses, yanking you to your feet, shoving you to the window. You realize now you're on the second floor of the saloon you saw when you entered town.

"You see that out there?" Ring says, pointing to a circle of burning torches in the center of town. You squint and see two men boxing inside the circle.

No—one man is boxing; the other is an undead circus clown being beat to a pulp.

"That's the circle," Ring says. "The arena. Gladiator-type shit."

"Gladiator-type shit," you say.

Ring nods with a wide grin. "Gladiator. Type. Shit. As you can see, I'm a sporting man, so I'm going to give you a choice here. You fight for Ring's Most Wonderful Circus Show, and I let the girl go free."

You look to Iris on the couch. Her teeth are clenched.

Ring leans in so close you can smell tequila on his breath. He grins, flashing yellow teeth. "Or," he continues, "I keep the girl, and you drive on outta here."

You hear Iris, breathing hard now. You eye Ring. His skin is dirty and pocked. His eyes twinkle in a cruel way. He has a thin, waxed mustache.

It'd be a pleasure to put his nose through his brain. But you have a choice to make.

If you'll agree to fight as Ring's gladiator so Iris can go free, turn to page 197.

If you'd rather drive out of town and attempt to get her back some other way, go to page 363.

ELEPHANT RIDE

You trek on. Through day and night.

You lie on top of the elephant, one hand around its side, gripping an open rib, the other holding the flagpole, which rests on the undead animal's head.

It's slow going.

You pivot the head on the stick when you have to, steering the animal to the left or to the right. The animal never stops. It just continues on, relentless, trying to get its teeth on the bobbing lump of flesh.

And you never get down. Never get off. As soon as you do, the beast will attack. You shift to the side to piss. Shitting isn't as easy and the animal's back is soon a filthy mess.

On the second day, you wake up to pounding rain. You turn over to drink. It washes you some, and you're thankful for that.

Outside Des Moines, a single zombie crosses the path ahead, startling you. And then more. Hundreds, crossing the road like a herd of wild animals. Bones crunch as the elephant stomps right over them.

For the elephant-monster, it's Ring's dangling head—the one single thing driving him forward. And for you, it's Iris, the mission, and the poison—intertwined, your blinding focus.

You remove your belt—tie one end to the animal's rib, another around your wrist. Best you can do to keep from tumbling over the side. You fall back asleep . . .

When you wake, rain is pounding again, coming down sideways. The stick is slipping. You tighten your grip, reaching, but it's too late—the pole slips from your hand and Ring's head drops to the ground.

The elephant immediately lowers its head to dine. The animal's hide is soaking wet, and you tumble off, landing on your wounded leg.

The elephant devours Ring's head in two bites, then turns toward you.

You take two steps back. The elephant-monster stampedes forward, trying to ram its tusk into you. You roll to the side, grabbing the gore-splattered flagpole. When the elephant attacks again, you swing the pole into its ear, into its brain. Its legs go out and it falls, making a sound like distant thunder.

"Thanks for the ride," you say, catching your breath.

Before you have time to ponder your situation and search for a new mode of transportation, you see it. Something so unexpected, so silly, but so goddamn perfect that it makes you grin.

The SPAM Museum.

And parked out front is the SPAMmobile—a large blue RV with a huge image of a SPAM sandwich on the side.

Head inside, explore the SPAM Museum, and find something to eat? Turn to page 89.

Go straight for the SPAMmobile and continue on your way? Turn to page 131.

CLOTHESLINE FROM HELL

No more of this "Toro! Toro!" action for you. You'll clothesline the girl. Knock her clean off that goddamn Harley, get up on it, and ride straight out of this shit city. You never did heart NYC . . .

Sonja speeds toward you.

You position yourself behind the zombie. The cuffs bend the monster's arm back. It moans loudly, thrashing, trying to jerk its arm free.

You lean out, watching Sonja hurtling down the avenue toward you. She raises the mace. Bits of blood and brain pour off it—a red streak, trailing in the air.

She's bearing down on you. The engine like thunder.

Forty feet. Thirty feet. Twenty feet.

And—

NOW! You leap out from behind the zombie, using the monster's arm and the cuffs as an improvised clothesline.

Sonja shrieks as her upper body slams into the clothesline. She's ripped off the Harley and the bike skitters down the avenue, sparking and screeching.

Your plan worked.

Almost . . .

In the same instant, the force of the impact yanks your own arm free from its socket. You stare down, mouth slack, at your open shoulder. Blood gushes, such a thick, dark red it's almost black—like you're leaking oil.

You turn and see your arm lying twenty feet down the street, still attached to the zombie's arm—also ripped from its body.

Shock will take over soon.

If you go into shock, you're dead.

Can't get dead.

Can't get dead.

You press your hand tight against your gaping shoulder wound and take a shaky step. But then—

The zombie in the cement block. It lunges out with its one arm, digging long, clawlike nails into your neck. You reach out with your remaining arm, whacking at the monster. Its fingers dig inside your open shoulder flesh, gripping muscle and tendon and scraping your scapula.

As you struggle to free yourself, you see Sonja marching toward you, blood pumping from a dozen cuts on her face.

You free yourself from the zombie, just in time to watch Sonja stomping closer, swinging the mace, caving your head in like a ripe melon . . .

AN END

You tug on the cuffs. The zombie lunges toward you, then topples over.

Hmmm.

You wrap the loose metal chain around your hand. The metal is cool in your palm. You grip tight, and you *tug*. There's an audible *pop!* as the zombie's shoulder bone breaks.

Its flesh is weak, muscle decayed and rotten. You raise your leg, pressing your boot against the zombie's crotch, and you *heave*.

SNAP!

Flesh, soft and gray, tears, and the zombie's entire left arm is ripped free.

You now have a sort of extra appendage, attached to your own via handcuff—one of the stranger weapons you've ever wielded.

The Harley roars louder and Sonja lets out a bloodcurdling howl as she swings the mace. Simultaneously, you step out from behind the zombie and swing the zombie's arm—along with yours—treating it like a fleshy nunchaku.

The zombie arm catches Sonja in the throat. There's a sharp choking sound as she begins to fall back—but she seizes the handlebars, barely catching herself.

She races ahead, the Harley's front tire wobbling, and then, after sixty feet, the front wheel jerks, the bike flips, and Sonja is flung. From alleyways and storefronts come dozens of zombies. That's why you saw so few earlier—they kept them hidden, probably chained up until the games began. Like Boss Tanner said, it's Roman—and now it's like someone opened the ground panels in the Colosseum and unleashed the tigers.

The monsters come at you.

An old, fat undead man, its stomach split open, intestines spilling out like sausage links, so long it's tripping on them.

You swing the zombie arm, cracking it in the face.

You snap the arm up into the air, grabbing it by the wrist. The humerus bone juts out of the open wound and you slam it into the eyeball of the next zombie reaching for you—a woman in a torn nightgown.

More come. Encircling you. You whip the arm around in a wide, circular swing, driving them back, allowing you to move to the Harley.

Sonja looks up as you approach. She's hurt bad. Leg is twisted around. Spine possibly broken. You nod. "Thanks for the ride."

You place your boot on the still-cuffed zombie arm and tug, shattering the wrist, ripping it free. No longer hampered, you right the Harley, swinging up, twisting the throttle.

Just before the engine barks, you hear Sonja scream as the zombies pounce and sink their teeth in . . .

If you choose to use your new ride to escape the city, turn to page 256.

Do like Eigle asked and play the game? Turn to page 186.

You turn away from the crying boy.

Iris is all that matters. The mission. During your lifetime, you've left a trail of bodies behind you, thinking only about the mission—and it's that thinking that propels you forward now.

You pass through the thick smoke, into the dark visitor's tunnel. Screaming pain in your leg as you limp through the bowels of the stadium. Far behind you, the cars battle, rockets and machine-gun fire tearing the stadium apart. There's a tremendous eruption as some very large, very powerful missile slams into the seating.

As you turn the corner, there's a flash of movement up ahead. A smile creeps across your face. "Hello, Ring."

He turns. A shadowy figure in the darkness.

"You seem to have found yourself on the wrong side of the stadium, Ring."

"Other side collapsed completely," Ring says. He's out of breath. Panting, like a dog. "Everyone dead. Ran the length of the stadium trying to find a way out."

"Oh, you were planning on leaving?"

Another explosion rocks the stadium. The walls shake and lights above you fall and thick dust sifts through rapidly growing cracks in the ceiling.

Ring's face is pale, scared; his long black hair is matted with sweat. "Jimmy, look—this whole place is going to come down. You got a beef, I know, but let's settle it later, huh?"

"I told you I'd kill you, Ring."

"Gimme a break, Jimmy! I was running a business! The train is my business! It provides entertainment! For people! And what the hell—you're still alive, ain't ya?"

You shake your head. "I told you I'd kill you."

Ring's eyes narrow. "Fine, then, if that's how you want it," he says, reaching around his back, pulling out a silver pistol, firing.

The shot misses.

Ring frowns.

His hand, shaking, scared, squeezes twice more. Two bullets hurtle past you.

You flash a deranged, sick grin and tramp down the tunnel like a man possessed.

Ring empties the clip. He doesn't hit you once.

His eyes go wide. He opens his mouth to speak, but you slam a heavy fist into his nose, knocking him back on his ass. He slides across the floor.

You're just twenty feet from the large exit. Daylight shines in. Explosions behind you. Ring was right. This whole damn stadium is about to implode.

A strange moan draws your attention. Through the door ahead of you, an undead elephant is rambling along, outside, in the sunlight. Must have stampeded out when the stadium began to collapse.

Ring tries to scramble to his feet. Tries to run. But you close the distance and stomp down on the back of his calf, shattering his fibula. He howls.

Outside, the elephant-monster hears Ring's howl and lets out a bellow.

An idea is brewing.

A long flagpole juts out from the wall, above the exit. A torn Packers flag hangs from it—at one time, it used to welcome visitors.

A minute later, you've snapped the flagpole from the wall and you're standing over Ring.

"Good-bye, Ring."

Ring looks up at you. Crying now. "Jimmy, please, be fucking reasonable. Be a goddamn man, huh?"

You raise the flagpole, then slam the tip of it down into Ring's throat. You pull it back out, now dripping with fresh gore, and bring it down into Ring's throat and neck another dozen times, until his head is nearly separated from his body.

More explosions shake the stadium. Need to move quickly.

You kneel down and use your hands to finish the job. You crack the vertebrae and twist and pull until, finally, Ring's head is removed.

You then hurl Ring's headless body through the exit door. It lands beneath the elephant-monster with a wet thump. The elephant looks down at the body, lowers its head, begins eating.

Next, you tie Ring's long, ratty hair to the torn Packers flagpole. In moments, you've got his head strung up.

You exit the stadium, out into the afternoon light, where the elephant-monster is nearly finished devouring Ring's body. You move slowly, circling around the side of the thing. The undead animal's entire rib cage is exposed. You jam your foot in its side, wedging your boot between two ribs, hoisting yourself up atop the elephant-monster.

The animal attempts to crane its neck but can't. After a moment, it seems to regard you only as a minor annoyance, and lowers its head again and finishes eating Ring.

You lean forward then and extend the flagpole out, so that Ring's head dangles in front of the elephant-monster's mouth.

The creature's mouth opens and closes. It wants to eat Ring's head, but it can't quite reach. So it walks forward, toward it, like the old donkey-and-carrot routine.

More explosions behind you as you ride the elephant-monster down a short flight of steps and out into the stadium parking lot. The sounds of screams and gunfire chase after you. But they sound wonderfully far away. You rest your head on the elephant's back and shut your eyes and think about Iris.

Outside of town, you hear one final, giant eruption—and you turn to see Lambeau Field crumbling, the stands caving in on themselves, collapsing, half the structure imploding and filling the sky with a cloud of debris so thick that, for a long while, it blocks the sun.

Did the implosion swallow Mr. King and his Lincoln? You hope so, but you doubt it . . .

There will be plenty of time to think about that later, once you've reached Iris. You lie on your side and urge the animal forward. Ring's head swings back and forth, back and forth, his eyes like two little beads.

"Ring, you sonofabitch, you and this big undead beast are going to take me all the way to that goddamn ball of yarn."

You light a cigarette, smoke half of it, then toss it. You drape your body over the flagpole, trapping one end beneath your belly, then put your head down and shut your eyes. Only nine hundred miles to go.

TURN TO PAGE 169.

Driving down Route 29, leaving DC behind you, you say to Iris, "We need guns. Lost most back there. Call Eigle."

Iris talks into the microphone. Eigle tells her to wait—a moment later, he comes back on. "Remington factory, in North Carolina. Closest thing to you."

"Don't need an entire factory," you say loudly. "Just enough to get us where we're going."

Eigle says, "Remington factory, Jimmy."

"Christ. Okay." You say nothing for a long time.

After a while, Iris says, "You like guns, huh?"

You don't respond.

"You do," she continues. "Why do men love guns?"

"Didn't know we did."

"Yes, you did. And *you* do. Why?"

"I don't."

"Sure you do."

You shake your head. "Open me up a new pack," you say, pointing to the carton of stale cigarettes on the floor.

"Tell me why you like guns first."

"Light me a cigarette."

Iris plucks your Zippo from the center console, lights a butt, and hands it to you. You smoke slowly, one arm out the window, and after a long moment, you say, "A gun is a tool. Does a carpenter *like* hammers? No. But it's a tool, and he's good and comfortable with it, because his job requires him to be that way."

"I just think you love killing."

"Okay."

"What do you mean, 'Okay'?"

"I mean, okay, you can think that."

Iris sighs, leans back in the seat, and puts her feet up on the dash.

"Can you keep your feet down?"

She kicks off her shoes. Just her bare feet. "Better?"

"Not really."

You reach for your flask. You unscrew it with your teeth, navigating around an overturned Greyhound bus.

After another few quiet minutes, Iris says, "Then what *do* you like?"

You don't respond.

"You like that?" she asks, nodding her chin at the flask.

Holding up the booze, you say, "This?"

"Yes. That."

You flick your butt out the window, turn to Iris. "What are you asking all these questions for, anyway?"

"Because I want to talk. Didn't think I'd want to—usually can't stand talking. Told you that, back at the garage. But all this emptiness, all this driving—it's new to me. Makes me feel like a different person . . . not so tight inside. Figured I'd make it easy on you by talking about something you're into. From what I can tell, guns and drink are about it. And the firearm chitchat didn't go far."

"Don't like to talk. Told you that."

"Well, I'm the one with the special fucking body that's supposed to save the world, and for the first time in a long time, I want to talk. So tell me—does it make you feel good?"

You don't reply.

"Come on, I said talk!"

"I am!" you say, barking it out. "I'm thinking. I'm trying to answer your question correctly. You ask me a question, you want to talk, fine, I'll try. I'll try to answer it. But give me a goddamn second to try to form the words."

"Not good with words?"

"Been alone in a cell for five years. I'm out of practice."

"Okay," she says.

A few minutes and a few swigs later, you say, "Booze doesn't make me feel *good*. It makes me feel *right*. My brain, it's like—I don't know, an old undershirt. Gets dirty, right? Gets shit all over it. So you need to wash it. Get it clean. That's the booze. It washes my brain, makes it right again—removes the dirt. Or more like, it helps me ignore the dirt. The dirt'll always be there, but I notice it less when I'm drinking."

"But every time you wash a shirt, it falls apart a little."

"Maybe," you say, turning to her and grinning, "but what are you gonna do, walk around in grimy clothes all the time?"

"I guess, but it seems like—"

"I'm done talking for now."

Iris nods. "Got it."

You find the Remington factory in Madison, North Carolina. You leave the car running. "Wait here," you say. "Keep the car locked."

You head inside.

Eleven minutes later, you return, splattered with blood, carrying a heavy automatic shotgun—like the military AA-12, but this is something new, state-of-the-art. A large drum beneath the barrel holds twelve rounds.

You pull a rag from the back of the El Camino and wipe the blood from your face and arms. Sliding into the driver's seat, Iris says, "Shit. What happened?"

"Cannibals."

"What did you—" she starts.

"They were grilling infants over a fire. They're all dead now."

Iris's face goes slightly pale. She tries to hide it, but you see it—it's bad in New York, but it's *hell* out here. You don't say much for a while after that—just continue driving south, hugging 85, looping around Charlotte, and then racing down back roads, staring at the pavement until it all begins to look the same. You want to drink more, but you don't.

TURN TO PAGE 276.

You throw it into first, alternating gas and brake, trying to rock the El Camino free, but the tires just kick up grass and dirt and—soon—flesh.

You throw it back into reverse.

Nothing.

Mud and dirt and grass and zombies, all together, chopped up and chewed up and spit out like fatty meat.

And then the howitzers start up again. You hear a single shell, whistling as it soars through the air.

The explosion is so tremendous, so loud, you hear only the pop of your eardrums shattering. You don't feel it. No pain. Just flashes. You see the ground. And the sky. You feel yourself flying.

When you wake, you're lying on wet grass. You see your own arm, a dozen feet away.

You open your mouth, but there's blood in your throat, gargling and bubbling with every raspy attempt at breath.

You manage to lift your head. Your legs are gone. Only two gory stumps remain, charred black. You must have been thrown fifty yards through the air.

A tall shadow falls over you. You see an undead hand, clutching a piece of paper. You can just barely make out a few words on it, written in fancy script: *Four score and seven years ago . . .*

And then a face appears. A zombie. One eye is gone, only a dark hole where it should have been. A tangled beard, dark hair, crawling with maggots. The thing towering over you, you realize, is an undead Abraham Lincoln reenactor.

It bends down and begins clawing at you. Its left hand has no fingers, and bony nubs paw at your skin. One rips through your flesh, poking at your windpipe.

And it really does look pretty accurate. That's what you're thinking as its nubs get hold of your Adam's apple and it tugs, turning your gasps to a soft, airy whistling.

It looks pretty damn accurate . . .

·:·꞉· AN END ·꞉·:·

Your mind races as you twist the throttle. Freedom feels close—but you don't want to die, not yet.

You make up your mind.

All right, Boss Tanner, you want me to play your game, I'll play your game.

And, Eigle, you want to offer me my freedom? But I need to slay a few zombies first? Maybe a few breathing folks, too? Will do.

You rev the engine, turning onto Fifty-Sixth Street, back toward Times Square. Roaring through the crowd of undead monsters, knocking one aside, rolling over another, and racing out into the street.

As you slide around the corner, they surprise you. Undead bodies, crawling out of open manholes, stumbling from the shadows of overhangs. Hands reaching through sewers.

One staggers out from behind a rusted delivery truck—this one long and tall, in a shredded camel topcoat. You get a glimpse of a dark face and broken teeth and then it's ripping you down, off the Harley.

You hit the ground, roll, and rise. Nothing broken.

A piece of splintered wood nearby. You grab it, flip it in the air, swinging as you catch it, snapping topcoat zombie's neck with the first blow. Two more swings and its head separates from its body. Another lunges—you jam the splintered wood into its brain.

You're near the Paramount Building, where this whole shit-show started—the building where Eigle offered you your freedom. Where you rebuffed him and tried to kill him. The crowd, leaning out windows all around you, hoots and applauds.

Now, far down the avenue, you see two cars dueling, veering back and forth, metal sparking and clanging, and you hear machine guns rat-a-tat-tatting.

Need to keep moving.

You round the corner, and there you spot a Jeep Wrangler. Rocket launchers on the side. Whopping fifty-cal on top.

This, you realize, is what Eigle was referring to when he said a vehicle was waiting downstairs.

He really did have it all set up, everything arranged. He must need you bad.

You climb inside. Wrap your hands around the steering wheel.

Another salvo in the distance. Explosions. All the action, together, forming some ungodly orchestra. It's time you added your own instrument to the tune . . .

You start the engine, stamp the accelerator, slipping it into second as you enter Times Square. Ahead of you, chaotic car combat and Boss Tanner's handpicked man—Mr. King—hurtling toward you in the Lincoln.

 TURN TO PAGE 205.

"The deal is," you say, sliding into the seat, "only *I* drive the El Camino."

You slam the key into the ignition as Iris climbs in beside you, then press your foot hard on the pedal, gas pumping through the engine like the adrenaline through your veins. You twist the wheel, steering your death machine toward the stable.

"You're driving *toward* him?" Iris says. *"Wonderful."*

"Want to kill King now, if I can."

You trigger the rockets—an instant later, twin spirals of smoke as they speed ahead, zooming toward the Lincoln with a piercing shriek. Your enemy cuts at the last moment and the rockets erupt harmlessly against an outcropping of trees in the distance.

You wrench the wheel, sliding, triggering the M134D mini-gun. Bullets pound the Lincoln's hood. Smoke erupts and the Lincoln's locked tires howl as it turns wildly, a spinning top, out of control—and then—WHAM—slams into the farmhouse.

Before you can stop the car and finish him, the front end of the El Camino goes up and over a zombie, dragging it beneath the chassis. You stomp the brakes, but the tire skates, hydro-planing on the monster's wet flesh.

The El Camino slips into the shattered horse stables, up and over the wreckage left by Mr. King. Inside, Dr. Splicer's monstrous menagerie is loose.

You drop it into first gear and steer the El Camino forward, four-wheel drive pushing you through the collapsing stable and through an army of strange creatures—the thresher chewing some of them up, pushing others aside.

Pigs run, squealing unnaturally, eyes darting—some seem to have the eyeballs of human beings. Undead toddlers stagger about, one covered in chicken feathers, another in goat hair. A zombified cow stumbles forward, its udders replaced with human fingers. You slam into it, threshing it to nothing but specks of red.

And there, at the end of the stable, is Dr. Splicer, hunched over his operating table, blood streaming from his lacerated belly.

He sees you. Horror on his face. You just grin and give the El Camino gas.

The El Camino smashes into the metal table and knocks Dr. Splicer back. He's scrambling to his feet, clutching his mangled gut, when the thresher gets him, taking his foot first, then more of him, the whirling blades devouring the man as his fists beat the hood, swallowing his torso, and he's howling, howling, howling still as the El Camino bursts through the back of the stable, out into the wild grass, Splicer still pounding his fists against the hood, wailing, until he's no longer there, alive, because the thresher has consumed him entirely.

Gone. Red mulch.

You circle around, searching for the Lincoln, but it's gone, too. You spot muddy tire tracks, headed east.

You ignore them.

Charging out into the street, nitrous pumping, supercharger pounding, the El Camino leaves behind a long trail of blood and pulp on the grass.

 TURN TO PAGE 308.

The scent of roasting animal is in the air as you move carefully through the trees, taking a wide berth around the house.

Coming around the rear, you catch a glint of light along the ground. Something reflecting in the afternoon sunlight.

Fishing line.

Kneeling down, following the line with your eyes, you see it leads to a tin-can alarm system.

You carefully step over it.

Twenty yards from the house now.

A loud creaking then, followed by a loose smacking—a screen door opening and shutting. A man steps out. He wears a filthy New Orleans Saints jacket. He has a thick gray beard, halfway to ZZ Top, and a greasy trucker hat on top of his head. Late forties. This must be Dewey.

You slide behind an oak tree, one eye around the side.

Dewey walks toward the section of fence nearest to you. There's a grill there. He opens it, smoke pours out, and he curses. Clumsily, he clambers over the fence, out into the woods.

He drops down to one knee and reaches through the fence to adjust something on the grill.

Slowly, quietly, you step through the dense brush. You raise the sawed-off, just a threat, not to kill. Another step, and—

SNAP!

You choke down a scream. Your eyes drop and you see rusty metal slicing through your boot into your right ankle. A bear trap.

Dewey turns. He holds a revolver. He has a wide, shit-eating grin on his face. "Hello there, fella."

You grit your teeth. The rusty blade cuts into your bone.

Leaning against the fence, relaxed, Dewey keeps the revolver on you. "Saw you coming a ways back, end of the path. Figured if I fiddled around here, you'd come up behind me—try to get the jump. Figured, too, that you'd step right into that there trap. I'm real good at figurin'."

"I need help," you say.

He chortles and nods at your foot. "You sure do, fella."

"I'm not here to rob you or hurt you. I need your skills."

"For what?"

"A woman. It's hard to explain."

"I saw a dead woman in your car."

"Yes, she died. But I think you can still help me."

"'Fraid not."

"Please," you say. "I can trade. Guns. Booze. Food."

"I got plenty of all three."

You see how this is going. So you jerk the sawed-off up and—

BLAM!

Dewey's shot punches you in your shoulder, knocking you onto your ass, your ankle snapping as you fall. You lie there for a long time, bleeding, before you lose consciousness.

You wake up in a dark, windowless room, strapped to a wooden table. Belts and chains around your ankles and legs.

Creatures surround you, staring at you. You blink. Realize they're taxidermied animals—squirrels and cottonmouth vipers and snapping turtles and big-ass alligators.

Dewey appears, leaning over you. "Fella, you were out a long time. Already finished work on your lady friend."

"Uh?" you mumble, groggy, confused.

"Go on, take a look," he says. "She lookin' real pretty now."

You sit up.

Iris is across the room, her dead body set in a rocking chair.

She looks alive—almost. Her legs are crossed and she's in a short pink skirt and a white top. Her hair is now thick and wavy. She's staring at you.

Christ.

"You stuffed her?"

Dewey just giggles.

"I'll kill you."

"You be nice, now—or else I might be tempted to make you look real silly when I do you up."

You try to lift an arm, grab his throat, but your hand is tied too tight. You're helpless.

Dewey taps your forehead twice, then crosses to a table. "Now, I'm about ready to get started. Hope you don't mind too much I keep you awake for the beginning. It's just, shit—well, I get awful lonely here. Having someone to talk to would be nice, while I work."

You don't say anything. You just watch as Dewey picks up a long fleshing knife and a curved skinning blade. He takes a swig from a bottle, then grins. "See, I'm gonna preserve you, fella. Then I think I'll pose you on the porch, out front, next to where I sit at night. Think I'll make you look like some sort of great zombie slayer. I figure that's what you s'posed to be, from that car you driving. Some sort of wasteland warrior? I'll have you posed all strong, with that hog leg in your hand."

He leans over and begins cutting into your belly.

"Yep," he says. "But don't worry. I'll keep your friend here right nearby, so you have some company. Just you two, posed all nice, 'til the end of time . . ."

AN END

You move quickly: jumping up, grabbing the thick branch, swinging the ax, and slicing their ropes. The couple falls to the ground, landing in a wet pile of their own waste.

You tend to the woman, Martha, first, gently pulling the rusty metal hook from her back.

Looking closer, you see the wounds have been tended to before. The hooks have been removed, then reinserted, many times over, and Martha's wounds have been stitched up, then torn open, again and again. Her feet are gnarled—animals have chewed them down to misshapen stubs. Raccoons, you guess.

"How long have you been like this?"

Martha's too dehydrated to cry, so her body simply shakes. You place a hand against her shoulder. She's hot and feverish. "A year," she manages. "More. Don't know."

Jesus.

"Why?" you ask.

"He keeps us. To attract them. He fixes us, heals us—just enough."

"Who?"

"The monsters," Martha says. She coughs, a mix of blood and phlegm and bile coming up, like some blackness seeping from a backed-up sewer drain.

"No," you say. "Who keeps you?"

"Doctor. The doctor."

"For what?"

"Experiments. On the monsters . . ."

Iris shouts then, from the car. "Jimmy! Behind you!"

Before you can turn, something hard and metal slams into the side of your face with force enough to kill most men. You tumble forward into the grass. Rolling over, you see a huge beast of a man, gripping a pitchfork. He tramps past you and begins jabbing the tool into Martha. As the man-beast stabs continually into what is now just fleshy pulp, the sound turns to a wet slapping. He moves on to the man then, attacking arbitrarily: chest, throat, face, arms.

They are both dead, and there is silence.

The man-beast turns to you. He's silhouetted by the full moon.

He moans. A sound like a horse neighing, almost, combined with the thick, guttural cough of someone very sick.

Out of the corner of your eye, you see the glint of the sawed-off lying in the grass. You reach for it, but you're too slow—the man-beast roars and brings the pitchfork down, piercing your wrist and pinning your arm to the dirt. It's a shrill pain, like fire inside you, and you hold back a scream.

Iris cries out, and you hear the car door open, but you don't hear anything else: the man-beast raises a booted foot and stomps your face.

TURN TO PAGE 342.

CELEBRATORY BOOZING

You grin at Major Eigle. At the man who offered you freedom but instead ran you through this bullshit derby—this test.

"I'm going to get drunk, Eigle. You can buy me a drink next time."

Boss Tanner slaps you on the back, says, "Attaboy!" and leads you away. You turn back, grinning at the bastard. Eigle stares at you. Whispers something to Hank. You spit.

You and Tanner hit the town. Hard. Some guys hit the town, but you throw it an Iron Mike uppercut.

It's a blur. You knock back booze with Tanner at an upscale joint, while his militiamen round up all the zombies that were used in the contest and clear the streets. Two hours later, Tanner gets an all clear, and you all make your way downtown, moving from spot to spot.

Bars.

Brothels.

Bars with zombies hanging in the windows.

Brothels with zombies for rent by the hour.

That's about all there is in this new version of Manhattan.

Just before five a.m., you pass out in a sex house. Room is on Boss Tanner's tab—anything for a Death Derby driver, they tell you.

They wake you just after dawn. Major Eigle, sitting across from you. The mechanic named Hank, with a big revolver trained.

Light is peeking through the windows. Your head is pounding.

You sit up, yawn, rub your temples. An empty whiskey bottle on the nightstand. "Where'd the girls go?" you say.

Eigle hands you a glass of water. "Jimmy, when I pulled you out of that cell, I told you I had a mission for you. You just had to prove yourself first. Yesterday, you did."

"I don't think I want your mission."

"Then you go back in the cell. And you don't ever come out."

You toss back some water. "You think so?"

"I do."

You look at Hank. "Sorry, fat man, but you won't be shooting me."

"I will," Hank says. "I don't particularly want to, but I will."

Eigle looks you in the eyes. "Jimmy, come quietly, or don't come at all."

If you'll go with them and undertake Eigle's mission, turn to page 216.

No thanks. You'd prefer to spend your life in Manhattan, driving and drinking and whoring. Go to page 264.

"Let the girl go," you say. "I'll stay."

Iris looks at you, head cocked, not quite sure how to react.

"Iris, don't say a word." Then, turning to Ring, you repeat, "Let her go, and I'll fight for you."

Ring rolls his waxed mustache between his fingers. His eyes move from you to Iris and back to you—like he's now rethinking the deal.

"It's that goddamn Boss Tanner," Ring says angrily. "He doesn't want the circus in the city. You know how much I could pull in, over in New York? But he says it's a damn distraction. Says it's no good. You know what that means—it distracts from what *he* offers. His fuckin' derby."

Finally, Ring nods to the man standing over Iris, and the man steps away, lowering the gun.

Iris reaches for your hand. You pull it away. "Go."

Reluctantly, she stands.

"Iris," you say slowly, carefully, "get the keys from the garage. I want you to drive to the place you always wanted to go as a child, okay? And wait for me. I might be a while, but you wait anyway."

Ring laughs. "You won't be going nowhere. Most likely, you'll be dead in an hour."

Iris ignores him. She looks into your eyes, you nod, then she's gone, out the door. You hope she knows what you mean— the World's Largest Ball of Twine. A damn stupid thing, you think, but she wanted to see it, and now it's a damn stupid rendezvous point . . .

Looking out the window, Ring says, "Folks are getting antsy out there. Looks like it's time we get this started."

You stand. "No."

"Excuse me?"

"Not until I see her drive out of town."

Ring chuckles softly. "What, you think I got a man down there, waiting to snatch her? Bring her to Tanner? Get my money's worth from both of you?"

"Possibly."

Ring laughs. "Fine, let these country boys wait."

You walk to the window and stare out. "Got anything to drink?" you ask.

Ring snaps his fingers. A moment later, you're drinking deeply from a glass of warm scotch. You light a cigarette and you watch.

Waiting.

Finally, you see the El Camino pull out from the garage down the street. Iris's at the wheel, alone. She guns it, nearly runs over a man carrying two loaves of bread. He slaps the hood and curses at her.

You watch her drive to the gate at the edge of town. It opens and she drives through. You don't see her for long after that, the El Camino soon disappearing into the surrounding ruins.

You keep watching, though, just in case. And you drink. You feel the warmth in your chest. The warmth fades as the liquor dissipates and as Iris drives farther and farther away.

"Ring," you say, turning to him. "One thing. When I get out of here, I will kill you."

Ring laughs. "Best of luck with that. Afraid you won't be going anywhere."

He's wrong. You'll get out of this place. You'll get Iris to San Francisco.

You think those two thoughts, over and over, a mantra, as

you drink your scotch—until finally Ring pulls it from your hands, pushing you out of the room, down the stairs, telling you the fighting begins now.

TURN TO PAGE 148.

GETAWAY

Sorry, Tanner, but I won't dance to your tune.

You rev the Harley, racing toward the flatbed. Standing, pulling back on the handlebars, the bike hopping up the back of the flatbed, gunning it harder, then launching yourself—over the truck cabin, through the air, over the barriers. The Harley thuds down on the other side of the wall—on the Queensboro Bridge—with a loud squeal.

A free man with sixty-five horsepower rumbling beneath.

The Harley charges into the monsters. You lower your body and grip the throttle—undead beasts are spun aside and knocked back. You rev it again, going faster—slow down and you're dead.

You can see the end of the bridge.

You can see Queens.

Freedom.

But there's something you don't see.

Two women in dirty shirts, perched atop the bridge tower, with semiautomatic rifles pointed at your chest.

You don't see the muzzles flash.

You don't hear them fire.

You only feel the bullets smash into your chest, ripping you off the bike, slamming you to the pavement.

In an instant, the monsters are on you. Tearing at you. Teeth digging into your face. Hands ripping at your chest, splitting your flesh. Claws inside your stomach, tugging on your ribs, spilling your intestines across the Queensboro Bridge.

Two hundred undead New Yorkers, devouring you—sucking you down, piece by piece . . .

WELCOME TO TOMBSTONE

Things look different now. The grass is greener. The air almost sweet. The sun is bright and warm but not blinding. You drive down long, flat roads, then onto Interstate 10.

Outside Benson, Arizona, you pass a sign pointing to Tombstone.

Like you told Suzie-Jean and Walter, you always were a Western fan.

You follow the signs and soon come upon *Tombstone: The Town Too Tough to Die.*

You take a belt of whiskey and step out. You see that the historical section of town—the tourist shit, the old Western setting where Doc Holliday and Wyatt Earp shot it out with the outlaw cowboys—is encircled by a fence, fifteen feet high.

There's a big metal gate beneath a wooden *Welcome to Tombstone* sign. A man in Western dress stands out front, holding a rifle and spitting tobacco.

The man approaches you, looking the car over. Half-confused, half-intrigued. "What brings you to town?" the man says in a drawl.

"Not really sure," you say honestly.

The answer seems to catch him off guard. "Man shows up at a town, he should probably know why."

"Hot meal. Hot shower. Cold drink. Can you do that?"

He nods. "Sure. Got places to stay, too—permanently. Market's booming."

You look at him, squinting. "Market?"

"Folks coming from all over, looking to live within the fence. Folks looking for a card game. Folks wanting to start a business. We got places for rent, places for sale. Barter economy now, although Mayor McCray 'spects that'll change soon enough."

You take another swig and light a cigarette. "Okay."

"But," the man says, "no cars. You leave that behind. No automatic guns, neither, but you can keep your sidearm. Those are the rules in Tombstone, 'n' we expect folks to obey them."

If you're not ready to permanently abandon your mission, turn to page 362.

That's it. No more. You're done with the El Camino, done with Iris, and done with trying to save the world. Go to page 209.

"Billy, I need your help."

"You do?" he says. He sits forward, looking excited.

"Yes. I need to get out of here."

He's scared now, stiffening. "No."

"Please, Billy."

"But . . . I can't."

"Billy," you say. "Get me out of here. I *have* to get out of here. It's so important, I can't explain."

"Mr. Ring told me no."

You curse and light a cigarette. "Go on, then. If you won't help me, then get out."

Billy walks to the far end of the car and begins climbing up to the small crack in the ceiling. "I'm telling," he says, looking back at you. "I'm telling Mr. Ring that you asked me to help you."

You pull the cigarette off your lips. "Don't do that, Billy."

"I have to. Mr. Ring'll kill me if I don't."

You swallow. You eye the small boy. If he tells, you may very well be dead, and then Iris will be, too . . .

If you'll do the unthinkable and silence the boy, turn to page 112.

To let Billy leave, go to page 254.

You floor the Jeep, quick-shifting, then flick the trigger and unload the fifty-cal. Bullets pound the Lincoln's windshield. The bulletproof glass spiderwebs but holds.

Mr. King, in the Lincoln, whips around, racing downtown.

You shift into third and the Jeep leaps forward, cutting through the chaos. Other vehicles battling around you, explosions, buckling metal, gunfire snapping and thundering. It's a war zone. Elwood's Dodge Monaco is spun around, roof on fire.

You catch a flash, a glimpse of Mr. King's eyes in his rearview. He's focused on your car.

He's making a move . . .

Instinctively, you veer to the right.

Motion on the rear of the Lincoln, and then you see a flash of steel in the sunlight. Tire spikes. Two dozen dropping out the back.

But your swerve worked, and you speed past the tumbling tire spikes unharmed.

The announcer loses his shit. *"Jimmy El Camino seemed to know what was coming!"*

You can't help but grin. The announcer is dead-on. And that's why you always won—in war and on the track. And that's why you'll keep on winning.

You cut back behind Mr. King's Lincoln, unloading with the fifty-cal, slugs battering the bulletproof rear windshield and the reinforced trunk lid.

You stomp the accelerator, keeping the pressure on and keeping your finger on the trigger, firing, firing, firing, until—

KRAKA—BOOM!

Your eyes jump to the rearview and—

FUCK.

You weave right, up onto the curb, as a rocket spirals past. It's the Desert Fox in the World War II Panzer, rumbling behind you. The massive main gun—the KwK—aimed at you.

You're forced to let Mr. King escape. You hit the brakes, downshift, and jerk the wheel, off the avenue, onto Thirty-Fifth Street. Tires squeal.

There's another **KRAKA—BOOM!** as the KwK fires. You catch a glimpse of the shell in your rearview, rocketing down the avenue you just left behind.

You avoided the warhead, but you're not in the clear. Zombies ahead, clogging up Thirty-Fifth. A fucking parade's worth—two hundred. Too late to slow down, so you floor it.

Turning up Seventh Avenue, you see two cars dueling ahead of you. Lucy Lowblow, in the lightning-fast Porsche, and Stu Bean, in the Ford van. The old Deadhead cuts it hard, trying to smack the Porsche off the road, but Lucy speeds ahead.

You can take out one of these guys, maybe, but not both. Which one will you hunt? Who will you murder in order to impress Eigle, get the mission, and get back your goddamn freedom?

Chase after Lucy Lowblow in the speeding Porsche? Turn to page 63.

If you'll choose to hunt down Stu Bean in his old Ford van, go to page 226.

You slow the El Camino and grab hold of Iris, pulling her over the shifter. At the same time, you open the driver's-side door and jump out—the car still rolling. "Iris, you drive around back, all the way, then meet me out front."

"You're mad!" she barks, sliding behind the wheel.

You ignore her, grabbing the fire ax and racing away from the already accelerating El Camino. The sawed-off slaps against your thigh as you dash through a splintered door into the White House—and you hear Lucy Lowblow coming around fast.

You sprint through the building now, past undead tourists and decaying tour guides, all swiping at you, moaning loudly in the cramped halls. An undead Secret Service agent lunges, and you swing the ax, barely slowing, burying the blade in its brain.

You cross the White House in barely a minute, coming to a stop at an exit on the opposite end of the building, kicking open the door just in time to see the El Camino racing past. Iris, eyes narrowed, focused, struggling to keep control of the vehicle.

And then she swerves.

There's someone in front of her.

The president.

Zombified.

She doesn't turn fast enough. She hits the president—its knees shatter, the thresher carves up its lower body, and then it's knocked aside.

And then the Porsche engine barks and Lucy is racing around the corner, chasing the El Camino, focused on it, machine guns blasting, as you step out onto the lawn, raising the sawed-off, and—

BLAM! BLAM!

Both barrels, directly through the driver's-side window. Lucy's face is blown apart, her golden hair mixing with brain matter and skull and painting the interior of the Porsche a wet crimson. The car careens across the lawn, slamming into a large tree, cracking the trunk.

You holster the gun and step over the writhing zombie body. "Mr. President," you say, giving a nod to the undead leader of the free world.

Iris climbs out of the El Camino. "I see why you like driving so much."

"Sure," you say, sliding behind the wheel. "Have a car, know how to drive, you can go wherever you want. Whenever."

"And where are we going now?"

"We're getting the hell out of Washington."

TURN TO PAGE 180.

"I'll be back before sundown," you say. "Need to settle a few things."

Outside Tanque Verde, you cut off the road, rumbling across the rough desert until you find a flowering palo verde tree.

You pull a collapsible shovel from the El Camino and begin digging. It takes you two hours to get to six feet deep. It's tough going, but it feels good—you feel alive, and you barely stop to catch your breath until you're finished.

You carry Iris's legless body from the El Camino. As gently as possible, you slide her down into the grave. She looks at peace. Maybe that counts for something.

Maybe.

Knowing she was religious, you feel you should say a prayer, but you don't know any. You think on that, then finally just say, "Good luck. Hope it's not too cold in there," and cover her with dirt.

Once you've filled the grave, you hack a thick piece of bark away from the tree and construct a crude headstone. With your combat knife, you carve the words: *Iris. Died age 19. Gave her life for something that mattered.*

From the car, you slide the sawed-off into your hip holster, slip the Smith & Wesson revolver into your belt loop, and stuff a bottle of whiskey in each pocket.

That'll be enough to start your new life.

You slide back into the car and pick up the microphone. "Eigle?"

A moment later, he comes on. "Jimmy? What's your status?"

"I'm done. That's my status."

"Wait, Jimmy, what—" he starts, but you don't hear him finish because you've put a bullet into the radio.

You remove the ax from the car, and then it's one last thing. You find a large rock beneath the tree, place it on the El Camino's gas pedal. The engine roars. You reach inside, shift the car into first, and jump back as the El Camino speeds away. You wonder where it will stop. You hope it crashes into a gorge somewhere and explodes. That part of your life is over.

Some hours later, you're back at the gate to Tombstone, drenched in sweat. It's dusk, and a blue haze is settling over the town. "I'm ready," you tell the man.

He nods and opens the gate, and you step into every Western fan's wet dream.

Main Street is lined with saloons and brothels. You notice a sheriff's office, with a big wooden badge hanging out front. There's also a barbershop, a church, a general store, and a livery.

And it's not fake. Not anymore. A few years ago, sure, it was a tourist attraction—but now, this is real.

You're approaching a saloon called the Brass Rail when you hear a commotion. The bat-wing doors fly open and five men—farmers, it looks like—tumble out, tripping over the steps, kicking up dust when they land on the dirt street. They scramble to their feet. One screams.

Six zombies stumble out behind them, quickly upon them. Women cry out and the street empties and doors lock. The men crawl over one another, trying to get away. One man swings a bottle at the monster that's pinning him to the ground.

You're twenty yards from the zombies and the men trying to fight them off. You watch the beasts claw at the men. You drop the ax to the dirt and draw your Smith & Wesson 500.

Six shots ring out.

Brains splash the dirt road and six zombies crumple to the ground.

You reload the pistol as you stride toward the men. They're just getting up, dusting themselves off, breathing heavily, confused, still scared.

"Mister . . . Christ, thank you," one says.

A younger man says, "Hell, you shot all of them? No misses?"

The oldest of the men sits up, holding his neck. Blood streams through his fingers.

"Oh hell, Wyatt, you're bit," the first man says.

The one named Wyatt looks up. He has a thick gray mustache and his hair is wet and matted and his hat lies beside him. Blood pumps steadily from his neck. He'll turn soon. There's a look of immense sadness on his face.

You look up from Wyatt to his friends. "This man have any family who should come say good-bye, 'fore he turns?"

The other men all shake their heads. "Had a brother, but he died."

You nod, then you place the reloaded Smith & Wesson to Wyatt's pale forehead and kill him.

Holstering the gun, you say, "Sorry I had to put your friend down like that."

"Mister, he wasn't just our friend. He was Wyatt Earp. He was the dern sheriff."

You look down. Brain matter is splattered across a silver badge.

"Wyatt Earp?"

"Sure. Well, he *played* Wyatt Earp, in the reenactments, for the tourists. But after everything happened, he took the name, became sheriff officially."

That's the silliest goddamn thing you've ever heard, you think.

"All those O. K. Corral shoot-outs," the man continues, "for the tourists, made him a helluva shot. He was a good sheriff."

A roly-poly sort of fellow comes running down the street, hollering, "What happened? What happened?" in a tinny voice.

"Goddamn things got in," the man says. "Crack in the fence. Came through the rear door of the Brass Rail. Stranger here put 'em down, but Wyatt was already bit."

The roly-poly man looks at you. "What's your name?"

"Jimmy," you say.

"Looks like you just killed our sheriff, Jimmy."

You don't say anything.

"I'm Mayor McCray. You just get into town today?"

"Not more than ten minutes ago."

"You planning on staying for a while?"

"Was thinking about it."

"Looks like you're something with that pistol. How'd you like to be sheriff? Pays in food and liquor. Barter economy. But you'll have room and board and we can give you something to gamble with, if that suits your fancy."

You think about that for a moment, then say, "Sure. That sounds just fine."

Mayor McCray smiles. "Good. That's real good."

The other men say their thanks and make their way back into the Brass Rail to continue drinking. A bony, crooked undertaker hobbles over, grabs Wyatt's body, and drags it down the dusty road.

You're sitting on the porch outside the sheriff's office. It's early morning and you're eating eggs, pork sausage, and biscuits—courtesy of Clara, owner of the brothel down the way. She brings you breakfast every morning. In exchange, you keep a close watch on rowdy customers and you hit extra hard if anyone messes with one of her gals.

You sip coffee, thick as syrup, and feel the weight of the pistol hanging at your side.

You put your feet up on the railing.

This is all right, you think, watching the sun rise over the row of shops and bars across the way. This isn't the beach house you dreamed of, but goddamn, this is all right.

AN END

"This way, Billy," you say as you begin racing across the muddy field toward the ambulance. The monsters are swarming. Not far from your position, an undead lion chomps the head of a zombie and swallows it whole.

You grab hold of the ambulance's twin back doors. You hope to find some sort of weapon inside—a fire ax, maybe.

But both doors fling open on their own, hitting you on the nose and drawing blood and spinning you aside. An undead football player leaps out at you like the thing was spring-loaded. Dreadlocks wave as the monster soars through the air, lands square on your chest, and drives you into the ground. Its jersey is stained with grass and blood.

The thing has its rotten mouth to your face, teeth snapping. The player's muscles have deteriorated, mostly, but it's still much stronger than any zombie you've faced before.

Reddish saliva drips down, and you turn your face. You push at its throat, trying to hold it back.

And then Billy's there, slamming a fire extinguisher into the player's head, over and over, until the thing rolls off and collapses and chunks of brain dot its dreadlocks.

You get to your feet.

Before you can thank Billy, the earth trembles and you see fire in the distance, and then the security gate at the far end explodes and a swarm of rockets zooms into the stadium . . .

TURN TO PAGE 234

An hour later, you're in an auto-body shop on the Lower East Side. It smells of oil and sweat and rotten meat. A single dim light flickers overhead. Maps cover one wall. You're sitting in the shadows in a back room, on a dirty couch with strands of orange fabric sticking out.

A moan sounds from the corner of the dark room.

A zombie. Once a man. It wears a torn suit, a necktie hanging loosely, splattered with brown blood. Its nose is missing—face looks more skeletal than human.

A chain around its neck leads to a water pipe not far above. It half hangs from it, half stands.

It moans again.

You look away from the zombie to Major Eigle. He stands near the monster, arms folded. Hank sits in a plastic folding chair, drinking a beer.

"I'm here. Now get to it," you say. "What's the job?"

"I want you to drive, Jimmy. The most important ride of your life."

You stare at him blankly.

Eigle turns and calls out, "Iris!"

A girl appears from the hallway at the far end of the room. Maybe twenty years old. Dirty blond hair, like hay. She looks beat to hell and run-down and tired of moving, like an old pickup pushed too far on not enough oil. But as she stands there, staring at you, you see she's got eyes that still sparkle just enough to make you want to know her story and maybe buy her a drink.

"Who's this?" Iris asks.

"This is Jimmy," the major says.

Iris sighs. "I told you, Eigle. I made it real plain and clear: I'd do this *only* if you got a real driver. A professional. Not gonna happen with some washed-up old booze hound."

"Washed-up old booze hound?" you say, reaching for the nearby bottle and pouring yourself a healthy-sized glass. "She's observant."

Eigle says, "Jimmy here—he's the only driver not loyal to Boss Tanner."

You take a pull from your big drink. "What's the drive? And what does this girl have to do with it?"

"You need to deliver Iris to San Francisco."

You shake your head. "No. From the little I saw out there, what you showed me? That's a one-way ticket. A suicide run."

"And not long ago you were in a cell, Jimmy. I'm offering you a chance at freedom."

You lean back, sinking into the couch. An old cigar case full of grease-stained, poorly rolled cigarettes on the table beside you, matches scattered about. You light a smoke. Exhaling, you say, "Why's she got to get to San Francisco?"

Eigle starts to say something but stops. "Easier if I show you."

Iris looks suddenly sick. "Just tell him," she says.

"What we're asking?" Eigle responds. "He needs to see."

"Just tell him—" Iris starts, but Eigle holds up his finger. She goes quiet.

Eigle grabs her; she resists briefly, then goes with him, toward the zombie chained to the pipe. You lean forward, sipping your drink, curious now. Hank taps his foot anxiously and looks down at the cracked cement floor.

Slowly, like a magician showing you that everything is on the level, Eigle begins rolling up Iris's sleeve. Her skin is milky white. Looks soft. You want to touch it.

He rolls her sleeve up further, past the elbow, and you see then that her skin there is scarred to hell. Like a junkie's.

The zombie moans.

"The stick," Iris says.

Eigle takes a short, thick wooden rod from a table at his side. He slides it into the girl's mouth, and she bites down.

Eigle wraps his long, bony fingers around Iris's wrist. She squeezes her eyes shut, and then Eigle holds her arm out to the zombie.

The monster's eyes flash and its head snaps forward and its teeth dig into her flesh. The wet sound of tearing tissue fills the room.

You start forward. Eigle holds his hand up. "It's okay," Hank says from across the room, still looking at the floor. "Watch. You need to see."

Iris squeezes her eyes tighter and bites her lip until it bleeds and her legs quiver—but she doesn't try to escape and she doesn't cry and she doesn't try to stop what's happening.

Blood drizzles from the zombie's mouth. Eigle says, "Hank."

Hank stands, crosses the room, and slams a heavy wrench into the zombie's head. He swings twice more, and the zombie's teeth release Iris's flesh. Another heavy blow to the face and the zombie's head whips back.

Iris's legs give out then, and her arm falls limp. Hank is there, catching her, helping her to a couch. He quickly wraps her bleeding arm in a towel. Iris looks like she wants to cry, but she never does.

"You just killed her," you say, getting to your feet, ready to tear apart Eigle and Hank. "You just sentenced that girl to death. She'll be one of those things now—undead."

Eigle shakes his head. "No. Iris is resistant," he says. "Her blood, her DNA, *something*—she *can't* be infected. We're in communication with San Francisco. There are scientists there: men and women who can study her body and, they believe, create a vaccine. We can end all of this. We just need to get her there."

Iris speaks up, her voice a faint croak. "Eigle. That's the last time. Never again. I've agreed to your plan—but no more of this show. I swear, you suggest it again, you try it, and I promise: *I'll fucking kill you.*"

Eigle ignores her. He's watching you.

You take another swallow of your whiskey—a big one.

"So you're asking me to save the world?" you say.

"In a way, yes."

"Why me?"

"Same thing I said yesterday—you can kill, and you can drive."

"But why so hush-hush?"

"If Boss Tanner learns about Iris, he'll kill her. Same goes for the men running every city from here to San Francisco. The apocalypse turned ordinary men into criminals, and it turned criminals into kings. They have power now. And they don't want to lose that power—even if it means letting the apocalypse march on, until there's nothing left . . . just unending death . . ."

Iris eyes you, holding the rag tight, but not tight enough—the blood still coming, pooling on the floor.

"One drive," Eigle says. "One drive, and the chance to save the world."

Will you accept your mission? If so, turn to page 107.

A suicide run isn't your idea of a good time. Go to page 307.

LAISSEZ LES
BONS TEMPS ROULER!

You drive over the Crescent City Connection, crossing the Mississippi, following the signs into New Orleans. You're looking for a hospital—that's where you'll find your backup generators.

New Orleans was in full swing, midcelebration, and suddenly, it just stopped when the apocalypse came to town. Monsters in elaborate costumes, slathered in face paint, stumble about. Abandoned floats clog avenues. Colored beads and feather masks scattered across the ground.

The engine growls softly as you prowl the streets, trying not to draw the attention of the undead.

You find the hospital near Bourbon Street.

You steer the El Camino down a winding ramp to the hospital's storage garage. You leave the car idling and step out, carrying the ax. You chop through a thick metal chain and lift the gate. The sharp stink of death fills the garage.

You find four wheeled generators in the rear. It appears there were more, but they've been taken. A few long-dead corpses lie on the floor, shot dead. A fight over the missing generators, you assume.

You're trying to figure out how you'll get the massive, five-hundred-pound generators back to Dewey's when you hear a booming voice from a megaphone outside.

You creep back up the ramp.

A parade float is rolling down Bourbon Street, the lane

thick with zombies. The slow-moving float knocks them aside and rolls over them.

The float is roughly twenty-five feet long and ten feet wide, the main platform raised eight feet off the ground. Squinting, you see that it's built atop the chassis of a pickup truck.

It's an anti-everything float. Signs read:

Homos in Life, Zombies in Death

Repent, Zombies!

Gays Become Zombies, God Becomes Happy

There are five people atop the float. The man in front holding the bullhorn looks to be the leader. He's in his late seventies and wears a blue track jacket and oversized slacks.

He holds a cigarette between his fingers and he alternates between dragging on the cigarette and yelling into the bullhorn. A white cowboy hat about three sizes too large sits on his head. Every few moments, it drops down over his eyes, and he has to push it back up. When he does, he ashes on his track jacket, and he curses into the bullhorn.

His speech comes out a little like: "THE HOMOSEXUAL AGENDA HAS—*shit*—BROUGHT ABOUT THIS—*cough*—RISING OF—*damn it!*—SATAN'S SPAWN!"

A middle-aged woman—the wife, you guess—stands proudly at his side, holding a rifle, at attention.

Two teenage boys, grandkids, maybe, walk around the float, hurling garbage at the zombies. One has a rattail. The other wears round sunglasses. Zombies reach up for their feet, but the undead hands are blocked by chicken wire.

A girl, maybe nine, sits at the rear of the float, atop a large papier-mâché structure depicting two men engaged in an explicit and, you think, intriguing act. She kicks her heels gently against the papier-mâché men and reads a comic book, not seeming to care about any of this.

There's someone underneath, too, driving. That makes six total: the old man, his wife, the two teenage boys, the young girl, and the driver.

As you watch the float roll down Bourbon Street, you suddenly know *exactly* how you'll get those generators back to Dewey's.

It's time to wreak a little havoc . . .

Confront the float head-on? Turn to page 376.

Use the element of surprise instead? Turn to page 15.

You race back toward Billy. The closest zombie to him is a football player, still wearing its helmet. You charge forward and throw your shoulder into it, bringing it down, then grabbing the face mask, wrenching it, twisting hard, cracking its weak neck, and then finally ripping its head off entirely.

You stand over Billy, holding the helmet—the zombie's head still inside, dripping gore.

A dozen zombies shuffle forward, blood pouring from their lips. Eyes dark and dead. You swing the helmet wildly, each strike cracking a skull.

A resilient one leaps forward. You swipe the helmet up, connecting with the thing's jaw. Its mouth clamps shut and its tongue is severed and you continue through with the swing, until the head inside the helmet finally slips out, soaring through the air. The attacking monster drops and the player's severed head rolls across the grass.

"Let's go!" you say, bending down to scoop up Billy.

But there, ahead of you, is a runaway undead elephant. It slams into the goalpost and there's a tremendous *crack*.

You see it happening, in slow motion. The goalpost breaking. Falling. Plummeting toward you. You try to dart to the side, but it's too late.

You hold Billy tight as the post slams into you. Billy cries out, then his cry is silenced as the heavy pole shatters his spine.

Everything goes dark.

Your eyes flicker open. Billy is on top of you, staring at you. It looks like he's attempting to speak but can't. Can't move his facial muscles or his jaw.

You try to tell him it'll be all right, that it's going to be okay, but you can't. Nothing happens. Your mouth doesn't respond to your brain's commands. You can blink your eyes. Nothing more.

With sudden, overwhelming terror, you realize your neck is broken. You're pinned beneath the pole, but it doesn't matter—you could be lying in an open field, and you still couldn't move.

Looking up, you see shadows fall over you. Zombies shuffling toward you. Two of the monsters in black-and-white referee uniforms.

They drop to their knees and begin. First pulling the flesh from your face. Wet teeth biting into the bridge of your nose. Killing you. And you don't feel any of it . . .

AN END

You eye the rear of Stu Bean's fat old Ford van, then reach down to the dash and tap it twice, a series of red switches appearing. Triggers. It's like the Aston Martin in *Goldfinger*—but with a helluva lot more firepower. And it's driven by you, red-blooded American Jimmy El Camino—not some martini-sipping Brit.

Hell, most of the Brits are dead now, far as you know. From what you saw on the TV, London fell quick.

Your eyes snap back to the road. You thumb the trigger, the armored van directly in front of you, and—

KRAKA—BOOM!

A rocket fires from the launcher on the side of the Jeep Wrangler and slams into the Ford, blowing open the rear doors and sending it careening across two lanes. The van goes up on two wheels as it turns off the avenue.

You follow.

The announcer: *"One of Boss Tanner's patented zombie traps is ready to be revealed. But where is it? Which driver is it targeting?"*

The announcer mentioned booby traps earlier, but you don't know what to expect. Don't know the extent of this absurdity. And then, turning onto Madison Avenue—

SPLAT!
SPLAT! SPLAT!

Zombies, slamming into the ground, pounding the street. One, then two, then five, then so many you lose count.

"ZOMBIE SUICIDE!" the announcer calls out. *"Boss Tanner's*

226

favorite! And if it's Boss Tanner's favorite, then it's our favorite, too!"

You look to the rooftops. A man is herding zombies off a ledge. The undead bastards plummet to the ground, the impact taking out the first few . . . but the others landing on the wet pile. Their bones might be shattered and their insides liquefied, but unless the brain is destroyed, they keep on coming.

SPLAT! SPLAT! SPLAT!

The zombies rain down from both sides of the street, body after body, like a lemming mass suicide.

You hit the brakes just as one monster drops onto the rear of the Jeep, crashing through the hard top, rocking the vehicle.

Instantly, cold hands reach for you, grabbing hold.

The zombie, once a woman, is now putrid and unrecognizable. One eyeball gone. No lips. Legs shattered, folded underneath it at impossible angles. Eyes mustard colored and hungry—hungry as hell, as it lets out a ferocious moan and its fingers dig into your shoulder.

You lunge across the car, reaching for the sawed-off, double-barreled Remington on the floor.

"No hitchhikers," you say, grabbing the big gun, spinning, raising it, and squeezing. The stowaway's head is blown off, leaving a cloud of red mist over Madison Avenue.

You blink away the blood, turn back to the streets, and—

Stu Bean's old Ford van is gone. All you see now is the Desert Fox and his Afrika Korps Panzer tank rumbling toward you.

BOOM!

You spin the wheel. The KwK fires and the massive shell rockets past you as the Jeep scrapes against a Duane Reade, bouncing off and slamming into a fire hydrant.

You throw it in reverse. The tires spin. That big Panzer tank barrel is turning toward you.

The tires spin again.

The Panzer rumbles.

Fuck it.

You open the thick, reinforced door and scramble out of the Jeep. You hear the heavy crank of the Panzer's cannon being repositioned. Need to hurry. Need to get away from the Jeep before it's blown to shit. You reach into the back of the overturned vehicle.

C'mon, c'mon.

CRANK CRANK CRANK

There.

Grenades. You stuff one into your pocket. You take the fire ax and the sawed-off, then you're sprinting away from the Jeep, into the middle of Madison.

The announcer screams: *"And Jimmy El Camino is out on the streets, on his own, running!"*

But where are you running to? Everywhere you look, zombies are shuffling toward you . . .

Charge the Desert Fox! Go to page 152.

Do anything but run toward the giant tank? Turn to page 275.

A NOSY FELLA

You bring Iris inside. In the rear of the museum is a large industrial freezer, previously used for storing wax. Igor sets her inside, flips some switches; a generator rumbles to life, and the freezing begins.

"Return with [REDACTED, LEGAL]," he says, handing you a map of the Hollywood Hills, "and I'll return your friend, in Popsicle form." You march out of the museum, slide inside the El Camino, and begin the hunt . . .

You follow the route on the map, driving past famous landmarks, most either destroyed or overrun with the undead. Zombies shuffle along the walk of fame.

It's strange, not having Iris in the seat next to you. It feels like you've abandoned her. Abandoned your mission.

And it would be so easy to leave it all now. You're close. You could hop on the Pacific Coast Highway and burn rubber to San Francisco—be there before sundown, maybe. Tell the scientists that bandits took Iris's body. Call Eigle, tell him, too. Demand the antidote. You'd get it, for sure. You'd force them to hand it over.

But you owe it to Iris to press on. Hell, you owe it to yourself.

In movies, characters always ask some villain or some cheating husband, *"How do you sleep at night?"* In the past, when you've asked yourself that question, you've always answered, "Like a goddamn baby."

But now you're asking yourself, "How will you sleep for *all eternity*?" After you're dead and gone, on the off, off, *off* fucking chance that some sort of consciousness remains—how will you sleep then? How would you sleep if you had the chance to save humanity, and you just turned your head, looked the other way?

Not well.

But you'll snooze wonderfully, you think, if you just do everything in your power to get Iris's body to San Francisco.

You hug the turns around Mulholland, charging up through the hills. It's a treacherous drive. Nature has teed off on the road in the four years since the Los Angeles sanitation department last tended to it. Fallen trees block the cracked roads and growing moss makes the turns slick.

You find the house at the peak of the Hollywood Hills. You can see the Hollywood sign, off in the distance, across the thick, tree-covered range.

The house is gated, but the gate has been destroyed. A truck sits in the front yard, pieces of wrought iron wrapped around the grille.

You park the El Camino and walk the drive, gripping the sawed-off. Nudge open the front door with the barrel, and immediately one is upon you. A monster in a once-white tuxedo, now torn and blood-splattered and dirty. It gets its arms up on your shoulders, like some emotional drunk trying to hug you.

You press the barrel against the monster's throat, just above its Adam's apple, pointed skyward, and pull the trigger. You turn and shut your eyes as it splatters your face.

You move further into the house. A thick layer of dust and dirt covers everything. Bottles of champagne on granite countertops. An Oscar statue lies on the floor. You pick it up. Feel its weight—surprisingly heavy.

Moaning from across the room. More men in tuxedos. Women, some in long dresses, some in short dresses, come stumbling through a shattered patio door. You swing, burying the Oscar statue in the head of a slobbering monster of a man.

And then you unload with the sawed-off. It's a quick slaughter. The heavy slugs tear through their strange, rotting faces. The rotten skin hangs oddly off some—too many filler injections—but the bullets end all that.

With the undead party guests finished, you're free to explore. You peer outside, through the patio door. Dead bodies in the swimming pool. Skeletal bodies scattered around—those that were never zombified simply died and were left to nature.

Stepping over the detritus of a four-year-old party-turned-massacre, you feel something crack beneath your feet. A retro Polaroid camera. Beneath it, a small pile of photos.

You bend down. And shit—you hardly believe it—there she is. [REDACTED, LEGAL], right there, in the first photo. Mugging for the camera, holding a glass of red wine in one hand with her arm around some hipster boob.

So she was here, in this house.

In a large bathroom—all granite and sparkly white—you find a note scrawled on the bathroom mirror in lipstick. "B. Going to the sign. My agent says helicopters are coming there. Come quick. xoxo.—[REDACTED, LEGAL]."

The sign.

The Hollywood sign?

From the back patio, you can see it—maybe five hundred yards away, through the sloping, wooded hills.

You walk that way. There once was a rough path, but it's overgrown. The hill pitches steeper upward, and you're forced into a climb. Panting, coming through the thickness, exiting the brush, the big letter H towers over you. A few monsters stumble around. You move quietly.

Could she be here? Still alive?

No. Not possible.

But her zombified body?

Maybe.

Or who knows, maybe the helicopter *did* come, and she's long gone.

Only one way to find out. You whistle, loudly, and the beasts come at you.

You check their faces, look for any sign it's her, clear them, and fire.

A man, an actor you recognize, not her. **BLAM!** The sawed-off slug blows its face apart, tearing flesh from skull.

A woman, rotted away, hard to make out—you check its neckline—no diamond. **BLAM!**

You continue around the thick base of the letters, firing, re-loading, leaving a trail of undead corpses behind you. But no sign of [REDACTED, LEGAL].

Coming to the end, the final letter, the towering D—you see a pile of zombies at the bottom. And a discarded shoe—a high heel.

You look up.

What would you do, if you were surrounded by zombies, waiting for a helicopter? With no weapon?

You'd climb.

Did she?

You'll find out.

It's forty-five feet. You climb it in three minutes.

Coming over the top, you feel a human bone. You hoist your-self up.

A body lies there, atop the big letter D, curled up in the fetal position. It's nothing but bones and tattered shreds of clothing now. The dress, though pounded by four years of weather, was clearly white.

You pull it aside, examining her clavicle, and there it is. The diamond necklace from the photo.

So that's how it went down. The zombies came. She ran from the house, through the hills. Climbed the D to escape them. There, she waited for a helicopter that never came.

She couldn't climb back down—there was an army of hungry monsters waiting below.

So poor little [REDACTED, LEGAL] stayed there until she likely died of dehydration.

Mystery solved. Good work, Marlowe.

You take the necklace and climb back down. You move quickly, back through the hills, through the house, to the El Camino, racing back to Madame Tussauds.

You've had enough of Hollywood.

TURN TO PAGE 391.

They found you.

You saw Mr. King chasing the train earlier, but you didn't think he'd make his assault here, in the stadium.

The Lincoln races through the thick smoke, guns blazing.

Behind him is Buzzy in the 1981 Chevy pickup, indiscriminately firing rooftop-mounted rockets.

The first rocket slams into a mass of undead beasts, vaporizing them.

The second rocket hits the stands behind you. Bodies explode. A piece of shrapnel stabs into your leg, hot and sharp. Blood running. You'll deal with it later.

The third rocket hits the scoreboard at the front end of the stadium, above the gate where you entered. There's a deafening crash as it slowly tumbles over, landing in the stands, that section of the stadium beginning to break, hundreds of bodies crushed by the impact. The entry gate cracks open and you wonder if—hope that—Ring is dead now, too.

But there's no time to go back and look.

You're closer to the visiting team's exit. It's still aflame, and smoke still billows out, but if you can make it, then you can lose the cars, lose the monsters.

The Lincoln rips across the field. The cannons don't let up. Bullets slam into the monstrous animals and the undead humans and it's now bedlam unlike anything you've ever witnessed: the stadium collapsing, bodies being blown to pieces, the heavy smell of gunpowder so thick in the air you can barely breathe.

Billy coughs and chokes and grips your jeans.

You can see the visitor's entrance—your exit. Forty yards. But Mr. King's Lincoln is turning, coming toward you.

And those forty yards will be the longest goddamn run of your life.

If you'll run for the exit, turn to page 156.

Attempt a leap into the stands? Go to page 273.

STORMING MOUNT RUSHMORE

Try to flee and the sniper will cut you down. If there's any hope of continuing this mad mission, you need to take him out.

When the next two zombies come shuffling around the side of the car, you shoot them point-blank with the sawed-off, splattering brain matter across the highway. You stack their bloody, lifeless bodies atop the car's undercarriage.

Iris, peering around the side, says, "Lot more coming. Whatever you're doing, fuckin' hurry."

The bodies function as a sort of makeshift sandbag wall, allowing you to grab a tire iron and begin removing the El Camino's front right tire. The sniper gets a glimpse of your head and a shot rings out. The bullet punches the zombie sandbag, hitting it with a meaty THWACK.

Moments later, you've removed the tire—then you're removing your undershirt, jamming it into the tire, sparking your Zippo, and setting the whole thing ablaze. You kick it out so it rolls across the highway and bounces into the Mount Rushmore parking area.

In moments, a torrent of black smoke fills the air, obscuring the sniper's view.

You grab Iris's hand, pain shooting through your shoulder, and rush out from around the car, pushing through the mass of zombies crowding the highway. You hold your breath, charging into the smoke, past the flaming tire.

A shot echoes as you come racing through the blackness

and down into the sprawling parking lot. Behind you, a car window shatters. You duck behind a rusted van.

"Where's he shooting from?" Iris asks, catching her breath.

"Gonna find out."

You wait three, four minutes until a zombie shuffles up and around the side of the van, arms out, fingernails dark and caked with dried blood. You swing the ax into its face, splitting it, and catch the body before it hits the ground. You prop the lifeless thing against the van, holding it there, your hand on its bloody throat.

"Iris, when I say, you kick the zombie. Right out into the open. Got it?"

She nods.

You press your face to the van's window, squinting through it, watching the massive hillside and the four faces of Mount Rushmore.

"Now."

Iris kicks the dead thing. It tumbles forward, then smacks the cement, nose breaking loudly.

You see the muzzle flash a moment before you hear the crack, just as the zombie is shot through the head.

The gunfire came from inside Lincoln's eyeball. This sniper has made a little home in there—a cutaway in the side of Mount Rushmore. Probably picks off passersby, feeds on them.

A scavenger.

The Sniper Scavenger.

Ahead of you, a short road leads to a three-level parking garage. Beyond that, a large cement gate—like the entrance at Disneyland—and then a long walkway leading to gift shops and a visitor's center at the base of Mount Rushmore.

Try to come through the front, the Sniper Scavenger will use you for target practice. You need another route.

Staying low, you and Iris creep down into the lower level of the parking garage, where you're safe from the gunfire. You cross the garage, and you can see the mountain again, and you can see Lincoln's eye, and you can see the reflection of the rifle's sight swinging side to side as the Scavenger hunts for you.

"I can distract him," Iris says. "Give you time to do whatever it is you plan on doing."

You think that over, then pull the sawed-off from your side and hand it to her. "Count to a thousand. At a thousand, you fire into the air, okay?"

Iris nods.

You get down on your belly and crawl away from the garage, gripping your beloved ax. You move slowly, low, behind a long line of cars, toward the thick woods surrounding the monument.

When you hit the trees, you start running—looping around the large rectangular area beneath the mountain base, boring to the left, shoulder howling. Zombie tourists shuffle about, stumbling around the center. Their moans echo off the mountain walls.

Soon the monument is directly ahead, a nearly sheer cliffside. Sixty feet up, squinting, you can see the sniper barrel jutting out from Lincoln's eyeball. A rope dangles down from the cutaway.

That's when you hear the shot go off, the thunderous sawed-off echoing from the parking lot. *Good job, Iris . . .*

You watch the sniper barrel swing right as the Scavenger searches for the source of the shot. He's distracted. This is your chance.

You grip the rope and begin climbing. Every pull is an exercise in pain. Your shoulder is on fire, blood pours down your side, your hands are slick with sweat, but your mouth is desert dry.

Hanging, catching your breath, you turn and look out at the parking lot and the mountains beyond it.

Shit.

Iris is out in the open. She's struggling, fighting off a zombie.

Ten feet above you, you see the barrel go steady as the sniper focuses on her, about to squeeze.

You pull, fighting through the hurt, climbing, up, up, up, and then reaching, grabbing the barrel, and tugging it, just as the Sniper Scavenger fires.

You hear a man's voice, a grunt, confused. The gun fires again, but by then you're gripping the ledge, pushing the barrel up, into the man. Your wounded shoulder screams as you throw your hand over the side, grabbing the ledge.

With your other hand, you blindly swing the ax, up and over the ledge. You hear a shriek. The ax hit *something*. You release the ax and pull yourself up, into the hollowed-out cave that the Sniper Scavenger has built inside Lincoln's stone eyeball.

The man's foot is bleeding from the ax blow. You stand—there's just barely enough room—and grab the ax again, swinging it into the man's back, turning him. He howls, but it's muffled behind a mask. Goggles, too, looking like he just stumbled out of a nuclear holocaust. Bleeding, screaming, he staggers toward you, swinging the rifle. His feet are caught up in a rope ladder. The ladder catches him, and he shrieks, then pitches forward, through the mouth of the cavern.

You lean out, one hand on the low ceiling, and watch the Sniper Scavenger plummet down sixty feet of near-sheer cliff face. Just before he hits the ground, the rope ladder pulls tight and there are two loud cracks: first, his ankle snapping, and second, his head splitting as it slams against the cliff wall.

Good night.

You take the sniper rifle, lie down, grab three deep breaths, and scan the parking lot. Iris is still fighting off the tourist zombie. You raise the gun, hold your breath, aim, and squeeze. The zombie's head explodes and it collapses. Through the scope, you watch Iris step back, confused, then look up at you. She squints.

You wave your good arm, indicating you want her to stay put.

You lie there a moment, letting the pain in your shoulder turn less hot, sliding from a burning pain to a dull ache. Then you examine the strange cave-hut. It's full of foraged items. Two dozen license plates, cigarettes, heavy jackets and hats, watches, boots, gloves, binoculars, edged weapons, and canteens.

Far beneath you, the Sniper Scavenger's body swings from the rope ladder. Zombies feed on him. You grip the sniper rifle, get into a firing position, covering Iris, and wait . . .

It's dusk when the zombies have finished with the scavenger's body, picking the last bits of flesh, the villain now looking like the aftermath in a nature show about piranhas. The monsters have scattered, and you've shaken his skeleton free from the ladder. Iris climbs, and you help her into the cavern chamber.

"Some damn afternoon, huh?" she says as she comes over the side.

"It gets better," you say. "Look."

You hand Iris a piece of paper. Scrawled on it, in scratched, maniacal handwriting, are the words: *1 man, 1 girl, '67 El Camino.*

Iris looks up. "He was looking for us."

You nod. "One of Tanner's men."

An HF radio sits in the corner of the cavern. Direct to Tanner, you guess. Iris sees it, too. "I want to call him," she says. "Tell him to go screw."

Not a bad idea. You pick up the microphone and key it. "Tanner," you say.

A second later, his familiar voice comes on. *"Is it done?"*

"Sorry, no. I'm afraid I killed your man."

There's a pause. *"Mr. El Camino?"*

"Yes."

"You still with that whore?"

You look to Iris. Her face is blank, unmoving.

"I'm with Iris, yes," you say. "And we're coming straight to San Francisco. You know my route now, and it's not changing. Bringing the girl over the Golden Gate. So call your drivers. Call Mr. King. Build a great wall, all I care."

Tanner snickers, but you hear something like fear behind the laugh. *"Bullshit. Why would you tell me all that?"*

"Because you don't think I can do it. You said it when we met, back in your Times Square ivory tower—'drunken bum,' something like that. Iris said something similar. Time to prove you both wrong. Thirty-six hours from now. Dawn. You'll see me coming, and you still won't be able to stop me."

"Jimmy—" he starts, but you've already turned the volume down.

You look to Iris. She's smiling, eyes warm.

"So, what do you think he's got to eat around here?" you ask.

TURN TO PAGE 331.

A VISIT TO FRED AND MARTHA'S FARM

Cannibals come for you in Indiana. They're posted outside a huge statue of a martini-drinking elephant, and Iris is quick to tell you that it's named just that—the Martini-Drinking Pink Elephant—according to her *Odd America* book.

The cannibals line the side of the road, armed with rifles, wrapped in layers and layers of clothing belonging to men now dead. They hide behind the large elephant statue, firing shots at the El Camino. One darts out into the road, stupidly, and you slam into him and snap him in two.

The sudden jolt of the man causes Iris's neck wound to open up and the bleeding to worsen. She finds a rag in the back of the car, presses it hard to her neck. No question now, she needs stitches.

Down I-74, past Indianapolis, you pull over and look at the map. A farmhouse is circled, indicating friendlies. Belongs to a couple named Fred and Martha.

Iris says, "Farmhouses are creepy as hell, huh? I've only ever seen 'em in horror movies, on TV, when I was a kid."

"Horror movies," you say, shifting the car into first and pulling out. "That's a good omen."

Two hours later, you're steering the El Camino up onto the thick, tall grass in front of Fred and Martha's two-story farmhouse. It's past midnight and a full moon shines down on the farm like a spotlight in a stage production.

The farmhouse is barely set back from the road, and behind

it is a large field, and beyond that acres and acres of corn. A metal wind pump towers over the house, rattling away. Fifty yards to the rear of the house you see a long horse stable, run-down, the wood rotten.

Iris gasps and points.

A large chestnut tree grows near the house. Hanging from the tree, swaying gently, are two bodies.

"Just the undead," you say. "Probably a warning to cannibals, like the ones we saw earlier."

But as you step out of the El Camino, you see they're not zombies. They're human. And the pained gasping sound and the smell of fresh shit and piss tells you they're still alive.

An older man and woman. They hang from the tree by hooks driven into the flesh of their lower backs. A large turkey vulture—the carrion crow—picks flesh from the woman's face. Much of her cheek tissue is gone, and you can see bloody gums and teeth. The vulture cocks its head, looks at you in annoyance, then flies off. You've interrupted his meal.

"Please . . . ," the woman whispers.

"Are you Fred and Martha?" you say, standing in front of the woman.

"Help . . . ," she chokes out. The man says nothing. He sways gently. Blood leaks from the hole in his back, down his ass, along his left leg, and then drips steadily off the heel of his boot. The blood gathers beneath him on the damp dirt, mixing with his feces. His eyes look nowhere, clouded in a pained, vacant fog.

"Are you Fred and Martha?" you repeat.

The woman manages a noise that sounds like "yes."

The house looms to your left. From your position now, you can see a barn around back of the house, one hundred yards opposite the stables. A candle burns in a stable window.

"What happened?" you ask.

The woman tries to speak but you only get a wet whimper.

"Speak," you say.

Mustering up energy, blood dribbling from her lips, her throat throbbing, she finally manages three words: "We . . . are . . . bait . . ."

Go. Now. Fast. If these two are bait, you're likely to be caught by whoever set this trap. Turn to page 288.

If you want to stay and help these poor bastards, turn to page 193.

A NEW DAWN

You're up before dawn, climbing down the rope ladder, crossing the parking lot, out onto the highway, and working to get the El Camino back on four wheels. Once the car has flipped, you steer the rattling, groaning thing to the upper level of the parking garage, far from any of the staggering dead.

The visitor's center was under construction. Around the rear, you find a stick welder, acetylene torches, multicutter saws. A handful of painkillers from the scavenger's den does just enough to numb the fire in your arm and allow you to work.

You find a pile of vehicles that belonged to men killed by the Sniper Scavenger, and you begin removing steel. Doors and roofs and hoods reinforce the front of the El Camino. You double-layer the inside, shielding the engine, then covering the windshield, leaving only a small space—the size of a license plate—to see through.

The sun is fully up and you're sweating like a demon when Iris comes shuffling up the ramp. She hands you a cup of coffee. "Found some in the cavern. Made this."

You take a long drink. The coffee is warm but not too hot. "Thank you."

She nods.

"Good morning," you say.

Looking at you, but not really, looking *through you*, at the mountain, and then turning to see everything else, she says, "Good morning."

"A few more hours. Then we'll leave."

"Sure," Iris says softly. She takes her coffee and walks to the edge of the parking garage. She sits on the ledge and stares up at the monument. She's small, on the ledge. The sun is massive and the sky is open and endless.

You could watch her all day.

You finish repairing, reinforcing, and rearming the El Camino. It's not as quick as it was, but it's fortified with steel ten times over. The guns are fully loaded and it's ready as it can be for a straight ride into the beating, revving heart of the enemy.

You light a smoke and cross the garage to Iris. "It's time."

"I know."

"You okay?"

"Not really."

You don't respond to that.

"But even if I die," she says, "whether we get there or not—I'm glad I got to see all this."

"It's filled with monsters."

She turns and looks up to you. "But it doesn't have to be. Not forever."

You smile. "That's your job."

It's a long drive and you barely touch the brake, gas pedal to the floor from South Dakota to California. Mercifully, you run into little trouble.

It's over twenty hours of driving. You stop only to refill the gas tank and to piss. Your wounded shoulder, wrapped and re-wrapped, hums with a steady, dull hurt.

You and Iris talk little.

You're delivering this girl to her death. Best-case scenario, you push through the gauntlet that awaits you and you get into

San Francisco and you're cured of Eigle's goddamn poison. And then some scientists, doctors, who knows what, cut Iris open and she dies.

So, really, what is there to say?

You light a cigarette and drink and you let her pick the music.

She finds an old Beatles eight-track. You were never a Beatles guy. But she puts it on and listens to "Here Comes the Sun" as she watches the highway and the undead monsters blurring by and you think, maybe, for a second, you see a slight smile on her face.

The Golden Gate Bridge links Marin County, and in turn, the rest of Northern California, with San Francisco—the last bastion of true civilization in the United States.

You take the Redwood Highway. It's lined with lush, green, and now thickly overgrown hills.

When you see the sign that reads *Golden Gate Bridge Ahead*, you decide that's close enough. You slip off at the next ramp, then pilot the El Camino through the tall grass, cutting the engine, coasting up one of the larger hills.

"What are you doing?" Iris asks.

"Not flying blind."

You roll to a stop beneath a towering redwood, step out of the car, and look around. A few zombies stumble around the bottom of the hill—far enough away not to be an immediate threat. One has long blond hair, not all fallen away yet, and it shimmers in the morning sunlight.

You lift a pair of binoculars to your eyes. From your position, you see the entrance to the Golden Gate Bridge, the six lanes of highway leading to it, and the sloping hills that line the northern side of the highway. The other side of the highway drops away, into San Francisco Bay.

It's more than just a gauntlet waiting for you.

It's a goddamn army.

Zombies, thousands of them, dot the hillsides and the highway. Thousands more fill the Golden Gate Bridge—so many that they don't look like individual things, but instead, one thick mass of death, swaying together.

And then the cars.

You stop counting at twenty. They line the highway, three cars deep, blocking the bridge entrance. A few you recognize from New York. Stu Bean, in his Ford van. Buzzy, in his 1981 Chevy pickup. Elwood, in the Monaco. The Panzer tank found some new neo-Nazi to pilot it, since you liquefied the last one.

They must have set out immediately after you, taken I-80 straight—with amphetamines and no sleep, it's less than a two-day drive. And it took you a good deal longer than that.

Other vehicles crowd the road. A yellow Ford Falcon, with a man leaning out the passenger window, holding a scoped rifle. A bus, armed to the teeth. An old station wagon with an array of rockets across the top. Motorcycles with Gatling guns fixed to the front. An ice-cream truck that appears to be aflame.

"Jesus Christ," Iris whispers, stepping out of the car and walking toward you. Then whispering a quick Hail Mary.

She squints and looks up at you. Her eyes are heavy, tired, but you get a glimpse of something eager and hopeful there. "What if I said, let's just drive to Canada—find a place, away from all this?"

You shake your head. "I'm dead in days . . ."

"So we swing around. Avoid this. What do you have to prove? There are other ways into San Francisco, right? There must be! They cure you—and we go someplace else. I don't even have to die. Ain't that a thought."

"I'm going straight through the front door. But, Iris," you say, "I won't force you to go. I'll take you someplace, get you a vehicle, you can go wherever you want. Anywhere. I won't force you."

"I should go. I know that. Just don't wanna."

Iris pours whiskey into the tin cup and takes a swig. Stands up straight. "All right, then. What's the plan?"

"You'll go on foot, toward the bridge. You're not coming with me. You stay on the hills—don't come down until you're at the bridge entrance."

Iris shakes her head. "Wha— No way."

"I'll keep that damn army busy," you say. "And you'll run, straight across the bridge. Take the footpath. Looks like most of the monsters are on the bridge proper. Any on the footpath will chew at you, but you just need to get to that gate at the end, then the doctors can take care of you."

"And you?" Iris asks.

"I just need to give you enough time."

"Damn it, Jimmy. We started this together, I'd like to finish it together."

You sigh and take a step back. You light a cigarette and look down at the massive, endless army.

If you'll bring Iris with you, turn to page 334.

Stick to your guns and go with your plan? Go to page 345.

ENHANCED
INTERROGATION

You drive slowly along the shadowy Virginia back roads. Any faster, and the thresher—even shut off as it is—will slice Greasy to shreds.

You pass Foamhenge—a full-size replica of Stonehenge made of foam. Iris mentioned that—one of the locations from the *Odd America* book. Zombies shuffle around it.

In a town called Blue Ridge, you take a turn into a large cemetery. Zombies stumble outside the tall, cement-brick walls. You drive down the winding cemetery roads, pulling to a stop in front of a tall oak tree.

You pull your flask from the glove box and knock back most of it with one hungry swig.

"All right," you say, stepping out of the car. "Time to get started."

Carrying the fire ax, you walk to the front of the El Camino. You raise the ax and Greasy shuts his eyes, expecting death.

You bring the ax crashing down. Four times, severing the bungee cords.

With the last cut, Greasy tumbles forward onto the grass. His back is torn up, like it's been attacked by a cheese grater.

Using the razor-sharp edge of the ax, you cut a slice in the duct tape covering his mouth. "Where does the train go next?" you ask.

"Go spit," Greasy says, gasping for breath.

You take a seat on a nearby headstone. You drink from the

flask and watch him curl up, holding himself, overcome by pain.

"The route," you say. "Tell me, I'll let you go."

"I won't tell you nothing."

"Sure you will."

You hear his pained breathing and you hear zombies moaning just beyond the cemetery walls. A few of the monsters mill around near the entrance. You place two fingers in your mouth and whistle sharply, causing the monsters to turn. Three or four begin stumbling toward you.

From the El Camino bed, you take a long coil of rope and tie it first to Greasy's sliced ankle. He kicks at you—tired, harmless. You throw the other end of the rope over a thick tree branch twenty feet above you. You catch it as it comes over and tie it to the El Camino's front bumper.

"Hey," Greasy says. His voice is shaky. "Hey, what are you going to do?"

"Play a game."

You slide into the El Camino, shift into reverse, and slowly back the car away from Greasy and the oak tree.

"Hey!" Greasy screams as the rope begins pulling at his bleeding leg. Soon, Greasy's leg is yanked up into the air. "Stop! Stop now!"

You lean out the window. "The train route," you say calmly.

"Fuck your father!"

"Okay."

You click on the old eight-track and turn the volume up as loud as it will go. Lynyrd Skynyrd blasts.

More zombies come stumbling now, shuffling toward the El Camino and toward Greasy.

"Don't!" Greasy says. "You can't!"

At first, it's just the sound that draws the monsters. But as they get closer, they smell his flesh and their undead eyes flash. One is nearly upon him.

"C'mon!" Greasy shouts at you.

You smile and give it some more gas, lifting Greasy fully into the air. He dangles like a side of beef as the monsters shamble toward him, arms raised.

"Tell me the route," you call.

"Fuck you!"

You release the brake. The car begins rolling down the hill, lowering Greasy. One of the zombies grabs hold of his stained suit jacket. A hand claws at his face, drawing blood.

"Okay, okay!" Greasy screams. "Just pull me up!"

"You going to talk?"

"Yes!" he says. "Yes! Yes!"

You shift back into reverse and lift Greasy so high into the air that his foot is wedged against the branch.

"Kentucky!" he screams. "Louisville! That's the next stop!"

"What's the route?"

"Tracks run along Route 64, through all that bluegrass nothingness. That's all I know!"

"Where will Iris be?"

"Huh?"

"The girl! Where will Iris be?"

"I don't know!"

You release the brake, rolling forward; Greasy plummets downward. One zombie grabs hold of his hand. The monster tries to bite it.

"With Ring!" Greasy screams. He thrashes his arms. "She'll be with Ring! Ring likes a girl in his car."

"Which car?"

"Second from the front."

Again you reverse, just seconds before one monster devours Greasy's face. "Was that so hard?" you say.

You put the car in park and pop the e-brake. A zombie is pawing at your cracked window. "Excuse me," you say, opening the door, slamming it into the undead thing. It stumbles back, and you bury the ax into its face.

You walk down the hill. Nine zombies are crowded beneath Greasy, reaching up for him, moaning.

You hold the sawed-off at hip level and fire, the wide blast catching four of them in their chests and knocking them back. You fire again, dropping the rest. Before they can get up, you're over them, swinging the ax, splitting their heads, one by one, like you're chopping wood.

Greasy dangles above you. "You're insane," he says.

"Brother, you ain't seen nothing yet."

TURN TO PAGE 318.

"Fucking go on," you say after a moment. "Do what you want."

"I will," Billy says.

You flick your cigarette butt at the boy. It hits his bare foot as he escapes through the roof.

You lie on your back and you drink what little is left of the bottle and you smoke until you fall asleep.

When you wake, the train is screeching to a stop. Minutes later, the big cattle-car door slides open, revealing Ring. Billy stands at his side, his head just peeking inside the car.

"He tried to escape," Billy says, pointing at you. "He asked me to help him. So I told you, Mr. Ring, just like you said."

"You did good, Billy," Ring says, climbing up into the car.

The two gunmen, as always, have their rifles trained on you. Ring pulls the bottle from your hand. You leap to your feet, about to tackle him, but he brings the heavy bottle crashing down, into the side of your skull. You stumble forward. He swings it twice more, and you drop.

When you come to, you're on your knees. You blink. Confused. Unsure. Head pounding.

After a moment, you realize you're on top of the train car. But the train is not moving.

Looking around, you see the train is stopped in the middle of a thick wood. Some carnies sit in the trees, watching, and others hang upside down from the branches.

Ring has his hands on your hair. Holding you. The edge of a knife presses against your shoulder.

"I'm gonna kill you," you growl. "I'm gonna kill you if it's the last thing—"

Ring jabs the knife into your shoulder. Twists. Pain explodes.

"You're not going to do nothing but die," Ring says.

Ring pushes you forward so you're looking through a sliding roof hatch, down into the car. Beneath you are the monstrous, zombified clowns. They fill the car entirely—a hundred bodies packed so tight you see nothing but their rotted, painted faces. The stench rushing up from the car is overpowering. Blood from your shoulder rains down on them, and they stare up, moaning, hungry. Their outstretched arms reach for you. Gnarled, rotten fingers grasping at air.

Ring stabs again, this time into your other shoulder, and he twists the knife and you pitch forward, through the open hatch, into the waiting arms of the clown-monsters.

You never even hit the floor of the car. There are too many of them. They grab at your flesh and they gnaw at your tissue.

And now?

Now you rise. Broken. Ripped of nearly all skin. Organs torn loose, devoured.

Undead.

Now you're part of this godforsaken undead circus.

Permanently.

Or at least until some other gladiator comes along. Someone like you. Someone who will kill you in front of the roaring, bloodthirsty crowd.

AN END

The Harley rumbles beneath you.

Fuck Major Eigle and his offer. Fuck Boss Tanner and his game. You can taste freedom now—sweeter than Southern whiskey.

You speed across Manhattan, to the east, toward the river. You twist the throttle and navigate streets swarming with monsters. The Harley hugs the corners as you dodge stumbling, lunging beasts. Explosions boom in the distance: other racers, locked in vehicular combat. If you can cross the bridge or the tunnel, you can get to Queens—that gives you options: head upstate, or maybe ditch Tanner and Eigle in Brooklyn, bide your time, get to Staten Island, then swim to Jersey— from there you can go anywhere you want, lose them for good.

The announcer's voice echoes off the buildings: *"It looks like Boss Tanner's newest driver, Jimmy El Camino, has decided to abandon the Death Derby! Our beloved ruler will not be pleased."*

A moment later, Boss Tanner's voice comes over the loudspeaker: *"Mr. El Camino, turn around. Understand, you cannot escape this island. Play the game, Mr. El Camino. Return to the game, or die."*

You've come to the Queensboro Bridge. The cantilever truss structure looms over you, towering and steely. Unlike the nearly abandoned bridge you and Eigle came in on, this one teems with zombies—a thick mass, covering the deck.

Concrete barriers block the bridge entrance. Beyond the barriers are tractor-trailer trucks, turned sideways—a second wall.

You need to get around them. Or over them.

You search, soon spotting a large flatbed truck with the bed raised, angled to the sky like a ramp—like a fucking gift from above. A way out.

You turn, ready to race the bike up the back of the flatbed, and Boss Tanner's voice booms again: *"Mr. El Camino, this is your last warning. Play or perish . . ."*

If you want to listen to the villainous Boss Tanner and turn around, go to page 186.

If you choose to ignore him and continue your escape attempt, go to page 200.

AT THE HIP

You tug at the ropes. They're wound tight around your wrists. You could maybe dislocate a wrist, free yourself, but the wound from the pitchfork jab won't let you.

"We wait," you say, finally.

Iris nods toward Henry. "Can he understand us?"

"Just be quiet," you say. "And wait."

It's your best bet. The scientist can be overpowered. He only needs to give you a second, and you can break him.

Above you, the zombies continue to moan and the wooden rafters creak. Strange animal sounds in the distance—freakish, tormented howls. You shut your eyes.

An hour later, Dr. Splicer returns. You flex your arm. Get your hands ready. You're eager to kill this man.

"Henry," Dr. Splicer says, "be a good monster and fetch the wheelbarrow."

A confused grunt from Henry.

"Wheeeeelbaaaaarrooooooow," Dr. Splicer says, like he's talking to an imbecilic child. Henry grunts again, then rises and leaves.

Dr. Splicer kneels down beside Iris. "You are so pretty, my dear. I hope you don't mind my asking—have you and this brutish thug, the man driving that odd vehicle, been intimate?"

Iris spits in his face.

Splicer smiles and smacks his lips together, tasting her saliva. "As you can see," he says, gesturing to the chunks of gore and animal intestine that cover him, "I'm not troubled by germs. Now—it's time for you two to take a short nap . . ."

Dr. Splicer reveals a syringe. Iris kicks and thrashes as Splicer places it to her neck and injects her.

"When you wake, my dear, you and your Stone Age friend will be more intimate than you can possibly imagine . . ."

Iris's head rolls to the side. She's out. Ketamine, you suspect. Complete temporary paralysis.

Splicer pulls another syringe and comes toward you. You pull at the beam. Tugging with everything you have. The zombies rattle above you.

Splicer chuckles. "Try all you want. I've had stronger men than you in—"

The beam cracks. Part of the ceiling fractures. The doctor's eyes go wide. As the ceiling breaks, the zombies tumble to the dirt floor.

You pull your arms free and rise, but Splicer is diving at you, his arm extended, the syringe like a small sword, poking at you. Splicer lands on top of you. You kick him in the balls and he sucks in air. But it's too late. His arm comes down, jabbing the needle into your neck, thumb pressing the plunger.

You punch Splicer hard, shattering his cheek. He cries out and falls back into the hay.

You stand.

And then you fall.

All around you, the zombies are rising.

You're beginning to fade out. Your vision is blurred. You can just make out Henry, returning with the wheelbarrow. He sets it down, then moves methodically through the barn, swinging his ball-peen hammer, delivering crushing blows to the zombies' skulls.

You waited too long . . .

You come out of the ketamine hole, half-dazed, trying to move. You're in the wheelbarrow, on your back, in a heap. Henry is pushing you.

You can move your eyes. You can swivel your head, just slightly. Your arms and legs are completely anesthetized.

A door opens and you're pushed inside the large horse stable you saw earlier. Your head hangs over the front of the wheelbarrow and you see everything upside down.

You pass stables. In each one, a grotesque, zombified beast.

A zombified man with the hooves of a horse.

A zombified horse with the head of a pig.

A woman with giant sagging cow teats for breasts.

There are two dozen stable stalls, and each one contains some malformed madness. Each creature moans and howls and cries, together forming a horrid symphony of pain—a cacophony of ungodly terror.

Candles dimly light Dr. Splicer's operating space. Iris lies nude on a long metal table. Her stomach is open in vivisection.

Henry lifts you up onto the table. You're touching Iris, though you only scarcely feel it. Iris can't speak. Her head hangs to the side, and she looks at you with wide eyes that beg for mercy and for saving but know it's not coming—eyes that are aware of the absolute maddening horror that awaits her but can do nothing about it. You can almost see her sanity escaping.

Dr. Splicer's face is red and already bruising from the blow you delivered. He uses a rusty hacksaw to cut open Iris's head and remove the top of her skull. Her brain is visible. Using an X-ACTO knife, Splicer slices into it. Chained to the wall behind you is a zombie, the top of its head removed, looking like a soft-boiled egg. Splicer removes one half of Iris's brain, sets it on the table, then crosses to the zombie, removes one half of its brain, then sets it inside Iris's skull.

Next, Dr. Splicer begins sawing away at your arm and, mercifully, you lose consciousness.

When you wake, your sense of touch has returned. But everything feels off, secondary, like navigating in a dream.

Iris's chin rests on your shoulder. No. Not *resting*. Terror overwhelms you as you realize her face is attached to yours. Sewn tight.

You look down. Your left leg is gone. Iris's right leg is gone. You now share a lower body.

He's combined you. You and Iris now share a broken, disfigured, half-undead body.

Craning your neck, you can just see Iris's eyes. They stare into yours, but there's no recognition there. Her eyes are hollow and dead and unmoving. Iris—who she was—is gone.

You open your mouth to scream, only to discover that you have no tongue . . .

AN END

You mash the pedal, looping around the White House, bursting through the gates, back onto Pennsylvania Avenue. Machine-gun fire hammers at the rear of the El Camino.

Into fourth gear, now charging down Fifteenth Street, swinging onto Constitution Avenue, hopping the curb onto the National Mall. The Lincoln Memorial looms ahead of you; the Washington Monument towers behind you.

You race past the World War II Memorial, bursting through an outcropping of trees, up a small incline, the El Camino hanging in the air for a moment, wheels spinning, then splashing down in the reflecting pool. Streams of rainwater shoot up as you wrench the wheel, slicing across the slick surface.

The Porsche follows, landing, guns blazing.

You cut the wheel, fishtailing, and Lucy does the same, the two vehicles mirroring each other, your bullets at her tail, hers at yours, a circular dance—a dogfight on water. Zombies, which fill the reflecting pool, are blown apart, spun aside, run down, limbs exploded.

You drift closer and closer to the Porsche, each of you circling the other, and then, suddenly, you cut the wheel in the opposite direction and the El Camino hydroplanes, spins, and a moment later you're on the heels of the Porsche. Lucy Lowblow tries to correct, but the Porsche just slides. You reach down, flick the red switch, and—

KA—BOOM!

A single missile hits the Porsche in the rear, lifting the ass end into the air, blowing apart the rear tires, and shredding the undercarriage. The blast sends zombies spiraling, aflame, then splashing down, sizzling when they land. Steam rises off the water.

The Porsche engine revs as Lucy tries to flee across the lawn, headed toward the Capitol. The rear tires—now just rolling on rims—shred the grass.

Finally, coasting down Maryland Avenue, the smoking Porsche rolls to a stop.

Fifty yards away, you stop the El Camino, step out. "Iris," you say, "grab me that big weapon there—the one that says M32."

She hands you the grenade launcher. You aim through the reflex sight, locking onto the Porsche first, but then aiming up—putting the Capitol doors in your sight, squeezing, firing a volley—the doors are blown apart, and out come the monsters.

Undead congressmen. Undead senators. Undead pages. Undead interns. Undead lobbyists.

The first wave is engulfed in fire, but they continue forward still—staggering toward the Porsche.

Lucy stumbles out of the car, looks around, frantic. Begins to run, but it's too late. Washington's most influential are upon the deadly young woman, pulling her hair out in bloody clumps, hands plunging into the flesh, stripping her bones, and finally dining.

TURN TO PAGE 180.

THANKS,
BUT NO THANKS

"All right," you say, standing. "You got me. Let's do it."

"Good choice," Eigle says.

But then, too quick for either of them, you're grabbing the whiskey bottle from the nightstand, smashing it against the wall, jamming it into Hank's throat, twisting it, pulling the fat man around as Major Eigle draws his gun and fires.

Five shots, all of them into Hank's chest.

Hank's hand tightens around the revolver. He pulls the trigger, firing into his own foot, blowing it to mush.

Your turn, pushing Hank forward, grabbing his hand and the gun. Raising it. Holding it up straight, pointed at Eigle.

Eigle fires again. The bullet causes Hank to tighten. Causes him to squeeze the trigger. You hold Hank's arm steady, and—

BLAM!

The big gun goes off.

Eigle is hit in the upper body—face and throat, point-blank range. His body is propelled into the nightstand and he's dead before he hits the floor.

You drop Hank.

You breathe.

Body heaving.

Ears ringing.

The smell of cordite in the air.

There's movement outside, then the door opens. It's the owner of the brothel and one of his girls.

The girl shrieks. The owner doesn't. He just looks tired.

"Get ahold of Boss Tanner," you say. "Tell him Major Eigle and his fat mechanic are dead. Tell him Jimmy El Camino has a hell of a headache and he's going back to bed."

When Boss Tanner wakes you up, two of his men are dragging the bloody bodies out the door. One of the brothel girls scrubs the floor. She doesn't appear to be enjoying her morning, particularly.

"What happened?" Tanner asks.

"Eigle wanted me to do something. Some job, mission."

"And you didn't want to?"

You shake your head. "Rather stay here and drive."

Boss Tanner nods and pats you on the arm. "Fine choice, Jimmy. Fine choice."

And you do drive.

You're damn good.

You drive every week.

In between, you drink and whore your way up and down Manhattan.

They throw you a big party when you kill your thousandth zombie in the derby.

You remember that zombie well. It was a child. A small girl, face rotted away. It was still wearing its backpack. It had one tiny red sneaker on. And a tiny Pittsburgh Pirates cap.

You mowed it down in a pickup truck. Ran it right over. It was so small, the truck barely bucked as your right tire flattened the girl's face.

It was your final kill.

The next race, you got behind the wheel so drunk you couldn't see.

That was a mistake.

Mr. King caught you in an alley.

Napalm.

You burned in your car. It took seven minutes for you to die. Seven minutes for your skin to melt and your insides to cook.

And you never found out what the mission was. Never knew you could have saved the world . . .

AN END

You roar, a screeching wail, as you force yourself to your feet, demanding your body listen to you. You pull the automatic shotgun as you stand, swinging it up, shooting.

It's the loudest handheld weapon you've ever fired. An automatic shotgun with a hair trigger. Twelve powerful rounds.

Your vision is blurred. Trails of light. Drunk with vertigo. Movement unfocused, unclear. The dim moonlight suddenly blindingly bright.

Goddamn Eigle. Goddamn his poison.

You try to fire slowly, steadily, deliberately, but your body is a herky-jerk machine on the fritz and adrenaline, which usually has you functioning at your peak, has been replaced by poison—suffocating your system, clouding your vision, obscuring your ability to kill with precision.

You simply squeeze.

BLAM!

Two purple robes torn to ribbons, bodies seeming to tumble in slow motion, globs of blood hanging in the air like confetti.

And then everything speeds up. You're moving faster than you're able to control, spinning, firing, whirling. Smoke in your eyes, watering, tears blurring things further.

BLAM! BLAM!

Purple-robed bodies tumbling back, looking almost comical to your warped mind—like a shoot-out in a silent movie.

BLAM! BLAM! BLAM!

Barely feeling the heavy gun jerk in your hands, you move through the structure, firing. Coming around one corner, shooting a purple body in the chest. He flies back ten, twenty feet. Rifle fire ricochets around you, glancing off and grazing the cement slabs.

You've turned the poison around. Flipped it, so it now fuels you.

BLAM! BLAM! BLAM! BLAM!

Men scream. Faces explode. Chests cave in. Bodies crumple.

At last the gun is empty and the men are dead and you collapse in the tall, dewy grass—other men's blood splashed across your face.

You cough and you catch your breath and you whisper, "Iris?"

"Jimmy?"

You crawl toward the voice, climbing over purple-clad bodies. Iris leans against a cement slab.

She's shot. Blood all over her topless body.

Her gut has been hit and the flesh is torn and open and blood gushes out.

It's not a rifle shot. It's a shotgun blast.

You shot her. *You* did this.

She looks up, her mouth twisted and bloody, eyes cloudy. She's gone into shock, and she seems to be smiling, almost. Relieved, maybe, that it's all over. "Jimmy, you killed me."

"No . . . I couldn't control it, Iris, I . . ."

"It was all for nothing?"

"No."

"It was."

"It wasn't. I swear, Iris. I swear, it wasn't."

"It was. We failed. It was all for nothing . . ." Then her voice fades out and her body trembles and a leg jerks and she's dead. You slump over. The poison overtakes you and you force your face down into the wet grass.

You come to. Dawn is approaching. The poison has faded some and your body feels like it belongs to you again.

Iris's face is frozen. Her mouth is open, her lips still forming her dying word. *Nothing* . . .

You killed her.

You can't let it all be for nothing now.

You can't.

Moaning behind you. Zombies? You turn.

No.

The Man in Antlers. He's gutshot but still alive. He's on his back, looking up at the pale yellow sky.

You struggle to your feet, staggering over to him, ripping the antler crown from his head. Beneath the antlers is a sweaty comb-over.

You press them down into the soft ground, bridging his neck, pressing harder, choking him.

"You're going to die now," you say.

"Yes," he whispers. "Happily. In death, I will meet the One. I will look down from heaven as the new world order marches on."

"There's nothing after for you. No heaven."

"Ha. I will find release. Eternal happiness. I'm ready for you to kill me, here, in the shadow of the temple. Eager."

You lift the antlers from around his neck and step back. "If that's the case, then I won't let you die."

"Nothing can stop my death," he says, a sick smile on his face. "It will overcome me in minutes."

Looking off at the fields, you see a few zombies stumbling about. "We'll see."

Moments later, you're grabbing the ax from the El Camino, then crossing Route 77 and wading through the waist-high grass. Three zombies shuffle around. You come up behind them. Two destroyed instantly, ax blade to the head, splitting skin and skull.

The last one stumbles toward you. It was a farm boy, tall and strong once, but now its eyes are a buttery beige color and blood covers its jaw.

The farm boy lunges for you, but you step aside and it falls. You press your boot onto its back, then raise the ax and swing twice, chopping off its arms. There's little blood. This one has been undead a long time.

You grab the zombie by its torn shirt collar and drag it through the field, across the highway, toward the Guidestones. The monster moans and its teeth snap at the air.

Gripping the collar, you soon hold the monster over the Man in Antlers.

"I will not give you easy death," you say. "I will give you an eternity of undying."

Suddenly, the Man in Antlers is horrified. The blood rushes from his face as panic overcomes him. "No. No, no. I can't! The plague is for the others. Not me! I believe! I *believe!*"

"Sorry, pal. Hell comes to believers and nonbelievers alike."

With that, you shove the zombie downward, driving the thing's gnashing teeth into the man's face. The armless monster feasts and blood foams and bubbles and the man howls and cries and shits himself.

You let go of the zombie and stumble back. It continues feasting. The man kicks and writhes. As you scoop up Iris's body and carry her back to the El Camino, you still hear him weeping.

Just before you enter the car, the crying stops. There's quiet in the fields, for a moment—and then you hear the moaning of *two* zombies.

You gently set Iris's body in the passenger seat. She continues to hemorrhage, blood seeping from her gut wound.

Something the Man in Antlers said runs through your head: *The woman, she is foul. Her organs and her blood are tools of the devil.*

You reach for the radio . . .

TURN TO PAGE 143.

You pick the spear up from the pavement. Grass growing through cracks in the street tickles the back of your hand as your fingers wrap around the wooden handle.

"He has chosen . . . *the spear!*" Ring shouts.

With that, the monsters rush forward. A thin one in front moans loudly. Its big red wig blows off as it comes at you, stumbling awkwardly, arms out.

You let it come. Let it get close.

Then you jab out, jamming the spear into the thing's chest. The spear hits its rib cage. As it continues rushing toward you, you lift, using its movement as leverage, raising the undead clown up into the air and over you.

Screams erupt as the body lands in the crowd. Blood splashes you from behind.

The remaining monsters come at you at once now.

You jab out with the spear, getting one through the mouth. You swipe up, shredding its palate, then you're yanking the spear out and jabbing again, through the clown's forehead, piercing the skull.

The other three lunge, arms extended, pushing you back against the metal fence. You hold the spear horizontally, struggling to keep them off.

And then, a sudden pain. A bottle, shattering against the side of your skull.

It's the boy.

Blood pours down over your eyes, blinding you, and more

hands grab at you. The crowd whoops. You struggle, but more hands grab on, holding you tight.

Launching that zombie into the crowd may not have been smart . . .

The crowd grips you as the clown-zombies throw themselves upon you. Their fingers rip flesh from bone and their teeth puncture your skin. One gets its hand in your mouth, clawing, pulling at your cheek, ripping it open . . .

Your knees give out, but you don't fall. The crowd holds you. The crowd holds you as the clown-monsters gorge themselves on your flesh and your blood flows and flows.

"Now, that's a show!" Ring shouts. "Now that is a goddamn show!"

AN END

LAMBEAU LEAP

Bullets crack, whizzing by you as you race toward the wall, Billy at your heels.

You jump over player benches, past discarded helmets and pads and empty Gatorade jugs.

And then you're at the stands. You grab Billy, still running, and toss him. His small body clears the wall and he lands among the screaming fans.

You charge forward and leap into the arms of the waiting crowd. "Pull me up!" you yell.

But the crowd doesn't seem to want this gladiator to survive.

One man—long hair, jagged yellow teeth—slashes you across the forehead with a razor. Blood pours down, over your eyes. Through the blood, you see Billy on the floor of the stands, watching, crying.

You try to wrestle free, but the crowd holds you tight, gripping your wrists. Some pour beer on you.

And then the sound of the Lincoln. The engine behind you, roaring.

You crane your neck. Blinking away the blood, you can just make out the battle-scarred vehicle barreling toward you. You try to rip your hand free, but the fans hold you tight, laughing wildly as the stadium crumbles. Soon, they'll all be dead—but all they do is cackle and slash and spit.

And then the Lincoln is there. Slamming into you, guns firing. Driving not just into you, but *through* you—demolishing your body entirely, turning you into something like chum, just bits and pieces of broken, red flesh.

AN END

KRAKA—BOOM!

The Jeep is blown to pieces. Shards of glass, chunks of brick, and hot metal rain down. A flaming car door nearly takes your head off.

You're in the middle of the street, two blocks from the Desert Fox and his big swinging dick of a tank. Zombies stumbling toward you from all directions. Shattered faces, hungry moans, closing in.

If you'll use the zombies to create an "undead shield," turn to page 284.

Choose to ignore the zombies and run toward the Desert Fox? Go to page 152.

THE GEORGIA GUIDESTONES

You're outside Anderson, Georgia, listening to Ry Cooder, Iris humming along to a song she doesn't know, when she suddenly says, "The Georgia Guidestones! Son of a bitch!"

"Uh . . . ?"

Iris pulls the *Odd America* book from the glove box. "This is it," she says, stabbing at it with her finger. "Jimmy, pull over. I'm not fucking around. Pull over."

"No."

"This is about me," she says, waving the map. "The Georgia Guidestones are *about me*."

You glance over at her. Something intense in her eyes. "What are you talking about?"

"Just stop the car, I'll show you."

You sigh and pull over to the side of Route 77.

Iris hands you the map. "See? That thing out there in the field, they're called the Georgia Guidestones. Says here they're a 'guide to future societies, designed to help provide a pathway to prosperity, happiness, and survival.'"

Oh Christ . . .

"What does that have to do with you?" you ask.

"I'll show you," Iris says, climbing out of the car.

You reach across, grabbing for her, but she's already out. "Goddamn it."

There's no guardrail alongside the barren Route 77. Sprawling fields border the road, and large groups of evergreen trees dot the distance.

Iris walks slowly toward the monument, like the weight of the world is on her shoulders. In a way, it is. You follow her, carrying the automatic shotgun, striding through the overgrown grass.

The monument sits a hundred yards from the road: six large granite slabs sticking out of the ground, each one twenty feet tall. It looks like some half-assed American version of Stonehenge.

As you step closer, you see there is writing on each stone slab—inscriptions in different languages: English, Hebrew, Arabic, Chinese, Russian, Spanish, Sanskrit, and what looks like Swahili.

You both stand in front of the English slab, reading. When you've finished, you walk a slow circle around the structure.

"I wonder what the other ones say," Iris states.

"The same thing."

"You can read it?"

"Not Sanskrit or Swahili, but the others, yes."

"You don't seem like a guy who knows a lot of different languages."

Coming around the other side, you smile. "I'm full of surprises."

"Do you see what I mean now? How it's about me?"

You shake your head and light a cigarette. "I do not."

Iris sighs and looks at you like you're dense. She reads the English text again, this time out loud, and she reads slowly, like a student uncomfortable speaking in front of her class:

"'Maintain humanity under five hundred million in perpetual balance with nature. Guide reproduction wisely—improving fitness and diversity. Unite humanity with a living new language. Rule passion—faith—tradition—and all things with tempered reason. Protect people and nations with fair laws and just courts. Let all nations rule internally, resolving external disputes in a world court. Avoid petty laws and useless officials. Balance personal rights with social duties. Prize truth—

beauty—love—seeking harmony with the infinite. Be not a cancer on the earth—Leave room for nature—Leave room for nature.'"

She lets out a relieved breath as she finishes. You stomp your cigarette butt out in the grass.

"This is how we're supposed to act now," she says. "If we make it to San Francisco and they're able to use my body to make a cure? Then this thing . . . it's telling us how to build a better future."

"Iris, it's just bullshit."

She glares. "Why would you say that?"

"It's just something some nutcase with too much money came up with. 'Maintain humanity under five hundred million in perpetual balance with nature.' Do you know what that means, Iris? The population before the plague was seven billion. So this thing is saying it would be plain fucking wonderful if near everyone on Earth just up and died."

Iris swipes a cigarette from your pocket. She lights it. "So these statues here—they're saying that the plague was *supposed* to happen?"

"Iris, it's nothing. Don't pay attention to it."

"It's important," she says coldly.

"It's the ravings of a cult."

"That's what you think. I think it's a sign. I think it's saying I'm not *supposed* to get to San Francisco."

You shake your head.

"But it could be."

"No."

"Like this is the rapture. Like the Bible says, Thessalonians: 'Then we who are alive, we who remain, will meet the Lord.' It *has* to happen, and this is it. Who am I to get in the way?"

"No."

Iris sits down and for a long while, she doesn't move, resting in silence. You find a stump and take a seat and pull from your flask. You notice a few zombies, far off in the distance, across 77.

They pay you no attention, but you grip the shotgun a little tighter.

The sun is starting to set, throwing deep orange across the field, when Iris comes and sits down beside you. "I feel safe here," Iris says. "This place feels like a temple. You think it's a big joke. I get that. That's fine. But I don't."

"Okay."

She looks up at you then. "We're going to stay here tonight. I want—"

"No."

"Don't fucking cut me off when I'm speaking. This feels like something sacred. And if I'm going to die in San Francisco, I want to be clean first. The things I've done to stay alive in New York . . . I'm dirty, inside."

"Iris, the last time you tried to go to church, it didn't end well."

"No shit! So I *need* this to end well. I need peace, before . . ."

"We can't—"

"Motherfuck!" she screams suddenly. "*Listen to me!* I'm giving my life! I'm giving *my fucking life* to end this plague!" Her eyes are wide and wet. She quickly gets ahold of herself and continues, "Jimmy. It's important that we sleep here tonight."

If you'll agree to stay for the night, turn to page 303.

If you choose not to risk spending the night in the field and instead want to get on with the mission, go to page 311.

You drive the endless, deserted roads, feeling madness crawling along the folds of your brain, infecting you. You drink whiskey until you can barely see—hoping your old friend will fight off this enemy.

But you get the opposite.

Pulling over. Stumbling, pissing, puking, heaving, clawing at the desert ground.

Driving again. Nearing Monument Valley, Route 163 grows thick with cast-aside vehicles, and you cut off the road—racing across the vivid, stark-red valley.

The poison is now throttling your insides, squeezing your stomach, like two hot hands, fingers strangling your intestines.

"Iris, I don't feel too good," you say.

Iris does not respond.

"How you feeling?" you ask.

You hit a rough patch of desert sage and the car jumps and Iris's body jerks and her head rolls to the side, like she's looking at you—two big, dead eyes staring at you—like she's saying, *Jimmy, how the hell do you think I'm feeling?*

"Yeah, well, that's about how I feel, too, I guess."

Coming toward the Grand Canyon, you turn to the freeze-dried body in the passenger seat. "Iris," you say, excited, sounding like some great, wholesome dad in a movie, taking his kids on vacation. "Iris, look! The Grand Canyon! You ever see it?"

No response.

"I saw it when I was just a pup—my dad was stationed at Fort Huachuca. Don't remember much, except it *was* grand."

You swoop across the sprawling plains and pull the car to a stop not far from the canyon edge. You're not alone, though; an RV is parked nearby.

"The hell is that?" you say, stepping out. There's a U-shaped cantilever bridge jutting out over the canyon. Very gentlemanly-like, you step around to Iris's side of the car, open the door, and carry her.

There's a single zombie leaning against the railing. From behind, you see he wears a green vest and a fishing hat. His body is thick, not long dead.

You come up behind him, slowly, ready to kill him—when suddenly, he turns.

"Hey there, stranger," he says.

Your heart nearly stops. "Shit, you're alive."

"For now," he says.

He looks at you, battered and bleeding, your eyes dilated from the poison so you surely look mad. He looks at you holding the dead girl's torso. And he just sort of shrugs.

You see now that there's a boy with him. Maybe five years old. Undead—red hair thinning, yellow eyes, blood on its lips. Rope tight around the legs, arms, and wrists.

"Name's Jim McCaugh," the man says, sticking his hand out. You take his hand and shake it. You see his wrist then, and see that the flesh there has been torn open.

"You're bit," you say.

He nods. "Yeah. I am."

"How long?"

"Few hours. Figure I got another half hour or so. I got careless. Didn't lock the bathroom door properly. He came out," he says, indicating the boy, "while I was driving. Didn't even hear him. Can't get careless out here."

"No, you can't."

"Always wanted him to see this," he continues. "I saw it when I was a boy—"

"Me, too," you interrupt.

He smiles solemnly. "I couldn't remember it, really. This wasn't here, though. This is new, for sure," he says, stamping his feet on the thick glass beneath you. "Read about it in the paper, when it opened some years back. Thought, *Lord, that's something.*"

You light a cigarette.

"Well, Danny, you seen it now, haven't ya," the man says, rubbing his undead child's hair. Hair drifts through the air, like he's scratching a golden retriever.

Looking at the canyons, cut by time, you wonder—how much time will it take to come back from all this? Is there enough time?

"Well," the man says, "I think that's about it. Mister, there's some food in the RV, and you're welcome to it."

You nod. "Appreciate that."

The man picks up his boy and holds it around the stomach, so they both face you. The boy's face is bloody and angry. The man doesn't look sad or broken, just ready. He smiles at you, nods good-bye, and then squeezes his boy tighter as he tumbles back, over the railing.

You watch him fall, end over end.

It happens so slowly, it seems.

On the ground, in Iraq, you saw a Ranger plunge from a chopper—got tangled up in his jump line. And you remember thinking then, too, that it seemed to take him so long to fall.

"Hey, Iris, you see that? You don't see that every day."

You pick up Iris then and carry her back to the El Camino.

Sitting in the car, facing the skywalk, you think about the smile on the dying man's face before he toppled over the side.

Your hand reaches for the shifter.

"We can do him one better, Iris," you say. "We could drive right through that damn thing. What do you think?"

Her eyes, milky and cold, look at you. They seem to be pleading with you. But pleading for what?

If you think Iris's eyes are pleading with you to end this and drive straight off the ledge, turn to page 382.

No, you believe Iris's eyes are pleading with you to press on and finish. Go to page 73.

The Panzer unloads again, the MG 13 cracking, smoke fill-ing the air. Need off these streets, fast. You spot a Gristedes supermarket—looks abandoned—and you race inside.

A single zombie shuffles outside the entrance. A onetime Gristedes employee—a teenager in torn jeans, a blue shirt, and a guts-splattered apron.

You whistle, getting the zombie's attention. It stumbles over, moaning. There's another loud crack, and an MG 13 bullet blows apart the monster's arm just below the elbow. It pays no attention to the wound; it's not even an inconvenience.

You wait inside the store for it and then—

THWACK!

You bury the fire ax in the thing's head. It falls to its knees.

You peek back around the corner.

Two more zombies coming—more former employees. One is charcoal black, burned head to toe.

Again, you whistle. They hear the sound of a living human: food. They shuffle.

The Desert Fox is sick of waiting. You hear the treads churn: the Panzer rolling toward you, only a block north now.

The two zombies make their way through the shattered slid-ing door, inside.

THWACK!
WHACK!

Two chops, two undead things fall to the ground.

Outside, the heavy crunch of the Panzer's turning tread grows louder.

You stuff the chopped-up zombies inside a grocery cart. The first one goes in easy. The second: you chop away at its knees, cutting off the legs. You then pile the legs on top of the upper body. The third one takes three hard cuts. You sit its torso up in the kids' seat, strapping it in using the little belt loop. You pile their heads on top.

Meat shield complete.

You take a deep breath, lay the ax and the gun on top of the bodies, and charge out into the street, pushing the cart. It's got a bad wheel and keeps trying to pull to the left.

The Desert Fox opens up with the MG 13. You keep your head low, pushing the cart, as the announcer screams, *"THIS MAY BE THE MOST INSANE THING WE'VE EVER WITNESSED AT A DEATH DERBY!"*

Bullets pound the meat shield. Chunks of flesh splatter. The first body is turned to pulp. The second will go soon.

RATTA! RATTA! RATTA! RATTA!

A bullet rips through the final piece of the meat shield. A CRACK as the next bullet snaps past your ear.

You give the cart a hard push, toward the Panzer, just as the huge KwK cannon fires. Still a block away and no time to—

KA—BOOM!

The meat cart is exploded, detonated, blown to bits. The ground around it, too. The eruption lifts you off your feet, somersaulting you through the air. You crash to the concrete.

No time to lick your wounds. The Panzer is turning. You scramble forward, crawling, then rising, sprinting, head lowered, closing the distance.

You shove your boot into the tank tread and slam the ax into the gray metal hull. It sticks, and you pull yourself up.

The announcer squeals, giddy, but you pay no attention, only focused on staying alive.

You tug at the pilot hatch. Locked. You bring the ax crashing down into the handle, twice more, and it cracks. You rip open the hatch and—

BLAM!

You leap back. A screaming bullet nearly gives you an unwanted nose piercing. The Desert Fox is firing from inside with a Luger.

You pull a grenade from your jacket pocket. Pop the pin.

"I'm liberating you of your vehicle!" you shout, just as another Luger bullet whistles past.

You drop the grenade into the tank, throw the hatch shut, and put your weight on it. Four seconds, five seconds, and . . .

The Desert Fox cries out. He weeps, sobs, pounds at the hatch.

Eight seconds, nine seconds, and . . .

BOOM!

"My God, Jimmy El Camino has just blown the Desert Fox back to hell!"

You lift the hatch. Smoke pours out. You let it clear, then hoist yourself down. Bits and pieces of the Desert Fox drip from the walls of the tank cabin. You've vaporized the Nazi bastard.

You glance over the tank controls. They're damaged from the blast but still usable. You rode in modern tanks during Operation Enduring Freedom. Never driven one, but you've seen it done.

You hit the gear switch with your foot and work the blood-soaked steering levers. The tank jerks, then rolls forward.

Just then, a shriek as Mr. King's Lincoln comes speeding around the corner ahead of you.

Mr. King. Boss Tanner's man. He's the one you want . . .

You unload with the MG 13, bullets pounding the ass end of the Lincoln.

Parked along the avenue are two large NYC Department of Sanitation dump trucks. As you roll toward them, the truck beds begin to lift. The rear hatches open, and dozens of zombies tumble out.

Another of Boss Tanner's booby traps. But this one is no

threat, the Panzer simply rolling over the monsters, pulverizing bone beneath the treads.

In an instant, you've wiped out two dozen of them.

The announcer calls out the score. You've paid no attention to it—too busy trying not to die.

"Ten seconds remaining, with Mr. King in the lead . . ."

Time's nearly up. But you want Mr. King dead. You trigger the guns. Cement explodes. Buildings splash brick on the escaping Lincoln.

"Five seconds remaining . . ."

Mr. King is now four blocks away, moving fast. You trigger the KwK cannon, the boom echoes, shattering nearby windows, and the shell rockets toward Mr. King, closing in just as—

He swings around the corner. The shell soars past him harmlessly.

"That's it, folks! Time's up! Game over!"

Shit.

Mr. King beat you. You don't like that. But you did like Eigle asked. You didn't get dead. Now, time to get out of this tank and into some fresh clothes—you're soaked in deceased psychopath . . .

TURN TO PAGE 161.

The woman groans and raises her hand, attempting to cry for help. You can't risk Iris. You certainly won't risk yourself.

You quickly march back to the car.

"What was it?" Iris asks as you slide into the driver's seat.

"Something bad," you say, shifting, pulling back out onto the dark country road.

"Can we help?"

"No. Goddamn hopes of humanity riding on you."

You drop it into second. The high beams light up the night.

You've gone just fifty feet when there's a *snap-bang* sound: the triggering of a small explosion. An instant later, a massive branch crashes down onto the road, directly in front of you. The El Camino's tires screech as you brake, too late, and slide into the sudden wooden obstacle. Your head slams into the wheel and Iris cries out.

You were merely a target. One of many, surely.

A huge, beastly man-figure appears, stepping up and over the branch.

Iris reaches for the shotgun, but it's fallen to the floor, at your feet. "Jimmy!" she barks. "The gun! I can't reach."

The figure steps around to the side of the car. He moves, methodical and quick, and he's suddenly standing there at your door.

You're dazed, dizzy from the impact. As you reach for the gearshift, the thing rams a pitchfork through the side of the car door. It slices into your left arm. Sharp pain.

And then he swings a hammer. Through the window. Into your skull.

TURN TO PAGE 342.

You drop the hot tommy gun to the ground and shout, "I'm empty!"

Dewey's in the small garden in front of the house, flipping over rocks. Beneath each rock, a grenade. He grabs an American MK2 from World War II, pulls the pin, and hurls it.

It skips across the dirt and then blows, launching four shattered corpses into the air. A wet stump of an arm lands on the El Camino's windshield.

"Watch the fucking car!" you shout from the doorway.

Soon, *finally*, you see the last of the monsters. No more coming up the path. Maybe fifty remain, surrounding the house. Dewey hurls another grenade, then shouts, "Go to the roof."

"Why?" you bark back.

A zombie is close, leaning over the fence, crooked fingers reaching out. "Just go!"

A rotted wooden ladder lies on the ground. You lean it against the house and climb.

On the roof you see the chimney and the big plastic Santa Claus.

The shingles are weak, it feels like you could fall through at any moment. You grab the plastic Santa and lift it.

A smile crosses your face.

The plastic Santa has no bottom. Dewey used it to hide an M134 minigun. The gun is mounted—screws and plates holding it to the roof.

You step behind the minigun, grasping it tight, and then—

KRAKA! KRAKA! KRAKA!

It's an absolute massacre: two thousand rounds per minute, the ground exploding in a fury of dirt and stone, stray shots filling the air with tree bark and splintering stone. Klan hoods tear apart. You don't even see entry wounds; you just see hoods suddenly—POP!—turn red as bullets explode the faces inside.

The sound is deafening. Hot shells rain down upon the roof. It's like gripping a jackhammer, your arms shaking and vibrating and going numb.

Under a minute, and it's all over. Two hundred Klansmen zombies. Dead. Actually dead. Bodies slumped in the woods, bodies piled in the drive, bodies draped over the El Camino.

And then a scream.

From below, inside the house. Suzie-Jean.

You jump down from the roof and land in the garden, turning and pulling open the door. Walter stands at the window, frozen. The back door hangs off its hinges. Four hooded zombies inside the house, moaning, frothing.

Two of the monsters are attacking Suzie-Jean, pulling at her, jerking her back and forth.

Two more are atop Dewey, tugging at his arm, digging long, gnarled fingers into his mouth. The one with his hands on Dewey's cheek wears no hood—just a pale, gory, crumbling face.

The sawed-off hangs at your hip, but it's the wrong tool for the job: pull it, and you'll kill just about everyone. Instead, you yank the rifle from Walter's shaking hands.

Suzie-Jean, seconds from death.

Dewey, just a moment from being bitten.

You swallow hard, realizing you can only save one of them . . .

Shoot the zombies hanging on Dewey? Turn to page 340.

If you'll instead blast the zombies about to devour Suzie-Jean, turn to page 313.

You shift into reverse, throw your hand over Iris's seat, and glance at the tight alleyway behind you.

You stamp the accelerator, and at the same time, you hear thundering on the cement as the rhino-monster charges.

"It's coming," Iris barks. "Coming fast."

You look ahead. The undead beast stampedes toward you, charging with a strong, almost-drunken gait. It lets out a deafening wail—a mixture of the undead moaning of the human zombies and its natural call.

You stamp the gas harder, hand tight on the wheel, as you race in reverse toward the end of the alley.

But then they come. Fifty zombies, at least, charging into the alley. Filling it. Ending any hope of rear escape.

"Jimmy . . . ?"

You slam the brakes. As you do, the rhino's massive hoof comes down on the El Camino's hood, snapping the rear of the car up into the air. You're tossed forward, into the wheel.

And then the rhino is on top of the car.

Its head lowers and the animal bucks. Its long, pointed horn pierces the windshield and rips into your throat, the tip pushing through your Adam's apple, exiting out the back of your neck, blood now fleeing your body.

Iris gets her hand on the door, swings it open—and is immediately tackled by the undead horde. She curses, punches, screams bloody fucking murder, then goes quiet. After that, you hear only the soft, wet sound of warm flesh being greedily swallowed down.

The rhino steps back and its horn slides from your neck. You fall back into the seat. You try to breathe, but your throat bubbles blood and there is a soft whistling sound as you gasp for breath that will never come.

And then the undead rhino's head comes through the windshield fully, turned sideways, destroying the glass and twisting metal—its mouth open wide, its thick, dirty teeth tearing your face to bits.

AN END

Ring puts you in your own cattle car, a cell, wooden-plank walls reinforced with sheet metal, keeping you from punching your way out.

You sit in the corner and the train rumbles on.

Every few days, it stops, you're dragged out, and you fight. You crush them and you impale them and you skewer them.

And then, at night, it's back into your cattle-car cell.

You remain focused. Your mind never drifts, always on Iris, always on your mission.

Through a small crack in the wall, you watch wasteland America race by. Crumbled buildings and distant smoke and gray skies and zombies loping like herds of wild animals.

Sometimes, hordes of zombies crowd the tracks and they need to be cleared off before the train can proceed. Other times, the train is assaulted by bandits and gunshots ring out and you do nothing but lie on your back and think about Iris.

In a small town called Fairbanks, you fight six zombies with your bare hands. Your knuckles are bruised and bone protrudes and you roar when you grip one of the monsters by its ears and rip its ugly head right off its shoulders.

In Milwaukee, you use a hammer to beat to death a zombie wearing a gray hooded sweat-shirt, torn and blood-spattered. After killing it, you remove the sweatshirt and pull it on. The crowd laughs and claps and goes wild.

You think about running, always. An escape. But there are the guards and the guns and you can't be reckless because it's not only your life at stake but Iris's, and—hell—the rest of goddamn humanity.

In a town outside Decatur, waiting for the night's fight to begin, you spot a boy who works on the train. He's not supposed to talk to you—Ring's rules: no talking to the gladiator, the killer, the monster. But there's a stick of gum in the gray hooded sweatshirt—watermelon—and you bribe him for water.

He brings it to you and smiles and says you're his hero.

That night, he climbs through a small crack in the ceiling of the cattle car. He shimmies down into the car and sits across from you. He hands you a bottle of whiskey.

You look at the whiskey, then up at him. "How'd you know?"

"Your face," he says. "You look like my dad. Your cheeks and your nose. They're red."

The boy is covered in freckles, with blond hair that's short in the front and hangs long in the back. He wears a grease-stained white shirt and pants that are two sizes too big for him.

"How old are you?" you ask.

"I'm seven and three quarters."

"Not very old."

"Well, how old are you?"

"Fortysomething. I forget, I think."

"You look older."

"I feel older."

"I'm Billy," the boy says, after a moment of silence.

You nod. "I'm Jimmy."

"Can I try it?" Billy says, pointing at the bottle.

You hesitate for a moment, then hand him the bottle. He takes a large swig, then coughs a few times and runs to the corner of the cattle car and vomits.

You laugh a little.

"Don't laugh!" he says.

You drink some more.

"I'm sorry I threw up," he says softly.

You shrug. "It's all right. Probably improves the smell in here."

You drink more, until you're finally tired, and you tell Billy to leave. He doesn't. You shrug, lie down, and soon fall asleep.

Nightmares come.

You've always had nightmares. Ever since Desert Storm.

But these are different.

You see children. Zombified children. Children robbed of life and turned into monsters.

You watch yourself, murdering them.

You see Iris, alone in the El Camino, surrounded by undead beasts, pounding at the windows. You see Iris in the driver's seat, the car parked, and the monsters swarming around it. You see Iris, strong, but you see that strength fading.

Iris in the passenger seat now. Numb. Running out of food. Running out of water. Wondering if you'll come. She did what she said she would. She made it. Will you?

She hopes you will.

She doubts you will.

You see her giving in. You see her pulling the sawed-off from beneath the seat, loading one shell. And then, finally, placing it in her mouth and pulling the trigger.

Because you didn't come.

Because you didn't make it.

You see Major Eigle being executed while Boss Tanner howls. Laughing. Winning.

You see the poison in your bloodstream, driving you mad. You see the world ending, never to return to what it once was. You see humanity erased, because you failed.

You feel a hand on you. A nightmarishly small zombie hand. The boy. Billy. Undead. Eaten.

And then you feel the hand shaking you.

Your eyes open. You taste booze and cigarettes.

Billy is shaking you awake. "Jimmy? Jimmy, you okay? You're making sounds."

You sit up. You're dripping, clothes soaked through with sweat. You inch back, into the corner of the train car.

Billy hands you the bottle. You shake your head, pushing it away. Billy pushes it toward you again. You growl and pick up the bottle and fling it against the wall. It hits with a thud, falls to the floor, and booze pours out.

You're struggling to breathe.

This happened to you twice before, when you first came back to the States after Afghanistan, and when you first woke up in Eigle's cell.

Need cool air.

You crawl to the corner of the train car. There's a break there, between the wooden boards. Night air rushes in as the train races along the tracks.

You press your face to the wood and you breathe in deeply and exhale slowly. Finally, your body begins to cool. The sweat feels like ice water. The wooden floor is comforting. Your heart stops racing.

But the images, when you shut your eyes—the images don't go away.

Iris.

Tanner.

The world, burning.

You sit up.

"You okay?" Billy asks.

You reach for your cigarettes. Light one with a trembling hand. Exhale, slowly, through your nose.

You need to get out of here. You can't spend another night in this fucking cattle car. You can't spend another night with this poison inside you. You can't spend another night not working to complete your mission—not getting Iris to the coast.

If you want to ask Billy's help in escaping, turn to page 204.

If you'd rather hold tight and try to escape later, go to page 67.

"I can't free my wrists," you say.

Iris curses. "We need to do something before that lunatic comes back."

Farm tools hang from the walls—shovels and spades and dike cutters. They'd all be deadly in your hands, but there's no way to get to them.

Iris swallows loudly. Then, "Henry," she says, almost cooing. "Hey there, Henry."

You glance over, not understanding.

"Iris . . . ," you start.

She turns and grins, a spark of something devilish in her eye. "He's half human."

You shake your head slowly.

"Henry, come over here," Iris says. "Come sit next to me. Please."

Henry the man-beast stands up. He stumbles forward, his joints all out of whack, moving like a tin man needing oil. He nearly falls onto Iris.

"Sit beside me," Iris says. Her voice is throaty and for a short moment, amidst the terror of dangling zombies and Frankenstein monsters, you wish it were directed at you.

Henry sits. His thick hand lands heavily atop Iris's head. He's trying to be gentle, but he practically slaps her. Iris leans back and you watch her jaw clench as she braces herself.

Henry paws her body, grabbing her soft denim shirt. Gets his fingers in it and rips it open. Buttons fall to the dirt floor. Her left breast slips out. He pulls at it.

You look up at Iris's face; she chokes back vomit.

Suddenly, Henry's hands stab downward, toward Iris's crotch. Iris scoots back. "Untie me," she says. She tries to keep her voice soft and gentle, but it quivers.

Henry looks confused.

"Untie me," she says again, slowly and clearly. "FREE. ME."

Henry grunts, then reaches around behind her. His thick fingers have no dexterity. He moans in frustration, then simply grabs hold of the rope and tugs.

Iris's wrist snaps and she bites back a shriek. He pulls again, jerking her hand through the rope. Iris yanks her wrist around, cradling it. It's broken, but not a compound fracture—you can set it when you get back on the road.

What matters is that she's free. Henry grabs for her breast again.

"The pitchfork," you whisper.

With her good hand, Iris takes hold of Henry's arm. Gently, she stands. She looks into his eyes.

Then you whistle.

Henry turns his head sharply, looking over to you, allowing Iris to dart away. She yanks the pitchfork from the wheelbarrow. Henry the man-beast is charging toward her, but she's raising the pitchfork, screaming—a roar, summoning strength from somewhere deep—and jamming it through his chest, snapping ribs, puncturing organs.

Henry whimpers—he registers pain, unlike full zombies—then begins pummeling her with his meaty fists. Strong blows that cut open her nose and cause blood to run.

Iris yanks the pitchfork from his chest and darts to the side, ducking as he swings his almost-concrete fists. Henry stumbles forward, off balance. When he turns around, Iris is bringing the pitchfork up, through the base of the monster's square chin, tines jabbing through his face and blood gushing from his mouth, nose, and eyes.

After a long moment, his legs give and he falls, his body

yanking the pitchfork from her hands as he tumbles. He lands on it, and it jabs further, popping through the roof of his skull, and then he lies still, in a heap, dead.

Iris collapses in the hay, breathing heavily, cheeks wet. She wipes her eye, then spits on the monster. Saliva splats on his face.

And then Iris, holding her injured bone, comes to untie you.

"Let me see your wrist. Quick, before that lunatic returns," you say. You're standing at the workbench, drinking from a water jug.

"It's broken."

"I know. Let me see it."

She lays it out on the bench. It's already turning purple.

"I'm going to set it," you say, wrapping your fingers around her narrow wrist and hand.

"Fine. Just be fucking quick about—"

SNAP!

Iris bites back a shriek and you throw your hand over her mouth. "It'll feel better soon. No noise. Let's go."

You put a boot on Henry's shoulder and yank the pitchfork from his face. Stepping out into the field, you see half-lobotomized zombies grazing mindlessly. You catch a glimpse of one—toothless, the product of Dr. Splicer.

You move quickly through the tall grass, toward the El Camino.

"What about the doctor?" Iris whispers.

"Not our problem."

"He can do it again—to the next people to come along."

"Doesn't matter. Only you matter."

You slide inside the El Camino and reach inside your pocket. Then you realize: Dr. Splicer has your goddamn keys.

Quickly, you're out of the car, moving back across the large field, toward the stables. Iris is at your heels.

"Go back to the car," you say.

"I'm coming with you."

"Go back to the damn—"

A howl stops you. Slowly, crouched, you move toward the twin stable doors. Inhuman moans come from inside. Just outside the large doors is a tall pile of discarded flesh and bone—some human, some not. The air above the pile is thick with buzzing flies.

You loop around the stable, peering through cracks in the wooden boards. Iris gasps as she peeks through.

Each stable stall is filled with some foul, inhuman thing—unnatural creatures born from the hands and mind of a madman.

Zombified men with the faces of pigs, and pigs with the faces of zombified men. Goats with human legs, rotten and diseased. Undead horses with exposed rib cages and, nestled inside those rib cages, human infants, sobbing.

You find a rear door and gently nudge it open.

From behind, you see Dr. Splicer, leaning over a body on a metal table.

On the floor beside the table is something that looks like a person, but the whole thing is so slick with fresh blood that it's nearly unrecognizable. It whimpers.

You hold your hand up, indicating to Iris to stay put. She nods. Then you kick the door open, as loud as possible, pointing the pitchfork at Splicer. He spins around, startled, gripping a scalpel. "Drop the blade, hand me the keys," you say.

"Where's Henry?" Dr. Splicer says.

The doctor steps forward, revealing the horror on the table behind him. It is a zombified man. His belly has been removed and replaced with a cow's udder. His hands have been hacked off. Where there should be a right hand, there is instead a baby rooster, crudely sewn on. Its wings flap and it squawks in pain. His left hand ends in a cow's hoof.

You look back to Splicer. "The keys."

"Henry!" the doctor howls like the madman he is. "What did you do to Henry?!"

"Keys," you say. "Give them to me now, or I run you through."

"No. NO!" he shrieks, running toward you, waving the scalpel. You jab out with the pitchfork and Splicer impales himself. The scalpel falls to the floor. Holding the pitchfork with one hand, keeping the madman at arm's length, you shake his coat. You hear keys jingle. You reach inside and take them.

That's when you hear the engine roar. That's when you hear Iris scream.

The stable doors fly open, splintering, half the barn imploding and the ceiling caving as Mr. King's Lincoln bursts inside.

One of Boss Tanner's men has found you . . .

King triggers the machine guns and the stable stalls are torn open by the fire. Dr. Splicer's mad creatures rush forth, free. Beams splinter and the ceiling crumbles and the walls break.

You drop the pitchfork and charge through the back exit, Iris close behind. Bullets punch through the wall and the door explodes behind you. The entire stable lurches, its final collapse imminent as the Lincoln reverses out.

"Get to the car, Iris!" you shout, pushing her forward.

Together, you race through the tall grass, Splicer's strange beasts roaring and howling behind you.

"I'll drive!" Iris calls as you reach the El Camino. "You take care of him!"

Try to take out King with Iris at the wheel? Turn to page 368.

You're Jimmy El Camino and you do the damn driving. Go to page 188.

You watch the zombies shuffling about, far off across the high-way. You eye the evergreens, beyond the field.

And you look to Iris—the woman who will soon give her life—and you say, "Fine. I'll stay up, keep watch."

"You won't sleep?"

"No."

"Your choice."

It's near four a.m. when the men come.

You're smoking a cigarette, leaning against the slab covered in Russian words, looking up at the stars. Haven't seen some-thing like this since you were across the world, in the desert land.

Past five years, looking up at the ceiling of that cell every night, all you saw were constellations of cracked concrete.

Iris doesn't toss and turn. No hard nightmares—surprising, for a person facing the gallows. She's at peace in this little temple.

But you get nothing: no sense of security, no impression of some higher power. This is roadside America. Cultish kitsch.

The full moon and the opening clouds shine gray-blue light on the field, allowing you a clear view of the men coming toward you.

You stamp out the cigarette and sit up, holding the gun tight, finger curled around the hair trigger.

Squinting in the darkness, you count thirteen, possibly fourteen men. They wear dark robes that whip around in the breeze as they stride toward you.

"Iris, get up."

She moans softly. Shifts in her sleep.

You don't want to stand. Don't want them to see you—though you suspect they already have. You nudge Iris in the side. She groans. "Up," you say.

She stirs and her eyes flicker open.

The men march closer. Most of them carry hunting rifles. The man in the lead carries no weapon, but he wears a large headpiece.

You're not going to fight fourteen men, even if you are gripping the cool steel that is Remington's latest and greatest. You try to stand, reaching for Iris, but—

PAIN.

Excruciating, burning pain deep inside your stomach. You buckle over.

Fucking Eigle and his fucking poison: *now* it kicks in, full force. You must have drank too much, slept too little, and now the poison is putting a hurt on you. Temporary, most likely, but the timing is fucked.

It takes everything you have to slide the automatic shotgun out of sight, between your ass and the slab.

The men stand in front of you, in a row. In the moonlight, you make out a few details. The one in the center wears a cultish crown adorned with moose antlers. His face is clean-shaven, with hollow cheeks. The moose antlers shoot out like twisted devil horns.

"Is this girl the one?" the Man in Antlers asks, to no one in particular. "Or is this just another simple trespasser?"

Iris is fully awake now. She squints at the group, puzzled but not panicking. "What?"

The Man in Antlers steps forward. "The plague is a blessing. Slicing population. Making room for the new world order. We await the one who will lead us forward, as foretold in the prophecy. So tell me, girl: Why you have come to our place of worship? To join? Or to lead? Or to die?"

Iris stands. "I think—I think I'm—oh shit, yes, God above—I'm the one who will lead. It's me."

"Iris, shut the fuck up—" you start, but your words come out as strangled moans. Your stomach is twisted and your heart feels like it's being squeezed by a fiery hand.

The Man in Antlers looks to you. "Who is this foul-mouthed shepherd who has brought you?"

"His name is Jimmy," Iris says.

The Man in Antlers looks down at you. "Silence, *Jimmy*. Or I will end you."

Iris steps forward, her movements eager and anxious. "This all sounds insane, I know. But I have a power," she says. "I mean, I'm different. Special."

"You are the one who will lead?"

"Iris, if you tell them . . . they'll kill you," you say, as you realize they believe in this bullshit—they think the world's population must be cut down, then rebuilt. Iris is the opposite—she truly could be some sort of savior. So they'll murder her.

"I said silence, shepherd!" the Man in Antlers barks.

"I am immune to the plague," Iris says, pulling up her sleeves. "Look. These bite marks come from the monsters. But I'm immune. I can end it. I *am* the one."

No . . .

Whispers among the group.

The Man in Antlers shakes his head. "The plague must *not* end. The plague must continue until only five hundred million remain. Nine in ten must die. Nine in ten. Nine in ten. If you do not come to further the plague, then you are not the leader. You are the enemy."

Iris swallows. Tight fear in her eyes as she begins to understand. "You're mad."

The Man in Antlers crouches down, staring into Iris's eyes.

The antlers cast eerie, disjointed shadows on Iris's taut face. "You are sin personified. You have come to end the greatness that God hath wrought. The woman, she is foul. Her organs and her blood are tools of the devil."

Iris shakes her head. "No. You don't understand."

"The girl can be used!" one of the men barks.

The Man in Antlers turns, thinks for a moment, then turns back to Iris. "What Brother Gary says is true. You might be used to bring forth the one who will lead. You will be sacrificed. And then the one who will lead will appear, to continue God's work and usher the plague forward. Only then may the new world order begin."

Iris punches the Man in Antlers in the mouth. The attack surprises him, and he slips back on his ass, and Iris is running for the car. But the Man in Antlers is powerful, and in moments, he's upon her, grabbing her by the shirt, ripping it.

Iris now stands topless in the moonlight. The men admire her body. They whisper. Anger builds inside you.

The poison has you near paralyzed. To best kill these men, you should wait for the pain to subside. But there may not be time to wait . . .

If you'll attempt to fight through the blinding pain and kill the cult members now, turn to page 267.

Wait it out, hoping a better moment will present itself? Go to page 352.

You swirl the liquid around in your glass, take a heavy slug, and say, "I think I'll try my luck here, Eigle. Being alive is a good thing, and I'd like to stay that way as long as—"

Eigle immediately shoots you in the gut. A Smith & Wesson revolver, from out of nowhere.

You buckle over and the glass shatters against the floor.

"Christ," you say, your voice a soft whisper. "You weren't messing around . . ."

"I gave you a chance! I gave you a chance to save us!" Eigle barks, his voice turning to a roar. "You selfish bastard!"

Eigle stomps over to you, grabs you by your neck, and drags you across the room, toward the zombie. Your knees land in the pool of Iris's blood.

Eigle yanks you up, slams your head into the chained zombie's face. The monster bites your face, ripping out a long sliver of skin. Its saliva mixes with your blood.

And as you begin to change, begin to turn, you think . . .

You think how they'll just get some other driver . . .

And they'll give that driver the same routine . . .

And maybe that time, *you'll* be the zombie on display, the zombie chained up, biting Iris to show how special she is. And well, shit—at least then you'll have played some small part in fixing this world . . .

AN END

You drive and drink, and drive and drink, roads blurring, days mixing, nights a jumble of speed and darkness. It all becomes a blur. Before you realize it, you've driven near a thousand miles, past horrible sight after horrible sight, run down so many monsters you can no longer count, raced past so many cannibal hordes you've lost track.

You see the sign for Mount Rushmore, and then, an hour later, coming around a winding, tree-lined road and up onto the highway, you see the monument.

"Look," you say.

Iris looks up. She gasps when she sees the carved figures of Washington, Jefferson, Roosevelt, and Lincoln. "Mount Rushmore?"

"Uh-huh," you say, reaching down to get a cigarette.

And that's when the glass shatters and your shoulder explodes and you're thrown back, wrenched hand twisting the wheel and the El Camino flipping, rolling, metal crunching and Iris hollering, and you thanking God for the reinforced roofing as the car flips six times before sliding to a final stop on the highway running in front of Mount Rushmore—fifty yards from the parking lot, two hundred yards from the entrance to the memorial, and four hundred yards from the base of the mountain.

The car is upside down. Blood pours from your nose, down over your eyes.

Eerie silence. Your brain stops rattling and settles.

Then, gasoline dripping.

Iris's hair hangs down over her face. You reach out, push it aside, expect to see her dead, face mashed. But she's not. Eyes open, looking back. Softly, you say, "What happened?"

"Somebody shot me. We flipped."

You release your seat belt, grab the shotgun, and crawl out through the door, onto the highway, inching your way out, peeking around the side, up at the monument, and—

KRAK!

The gunshot echoes off the mountainside, and the cement just inches from your hand kicks up. A bit of pavement nicks you.

"Where are the shots coming from?" Iris asks as she crawls out behind you. You both crouch behind the overturned El Camino. You know it's only a matter of time before a shot finds its way into that gas tank . . .

"Somewhere up in those hills," you say. "Near the monument."

You hear moaning then. You grab your cracked sunglasses and hold them around the side of the car. Watching the reflection, you see zombies coming toward the car, shuffling up from the monument parking lot.

You pull Iris next to you, close.

You have your back to the car. You hold the shotgun tight to your chest. The moaning grows louder and louder.

One comes around the car—a twisted, disfigured tourist zombie. It wears a cheap cowboy hat. It's a thin thing, and its intestines hang like sausage links. It trips over them.

You shoot it in the face. The cowboy hat hangs in the air for the briefest instant, and then the zombie tumbles onto its back.

More moaning. Louder.

More monsters coming. And you, there, with nothing to hide behind but a goddamn busted-up El Camino with an exposed gas tank . . .

To escape your position and search for better cover, go to page 236.

If you'd rather hold tight and try to hold off the zombies, turn to page 101.

NO STONES

You take in your surroundings. Nothing but open field, all around you; zombies graze in the distance like animals.

"No," you say finally. "This is an ambush waiting to happen. They hit us here and we're dead."

So you walk back to the El Camino. Iris doesn't follow, but you don't stop to grab her, don't force her. You simply slide into the car and put it in gear.

"You'll die without me!" Iris finally calls, walking toward the car. "Get to San Francisco without me, and you don't get the antidote."

You roll down the passenger window. "I leave you here, you're good as dead. And that death—*that death* is for nothing."

Iris runs her hand through her hair. Looks back at the stones. Her head drops for a moment, then she marches toward you, slides into the car. You give her a small grin, happy she wised up, and—

She punches you. A quick cross—strong hands and bony knuckles drawing blood, your nose opening like someone turned on the faucet.

"You're a motherfucker," she says. "Now drive."

You wipe the blood on your sleeve, shake your head, and hit the gas.

The horrific sights grow repetitive: the undead, burned bodies, everything a crisp.

Lexington, Kentucky—an entire city on fire. The smoke clouds the horizon, forcing you so far north you're practically back where you started. You don't talk. And as you drive and drive and drive, you think not talking is just fine with you.

TURN TO PAGE 242.

You fire twice. One bullet through each of the Klansmen hanging off Suzie-Jean. Brain splatters her face.

You whirl, gun raised, but one Klansman has its teeth in Dewey's neck and the other is clawing at Dewey's chest, ripping at his flesh. Dewey thrashes at the things, trying to knock them away, but he's dead, so you squeeze.

The bullets slam into the first Klansman's back. Dewey and the monster tumble backward onto the coffee table, one leg breaking, both crashing to the floor. You squeeze again and the Colt cracks like thunder in the small room as you put two into each Klansman's head.

And then Dewey is up, charging toward you. His eyes are red and burning like fire.

You step back, squeezing, but—

CLICK.

CLICK.

Dewey hits you head-on, tackling you, your head slamming against the floor. You drive a hard fist into zombie Dewey's chin, shattering his jaw.

And then, suddenly, blood splashes down onto your face, into your eyes.

You blink. Get your fingers over your eyes, wipe the blood away.

Walter stands above you. He ran the fire poker through Dewey's skull—into one ear, out the other. His hand shakes, as does Dewey's head.

"Walter," you say, removing blood from your cheek, "please get him the fuck off me."

Walter tugs on the poker, and Dewey's head jerks to the side, then drops as Walter releases the weapon.

You get to your feet, spitting, wiping Dewey's blood from your face. Suzie-Jean is in the corner, sobbing.

"You okay?" you ask. "You hurt?"

She shakes her head no.

"Which one?"

"Yes, I'm okay," she says after a moment. And then, "No, I'm not hurt."

"You sure?"

She nods once, hard. "Yes."

You collapse onto the couch. Grab a beer from the table, pop it open, and drink it down. The kids watch you with their big, wide eyes—scared and confused and overwhelmed.

You light a cigarette then, and say, "Okay, little superheroes, we need to get Iris into the car. We need to drive."

It's a miserable journey out of New Orleans, headed west. Iris sits in the passenger seat and the kids are squeezed in beside her.

Most of the bridges are out—either too full of old cars to cross or too full of zombies. The Huey P. Long Bridge is just a frame—girders and cracked cement and twisted metal.

You double back, up along the Mississippi. At Jackson, atop a great hill, you spot four tanks, flying black flags. Not the type of trouble you want right now. That forces you north, instead of west.

You pass a farm. In the tall grass field, undead cows stand, unmoving. The kids stick their heads out the window and yell, "Moo!" The undead cows don't moo back.

You try I-55. You make it nine exits before the rusted, abandoned cars force you onto the back roads.

The kids play Twenty Questions. You pick "zombie." No one's sure if it's animal or vegetable, so you stop playing.

After a time, Suzie-Jean goes quiet.

"I'm carsick," she says.

You pull over. She vomits five times while you load up the gas tank.

The sun is long since down when you pull into Tennessee. Thirteen fucking hours of driving—to a place that should have taken you half that.

A sign points to Graceland.

You get a glimpse of Elvis's house, in the distance. Figures stumble in the darkness. You turn off the street, into the Anything Is Paradise parking lot.

You find a spot, wedged between two long-since-forgotten minivans, and shut off the engine. "Time to get some shut-eye, kids."

Suzie-Jean is already asleep. Walter smiles. "Good night, Mr. El Camino."

It's nearly dawn when you wake up, and the first light of morning is fighting its way through the clouds—struggling to add just the slightest bit of brightness to this gray, rotten world.

Walter's sleeping soundly. Suzie-Jean is mumbling. Nightmares. You want to wake her, but you imagine the nightmares are about you killing her family—so it'd be a bit fucked to have her come to and see your smiling face.

So you decide: Graceland.

You fill your flask, step out, locking the door behind you. At the gate, you peek out onto the street.

You hug the fence and walk up a short hill along the side of the road. You take a seat there, back against a tree, staring out at Elvis's mansion.

Most of the zombies are inside the compound's open gates.

All of them diehards, you figure. You can imagine it: them hearing the world was ending, making a pilgrimage. Some of them figure, *Hey, hon, the one thing I always wanted to do—Graceland.* Others, been here a dozen times, this is their place—where they're happiest. So they go to die—or, rather, to become undead.

And they look happy, almost. It's your mind playing tricks on you, you're sure—but something makes you think these ones look just a bit more content than the others.

You drink and smoke a cigarette and think on the absolute fucking strangeness of that.

You never liked Elvis much. You're more of a country guy. Some Southern rock. Zeppelin always got you going.

"Well," you say aloud, to no one but the ghost of the King, "now I've seen it."

Back at the El Camino, you flick your butt, toss the empty bottle, and slide inside the car.

"All right, time to hit the—"

Suzie-Jean has her mouth on her brother's throat. Her dim, milky eyes stare at you. Her skin is pale and veiny.

For the first time since this mess started, you're truly terrified—your skin crawls and your heart pounds.

Suzie-Jean crawls over her brother's body and up into the driver's seat, moving jerky and frenzied. Walter's flesh hangs from her lips and blood pours down. Suzie-Jean reaches out a red hand and swipes at you.

You push back against the door, still open, part of you falling out of the car.

She lied. She fucking lied. She was bitten by that goddamn Klansman in the house.

You reach for the sawed-off as she grabs hold of your jeans

and then your shirt, dragging herself along your body. Mouth open impossibly, terrifyingly wide, about to bite.

You pull quick and fire both barrels and—

Shit!

One shell hits Suzie-Jean in the face, blowing away a chunk of her head. The other load clips your side. Can't fucking believe it. A load in your gut from your own goddamn gun. Blood everywhere now.

She's coming for you again. Part of her face is gone, so it looks like a half-eaten tomato. Her brain still operates.

You push back, out onto the pavement, and slam the door shut. Suzie-Jean's twig-like arm snaps in two. You limp around to the other side of the car, rip open the door, and grab Walter by the back of the collar, throwing him out onto the parking lot.

Suzie-Jean crawls forward, over Iris's body. You wait for her to tumble out of the car, then you place your boot on her chest and fire. This time, you don't miss.

Then it's Walter, a mercy kill, standing over him, firing, splattering him across the Anything Is Paradise parking lot.

You sit down on the cement.

What to do?

What now?

Well, now you press on. And it'll go quicker. A blessing in disguise, maybe, that the children are dead, a terrible person would say.

But it doesn't feel like that.

As you wrap the wound and get back in the car, it sure as hell doesn't feel like that . . .

 TURN TO PAGE 27.

Sitting in the El Camino, one arm out the window, a cigarette burning, you look over a map of Kentucky. There's a stretch of empty field outside a place called Licking River.

That's where you'll attack the train. That's where you'll take back Iris.

You key the microphone. "Eigle, it's Jimmy."

After a moment, *"Go."*

"Iris's been taken."

Another moment. *"By who?"*

You sigh. "A fucking circus train."

"Ring's?"

"Yes, you know it?"

"I do."

"Do they know what she is?" you ask. "What she's worth?"

"Only that Tanner will pay for her. You need to get her back, ASAP."

"No kidding. Or else I die."

"That's right."

"You saw to that, too, sure as hell, didn't you?"

"I did."

You slam down the microphone. More than anything, you want to turn the car around, drive straight to New York City, and strangle Eigle with that goddamn radio cord . . .

But you don't.

Iris is the mission, and the mission must be completed.

You don't let off the gas until you're nearly into Kentucky. You do four hundred miles in just over five hours, including back roads, hitting the nitrous on straightaways. Greasy is in the back of the El Camino, flat on his back, chained up like an animal, groaning with every hard bump and sharp turn.

Outside of Covington, you spot the long circus train, thundering down the tracks. You drop down onto a parallel tree-lined road and stamp the accelerator, charging ahead.

You stay hard on the gas, getting out far in front of the train. Coming into Kentucky, bluegrass farmland stretching out on either side of you like ocean water, you pick up the tracks again. They're the only ones recently greased—the only ones used in years.

You pull to a stop alongside the rail. You guess you've got fifteen minutes before the train arrives. Need to work quickly.

Zombies shuffle through the bluegrass fields—huge groups of the monsters, grazing like herds of wild animals.

You walk around the back of the car. Greasy watches you, eyes wide, terrified. You tug on the rope still attached to his ankle and say, "We're going to play one more game."

"What are you doing?" he asks. His voice is shaky.

"Stopping a train."

He tells you to let him go. Tells you all the things he'll give you: guns, food, electronics to barter. Begs. Threatens.

"Keep making noise," you say. "It'll only bring them quicker."

You tie the rope around Greasy's bloody ankles, give it twelve feet of slack, then double-knot the other end to the El Camino's rear bumper. You drag Greasy from the bed to the ground. He struggles to get to his feet, shrieks as his ankle gushes blood, and quickly falls, smashing his nose against a rock.

"Hey," you say.

He turns, panting hard—anger is getting in the way of his breathing.

"What?" he says. When he talks, the blood from his nose mixes with the soil on his face and sprays a dirty sort of mist.

"It's been nice chatting with you."

"Don't!" he shouts. He gets up again, charging toward you—but you step to the side and the rope tangles his feet and again he falls.

You slide into the El Camino, shift into first, and drive. The rope goes taut and you hear Greasy yelp as he's dragged through the field like some Wild West outlaw caught horse thieving.

"We'll try some different tunes this time!" you yell. "Don't want you getting bored!"

You take out the Lynyrd Skynyrd eight-track, toss it behind the seats, and pop in a Rolling Stones tape. You turn it up as loud as it will go.

The zombies turn at the noise. They shamble forward. They get a whiff of human flesh, of Greasy, his bloody nose, and they hear his hollering.

The thresher spins as you drive, slicing up the overgrown bluegrass, and you give the field a fine mowing as you steer toward a large horde of the monsters.

As you drive through the pack, they slap at the windows like some undead car wash. They reach for Greasy, stumbling after him. You shift into third and pick up speed, pushing it to 15 miles per hour. The monsters give chase. In the side mirror, you watch Greasy kick and thrash, trying to free himself.

One zombie gets hold of him and hangs on, pulled along with him.

The El Camino bursts through a rotten fence and into the next farm. You drive slowly, giving it gas when you need to, gathering a trail of the undead like you're the Pied Piper, collecting rats.

Undead cows—ugly, bony things—watch you, uncaring.

You weave through four more farms. The horde of zombies

shuffles after, growing in number until there are nearly two hundred monsters chasing the El Camino.

You steer up onto the rails, then toward the train. You hear the loud, pained *bump, bump, bump* of Greasy's body banging against the wooden tracks.

In the distance, you see smoke rising off the locomotive engine, over the trees. The train will be here soon. You slow the El Camino, shifting into neutral.

Gripping the fire ax, you march around the back. Greasy is horribly battered and soaked in blood; he's been bitten a dozen times, and his face is a pulpy thing.

"Bye now," you say.

With a hack, you sever the rope. Then you're back in the El Camino, steering away from the track, letting the monsters congregate and dine on Greasy's flesh.

You stop the car behind a farmhouse not far from the tracks, and you sit up on the hood, waiting.

The train comes around the bend and there's a sharp screech as the massive locomotive begins to brake. It can't simply plow through the undead—there are too many. It would derail.

The train finally stops mere feet from the remains of Greasy and the zombie mass.

The second train car is the most ornate. Even without Greasy's help, you probably could have figured out that it belonged to Ring. The side of the car slides open, and Ring appears, peeking his bulbous head out.

Crouched down, you creep through the waist-high bluegrass until you're just twenty feet from Ring's car. Other windows open—carnies looking out.

Ring looks back into his car, saying something. Talking to Iris, maybe.

Ring then hops down, immediately spots the zombies, and quickly climbs back into the car. "Christ, it's a goddamn herd," he says. He calls out to a guard, "Clear them shits out of the way, goddamn it!"

You quickly cross toward the train. Someone points at you. Someone else yells something, but Ring doesn't hear.

"Just a herd on the tracks. We'll have them gone in a minute," Ring is saying as he's closing the door.

But it won't close.

Your hand is there.

He turns. "Huh?"

And you're stepping up, inside the car, sawed-off pressed against his chest.

"Miss me?" you say.

Ring stumbles back, falling into a plush purple seat. Iris sits on a chair in the corner. She eyes you curiously—not scared, not angry—just . . . curious.

The car is lush and opulent. Full of gold and silver and bronze. An oriental rug on the floor and mounted zombie heads on the wall. A TV set in the corner plays *Dumbo*.

"What happened to Bob?" Ring asks.

"He the oily-looking guy?"

Ring nods.

"I happened."

Ring wipes sweat from his brow.

"Come on, Iris," you say.

Iris doesn't move.

"Iris," you say, "now. We don't have much time."

Ring's lips curl into an ugly grin. "Mr. El Camino, I'm afraid your friend may not *want* to leave. I've told her all about life aboard the train. She'll want for nothing here."

"Bullshit."

You grab Iris by the wrist, but she pulls back. She swallows. "I like it here, Jimmy."

Ring grins.

"Iris," you say, "you're coming with me. Now."

She shakes her head, sharp and hard. "I don't want to die, Jimmy."

You speak slowly, so you're very clear. You raise the gun and aim it directly at her. "You're not leaving me any choice, Iris. Even if you're dead—even if I *shoot you*—the scientists may be able to pull a cure from your body. Do you understand what I'm saying?"

Iris looks at the gun and nods. "I understand. But, Jimmy, I really don't think you'll do that."

If you want to continue arguing with her, trying to convince her to come with you, go to page 159.

No. No more arguing. Turn to page 389.

You reach down, flick the red metal switch, and—

FA—SHOOOM!

Four rockets spiral through the air, streaming smoke, zooming toward the nucleus of the rat king. The explosion rocks the tunnel. Thick, wet chunks of New York City rat rain down, splattering the ground and the walls and the car. You hit the windshield wipers, smearing blood and fur, speeding through the cloud of black vermin hair and still-falling viscera.

You steer the El Camino out of the tunnel and into New Jersey. You're lucky: a hard rain begins to fall, cleansing the windshield some, allowing you an image of the road. A few old apartments, still lived in, loom over you. People eye you. Live music from somewhere: guitars and drums and something with a horn. On street corners, zombies stumble about.

After a long moment, Iris says, "That was the worst thing I've ever seen. And I've seen a lot of horrible shit the past few years."

"There will be plenty more bad before we reach the end."

Iris reloads the sawed-off, then leans back, tugging the seat-recline lever. "Fun."

You take the highway, briefly, before exiting and heading for the open road, driving west.

You can't forget about Tanner or his drivers. Good odds they'll be following you. They don't know your route, but that doesn't mean they won't be searching. But you push that thought to the back of your mind as you focus on the blurring pavement ahead.

You felt it before: the freedom, when you were driving in the derby. But now, on the wide, curving roads, it's different. It's more than freedom. You are yourself again.

You are Jimmy El Camino.

One hand on the wheel, another on the stick, you feel a great tension in your chest releasing—a darkness surging forth, rushing through you like black energy and escaping through the tips of your fingers and your boot on the gas.

You're driving again.

You're in control of your own destiny.

It's fucking fantastic.

Behind you is Manhattan, buildings reaching up to the sky like jagged spikes: a bloated corpse of a city. The Death Derby. Boss Tanner. Major Eigle. Your jail cell. All of that gone now. Tanner might chase you and his thugs might gun for you, but New York City is in the past.

Knee on the wheel, you reach across Iris and open the glove box. Grab the bottle of whiskey and fill your trusty flask. Drink. Drink again.

The roads are cracked. The grass is greener and taller than any you've ever seen in the Northeast. Reminds you of the jungles in Colombia. Overgrown trees hang over the highway. Cars on the side of the road are rusted and broken.

Zombie bodies hang from trees like warnings.

Far outside the city, headed toward Pennsylvania, you drop it into fourth. The powerful engine roars, the machine happy to be used. You haven't been on a road this open in a long while. You race around corners, hugging bends, leaving a growing cloud of dust in your trail.

You push the El Camino, pistons churning, carrying your old friend up over 100 miles per hour. You hug a bend, hands loose on the wheel, then ease off the gas, downshifting into third, and the wind through the cracked glass softens and you feel your chest, up and down, up and down, breathing almost in time with the pistons. You reach into the console, pull a cigarette, light it, and exhale deeply. Better than sex. Better than any you ever had, at least—but maybe you just never knew how to screw right. Wouldn't discount it.

Iris smiles nervously—you can see her feeling the rush of the ride, almost see her heart beating against her chest.

"Y'all alright?" you say.

"Yes," she says. "I've never been this far out of the city before. Never seen the countryside, or whatever you'd call this."

"How old are you?"

"Nineteen."

"So you were . . ."

"Fourteen or so when it happened. When I was real young, we went south a few times. Family. But I don't remember that too much."

"Maybe in San Francisco you can drive. Maybe it's safe."

After a moment, Iris says, "I learned how, on my father's box truck. I think I might enjoy doing it again."

Coming into Pennsylvania, the roads narrow and zombies occasionally stumble out, like deer. You spot one far up ahead, beneath an off-ramp exit sign.

"Take that one," you say to Iris.

"What?"

"That one, up there. Take it out when I drive past."

"I never did."

"A zombie? Neither did I, until a day ago," you say, slowing down the El Camino, shifting into second, so you're rolling along at just over 20 miles per hour. "Go ahead," you say. "Grab the door handle and just *pop* it."

Iris grunts an "okay," grabs the handle, and then as you pass the shuffling monster, she snaps open the door and—

POW!

The metal door knocks the monster onto its back, arms splayed out, then rolling, legs breaking. The right front tire rolls over one arm with a vicious crunch. You light a smoke. "Fun, isn't it?"

"Not fun," she says, "but . . ." She takes a while, looking for the right word: *"Satisfying."*

You nod. "I know it. Once you get a taste for it, well . . ."

Outside of a town called Loag is an ugly little roadside joint named Piggy's. You pull over to take a leak and look for supplies.

When you come back out, Iris's sitting on a rotted wooden picnic table, flipping pages. "Look at this here," she says, holding up a book. It says *Odd America*. It's a travel guide, with a big foldout map, listing a mess of the country's strange and kitschy roadside attractions.

"I had a copy of this," she says. "At home, when I was younger. Not the exact same one, but like this. My father brought it back from a trip down south—before everything happened. When the city became locked down, I used to read it. Look at all the stuff. I was just a kid, but I'd think about going to these places. Traveling. Like this here: the World's Largest Ball of Twine. My mom used to talk about it. She did some sort of Fresh Air Fund kid thing, spent a month in Kansas. Said this ball was the dumbest fuckin' thing she ever saw. As a kid, I always wanted to see it—see the dumbest thing. Wouldn't you rather see the dumbest thing than see something that was just all right?"

"Get in the car, Iris."

"Foamhenge. Weird shit in this country, huh."

"That's south."

"How do you know?"

"I've been all over this country, driving."

"Well, aren't we going south?"

"Not the plan right now. Might change."

"Well, if the plan changes, maybe we can see it."

"Get in the car."

"Don't gotta be a prick. Just the ball of twine. Drive past. No harm."

"No."

"You're an asshole."

"It's not news."

Past the Susquehanna River, the rain comes down in sheets, hammering the road, drubbing the windshield, water whipping about the cabin. The radio hisses on. *"Jimmy, it's Major Eigle. Something I need to tell you."*

Picking up the microphone. "Go."

"I poisoned you, Jimmy."

Silence. After a moment, you key the mic. "What are you talking about?"

"I poisoned you. The scotch, in the garage. You make it to San Francisco with Iris in less than one month, the poison is treatable. Antidote waiting."

You think back. He handed you that drink in the garage. You noticed a look in his eyes. You shared the bottle. But the poison must have been in the glass.

"Only way I could make sure you wouldn't toss Iris from the car and head for the hills."

"You sonofabitch," you growl, slamming the brakes, tires sliding and squealing. "I'm turning around, and you're making me right again."

"Not going to happen, Jimmy."

"The hell it isn't."

"I don't have the antidote. It's only in San Francisco. Couldn't help you even if I wanted."

You want to put your fist through the radio.

"What if I don't make it in a month?" you say.

"One month is plenty of time. Good luck, Jimmy. We're here if—"

You slam the microphone back down and glare at Iris. Her face is blank. "I didn't know," she says with a cold shrug. "Doesn't make any difference, but I didn't know."

TURN TO PAGE 8.

The sun sets, a sprawling pink hue over the mountainous South Dakota horizon. In the distance, staggering zombies cast long, eerie shadows and you're goddamn thankful you're up here and not down there.

You find cans of beans and skinned muskrats. You build a small fire and cook the muskrat and beans. The cavern quickly fills with smoke, and you and Iris laugh like old friends as you use blankets to wave it out.

You try to eat slowly, but it's not easy, and soon you're shoving food in your mouth, and again the two of you are laughing.

Iris finds the Sniper Scavenger's moonshine. You take the thick bottle, go to swig it, but Iris touches your hand, stopping you, handing you a tin cup. You shrug and fill the cup. She finds a glass jar full of buttons, empties it, and you pour a glass for her.

The moonshine is hot and thick and Iris nearly gags, but you don't laugh at her.

It's a good meal. Freshly grilled meat washed down with burning stiff drinks. It's what a last meal should be.

When you've finished eating, you sip your moonshine and lean against the cavern wall, and Iris slides under your arm. Nothing sexual about it, but not like a father and daughter, either—something in between, like two strangers, forced into something more, with a single long last moment before they go off to most likely die.

You sit and you stare out at the beautiful horizon— beautiful, despite the monsters with their rotting flesh and their tattered clothes, proof of previous lives that ended too early and too violently.

"Why are you doing this?" Iris asks after a long silence. She sips her moonshine slowly and winces, but doesn't choke so much anymore.

"Because if I don't, I die. Eigle saw to that."

She looks up at you. Her eyes are narrowed. She's searching for something. "But why are you really doing this? Something's changed."

You take a bigger gulp and light a cigarette. Your arm hurts and blood steadily oozes through a makeshift bandage.

"I was a soldier."

"I know."

"My old man was a soldier, too. Growing up, as a kid, I never wanted that. He dragged us all around the country. Never made much money. I couldn't understand that. Why put your family through that? I wanted to be—you'll laugh—a short-order cook. Seemed simple. People need to eat. You serve them food. They go home happy, you empty the register, shut off the lights, and you go home, too. So simple."

You sip from your moonshine. Pacing yourself.

"But then Dad died in Desert Storm. He was a good man. And he died in fucking Desert Storm. Damn near no one died in Desert Storm. It was an accident. On a base, some kid tripped, carrying a warhead. Blew himself up, along with my old man."

"I'm sorry," Iris says.

"Long time ago."

You drink some more. "I changed then. I figured, hell, he's a good man—and he dies like that 'cause some kid didn't tie up his laces? If life's that flimsy, then you might as well do some good while you can. Make it count. So I joined up in 1991, just a teenager."

"Have you done good?"

"No. I don't know. No. Maybe. Sometimes I think no, sometimes yes—most times, I don't think about it at all. I caused a lot of goddamn hurt and pain—"

"Don't," she says. "The Lord's name."

"I caused a lot of *damn* hurt and pain. I suspect, maybe, you try to balance all the bad I've done with all the good—and the scale's gonna tip over to the bad side."

Iris knocks back a slug of her moonshine. "I know that feeling."

"So maybe this is my chance. Before it all went to hell—I drove. And I liked it. Finish line, you won. Didn't make it, you didn't win. Like the short-order cook, real simple. So this is my last drive. And if I'm lucky, it'll be a final drive to tip the balance in my favor—over to the good. Y'know, just in case there is some big bearded man upstairs, maybe he'll look the other way while I sneak under the pearly gates."

"You'll make it."

"Will I?"

"Yes."

Iris knocks back the rest of the moonshine. She reaches, crawling over you, to the CB radio. Turning up the volume, keying the mic, she says, "Tanner."

You look at her, confused.

A second later, Tanner growls, *"What?"*

"This is Iris. The woman you've been trying so hard to kill. Just wanted to let you know—I'm gonna end your whole fucking existence."

And before he can respond, she hurls the radio over the side. You hear it crash to the concrete far below. Then you both fall asleep, you in her arms. One last good sleep before you go to die.

TURN TO PAGE 245.

"All right," you say at last. "We'll go in together. Get in. No point in waiting any longer."

You drive down the hill, car shuddering as you coast back onto the highway. You take a deep breath, then downshift, coming slowly around a bend, and then they're in front of you: this godless gauntlet. Forty cars. Thousands of the undead.

You stick a cigarette into your mouth, light it, and look to Iris. "Time to go raise a little hell."

Iris nods. "Raise it high, please . . ."

You floor it, your boot heavy on the pedal, quick-shifting through second, third, and into fourth, and then it all opens up at once—hard, fast, deafening, heavy-metal explosive.

Armored cars racing toward you, guns unloading like guns do, hot metal ricocheting off the El Camino's thick, steel-clad hide, and the sound inside the car and sound inside your skull just a screeching mix of screaming bullets and shredding iron.

You're firing back, thumb down, slugs screaming and zombie flesh ripping and tearing and bursting. Tough to aim, peering out through the slice in the reinforced metal—but you keep your thumb on the trigger, laying waste, bringing pain, each shot like a tiny, hot, angry piece of your insides happily ripped out and flung forward.

There's Elwood, gumball sirens wailing, charging toward you in the old Monaco. Last you saw him was in Times Square. Boss Tanner sent him all the way out here to take you down and you almost feel honored as you wrench the wheel, swinging on the pavement, sweeping past him. Eyes to the side mirror, he's turning, dust swirling, coming back around right on your tail.

Ahead of you is the Panzer, the big main cannon looming and you charging toward it—fifty yards, forty yards, thirty yards.

"You do *see that*, right?" Iris asks.

"I do."

At the last second, you twist the wheel, the tires locking, screeching furiously, and then the Panzer cannon BOOMS and the shell soars past you. An instant later, an ear-shattering explosion as the trailing Elwood and his squad car erupt in a ball of flame, white-hot scrap metal skipping across the dusty pavement.

You trigger the rockets and two cars—not armed like the ones you saw in New York—burst, breaking, hoods popping and engines catching fire, raining shrapnel down upon you.

Suddenly, two cars banging into you from either side: a souped-up Trans Am and a Ford Explorer. Jockeying against you, and you swerving, side to side, banging, bashing, metal crunching and sparking as you try to free yourself, finally wrenching the wheel hard left, the enemy Trans Am weaving, tires locking, body swinging and spinning off the highway in a swirling screen of dirt. And then you hit the brakes, seat belt punching like a baseball bat to the chest, Iris shrieking and gasping. The Ford Explorer tries to stop, but instead it just skids past you and then you have him, dead to rights, and you open up with the minigun, hammering the Explorer, firing, firing, until it flips, hopping the guardrail, sliding across the overgrown, grassy cliff ledge, dirt kicking up, and then it's gone, dropping over the side, and you've turned the wheel, back at it even before it's splashed down into San Francisco Bay.

Ahead of you, the zombies still wait—an army so thick you see nothing but the rotting beasts. You drop it into third and ease off the gas, letting the thresher hungrily consume the dead, leaving red paste in your wake.

And then you're there, crossing onto the Golden Gate Bridge, bursting through a wooden tollgate arm and plowing through a zombie in a yellow reflective jacket. You shift gears, speeding ahead, racing through them until the mass of undead bodies becomes so dense the thresher can no longer spin. Too many bodies, the El Camino slowing to a crawl, monsters slapping at the windows. Behind you, vehicles struggle to get through the tolls and continue their attack.

Iris watches the monsters silently. She knows what you know—you're not going to make it.

You grit your teeth and shift it into first. You stomp the gas, let off, and hit it again—a pulsing sort of movement carrying you nearly halfway across the bridge, but that's as far as she'll go—the El Camino stops completely. Eyes to the side mirror: enemy vehicles, slowly but steadily, pushing through. You'll soon be within firing range.

And that's when the big guns open fire from atop the massive wall on the San Francisco side of the bridge.

Your saviors.

The good guys.

The San Francisco cannons continue the salvo: zombies are blown apart, hundreds destroyed in seconds, pulverized, and the chasing vehicles hammered and blasted.

The radio zaps on. *"Jimmy El Camino, this is San Francisco Defense Unit number two, clearing a path for you. Get to the end of the bridge, and we'll open the big gates. See you in a few."*

Your heart pounds, swelling, a rush of happiness like nothing you've ever felt. Dead one moment, alive the next. Iris's fingers dig into your forearm, then she punches the roof, overjoyed curses rushing from her lips.

The next heavy cannon blast shakes the bridge. Blows a small crater in it. A pack of zombies is vaporized.

But as the cloud of red mist clears, you see him, at the very end of the bridge.

No zombies between you. Just you and him.

Mr. King, in his Lincoln.

He's been hiding there. Waiting for you.

And suddenly, he's charging.

In Times Square, the first time you did battle, he won.

So this is it.

You flick the nitrous and the El Camino is launched into overdrive, the engine screaming, your head yanked back, the force tugging at you, pushing you down into the tattered leather seat as the El Camino tops 120 miles per hour.

Mr. King charges toward you at an impossible speed.

You grip the wheel. Iris screams.

In seconds, there will be no turning back. If you collide head-on, you'll be dead—all of you.

So this is it: a single game of chicken, with, quite possibly, the future of all humanity at stake. The future of humanity in your hands—the hands that grip the wheel of the charging El Camino.

What will you do?

To stay hard on the gas, turn to page 397.

If you'll cut the wheel, hoping to avoid the head-on collision, go to page 114.

DINNER GUEST

You follow the girl up the front steps. The door creaks open. The house is dim and smells of sickness. "They're just through here," she says.

She pulls back a curtain, and the stench hits you full-on. Her family sits around a dining room table.

They're undead, all of them.

A father, a mother, and a brother. The father is a fat, rotten thing, with one arm and no legs. The mother is bald and has a crooked nose, and its jaw hangs loose. The brother is no older than four or five, and it rocks and convulses, chained to the wall.

You drop the food and reach for the sawed-off. "You said you needed food for your family," you say, drawing the gun and turning.

The girl is holding a massive shotgun, pointed at your chest, the weapon as big as her.

"I did," the girl says. "The food is you."

And then she fires.

AN END

You squeeze the trigger and put a hard round through the head of the Klansman draped over Dewey. Another shot, through the nose of the Klansman clawing at Dewey's retina.

You wheel to your right, but it's too late.

Teeth are buried in Suzie-Jean's scalp. She's screaming. Tears rush down her face and she looks at you with wide, wet eyes.

You fire twice more, into the girl. Her eyes, fast turning cloudy, stare at you, blaming you. And then she topples over.

You fire two more shots, killing the monsters, and then the gun hangs at your side. "Walter," you say, turning to the boy. "I—"

You stop.

Walter's grabbed his sister's rifle and is now pointing it at you. His eyes are narrow and his mouth is a hard, stiff line. "You shot my sister. Killed my family! They were worthless and awful, but they were my family!"

"I had to."

"Not my sister! You could have shot the man! You could have shot Dewey!"

"Walter, if I did that, there'd be no one to take care of you. Soon, you'd both be dead."

"You could have taken care of us! You could have brought us with you!"

"I can't do that. It's not—"

BLAM!

The shot punches you in the gut, your knees buckling, and

you stagger back onto Dewey's green couch. Before Walter can reload, Dewey is stomping across the room, knocking the boy aside, yanking the gun from his hand.

Walter falls to the floor. He looks up at you for a moment and then begins sobbing, full-body heaves.

"You hurt bad?" Dewey asks.

You pull up your shirt. There's no exit wound—not a through-and-through. "Be all right. I need to go. Need to drive."

"Need to get that bullet out of you first, Jimmy."

"No. Wasted enough damn time," you say. You grab a towel from the floor and blot the wound, then stuff fabric into the hole.

Dewey cracks a beer and retrieves Iris's now-legless body from the basement, and together you walk to the El Camino, stepping over and around the mass of Klansmen littering the drive.

"Thanks for not shooting me like you did that girl," Dewey says.

Wincing, holding your side, you say, "Just take care of the boy."

"I will."

"Sometime later, let him know I'm not mad he shot me."

Dewey nods. "Good luck. Counting on you to save the world."

"Easy."

You slide into the car. Dewey places Iris into the passenger seat, and you lean over and buckle her in. You pull your flask from your back pocket and clink Dewey's beer. And once again, you hit the road—this time, with Iris's freeze-dried torso beside you and a bullet in your gut . . .

TURN TO PAGE 27.

You come to, groggy, head feeling like it does when a man that size puts his force behind a blow.

You're in the barn, sitting on a hay-covered floor, your back against a wooden beam. Your wounded arm has been bandaged and your wrists are tied tight around the beam.

Iris is tied up, same as you, to a beam ten feet away.

You hear choked moaning. You look up. Above you, hanging from the rafters, are zombies. Dozens of them, ropes around their throats, groaning and twitching and kicking.

You turn to Iris. "You okay?"

She has a big red mark on her head, fast beginning to bruise. Her eyes are spacey. "Not my best."

The man-beast steps out into the dim light. You see him fully now, and he's a twisted take on Frankenstein's monster. He appears to be constructed from bits and pieces of different men. One arm is thick and muscular and black, the other bony and white. His face is covered in scars and stitches. One leg is longer than the other, so he walks with a pronounced limp. His denim overalls are splattered and stained with old blood.

He stomps through the hay, toward Iris. She closes her eyes and you see her shoulders tense—scared, but not panicking. Not once on your journey have you seen her panic.

The monster reaches down and wraps his thick fingers around her wrist, lifting it, sniffing. His hand paws at her face. He strokes her hair, almost gently.

"Henry!" a sudden voice barks. "Off!"

A door slams shut and you hear footsteps on the hay. The

monster—"Henry"—looks up at the entering figure. Henry growls, then reaches down, again pawing at Iris, now grabbing her exposed thigh.

"Ah, hell, *Henry*!"

The owner of the voice appears, stepping out into the center of the barn. The man holds a small buzzer, the size of a garage door opener. He presses it. Henry yelps like a hurt child and takes four quick, clumsy steps back, then turns and trudges to the corner of the barn. You see that a sort of shock collar is plugged into the monster's brain, by way of a rough drill hole in the back of his head.

"Please excuse him," this newcomer says to Iris. "I'm afraid we don't see a lot of *live* women around here. It gets him a little worked up. He can get, well . . . rowdy."

This man wears a butcher's apron, cut down the middle to resemble a scientist's laboratory coat. He's covered in blood. Some of it fresh, most of it old and black.

"What is it?" Iris asks, nodding to the monster.

The man looks back. "Henry was Fred and Martha's youngest. You saw Fred and Martha, out front. The nice old couple, just hanging around?" His terrible joke makes him chuckle. "A big hulking farm boy, Henry is. All-American! Isn't that right?" the man continues, crossing the barn floor and slapping Henry on the back. He applies some pressure to his shoulder, and Henry reluctantly takes a seat on a milking stool. He looks comically large, perched on the tiny four-legged seat.

"Henry was one of my earliest experiments," the man says. "Two brains. While Henry was still alive, I removed the left cerebral hemisphere and replaced it with the cerebrum of one of these local zombie hayseeds. Henry is now half-and-half: left brain human, right brain undead."

"So you're some sort of horseshit Dr. Frankenstein?" you say.

The man thinks about that for a moment. "No, no. Not quite. I'm more in the vein of Dr. Moreau, I'd suppose."

"Never heard of him."

"No matter. I go by my God-given name—Splicer. *Dr.* Splicer."

His name means nothing to you. You only know that he's clearly insane, you need to get out of this place, and that probably means killing him.

"I'll be back shortly," Splicer says. "Finishing a procedure. Combining a human torso with the lower body of a horse. The centaur project. Henry will keep an eye on you while I'm gone. Won't you, Henry?"

Henry grunts.

"Don't worry about him, by the way. I've removed his teeth," Dr. Splicer says. He reaches inside Henry's mouth and there's a wet, smacking noise as he lifts up Henry's lips, revealing the toothless orifice.

Dr. Splicer beams, proud of himself. "I'll be back in a bit. You two have given me an idea. I wonder—have you ever seen conjoined twins in person? Quite captivating . . ."

With that, he crosses and exits.

Across the barn, Henry sits, unmoving, staring at you with his cold, half-dead eyes.

"Jimmy," Iris whispers. "Let's get the fuck out of this madhouse, huh?"

You nod. "I'm thinking."

If you want to wait it out and try to escape when Dr. Splicer returns for you, turn to page 258.

Attempt to free yourself now? Turn to page 298.

"Trust me, all right? I got you this far. I'll see you soon, in the city. Beyond the bridge."

"You sure?"

"Positive."

At last, she nods.

You reach into the car and take out a map of San Francisco. You detail the route she'll take on foot. "You're going up and around this big, overgrown hill, here. Grass is so tall that no one will be able to see you. You'll come down the bottom then, and you'll find the guardrail to the bridge. Hop that. That'll put you behind the army. And then you stay on the pedestrian path; it's walled on either side, shouldn't be so thick with the zombies—and you just goddamn sprint to the gates at the end of the bridge. Head down, move quick, all the way to the city."

Iris looks up from the map. "And you?"

"I'll keep driving, keep battling long enough to let you get across the bridge. Got it?"

"They're going to know. They'll see I'm not with you. And that leaves me dead. All this, for nothing."

"I'll make sure they think we're together."

"Will I see you again?"

"Yes. Now go."

She begins to walk, then stops. Two quick steps back, and she throws her arms around you. You don't know how to respond. After a second, you wrap your arms around her and hold her tight.

A moment later, she steps back. A sad smile, and then she's gone, running across the hills. San Francisco's pale skyline is just visible through the mist in the distance.

Time to get to work. Only way this plan succeeds is if they're convinced you and Iris are together.

Gripping the sawed-off, you march down the hill, right up to the three zombies shuffling around below. You execute the two zombie males, leaving the undead blonde. It lunges for you. You step back, club the zombie with the grip, knocking the thing to its knees, then dragging it back up the hill.

While it struggles to stand, you retrieve duct tape from the car. When it's finally back on its feet, you step around behind it and fire the sawed-off—the blond zombie's body is blown forward, again, to the ground. You jump on its bloody back and wrap duct tape around its mouth before it has a chance to bite. Ten, fifteen times around, until it's mostly harmless. Then duct tape around the arms, so it can't claw you.

You stand up, wipe the sweat from your forehead. It's been six minutes. Iris should be about a quarter of the way to the bridge.

You push the blond monster into the passenger side of the El Camino, then belt it in. Through the duct tape, it still moans. You tug your shirt up, over your nose, blocking some of the undead stench.

Shifting into gear, back down the hill, onto the 101, and down the half mile of highway toward the awaiting army. When you turn the corner, the throng of hired guns stretches out in front of you, two hundred yards away. A line of vehicles blocking access to the bridge.

Gripping the sawed-off, you step out of the car, walk around to the passenger side, and grab the blond-haired zombie. You muss its hair so it falls over its face. Then you pull it up by its shirt, standing it up straight, so the drivers can see it. On the quick look you offer them, the undead beast will appear to be Iris.

You fire the gun twice in the air—the two hollow booms letting the enemy know you're coming—then push the monster back inside.

The cars begin charging—one thick mass of vehicles, thundering toward you. There's a crack as the first bullet fires, and then it's a storm of shots, thundering and snapping.

You slide into the El Camino, take a long swig of whiskey, and decide it's time to get on with it. It's been eleven minutes. Iris should be halfway to the guardrail now.

Teeth clenched, then, shifting into first, stamping the accelerator, using up every last bit of power this dying muscle machine has—leading the old girl into a stampeding charge of cars, trucks, motorcycles, and undead bodies.

Your reflexes are quick and you feel sharper than you have in years, gripping the stick, triggering the minigun—glorious and deafening—and you're smiling now, grinning, blowing them apart, the bullets non-stop thudding and pounding at the armed onslaught.

A souped-up Camaro is the first car upon you, zooming fast, veering from side to side. You fire a rocket. It explodes at the ground just in front of the Camaro—the front tires burst, melting instantly, and the vehicle skids, flipping past you.

Two motorcycles hurtling toward you. The riders fire AK-47s, but the bullets *tick tick* harmlessly off the El Camino's metal plating, and it feels good, the machine eating up what the enemy throws at it. You swerve hard into the leading motorcycle—the thresher catches the front tire, chewing, and the rider is catapulted over the back of the El Camino. You imagine you hear the sound of him hitting the ground and breaking, but it's only in your head.

Pop, pulling the emergency brake, cutting the wheel, swinging the tail end of the El Camino around, connecting with the second bike. There's a heavy thud as the El Camino plows into the motorcycle like a right hook, swinging through it.

You gun it then—turning, continuing forward, toward the

bridge, the army of cars firing at you from all sides. Concrete explodes. Fire rains down. You slam into the flaming wreckage of a Ford Taurus, ramming it, spinning the husk aside.

If you had Iris with you, this would be a straight ride into the gauntlet—a direct assault. But this is different. Your only job is to stay alive as long as possible.

But how far along is Iris?

Nearing the bridge, explosions bursting all around you, you skid to a stop. Bullets pound the car's metal hide while you lean over your blond zombie passenger—the idiot thing moans—and you peer through the window.

Searching.

Searching.

There!

You spot Iris, crouched down, at the base of the bridge.

But where's Mr. King?

Where would *you* be? At the far end of the bridge, a last line of defense.

That's almost certainly where he is, too. That mass of zombies on the bridge—that crowd so thick you can't see anything? You're sure that Mr. King is waiting at the very end. You'd bet the future of humanity on it. In fact, you have.

You need to draw him out, or Iris's dead.

Quick shifting, mashing the accelerator now, steering away from the bridge so it looks like you're fleeing the heavy fire. You push the El Camino across the highway, toward the hills, firing two rockets into the guardrail, then hopping over the twisted, burning metal and charging up the thick-grassed hills that line the highway and overlook the bridge. You tug the wheel, drifting, so the passenger door is facing out and you brace yourself for the next volley. Bullets pound the door as cars race after you, up the embankment.

To the undead blonde: "This is your stop."

You reach over it, snap open the passenger door, extend the

sawed-off, and fire it into its face. The shot blasts it out, onto the grass.

You bring the car to a full stop, tearing up dirt, sliding across the grass. Then, very slowly, you step out, arms raised. You see the blond zombie, now nearly headless—brain everywhere, its face like someone took a pickax to a watermelon.

You kneel down and hold it, like it's something that mattered to you.

A dozen cars encircle you as zombies shamble forward through the cracked guardrail and up the hill. The ring of cars keeps the monsters at bay.

Looking out into the distance, you see movement on the bridge. Zombies being pushed aside.

Mr. King.

The Lincoln, rolling through.

You were right—he was waiting at the end of the Golden Gate for you. And now he's coming.

The men step out of their cars. All of them in heavy clothes, leather jackets, two or three layers. Hired guns. Beards on most of them. One of them raises a rifle, but another says, "Hold. Wait for Tanner's man."

A minute later, the Lincoln rumbles up the hill and Mr. King gets out. You see him for the first time since Times Square—face scarred and twisted and burned.

He takes out a zombie that gets close as he steps up and over the hood of an old VW and into the circle.

"Took a while for us to get you," he says. His voice is a hard growl.

"It did."

"Nice driving."

You don't respond.

"So this is Iris, huh? This is the lady who caused all the fuss. The blood that launched a thousand cars."

"No," you say, "it isn't."

You look up at him, a smirk on your face.

His face twists. He steps over. Grabs the zombie's blond hair. Sees its shattered face. Sees what little remains of the duct tape on its mouth. He pulls up its sleeves and sees its arms, rotted away to nothing. "She's one of them," he says.

"Gotcha," you say, raising a finger, pointing, winking, sounding like a bad game show host.

Mr. King roars and kicks you in the face, snapping your nose, loosing teeth. You tumble back. When you sit up, he's pulled a revolver from a hip holster and has it against your left eye. "Where's Iris?"

"You want to see Iris?"

"Yes."

"You sure?"

"Yes."

"Okay," you say, standing. Very slowly, you reach inside the car. You pull out your binoculars and focus on the bridge.

There she is. Running past the thick horde of monsters, pushing through the few that get in her way. She's close to the end. The big gates are opening. Men welcome her in. Soldiers fire shots at the zombies that get too close.

Smiling, you hand the binoculars to Mr. King. He looks. Sighs. After a second, he brings them down.

"You're useless," he says to the men. "He fooled you."

"What about our payment?" one of the drivers calls out.

"There is no payment," Mr. King says. "You failed."

"Do we get to kill him?"

Mr. King turns back to you. He's thinking. "No," he says after a moment. "No, we don't. He had a job to do. So did we. He finished his. We did not."

And then Mr. King swings, his thick, scarred fist connecting with your jaw and knocking you to the ground.

"But blow the fucking El Camino to hell."

You get to your feet as a man hurls two grenades inside the El Camino. You make it only a few yards before it erupts, the blast lifting you off your feet and plunging you down the embankment.

And for a while, you just lie there. You lift your head and watch the cars leave. The Lincoln rumbles away as well, into the distance. Good-bye, Mr. King.

When the fire dies down, you examine the wreckage of the El Camino. Somehow, you find the sawed-off shotgun intact, buried beneath the rubble. You load it and stuff the few remaining shells into your pocket.

You light a cigarette and begin limping toward the Golden Gate Bridge.

Maybe you can make it across the bridge without being bitten.

Maybe.

You hope you can.

You'd really like to see Iris one last time, before the scientists cut her up . . .

AN END

BIDING YOUR TIME

The Man in Antlers pulls Iris to her feet and drags her toward the trees.

A cult member kicks you in the side. "C'mon. Move it."

You struggle to your feet. The pain is blinding. The man pushes you forward. You stumble, then pitch over into the dirt. He yanks you up and shoves you along. Your gun lies in the grass, behind you.

The Man in Antlers pushes Iris along, but she never cries or begs or calls for help.

You walk nearly a half mile through the trees, stopping at a run-down barn in a field. The wood is chipped and rotting.

The Man in Antlers orders a robed cult member to open the door, and you're led inside.

This barn appears to be the cult's base and home. Large crucifixes are spray-painted on the walls. Candles, a few hundred, placed throughout. Dead animals, drained of blood, hang from the rafters and the walls.

And zombies. You hear them. You smell them. But you don't see them . . .

You're kicked forward, so you're standing beside Iris. Cult members with their rifles on either side. Iris looks at you, terrified.

That's when you see the zombies.

You're standing over a large, circular pit dug into the center of the barn floor. Fifteen feet deep, forty feet around. Zombies fill the pit. Howling, hungry, reaching things. Your stomach roils, the poison rushes to your head, and you nearly pitch over the side. Iris grabs your arm, steadying you.

352

The Man in Antlers crosses to the opposite side of the pit, then speaks like some mad preacher. "This place contains the rotting bodies of men who visited the temple—men who were *not* the leader. Men who would *not* bring us forward, into the new age. The girl will join them, though her death will be a true and final end. We pray that her inhuman, unnatural, foul biology might bring forth the True One."

He lowers his head and prays silently. The cult members join him.

You focus.

If you can ride out this pain, get back half a fucking grip on reality, there's a chance you can get Iris out of here alive.

Suddenly, a hand on your collar, pulling you back, dropping you onto the ground. "You watch," a cult member says.

The prayer has finished, and the Man in Antlers now walks around the pit, toward Iris. He grabs hold of a dangling pulley, a large rusted hook at the end. He slips the hook through her belt. Her shirt is still torn and her breasts are bare. One cult member begins to raise the pulley. Rusty metal squeaks as Iris is lifted into the air.

Iris is silent, stoic, as she spins around helplessly.

You concentrate only on the blinding hurt. You can fight this. You've fought worse. You breathe into the agony. Deep breaths, sucking in air, directing the oxygen toward the pain points.

It begins to fade. The poison retreats.

The cult member who knocked you to the floor stands over you. He watches with intensity as Iris dangles, rubbing at his crotch through the robe.

You'll kill him first, you decide.

Breathing slowly, accepting the pain, defeating it, you rise. Farming tools hang from the barn walls. You spot a sickle. That'll do.

The cult members are all focused on Iris, being swung out over the pit.

Quietly, you pull the sickle from the wall.

She's being lowered into the pit now.

The men watch, entranced. The Man in Antlers has his eyes closed and he holds his arms out, embracing the bullshit.

Time for you all to die, you think.

You tap the closest cult member on the shoulder—the one who is watching Iris with a perverted intensity.

"Uh?" he grunts, turning.

You swing the sickle, slashing his throat, his head dropping from his shoulder. A geyser of blood erupts from his neck and he collapses onto the floor.

Chaos then.

Men yelling. Guns firing.

You swing the sickle low, severing the next cult member at the legs. He falls, bloody stubs kicking.

"Stop him!" the Man in Antlers demands.

You take on a human shield—a bullet sponge. You work your way around the circular edge of the pit, disemboweling one cult member, slicing open the next one's face, swinging the sickle through the next man's gut so it exits his side trailing blood and viscera and purple fabric.

The blade slashes the next man's arm, and he cries out, reaching for a limb that's no longer there. And then, blood splashing, he tumbles back into the man gripping the pulley.

There's a high-pitched whine as the rope rushes through the pulley and Iris plummets into the pit. "No!" she screams, and then there's a whack as she hits the ground, and then she goes silent. The moaning of the zombies grows louder.

All around you, the remaining cult members raise their guns.

And beneath you, Iris fights and thrashes and kicks as the undead begin mauling her.

You kick the bloody bullet sponge to the floor, mind racing . . .

To jump in after Iris, turn to page 124.

If you want to kill the remaining men first and
then try to rescue Iris, turn to page 164.

Dewey leaps into action, flinging open the door, dropping to one knee, shooting steadily with a Remington Woodsmaster. He fires in three-round bursts. Burst. Kill. Burst. Kill. Burst. Kill. Nothing wasted.

Walter and Suzie-Jean aren't screaming. You glance over, and they don't even seem scared—eyes just narrow and almost eager.

You don't pull the sawed-off. Beyond twenty feet, it's near useless.

An old Winchester Model 100 is mounted above the fireplace. You pull it down. Check the magazine. Loaded. You yank open a window, set the stock down on the sill, and aim down the sight.

It's worse than you imagined. Two hundred monsters. Some already past the El Camino now, nearing the fence.

You fire steadily. BLAM! One hooded face erupts in a shower of red fluid and gray matter. BLAM! A hooded child crumples. BLAM! A round spirals through two of the monsters, drilling through their skulls, killing them both.

You glance back, see that Walter has his fingers intertwined, helping Suzie-Jean up to the gun rack on the far wall. "What are you doing?" you shout.

"We can shoot!" Walter says.

And they *can* shoot. Their bigoted, survivalist family taught them well. They each grab a .38 and take up spots at windows on either side of you. They're slow but accurate. Shoot. Reload.

Breathe. Shoot. Reload. Breathe. Each shot takes about fifteen seconds. Two out of three shots hit a zombie in the head.

But the onslaught doesn't slow, the monsters keep on coming, and there's no rear exit, just swamp and gators behind you.

"Dewey," you say as you reload, "you got traps out there, anything like that?"

"Course I do," he says—and as he says it, there's a deafening blast. An explosion in the woods. Four zombies, blown apart, clumps of meat raining down.

"Russian land mine!" Dewey calls out.

"Gonna need a lot of land mines," you say, squeezing, killing one so it drapes over the fence and its hood falls off and its brain oozes down onto the lawn.

Dewey sets down his gun, quickly crosses to a large leather trunk. You follow. Inside: an old Al Capone–style tommy gun and a collapsible RPG.

Take the RPG? Go to page 378.

Choose the old tommy gun instead? Turn to page 49.

THE DREAM IS DEAD

You pull the trigger, blowing Iris apart, ending her and, in this dreamscape, all hope for a future free of monsters. And as Iris's face shatters and blood splatters your face, your eyes open.

You're back in the tent. Smoke fills the air. The healer leans over you.

"You are cured," the healer says.

You groan.

"Your blood," the healer says. "It is better now."

"Impossible . . . ," you mutter.

You sit up. Then stand and take a few steps. There's still pain in your side from the gun wound, but it's true . . . you feel different. Alive.

And you realize then that you can abandon all this.

You killed Iris in the dream because you felt it was right— that a world of death and destruction was better than the one you'd been living in: a world of drones and attack helicopters and rat races.

And now you can live in that world. Permanently. You no longer need to finish your mission to stay alive. The poison is gone.

You smile. *Fuck you, Eigle. I win.*

You don't say much to the healer. You simply walk back to the El Camino and climb inside. You're groggy, slightly, but you feel good.

Turning the key, the leader appears at the car window. He hands you a bottle. "Mescal," he says. "It's very strong."

"It's that obvious?"

"You drink. Some men change. Some don't. You won't. Accept that, and I bet you'll be happier."

You reach out and shake his hand. "I wouldn't worry about those monsters out there," you say. "I don't think anyone's going to stop this apocalypse. Not for a long time."

He nods. He seems to be quite okay with that.

TURN TO PAGE 202.

The Lincoln bursts through the vines and into the clearing.

You don't run. You don't hide. You simply raise the heavy Smith & Wesson, arm extended, and squeeze.

You put five bullets into the Lincoln's reinforced glass. It spiderwebs and cracks.

One bullet left.

You aim for the splintered glass. Through the crack, you see Mr. King's face.

And as you squeeze, a zombie seizes you from behind. The monster sinks its teeth into your shoulder. You howl, staggering forward, your hand contracting and the Smith & Wesson firing into the ground.

And then the Lincoln is upon you.

The three-ton vehicle hits you in the gut at 55 miles per hour, shattering your lower body, smashing both your legs, and yanking you underneath. The left tire rolls over your right arm, crushing it while the undercarriage catches your nose and tears it, ripping off your face.

Zombies shuffle toward you, smelling their next meal.

Your head rolls to the side. Through the trail of broken grapevines, you see Mr. King step out of the Lincoln. You expect him to come kill you. Instead, he disappears into the towering rows.

Zombies surround you. Hungry mouths descend upon your body. Flesh is sucked off the bone.

You feel your body turning. Your blood feels hot. What little skin that hasn't been torn off is burning up.

You maintain consciousness just long enough to see Mr. King stomping back through the orchard. You swallow. Blood in your throat.

Mr. King is dragging Iris's body.

You see him pull a machete from the Lincoln, stand over Iris, and begin hacking her to pieces, officially ending any hope of completing your mission. And then you don't see anything at all, because your eyeballs are ripped from your skull . . .

AN END

REVERSING COURSE

Leave the El Camino?

You had to make your peace with abandoning the mission. With letting Iris go. But the El Camino? The thought of leaving it suddenly sparks something in you, a need to push forward and finish what you began.

"Can't leave the car," you say to the guard. "She's my best friend."

You walk back to the El Camino. Sliding inside, you say, "We're not giving up yet, Iris. Not yet."

Zoning out along Interstate 10, you slam into an undead body. It's a big boy and the thresher doesn't devour it completely. The wheels roll over it, shaking the car. Rattling your brain.

And suddenly, the pain is back. The poison has returned.

The Native American healer, whatever he did—his bargain with God-knows-what—it's over and done with. You're no longer free of Eigle's death tonic. Once again, your life depends on getting to San Francisco.

"Hang on, Iris," you say, stamping the accelerator. "We'll be there soon enough."

 TURN TO PAGE 73.

"Take the girl," you say.

Ring's lower lip juts out in surprise. "Well, all right, then. Guess chivalry really is dead, huh," he says, laughing loudly.

"You mother—" Iris starts, leaping up, charging across the room, swinging at you.

"Sorry, hon, but I'm not dying for you."

"You're gonna die anyway!" she says.

You shrug. "I'll figure something out."

Iris cocks back her fist, but Ring bear-hugs her, pinning her arms to her sides. Iris barks at you—all the fun words you never hear at church. Finally, Ring shoves her across the room, toward one of his men.

"Take her to the train," Ring says. "My car."

Iris gives you one last look as she's led from the room—one of not anger but fear. You don't say it—you can't—but you'll get her back. Shortly, with any luck.

Ring turns to his remaining henchman. This man has a rectangular face and oily, slicked-back hair. He wears a shiny suit, but it's covered in stains. Dry cleaner must be closed. You spot your gun, tucked into his waist. "Lead Mr. El Camino to his car, please," Ring says.

Greasy gives you a shove, pushing you into the hall.

"Be seeing you," you say to Ring.

"I doubt that," Ring calls after you as you're led down the steps and out into the street.

When you step into the garage, the pimply-faced kid is gone. The El Camino is one of six cars being stored.

Greasy will make his move any moment now. You know that. There's no way they'll let you leave alive.

So you make your move first.

As he pushes you toward the El Camino, you spin, grabbing his wrist, wrenching it. You twist his wrist harder, dropping him to his knees, then go behind his back and pluck your sawed-off. "This is mine," you say, "and you shouldn't have taken it."

Greasy opens his mouth to scream, but you throw a vicious cross, knocking out two teeth.

"I'll show you what happens to people who take things that don't belong to them."

You pull a hacksaw from the workbench, then yank Greasy to his feet. You swipe the hacksaw low, across the back of his ankle, slashing open his Achilles tendon. His eyes go wide and tears rush out.

"You'll never walk right again," you say. "But you can still live, if you do like I say. Got it?"

He nods twice. Fast, almost spastic.

"Good."

You let go of him, and he tumbles forward, throwing himself over the hood of the car, just above the thresher. He's unable to hold his own weight.

From the wall, you grab bungee cords and duct tape. You wrap the duct tape around his mouth, then begin attaching Greasy to the car. Using the bungee cords, you get him draped over it, facing out—his wrists and ankles pulled taut, so he's strapped to the front of the car like a big X. The thresher blades cut into him, drawing blood.

Inside the car, you flick the kill switch, shutting off the thresher so it won't grind him up as you drive.

You drive slowly toward the town gate.

People gawk and stare. Some gasp. Someone shouts for Ring. But most just get out of the way and watch.

You go over a bump, and Greasy's body jostles. His head thrashes in pain.

"Hold it!" the armed guard at the gate shouts.

"Open it," you shout, "or the man dies."

The guard is unsure.

You shift into neutral and rev the engine. Greasy jerks, terrified, and his head raises. He nods at the guard, fast and hard. He's trying to shout through the duct tape.

The gate is opened.

You light a cigarette and drive out into the zombie wasteland—now minus one girl, but with one hell of a hood ornament.

TURN TO PAGE 250.

You raise the sawed-off and fire, blowing back a horde of the monsters, then you're kicking open the door, darting out. You run back, past the El Camino, grabbing the ax from the truck bed and swinging, cutting a swath, giving yourself some room.

You can free the El Camino later. Need to survive this first.

"He's running!" a voice hollers. The men standing by the howitzer cannons, in front of the gift shop, watch you.

You duck behind the base of a towering statue of a man on a horse. Peeking around, you see your predicament. If you run right at the men, they'll blow you to hell.

They fire again, and a dozen undead soldiers explode in a fiery blast—a mess of bloody limbs and splattered insides.

You need to flank the men. Come around the side of the gift shop, kill them, and then retrieve Iris.

Not far from your current spot is a small hill. Little Round Top, if you know your Civil War history. You can lose the men there, in the trees, then loop down behind them.

You holster the sawed-off, grip the ax, and move from headstone to headstone, ducked down, avoiding the gaze of the Confederate soldiers, one hundred yards away.

Twenty minutes later, you're scrambling into the trees at the bottom of Little Round Top. You start up the hill—after that, you only need to come down the other side—then you'll be on top of your enemy.

Creeping past a tall oak tree, an undead soldier lunges out. It had a beard, but its face is now rotted away and the flesh is singed and hair is gone. You decapitate it.

Five more stagger through the trees. You could pull the sawed-off, but the noise would alert the men working the howitzers.

So you swing the ax like fucking Conan the Barbarian.

Into the face of one rebel, splitting it open, then turning, bringing the hilt of the ax up into the next, driving its nose bone into its skull, stepping out of the turn, spinning the ax, slamming it down onto the third rebel's head. You kick the next one square in the chest, your boot caving in its chest cavity and sending it tumbling, end over end, down Little Round Top. The final one swipes at you, and you meet it with the ax, taking the top of its head off with one red swipe, just above the nose. You move swiftly to the base of the hill, burying the ax in the one with the caved-in chest cavity before it can rise.

You're close to the rear line now. You can see the four men working the two howitzers. You move forward, eager to make them bleed.

TURN TO PAGE 103.

You toss her the keys and bark, "Just get us out of here!"

You climb into the bed of the El Camino, reaching through the opening, grabbing both the sawed-off and the ax.

Iris floors it, too much gas, sliding over the dense field like the ground is made of ice. Wild blades of grass whip your arms as you hold the shotgun out the rear of the El Camino, firing to keep the monsters away.

Four zombies stumble in front of the car. Iris cuts the wheel and the car spins out, dirt kicking, rotating 180 degrees, now opposite the Lincoln.

You throw yourself to the floor of the truck bed as the Lincoln unloads with the machine gun. A long-haired zombie alongside the car is hit in the head, its face exploding, splattering you with skin and brain.

"Drive!" you shout, pounding the glass. The engine roars. You're knocked back onto your ass as the El Camino charges forward, toward the Lincoln, and then screams past it toward the still-crumbling stables.

Splicer's demented monstrosities are on the loose now— driven to the point of ferocious, flesh-hungry insanity. A zombified cow with a poorly stitched-on horse head lumbers in front of the car, jaw snapping. You square the sawed-off and fire, exploding its moaning, neighing head.

A lumbering zombie man with the head of a mountain lion dives up over the thresher. The monster rolls over the top of the El Camino, landing in the truck bed, hands instantly reaching, pawing, grabbing, then pinning you. The mountain lion's blood-matted mane shimmers in the moonlight. It opens its mouth, about to sink its long teeth into you. You squeeze the trigger, blasting the monster in its human gut and blowing it back—hurt but not defeated.

It claws forward, blindly searching the truck bed for you.

You grab the ax and as the car turns, you swing—turning your wrist and feeling the almost limitless power in the ax's wooden handle and seeing the flash of sharp steel—and then the mountain lion man's head is split in half and gore hangs in the air.

The El Camino rips around the barn, Mr. King still trailing, guns blazing. A bullet snaps past your ear, cracking like a whip. If you don't make a move, quickly, *now,* you're a corpse.

Coming toward the house, you spot a large propane tank, red and rusted. "Iris, the house!"

Bullets fly. Flat on your back, you drop two more shells into the sawed-off while the El Camino's reinforced tailgate absorbs the Lincoln's slugs.

The car shakes as Iris mows through creatures. Chunks of strange flesh—pig parts combined with human, a small child covered in horsehair—whoosh past as the thresher grinds them to bits.

Iris wrenches the wheel, slicing around the house, putting you next to the large propane tank, and then you're charging past it. You wait until Mr. King's Lincoln is directly alongside the tank, and then you spring up, triggering both barrels, and—

KRAKA—BLAM!

A sonic boom. The propane tank explodes with deafening force, rolling the Lincoln. It flips twice, then stops, upside down, wheels still spinning.

Mr. King is out of commission, for now.

You catch your breath. Lean through the window, give Iris a squeeze on the shoulder. Nice driving.

"Look," she says, pointing.

Dr. Splicer is in the middle of the street, being chased by one of his creatures: a goat with the head of a man. Splicer limps around, trying to avoid the thing, grasping his lacerated abdomen.

"Stop the car."

Tires screech, and you're thrown into the partition.

"Hand me my flask."

Iris does. And together, you sit and watch. You watch the goat man chase down Dr. Splicer. You watch this strange, ungodly, nonanimal thing tear Dr. Splicer apart. Rip flesh from his face. Pull his ears off. Devour his bleeding stomach and leave his entrails strewn across the road. You listen to Splicer scream and cry and moan like a woman in labor. An appropriate sound, maybe, since he gave birth to this beast.

Once Dr. Splicer is good and dead, you climb out of the truck bed, Iris slides over, you get behind the wheel, and you drive as fast as the dark, narrow roads will allow.

TURN TO PAGE 308.

You call out, "Dewey! Anyone in there?"

You hold the sawed-off down by your side—not hiding it, but not showing it off, either.

A speakeasy grille on the front door swings up and a rifle barrel pokes out.

"State your business," a voice calls out.

"You Dewey?"

"I said state your business."

"Need help."

"None here," the voice says.

"I need a taxidermist who can freeze-dry and preserve a body."

"Whatcha goin' need is a doctor if you don't remove yourself from my property. Three seconds 'fore I shoot. I don't wanna—it'll draw those stumblers in—but I will. I will protect my land."

You scan the front porch: three stuffed and posed zombies—all of them bearded men—a tin coffee mug, two ashtrays. Stacks and stacks of skin magazines. Guess when there's nearly no one left on Earth, you can just jerk off on your front porch. Silver linings.

"It's about a girl," you call back. "A real pretty girl. Pretty like the girls in your magazines."

After a moment, the gun slides back and the speakeasy grille shuts. The door swings open and a man appears, rifle up at his shoulder now, still aimed at your chest. He's medium height, very thin—though the thinness doesn't fit him, clothes hanging off his frame. Lost the weight after food became scarce, you figure. He has a thick, gray beard and he wears a grease-stained New Orleans Saints warm-up jacket, open, showing a hairy stomach.

"Yes, I'm Dewey," the man says. "Now, what girl you talkin' about?"

You nod to the El Camino. "In there."

Dewey takes his eyes off you and slowly looks over to the El Camino. "Hell kind of vehicle is that?"

You glance over at the El Camino. Bullet damage everywhere. Blood and gore coat the thresher. A mangled zombie arm sticks out from between the blades. Turning back to Dewey, you say, "The fun kind."

He smiles at that. "Put the scattergun down and we can talk."

You holster it, put your hands up, palms out. "How about that?"

He lowers the rifle just slightly, stepping off the porch, and crossing to the fence. "What'sa matter with the girl?"

"She's dead."

He throws his head back and does a full-body sigh, like he walked all the way across the lawn for nothing and that's some great catastrophe. "Damn. Had me all excited," he says.

"Sorry for that."

"Nothing I can do for a dead girl. Or for you, then."

"You can preserve her. You do freeze-dry preservation. Saw the ad in the yellow pages."

"To a full-grown woman? Fella, you're nuttier than squirrel shit. Ain't possible."

"Come see."

"I seen a woman before."

"Come," you say, and you begin walking. You hear the gate open and shut as he follows.

Reaching through the passenger window, you pull down the fabric that covers Iris's lower body.

"Yep," Dewey says. "She's a woman, all right."

You grab hold of her arm. "What's that look like?"

Dewey leans in and squints. "Stumbler bite."

You shift her body, showing her shoulder. "And that?"

"Two stumbler bites."

"But she's dead," you say. "Dead for real. Not undead. Why do you think that is?"

Dewey's pupils roll up to the corners of his eyes as he thinks. "Suppose that's a good question."

"She's immune."

He squints. "Horseshit."

"Not horseshit. No kinda shit. The girl can end all this. I was taking her to San Francisco. Some smart people there can use her to create a vaccine. But then she got dead. It may be all fucked now, but if you can do what you do—preserve her organs—there's still a chance."

He thinks for a long moment. Too long.

"Christ!" you bark. "Do you hear what I'm saying to you? This dead girl is important. I need your help."

Dewey looks up at you slowly. At last he says, "Bring her inside. We'll talk."

The interior of Dewey's Taxidermy and Freeze-Dry Preservation is full of mounted and preserved animals. A full-size stuffed alligator rests in the corner. Cougars and bobcats loom. It smells of smoke and meat and mold.

You lay Iris down on a ratty green sofa.

Dewey leans back in a rocking chair. "Now, I could stuff her for ya," he says as he lights a pipe. "That's not a problem."

"No. Can't lose the blood. I need her frozen. Organs maintained."

Dewey shakes his head. "That's for dogs, cats, birds. Folks who want their pet in their living room for the next fifty years."

"So do the same thing to a human being."

"Too big, fella! Take too much power. It ain't possible."

You take a drink. "So what? You need a generator? I'll get you a generator."

Dewey sighs. "Bud, I'd need three, four generators. Big ones. And even then it'll take two months, even with 'em clocking overtime. And probably the freeze still won't take and her insides'll melt like Blue Bell in August."

You swallow. You'll be dead in two months. But you don't tell Dewey that. "Okay. I'll get you four generators. What else?"

"Where you gonna get four industrial-size generators?"

"Leave that to me. What else?"

"She's too big. Full-sized woman, still not possible."

You take a swig from your flask, then say, "What if we cut off her legs?"

Dewey's eyes narrow and he rocks back in his chair, puffing his pipe. "You serious?"

"Whatever it takes."

Dewey leans forward. Rubs his hands together. "Four generators, no legs—I could maybe have her done in a month. Maybe."

"Then we do it."

Dewey sets his pipe down. Looks at you like you're a hundred percent certifiable. Then says, "All right, let's get started."

There's a hatch in the floor. Dewey pulls it open, then steps down a staircase to the basement. He carries a lantern and you carry Iris.

Along the wall are four tubes—like body storage in a morgue, but electronic. There's a cat in one, in the process of being preserved.

You lay Iris on a sort of wooden operating table. Dewey picks up a large hacksaw and stands over her body. "Sorry I don't have anything more surgery-like. Just never dealt with a body so big."

You shrug. Doesn't matter.

Dewey lays the blade over Iris's upper thigh, just below her privates. He begins cutting.

After a moment, you turn away and walk up the stairs.

"Where you off to?" Dewey calls. "Isn't you goin' watch? It's fascinating."

You light a cigarette. "I'm going to find your generators."

As you drive toward New Orleans, a thought enters your mind. The poison.

What if Eigle's bluffing? You know the poison is *real*, sure—you've felt it, no question, but you don't know if it'll kill you. Could just make you sick for a while, then exit your system. Maybe you could even find a doctor who could remedy you.

Could it be a bluff?

If it is, you could forget about all this. Try to create some sort of real life for yourself in this screwed-up world. This plan—Iris, the freezing—it's half-cocked anyway.

You take a pull from your flask and think . . .

If you want to abandon the mission and just drive, turn to page 157.

No, you'll continue on, searching for the generators. Go to page 221.

You wait at the ramp until the float is within firing range, then spin out.

It's a massacre.

You give both barrels of the sawed-off to the man with the bullhorn, and he responds with a shriek, suddenly cut off as he tumbles over the side.

The wife shouts, *"Lou!"* and leaps down onto the street, there for a moment, alive, then tackled by a zombie and she's crying and kicking and then silent.

You duck back behind the wall and reload.

The two teenagers—Rattail and Sunglasses—look around, confused, trying to figure out where the firing came from. You whistle, Rattail turns, and you fire, the shot punching him in the chest, launching him back into his brother, and then they're both toppling over the side.

The girl watches it all in shock.

The float picks up speed now, weaving back and forth. Whoever's behind the wheel is attempting a getaway—a getaway in a giant float down zombie-packed Bourbon Street. You need to stop it before the whole thing flips.

Behind the float, the two teenage brothers are lying in the street. Rattail is very much dead. Sunglasses is being devoured. He tries to fight off the horde of costumed monsters, waving a pistol, firing shots into the air while the monsters tear him apart.

You race out now—hopping up onto the float. Ignoring the girl, you kick away the chicken wire above the driver's cabin and drop down, leaning over the float and sticking your gun into the driver's face.

It's a boy, no more than seven.

You pull the gun back a few inches, so it isn't pressing into his cheek. He's got books tied to the gas and brake pedals, so he can reach them.

Suddenly, the young girl is on your back, tackling you, and your gun simply fires. The boy's small skull is blown all over the inside of the truck. He falls forward; his foot stomps the brake.

You're thrown from the vehicle and you land hard on the cement, bones snapping. Your hear a wet growl and then a hungry moan—and then, above you, crouching down, an undead clown, purple and green and gold.

And then another clown, shambling over.

And then one more.

And at once, a frenzy of hands and teeth, puncturing your flesh, clawing, pulling, tearing, and your blood is flowing and pooling, and you see your insides, tumbling out, and you see a long-nailed hand, for a moment, and then that long nail is digging into your eye socket, digging, pulling, popping . . .

AN END

You charge out of the house, lifting the RPG to your shoulder as you come through the door, taking aim at a throng, triggering the rocket—but then, suddenly, a skull slamming into your gut, an undead Klansman tackling you as you fire. The rocket spirals toward the El Camino.

You hear the explosion. You don't want to believe it. Need to see it. You pull the sawed-off, blowing the Klansman off you, scrambling to your feet.

The thresher has been blown open, split down the middle, and the hood has popped and flames are beginning to spread.

"No!" you scream. "My baby!"

You watch the El Camino burn from the inside out. Stunned, unable to move—and then the next hooded monster is there, draping itself over you, pressing its teeth into your flesh.

And as you fall, as you die, you watch your beloved El Camino burn. Your machine up in flames, along with your mission, along with any hope for the future of this damned world.

AN END

You make it halfway to the smoke signals before the pain in your side causes your head to go spacey, your vision to go black, and your body to slump over.

When you wake, the seat is fully reclined, and the El Camino is moving.

You sit up—and pain once again shoots through you. The poison will soon end you.

"Lie back," a voice says.

You crane your neck. The El Camino is being pushed by eight Native American men. They wear an incongruous mixture of traditional tribal wear and Kmart garb—jeans and sneakers.

Stranger still is what lies beyond. You're encircled by zombies—a full ring of the undead. But none of them is closer than one hundred yards.

"The dead . . . ," you start, before the poison grabs your throat and shuts you up.

"Don't worry. They won't come close," one man says. He appears to be the leader. "This place is safe."

Spiritual mumbo jumbo, but you're too tired to do anything about it.

Everything goes black again.

You wake up in a wickiup, a nineteenth-century-style home. A heavy blanket hangs over the door, and you push through. Gripping your bloody side, you step out onto a reservation.

You've spent time on reservations—had an old drinking buddy who lived on one. Used to swing by, get shitfaced, and load up on cheap cigarettes. They're sad places, mostly, poverty like a cancer, infecting everything—forgotten, ignored for the sake of convenience.

But this place is different. This reservation is in the process of returning to a more natural state now—truer to original customs. Concrete buildings are being disassembled, block by block. Trees here and there, dotted with yucca flowers.

"You're sick."

It's the man you saw before, when you were being pushed in the car. He places a hand on your shoulder.

"Yes," you say. "I'm shot and there's—there's poison in me." You have trouble speaking. Each word shaky, unsure. It's a foreign feeling. You've always been strong, stable, even when drunk. But that has left you.

"C'mon, have some food," he says, directing you to a wooden picnic table. You step over and gingerly sit down.

"Not hungry."

"You should eat," he says, sitting down across from you.

You shake your head. He shrugs and takes a bite of fry bread.

"Some car you've got there," he says. He pushes water toward you. You sip it. "What are you doing out here?"

"Trying to save the world."

"Tall order, man."

"Learning that the hard way."

It's morning and the reservation is coming to life. You see more people. Some of them eye you curiously. Most go about their business. They tend to animals—livestock grazes not far away, and crops grow beyond their longhouses.

You look out to the land beyond, where zombies surround the reservation. Their bodies flicker amidst waves of heat rolling off the plains. You thought they were a dream earlier, but no. They form a full ring around the reservation, undead eyes staring in.

"I shouldn't have come here," you say.

"Why not?"

"I'm trying to do something. I need to finish. I need to leave."

"Up to you," he says with a shrug. "But if you want us to help you, we can try. You seem like a broken man, in many pieces. I believe we might be able to make you whole."

To let them help you, turn to page 93.

To get back in the El Camino and continue the journey to San Francisco, turn to page 384.

You reach out and wipe away a stray strand of hair that hangs over Iris's eye. "It's been something," you say. "It's sure been something."

You take a long swig of whiskey, toss the flask out the window, shift into first, stamp down on the accelerator, and floor it across the desert surface, charging toward the skywalk.

And then the El Camino is blasting through the guardrail and sailing, out, over the canyon. The wheels spin in midair and the vehicle tips forward, plummeting downward.

Through the cracked windshield, you have a clear view of the imminent impact and your impending death as the El Camino drops. The ground rushes up fast. Zombies fill the canyon bed. Broken things, scattered about, their brains smashed open. Rodents pick at them.

And after a moment, the speed spinning your head, you seem to see undead monsters stumbling around the canyon bed—but that doesn't make sense—they'd be dead from the fall—and then you realize you've already blacked out, the El Camino has blasted right through the canyon floor, and the stumbling figures you see are simply the inhabitants of hell . . .

AN END

THE PRICE

Gripping Iris's hand, you slowly pull the gun away. "I'm going to complete the mission," you say. "I'm going to get you to San Francisco."

And then a piercing scream wakes you, slicing through the cool night. Your eyes snap open. The dream is over. You stumble from the tent.

The circle has broken and thousands of zombies, previously held at bay by some unknown force, are now rushing forward, stampeding into the reservation. All around you, residents fall. The zombies feast.

The healer grabs you by the shoulders. "The cure is not complete! Your blood is still foul!"

Fuck it. This isn't about you.

You just need to live long enough to get Iris to San Francisco. That's all that matters.

You turn away from the healer and charge toward the El Camino. You dive inside and turn the key. Iris's body is slumped against the passenger-side door.

There are so many monsters. The town will be overrun. These people will die. And when you deliver Iris, any attempt the survivors make to return to a different way of life will be for nothing.

That's the price of saving the world, you think as you hit the gas. *That's the price.*

TURN TO PAGE 73.

You stand up and finish your water. "I need to leave. I'm sorry."

"Why are you sorry?" the leader asks.

You're sorry because if you complete your mission, this man and his attempt to return to an older way of life will be destroyed. Cut down. Hell will return, with its heavy boot, stomping them out once again. But you don't say that . . .

"I'm sorry I've wasted your time," you say. Turning, you eye the ring of zombies one hundred yards out.

"They won't bother you until you leave our grounds," the leader says.

You nod.

"Take this. It won't fix you. But it will help the pain for a few days."

He hands you a clay cup full of thick, brown liquid, like mud. You drink it down. Nearly vomit. You quickly yank your flask from your rear pocket and wash the liquid down with a swallow of whiskey to settle your stomach.

"Good luck," he says.

"You, too," you reply. Silently, you walk to the El Camino, start it up, and drive. Very slowly, you approach the ring of zombies. You pull to a stop just in front of them.

It's strange, watching them watch you. These undead are like pieces of the landscape. Moaning, swaying animals that are no true threat. You honk twice, hard and loud, and the zombies shuffle to the side.

But the moment you get beyond their circle, they change.

They become what they were. Monsters howling and attacking the car.

But you don't trigger the thresher. You don't raise the sawed-off. You just drive. You'll do no violence today, if you can help it.

The thick liquid has you feeling better and the pain has subsided somewhat when, ten hours later, you cross into California. San Francisco is just a little over four hundred miles away.

TURN TO PAGE 73.

You want nothing to do with this madman.

You'll make it to San Francisco—and Iris will, too. You just need to drive hard and fast. And you can do that. Because you're fucking Jimmy El Camino, and no one's better.

Back in the driver's seat, you stamp the accelerator and race through Los Angeles.

You pass the TCL Chinese Theatre, which is damaged from fire. The Whisky a Go Go, where zombies with long black hair stumble about.

Coming around Wilshire Boulevard, you see the all-black Lincoln, lying in wait.

Mr. King.

Two puffs of smoke erupt from beneath the Lincoln's front bumper, then two rockets, in flight. You wrench the wheel, tires protesting, but it's too late—the bastard was camped there, waiting to end you.

The first rocket slams into the front of the El Camino. The second into the driver's-side door, ripping it apart. Hot metal slices through your leg. The El Camino flips, rolling across the sidewalk, crashing through a fence, and tumbling down a small hill. You hear an odd, hushed splash, and the car stops.

Blackness fills your vision. Black, covering the windows. Black, rising up, all around you.

You try to kick open the door, but there's resistance. Thick, black liquid. No. Not liquid. Something else. You quickly roll down the window and the blackness begins to seep into the car. You grab Iris's body and pull her out with you, squeezing through the window.

The black sludge surrounds you. Struggling to swim away from the El Camino, you see the sign: *La Brea Tar Pits and Museum.*

A fucking tar pit. And you've landed directly in the center of the millennia-old thing. The tar bubbles and burps, slowly pulling the El Camino under. You try to swim, but it's too thick—like moving through molasses.

The monsters come for you then. Moaning beasts, rushing forward from the museum parking lot, stumbling down the hill, into the pit. Fat men in bad shirts. Asian women, their faces blood-splattered.

Some land headfirst, sinking, their feet kicking wildly. Others topple down from the viewing area above, then begin the slow tread through the tar toward you.

You have an arm wrapped around Iris and you use your other arm to try to swim, but the tar is too damn thick.

More bubbling, as Iris is pulled under. Her face—it's like she's watching you, accusing you of failing. And she's not wrong. Some small part of you is almost happy when she slips under, completely, into the darkness. You won't see those accusing eyes again.

The tar is up to your neck now.

Standing at the broken railing above, Mr. King watches with a smile on his scarred face, smoking a cigarette and enjoying the sight of your death.

The monsters close in from all sides. The tar tugs at you from below.

And as hands grip you and the tar pulls you, you wonder: Will some scientist in the year 2200—if the world manages to right itself—excavate you? Will they wonder how you wound up in this pit of shit? What will they think of the girl with no legs? And what will they say of the El Camino?

You wonder if you'll go down in history, while, at the same time, you're going down, down, down—zombies on you, tearing at your tar-coated flesh, as you're swallowed whole by the thick liquid like some ancient woolly mammoth.

At last, your head goes under and the thick tar fills your lungs . . .

AN END

MISFIRE

You level the gun at Iris's belly. She stares you down, almost daring you to do it. *The balls on this woman*, you think. *The goddamn balls.*

Your eyes narrow, telling Iris, *I'll do it. I'll shoot you and I'll take your dead body to San Francisco and maybe that'll be enough to keep me alive.*

And she just stares back.

Your finger curls around the trigger. Tightens.

But you can't.

You can't pull it.

Iris exhales. You're lowering the gun when Ring attacks—leaping to his feet, launching himself into you.

And the gun goes off, deafening in the small car.

Iris is shot in the belly. Blood explodes and she's thrown back, slams into the wall, then pitches forward off the bed. Ring goes for the door as the gun clangs to the floorboards. You spin, swinging the ax, slicing Ring's right leg clean off.

You look to Iris: dead.

"You did this!" you bark at Ring. Then, with a sharp swing, you split his face in half.

There's a commotion outside. Someone calls out, "Everything okay in there, boss?"

Back to the wall, you thrust the door open. The men outside see the blood splattering the walls.

"Boss?" one squeaks.

And then you step into the doorway, holding Ring. You throw his body from the car, into the men, knocking them aside.

You grab the gun, reload, then leap down, carrying Iris's dead body over your shoulder.

Someone raises a rifle. You fire the sawed-off, blowing the man apart.

Moving quick now. Gunshots ringing out as you race across the field, toward the El Camino, rifles cracking, bullets whistling past you. The barn splinters as bullets hammer it.

You dump Iris in the bed of the El Camino, hop into the car, and floor it, bursting out from behind the barn, leaving Ring's Most Wonderful Circus Show behind you.

A mile from the train, you stop the car and walk around to the bed.

Iris's mouth is open and her dead eyes stare up at nothing.

You curse Iris for resisting. You curse yourself for raising the gun. You curse Ring for the whole fucking mess.

And then you get to work, wrapping her, bandaging her belly wound. You don't know what the scientists in San Francisco need, but you hope that Iris's body—even her dead body—is enough.

You take a long swallow of whiskey and slide into the driver's seat.

TURN TO PAGE 143.

Igor is pulling hunks of meat from a plastic bin and feeding the zombified husk of a former action-thriller actor. When he sees you enter, without the girl, disappointment crosses his wrinkled face.

"She's dead. Actually dead. Not like this shit," you say, indicating the monsters in the room.

Igor's shoulders sag. For a moment, you think he might cry. But then he looks up, angry. "You lie," he barks. "You didn't even look for her!"

You slap the necklace into his open palm. "Here's your proof."

Looking down, the realization that you're telling the truth hits him, and he does begin to cry then. Big tears pour down his cracked face.

"I was so hoping you'd find her," he says, sniffling, then wiping at his nose with a dirty sleeve.

"I completed my part of the deal," you say coldly. "Give me Iris."

"What?" he says softly, and then, "Oh. Yes, yes . . ."

He disappears into the back. A long moment later he returns, carrying Iris. He hands her over. She's icy cold and stiff. Her lips are now as blue as her eyes.

"Nice doing business," you say.

You carry Iris back out to the El Camino and, for what you hope is the final time, buckle her into the passenger seat.

No more stopping now.

This is it.

You have a full tank of gas, half a bottle of whiskey, and Iris's frozen body. Nothing to do but drive.

You travel up the Pacific Coast Highway. Rusted and wrecked cars line the road. Vehicles overturned. Belongings, lives, spilled across the ground.

You get into a rhythm, sliding from lane to lane, handling the El Camino like an instrument, finely tuned, your hands piloting without really thinking. Stereo music howls and you smoke cigarettes and, every once in a while, you pat Iris on her frozen shoulder.

When you pass the sign that reads *San Francisco—25 miles*, you turn down the stereo and pick up the microphone. "Eigle," you say.

After a moment, he comes on. "Long time. Thought we lost you."

"I'm still here. Getting close. Call your men. Tell them to get my antidote ready."

"How's Iris?" he asks.

"Cold."

You hang the microphone on the radio and glance in the side mirror. Wreckage and blight behind you—nothing else. Your long, cross-country hell ride is nearly finished. You couldn't keep the girl alive—no, you failed mightily at that— but you'll deliver her. You'll get her to your destination. That's something, isn't it?

That's when you hear the roar. Gunfire explodes, bullets ricocheting off the rear of the El Camino, and you know, instantly, that your journey is far from finished.

Coming around a bend, you crane your neck. It's Mr. King, behind the wheel of the Lincoln, putting the heat on, closing in.

He's followed you across too many goddamn states to count,

doing Boss Tanner's bidding. And now he's here. One last obstacle to overcome before you reach your mission's end.

You mash the accelerator and the engine growls, charging forward, speeding up even as you take the next bend, sweeping across three curving lanes, far door grazing an overturned tractor-trailer, so close the metal on metal shrieks.

Coming out of the turn, you see a mess of wreckage ahead, crashes, debris, hot metal shiny in the sunlight, scattered across the road.

Stomping the brake then, wrenching the wheel so you swerve off the road, thudding and screeching down into the parking lot of a roadside joint called the Deuce Deuce. Here, zombie bikers shuffle about amidst the shattered remains of two dozen Harley-Davidsons. One gets caught in the El Camino's thresher, leather shredding, and then a fat one, tattoos covering his swollen and bloated belly, is hit and bounces off.

You jerk the wheel, throwing the zombie off, then flicking the nitrous, hurtling around the roadhouse in a swooping drift. You swing back around front, the Lincoln directly ahead of you now, and you trigger the M134D minigun, unleashing a barrage of bullets on the enemy's driver's-side door.

Mr. King's head snaps to the side, then ducks as his bulletproof window cracks, finally weakened.

The Smith & Wesson. If you could stick that big mother through that cracked glass, you could blow Mr. King's goddamn head right off.

You punch it, whipping past the Lincoln, the El Camino leaping back out onto the highway. You quickly hit 90 miles per hour, weaving around an abandoned pickup and clipping a rusted motorcycle, sending it spinning back toward Mr. King. The Lincoln plows through it, charging forward, traveling in your slipstream.

A hard turn ahead, tight—the wreckage of a half-dozen vehicles crowding the road. You release the gas and slide, drifting across the turn, through the scattered obstacles, the ocean stretching out far to your left, a jumble of wreckage to your right.

Coming out of the turn, straightening the wheel, a second to breathe—and then suddenly, filling the road, filling your vision, a hundred rotting, undead beasts—too many to thresh through, plow through, or slam through. You jerk the wheel, one tire bursts, and then the El Camino is careening off the road, smashing through a wooden sign, hanging in the air for a brief moment before tumbling down a grassy embankment.

The car rolls three times, then lands on its wheels with a heavy, shuddering thud. The engine cuts out. You twist the keys, but the machine has shit the bed. You jam the Smith & Wesson 500 into your belt, scoop up Iris, and run like hell.

You hear the Lincoln racing down the hill behind you. Ahead of you are massive, overgrown grapevines and stalks. A building to your right has the words *Foster Family Vineyards* across the top.

As you charge into the winery's thick, nearly impassible rows of rotting grapes, you hear the whistle of rockets and then a deafening blast. You grip Iris tight, waiting for it—and then the heat is white-hot on your back as the El Camino explodes and the blast hurls you thirty feet through the air, into the grape fields.

You hit the ground and your arm snaps and your bone rips through the skin. Iris's torso falls beside you.

No time to tend to your wound. Moans drift through the rows of grapevines ahead: zombies in the fields.

You limp to the end of the row and peer around the corner. The Lincoln had stopped beside the flaming wreckage of the El Camino, but now it continues on, slowly entering the sprawling fields. You're being hunted.

You set Iris's body on the ground, hiding it among the towering, overgrown grape stalks, and then you move. Coming through the next row, an undead beast pounces on you. You don't fire the gun for fear of drawing the attention of Mr. King, more monsters, or both.

Instead, you swing hard, punching the thing in the jaw, snapping its head back. You tackle it, pulling the pistol and whipping the monster, feeling its skull crack, until, at last, its brain begins to seep from its ears.

Another comes, and you just run.

You come out into a large clearing, the grass waist-high. Monsters roam here as well, most of them wearing torn jeans and bloody denim shirts.

Behind you comes the rumble of the Lincoln. You turn. Grape stalks are ripped from the ground as the vehicle prowls, drawing closer, the sound telling you it will be into the clearing in moments.

If you want to hold your ground and unload with the Smith & Wesson, turn to page 360.

If you'd rather wait, hoping and praying that some inspired plan enters your rattled brain, turn to page 40.

BACK TO IT

The house looks like an invitation to death. So you continue on, leaving the girl behind. But as you watch the little one in the rearview, alone, surrounded by nothing but hell, you think of Iris. Iris, who agreed to give her life—to walk alone, into the open arms of death . . . for something bigger.

And you can't let that go unrewarded.

You need to finish what you started.

So you turn around. New Orleans it is . . .

TURN TO PAGE 221.

Your boot mashes the pedal until pain shoots up your leg—pushing the El Camino on—faster, harder, thundering toward the Lincoln with pistons pumping, every bit of the machine pushed to its limit—metal howling, bolts rattling, and the thick grille of the Lincoln growing in size as you storm toward it.

Two hundred yards.

One hundred yards.

Fifty yards . . .

At the last possible moment, Mr. King flinches. The Lincoln goes into a screeching slide, clipping the side of your car, you correcting, the Lincoln spinning, and then two bangs as the Lincoln's tires burst and the car flips, tumbling into a high-speed barrel roll, hurtling down the bridge.

You skid into a stop, turning to watch the Lincoln roll six, seven, eight times. Metal and glass explode.

On the ninth flip, Mr. King is tossed from the car, his body a rag doll, tumbling through the air, hanging there for a short instant, then crashing hard on the bridge.

Yet he's still not dead.

He struggles to stand, but he quickly falls to the pavement—his leg is shattered and his femur protrudes through the flesh. Bloods pours from a massive gash on his forehead. But through the gore, you see him watching—can feel his glare penetrating, staring at you through the El Camino's shattered passenger-side window.

He pulls a pistol.

Raises it, shakily.

Points it at you.

And then the monsters tackle him. Six zombies upon him, dragging him to the ground, tearing at him. The report of the pistol, twice, and Mr. King gives in, crumples and allows himself to be devoured.

Iris places her hand on yours. You nod, turn the wheel, and drive. Approaching the end of the bridge, two makeshift gates begin to open. Soldiers rush out, holding off any nearby zombies while men in uniforms usher you inside.

An excited scientist in a lab coat, like he just ran out in the middle of his research, hurries forward. He speaks to other men in hushed tones. It seems no one thought you'd make it.

You stumble out of the El Camino. Using your good arm to brace yourself, you limp around the car, then open the passenger-side door for Iris.

"Always the gentleman," she says, climbing out.

"Iris?" the man in the lab coat asks. "This is Iris?"

She nods. "Yep," she says, sounding a bit proud but also like she'd rather not admit it. "That's me."

"Oh thank Christ in heaven," he says. "Please, come with us. We'll tend to those wounds."

"No," she says coolly. "No, I'm not coming with you."

Your heart just about seizes up. She's come so far. She can't back out now. It's too important. You understand the fear of death that grips her now, but it must be done. The horror you've seen on your journey—the hell on earth this land has become—it must be ended.

"I'm sorry?" the man says.

"Not until you give Jimmy the antidote."

The man in the coat exhales, relieved. "Of course," he says, turning. "Admiral?"

A navy admiral—full dress blues, square jaw, thick head of hair—steps forward, looking you up and down. "It's an honor, Mr. Casey."

"Mr. El Camino."

"Mr. El Camino. The poison . . . ," he says, trailing off, then picking back up. "I'm sorry we were forced to do that. Eigle's idea."

You shrug. "It got me here. So, oh well."

The admiral cracks half a grin. He pulls three pills from a pouch at his side, then calls for someone to bring water. A moment later, a young soldier appears, holding a bottle, and you down the pills.

"The water will give you the runs—still working on good, clean water—but your system will be clear in two days," the admiral says. "Thank you for your service."

You say nothing. You sit on the hood of the El Camino, rest your arm on the hot barrel of the M134D, and watch Iris's time on this Earth draw to a close.

"Iris," the man in the lab coat says, almost timidly. "Could you please come with us now? It's time."

Iris turns to you. Her face is ashen, but her eyes are dry and her mouth firm.

She keeps her head raised and begins walking with the scientist—her first few steps shaky. Then, suddenly, she turns and runs back to you. She throws her arms around you, tight, like she's trying to squeeze the life out of you—maybe take a little bit of it for herself, to hang on to.

"I'm going to die now, Jimmy," she says.

There's not much to say to that. You hug her, then push her away. "I'll see you, Iris. Sooner than later, I'm sure."

"Good."

Then they lead her down the street, toward the California Pacific Medical Center campus. People watch. Some lean out the windows, cheering. It seems everyone knows what's happening, realizes the importance of this moment.

And you?

You're done.

Free.

You had planned for the beach. The house, where you'd sit and do nothing but drink yourself to death.

But now—now you think maybe you'll climb back in the El Camino. Head back east. Find the man named Boss Tanner. And slice the skin from his bones.

THE END

ACKNOWLEDGMENTS— AND A FEW THOUGHTS . . .

So . . . this was a difficult project—I'm just gonna go ahead and throw that out there. The first *Can YOU Survive* was well received and has become a bit of a fan favorite (I say, quite humbly). So when the idea of a sequel came up, I was intrigued (writers are *always* intrigued by paychecks!). But I had little interest in, basically, remaking the first book. I wanted to take this someplace very different. It sounded easy. It was not. And that fully caught me off guard. I wanted this new thing to feel pulpy, old-fashioned: a loving nod to my favorite films and stories of the seventies and eighties—but I never wanted it to feel archaic or antediluvian (big-word alert—thanks, Apple Thesaurus!). I wanted it to be mean and tough but never simply *mean*. And for me, that was a tough tightrope to walk. Was I successful? In parts, I think, yes. But in other sections, I'm less than sure. But that's the process, that's the game, and I suppose that's the risk.

In getting this thing to the finish line, I had a lot of help from a lot of great people. First, my editor, Ed Schlesinger. Other editors, too: the book wouldn't be here if it weren't for all the maestros who handled this project prior—thank you all! Also . . . Wesley Ryan, my consultant for all things military. Matthew McArdle, for a great many things—particularly for listening to me sing (many times) my quite lame Jimmy El Camino theme song, but more importantly for plot help, story aid, and some great notions. Christopher Mitten, for illustrative goodness, and for just being a generally really nice and solid guy. My parents and my sister, as always. And last but furthest from least: my wonderful wife, Alyse Diamond, for brutally honest feedback and anxiety-squashing back rubs. Love you.